GHOST STORY

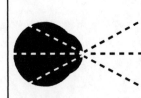

This Large Print Book carries the
Seal of Approval of N.A.V.H.

GHOST STORY

A NOVEL OF THE DRESDEN FILES

JIM BUTCHER

THORNDIKE PRESS
A part of Gale, Cengage Learning

GALE
CENGAGE Learning

Detroit • New York • San Francisco • New Haven, Conn • Waterville, Maine • London

GALE
CENGAGE Learning™

LIBRARY OF CONGRESS CATALOGING-IN-PUBLICATION DATA

Butcher, Jim, 1971–
    Ghost story : a novel of the Dresden files / by Jim Butcher.
        p. cm. — (Thorndike Press large print basic)
    ISBN-13: 978-1-4104-4209-3 (hardcover)
    ISBN-10: 1-4104-4209-8 (hardcover)
    1. Dresden, Harry (Fictitious character)—Fiction. 2.
Wizards—Fiction. 3. Chicago (Ill.)—Fiction. 4. Large type books.
I. Title.
PS3602.U85G48 2011b
813'.6—dc22   2011030318

Published in 2011 by arrangement with NAL Signet, a member of Penguin Group (USA), Inc.

Printed in the United States of America
1 2 3 4 5 6 7 15 14 13 12 11

To Air, for introducing me to
Mab by onion-colored light

ACKNOWLEDGMENTS

As always, there are too many people to thank and only a little bit of space to thank them in. This time around, I must especially thank my editor, Anne, for putting up with my delays in writing. I'm sure I gave her, along with several of the folks trying to schedule things at Penguin, headaches. My agent, Jenn, was invaluable in getting everything straightened out, as well as in helping me through the bumpy bits, and I owe her my thanks, as well. I would apologize to you all abjectly if I were sure it would never happen again. Seems sort of insincere to do it otherwise, all things considered, so I'll just thank you for your patience and understanding.

To the inhabitants of the Beta Asylum, many more thanks than usual are owed, especially for everyone who sacrificed so much of their time and focus in the last few weeks before the revised deadline. Your feedback, support, and advice were particularly invaluable.

To my dear patrons, the readers, I can only thank you for your patience, after leaving the last novel the way I did, then making everyone wait another three months past the usual delay while I made sure this book was ready to go. Enjoy! (And, technically, guys, *Changes* did NOT end in a cliff-hanger. Seriously.)

And to Shannon, who had to live with me during this more-frantic-than-usual period of insanity: I'm almost certain I'll be sane again at some point in the reasonably near future. I'll try to make it up to you.

CHAPTER ONE

Life is hard.

Dying's easy.

So many things must align in order to create life. It has to happen in a place that supports life, something approximately as rare as hen's teeth, from the perspective of the universe. Parents, in whatever form, have to come together for it to begin. From conception to birth, any number of hazards can end a life. And that's to say nothing of all the attention and energy required to care for a new life until it is old enough to look after itself.

Life is full of toil, sacrifice, and pain, and from the time we stop growing, we know that we've begun dying. We watch helplessly as year by year, our bodies age and fail, while our survival instincts compel us to keep on going — which means living with the terrifying knowledge that ultimately death is inescapable. It takes enormous effort to create and maintain a life, and the process is full of pitfalls and unexpected complications.

Ending a life, by comparison, is simple. Easy, even. It can be done with a relatively minor effort, a single microbe, a sharp edge, a heavy weight . . . or a few ounces of lead.

So difficult to bring about. So easy to destroy.

You'd think we would hold life in greater value than we do.

I died in the water.

I don't know if I bled to death from the gunshot wound or drowned. For being the ultimate terror of the human experience, once it's over, the details of your death are unimportant. It isn't scary anymore. You know that tunnel with the light at the end of it that people report in near-death experiences? Been there, done that.

Granted, I never heard of anyone rushing toward the light and suddenly hearing the howling blare of a train's horn.

I became dimly aware that I could feel my feet beneath me, standing on what seemed to be a set of tracks. I knew because I could feel the approaching train making them shake and buzz against the bottoms of my feet. My heart sped up, too.

For crying out loud, did I just *say* that death isn't scary anymore? Tell that to my glands.

I put my hands on my hips and just glared at the oncoming train in disgust. I'd had a long, long day, battling the forces of evil, utterly destroying the Red Court, rescuing my daughter, and murdering her mother — oh, and getting shot to death. That kind of thing.

I was supposed to be at peace, or merging with the holy light, or in line for my next turn on the roller coaster, or maybe burning in an oven equipped with a stereo that played nothing but Manilow. That's what happens when you die, right? You meet your reward. You get to find out the answer to the Big Questions of life.

"You do not get run over by trains," I said crossly. I folded my arms, planted my feet, and thrust out my jaw belligerently as the train came thundering my way.

"What's wrong with you?" bellowed a man's voice, and then a heavy, strong hand wrapped around my right biceps and hauled me off the track by main force. "Don't you see the damned train?"

Said train roared by like a living thing, a furious beast that howled and wailed in disappointment as I was taken from its path. The wind of its passage raked at me with sharp, hot fingers, actually pulling my body a couple of inches toward the edge of the platform.

After a subjective eternity, it passed, and I lay on flat ground for a moment, panting, my heart beating along lickety-split. When it finally began to slow down, I took stock of my surroundings.

11

I was sprawled on a platform of clean but worn concrete, and suddenly found myself under fluorescent lights, as at many train stations in the Chicago area. I looked around the platform, but though it felt familiar, I couldn't exactly place it. There were no other commuters. No flyers or other advertisements. Just an empty, clean, featureless building.

And a pair of polished wing tip shoes.

I looked up a rather modest length of cheap trousers and cheap suit and found a man of maybe thirty years looking back at me. He was built like a fireplug and managed to give the impression that if you backed a car into him, he'd dent your fender. His eyes were dark and glittered very brightly, hinting at a lively intellect, his hairline had withdrawn considerably from where it must have been at one point, and while he wasn't exactly good-looking, it was the kind of face you could trust.

"Southbound trains are running pretty quick lately," he said, looking down at me. "I figured you probably didn't want to hook up with that one, mister man."

I just stared up at him. I mentally added twenty years and forty pounds to the man standing in front of me, subtracted more hair, and realized that I knew him.

"C—" I stammered. "C-c-c—"

"Say it with me," he said, and enunciated:

12

"Carmichael."

"But you're . . . you know," I said. "Dead."

He snorted. "Whoa, buddy. We got us a real, gen-yoo-wine detective with us now. We got us the awesome wizardly intellect of mister man himself." He offered me his hand, grinning, and said, "Look who's talking, Dresden."

I reached up, dazed, and took the hand of Sergeant Ron Carmichael, formerly of the Chicago Police Department's Special Investigations division. He'd been Murphy's partner. And he'd given his life to save her from a rampaging loup-garou. That had been . . . Hell's bells, more than ten *years* ago. I saw him die.

Once I was standing, I stared down at him for a moment, shaking my head. I was a lot taller than he was. "You . . ." I said. "You look great."

"Funny what being dead can do for you," he said, widening his eyes dramatically. "And I tried Weight Watchers and everything." He checked his watch. "This is fun and all, but we'd better get moving."

"Uh," I said warily, "get moving where, exactly?"

Carmichael stuck a toothpick in his mouth and drawled, "The office. Come on."

I followed him out of the station, where an old, gold-colored Mustang was waiting. He went around to the driver's side and got in.

It was dark. It was raining. The city lights were on, but the place looked deserted except for the two of us. I still couldn't tell exactly where in Chicago we were, which was damned odd; I know my town. I hesitated for a moment, looking around, trying to place myself by spotting the usual landmarks.

Carmichael pushed open the door. "Don't bother, kid. Out there're all the buildings that coulda been, as well as the ones that are. You'll give yourself a headache if you keep thinking at it."

I looked around once more and got into the old Mustang. I shut the door. Carmichael pulled sedately into the empty streets.

"This isn't Chicago," I said.

"Genius," he said amiably.

"Then . . . where are we?"

"Between."

"Between what?" I asked.

"Between what?" he said. "Between who. Between where. Between when."

I frowned at him. "You left out *why.*"

He shook his head and grinned. "Naw, kid. We're real fond of *why* around here. We're big fans of *why.*"

I frowned at that for a moment. Then I said, "Why am I here?"

"You never even heard of foreplay, didja?" Carmichael said. "Cut straight to the big stuff."

"Why am I here as opposed to — you know

— wherever it is I'm supposed to be?"

"Maybe you're having a near-death experience," Carmichael said. "Maybe you're drowning, and this is the illusion your mind is creating for you, to hide you from the truth of death."

"Being here? With you? I've met my subconscious, and he's not that sick."

Carmichael laughed. It was a warm, genuine sound. "But that *could* be what is happening here. And that's the point."

"I don't understand. At all."

"And that's the point, too," he said.

I glowered.

He kept on smiling and said, "Kid, you're allowed to see as much as you can handle. Right now, we're someplace that looks a lot like Chicago, driving along in the rain in my old Mustang, because that's what your limits are. Any more would" — he paused, considering his words — "would obviate certain options, and we ain't big on that around here."

I thought about that for a moment. Then I said, "You just used *obviate* and *ain't* in the same sentence."

"I got me one of them word-a-day calendars," he said. "Don't be obstreperous."

"You kidding?" I said, settling back in the seat. "I live to be obstreperous."

Carmichael snorted, and his eyes narrowed. "Yeah, well. We'll see."

CHAPTER TWO

Carmichael stopped the Mustang in front of a building that reminded me of old episodes of *Dragnet.* He parked on the empty street and we walked toward the entrance.

"So, where are we going?"

"Told you. The office."

I frowned. "Don't suppose you could be more specific?"

He looked around, his eyes narrowed. "Not here. We aren't in safe territory. Ears everywhere."

I stopped on the completely empty sidewalk and looked up and down the motionless, vacant street, and saw nothing but lonely streetlamps, traffic signals, and windows unmarred by light or curtains, staring more blankly than the empty eyes of a corpse.

"Yeah," I said. "Real hotbed of intrigue around here."

Carmichael stopped at the door and looked over his shoulder. He didn't say anything for a few seconds. Then he spoke quietly, without a trace of affectation in his voice. "There are Things out here, Dresden. And some Things are worse than death. It's best if you get inside."

I rolled my eyes at him. But . . .

Something about the emptiness around me was suddenly extremely nerve-racking.

I stuck my hands in my pockets and tried to saunter inside. The effect may have been slightly sabotaged by my desire to get some solid building between that emptiness and me. Carmichael used a key to open the door and let me in before coming in behind me, his face directed back toward the street until he had shut the door and locked it.

He nodded to a guard, a beat cop in dress uniform, who stood just to one side of an elevator, his back in an entirely rigid position of at-ease, his hands clasped behind him. The guard's uniform was literally perfect. Perfectly clean, the creases perfectly sharp, his gloves perfectly white. He wore a silver-plated, engraved service revolver in a gleaming black holster at his hip. His features went with the uniform — utterly symmetrical, strong, steady.

I stopped for a second, frowning at the guard, and then reached for my Sight.

Professional wizards like me have access to all kinds of wild things. One of the wildest is the Sight, which has been described in various times and cultures as the second sight, the third eye, the evil eye, and a host of other things. It allows a wizard to look at the true nature of things around him, to see the unseen world of energy and power flowing around him. It's dangerous. Once you see something with your Sight, you never forget it, and it never fades with time. Take a look at the wrong thing and you can kiss your sanity good-bye.

But this entire scene was so Rod Serling, I had to find *something* about it that I could pin down, something familiar, something that wasn't being spoon-fed to me by a person who looked like a younger, thinner Carmichael. I decided to try to identify the single object that was most likely to tell me something about the people around me — a source of power.

I focused on the guard's gun.

For a second, absolutely nothing happened. And then the black and silver of the gleaming weapon changed, shifted. The holster elongated, trailing down the length of the guard's leg, and the pearl-handled revolver changed as well, the grip straightening. The silver of the barrel and chamber became the pommel, handle, and hilt of a cruciform sword. Light gleamed from the weapon, not reflected from the illumination in the entry hall of the building, but generated by the weapon itself.

The guard's blue eyes shifted to me at once.

He lifted a hand and said in a gentle voice, "No."

And as suddenly as a door slamming into my face, my Sight vanished, and the weapon was just a gun again.

The guard nodded at me. "My apologies for being abrupt. You might have harmed yourself."

I looked. His name tag read AMITIEL.

"Uh, sure," I said quietly, lifting empty hands. "No problem, man. I've got no problem with you."

Carmichael nodded respectfully to the guard and jammed a thumb down on the button to summon the elevator. It opened at once. "Come on, mister man. Time's a-wasting."

Officer Amitiel seemed to find the statement humorous. He smiled as he touched two fingers to the brim of his cap in a casual salute to Carmichael. Then he went back to his relaxed stance as a guardian, calmly facing the emptiness that had unnerved me.

The elevator doors closed, and the car rattled a little before it started moving. "So," I said, "now that we've got at least one guardian angel between us and whatever it is you were nervous about, can you tell me where we're going?"

Carmichael's eyes crinkled at the corners. He grunted. "I'm pretty much a tour guide at the moment, Dresden. You need to talk to

19

the captain."

Carmichael took me through a precinct room, the kind with a lot of unenclosed desks as opposed to cubicles, where cops worked. It looked a lot like the Special Investigations headquarters in Chicago. There were several men and women at the desks, reading through files, talking on phones, and otherwise looking like cops at work. All of them were about Carmichael's apparent age — right at the line where youthful energy and wisdom-creating life experience were reaching a state of balance. I didn't recognize any of them, though Carmichael gave and received nods from a couple. He marched over to the only other door in the room, leading to a private office, and knocked.

"In," said a clear, quiet baritone.

Carmichael opened the door and led me into the room. It was a small, well-used office. There were old filing cabinets, an old wooden desk, some battered wooden chairs. The desk had an in-box, an out-box, and a message spike, along with a rotary telephone. There was no computer. Instead, on a table next to the desk sat an old electric typewriter.

The man behind the desk was also more or less Carmichael's age, and he looked like a professional boxer. There was scar tissue here and there around his eyes, and his nose had been frequently broken. He had hung his suit

20

jacket over the back of his chair, and his shoulders and biceps strained the fabric of his white shirtsleeves. He had them rolled up to the elbows, revealing forearms that were approximately as thick as wooden telephone poles, and looked every bit as strong. His hair was blond, his eyes blue, and his jawline was heavy enough to make me think of a bulldog. He looked familiar somehow.

"Jack," Carmichael said. "This is Dresden."

Jack looked me up and down, but he didn't get up. He didn't say anything, either.

"He's always this way before he's had his cup of coffee," Carmichael told me. "Don't take it personal."

"Hey, coffee," I said into the silence that followed. "That sounds good."

Jack eyed me for a moment. Then he said, in that same mellifluous voice, "Dresden, are you hungry?"

"No."

"Thirsty?"

I thought about it. "No."

"That's because you're dead," Jack said. His smile was brief and not particularly reassuring. "You don't need to drink. You don't need to eat. There's no coffee."

I eyed Carmichael.

"I stand by my statement," said Carmichael. He looked at Jack and hooked a thumb at the door. "I should get back to that rakshasa thing."

Jack said, "Go."

Carmichael slapped my arm and said, "Good luck, kid. Have fun." And he strode out, moving like a man on a mission. That left me sharing an awkward silence with Jack.

"This isn't what I expected out of the afterlife," I said.

"That's because it isn't," he said.

I frowned. "Well, you said I was dead. Ergo, afterlife."

"You're dead," Jack said. "This is between."

I frowned. "What, like . . . purgatory?"

Jack shrugged. "If that works for you, call it that. But you aren't here because you need to cleanse yourself. You're here because there was an irregularity with your death."

"I got shot. Or drowned. Ain't exactly rare."

Jack lifted a big, square hand and waggled it back and forth. "It isn't about the physical. It's about the spiritual."

I frowned. "Spiritual?"

"The opposition," Jack said. "You died because they cheated."

"Wait. What opposition?"

"The angel standing guard at the elevator is what we cops think of as a clue. You need me to draw you some pictures?"

"Um. Hell, you mean? Like . . . actual Fallen angels?"

"Not exactly. But if you want to think of it that way, it works. Sort of. What you need to know is that they're the bad guys."

"That's why I'm here," I said. "Because they . . . broke some sort of cosmic rule?"

"You were getting in their way. They wanted you gone. They broke the law to make it happen. That makes you my problem."

I frowned at him and looked down at myself. I noticed idly that I was wearing jeans, a plain black T-shirt, and my black leather duster — which had been torn to shreds and consigned to the waters of the lake an hour or three before I got shot. I mean, my duster had died.

But I was wearing it, whole and good as new.

Which was when it really, really hit me.

I was dead.

I was *dead.*

Chicago, the White Council, my enemies, my friends, my daughter . . . They were all gone. Obsolete. And I had no idea whatsoever what was going to happen to me next. The room felt like it started spinning. My legs started shaking. I sat down on a chair opposite Jack's seat.

I felt his steady regard on me, and after a moment he said quietly, "Son, it happens to all of us. It's hard to face, but you gotta relax and focus, or there's nothing I can do for you."

I took some deep breaths with my eyes closed — and noticed for the first time how absolutely incredible I felt physically. I felt

23

like I had when I was a kid, when I was full of energy and the need to expend it doing something enjoyable. My limbs felt stronger, quicker, lighter.

I looked at my left hand and saw that it was no longer covered in scar tissue from the burns I'd received years ago. It was whole, as if it had never been harmed.

I expanded the logic and realized that I didn't actually feel all that incredible — I was simply missing an entire catalog of injuries and trauma. The faded, years-old scar I'd given myself on my right forearm, when my knife had slipped while cleaning the fish my grandfather and I had caught, was missing also.

The constant, slowly growing level of aches and pains of the body was simply gone. Which made sense enough, since my body was gone, too.

The pain had stopped.

I mopped at my face with my hand and said, "Sorry. It's just a lot to take in."

The smile appeared again. "Heh. Just wait."

I felt irritated at his tone. It was something to hang on to, and I planted my metaphoric heels and dragged the spinning room to a stop.

"So, who are you?" I asked. "And how can you help me?"

"You want to call me something, call me Captain. Or Jack."

"Or Sparrow?" I asked.

Jack looked at me with a cop face that showed nothing but the vague hint of disapproval. He reached across the desk and slid a file folder to the blotter in front of him. He opened it and scanned the contents. "Look, kid, you're stuck here. You aren't going anywhere until we get this discrepancy sorted out."

"Why not?"

"Because what comes after isn't for people who are rubbernecking over their shoulders or bitching about how unfair they had it," Jack said, his expression frank. "So, we sort out how you got screwed over. Then you get to move on to what's next."

I thought of being trapped in the hollow shell of the city outside and shuddered. "Okay. How do we fix it?"

"You go back," Jack said. "And you catch the scum who did you."

"Back?" I said. "Back to . . ."

"Earth, yeah," Jack said. "Chicago." He closed the folder and dropped it into his outbox. "You gotta find out who killed you."

I arched an eyebrow at him. "You're kidding."

He stared at me, his expression as jovial as a mountain crag.

I rolled my eyes. "You want me to solve *my own* murder?"

He shrugged. "You want a job here instead,

25

I can set you up."

"Augh," I said, shuddering again. "No."

"Okay," he said. "Any questions?"

"Uh," I said. "What do you mean when you say you're sending me back? I mean . . . back to my body or . . . ?"

"Nah," he said. "Isn't available. Isn't how it works. You go back as you are."

I frowned at him and then down at myself. "As a spirit," I said.

He spread his hands, as if I had just comprehended some vast and weighty truth. "Don't hang around for sunrise. Watch out for thresholds. You know the drill."

"Yeah," I said, disturbed. "But without my body . . ."

"Won't have much magic. Most people can't see you, hear you. Won't be able to touch things."

I stared at him. "How am I supposed to find anything out like that?" I asked.

Jack lifted both hands. "Kid, I don't make the law. I make sure it gets observed." He squinted at me. "Besides. I thought you were a detective."

I clenched my jaw and glared at him. My glare isn't bad, but he wasn't impressed. I exhaled slowly and then said, "Solve my own murder."

He nodded.

Anger rose from my chest and entered my voice. "I guess it isn't enough that I spent my

26

adult life trying to help and protect people. There's something else I have to do before going off to meet Saint Peter."

Jack shrugged. "Don't be so certain about that. With your record, son, you might just as easily find yourself on a southbound train."

"Hell," I spat. "You know what Hell is, Captain Sparrow? Hell is staring at your daughter and knowing that you'll never get to touch her again. Never get to speak to her. Never get to help her or protect her. Bring on the lake of fire. It wouldn't come close."

"In point of fact," Jack said calmly, "I do know what Hell is. You aren't the only dead guy with a daughter, Dresden."

I sank back into my chair, frowning at him, and then turned my head to stare past him to a simple landscape painting on the wall.

"If it makes any difference," Jack said, "three of the people you love will come to great harm unless you find your murderer."

"What do you mean, harm?" I asked.

"Maimed. Changed. Broken."

"Which three people?" I asked.

"Can't tell you that," he said.

"Yeah," I muttered. "I bet you can't."

I thought about it. Maybe I was dead, but I was sure as hell not ready to go. I had to make sure the people who'd helped me take on the Red King were taken care of. My apprentice, Molly, had been badly wounded in the battle, but that wasn't her biggest problem. Now that I was dead, there was nothing standing between her and a summary beheading at the hands of the White Council of Wizards.

And my daughter, little Maggie, was still back there. I'd deprived her of a mother, just as someone else had deprived her of a father. I had to make sure she was taken care of. I needed to tell my grandfather good-bye . . . and Karrin.

God. What had Karrin found when she came back to the boat to pick me up? A giant splatter of blood? My corpse? She was misguided and stubborn enough that I was sure she would blame herself for whatever had happened. She'd tear herself apart. I had to reach her somehow, and I couldn't do that from this spiritual Siberia.

Could they be the ones the captain was talking about? Or was it someone else?

Dammit.

My self might have felt full of energy and life, but my mind was weary almost beyond measure. Hadn't I done enough? Hadn't I helped enough people, rescued enough prisoners, defeated enough monsters? I'd made enemies of some of the deadliest and most evil things on the planet, and fought them time and again. And one of them had killed me for it.

Rest in peace, it says on all those tombstones. I'd fought against the rising tide until it had literally killed me. So where the hell was my rest? My peace?

Three of the people you love will come to great harm unless you find your murderer.

My imagination conjured scenes filled with the anguish of the people I cared most about. Which pretty much settled things. I couldn't allow something like that to happen.

Besides, there was one more thing that made me certain that I wanted to go back. At the end of the day . . . some son of a bitch had freaking *killed* me.

That's not the kind of thing you can just let stand.

And if it would let me get out of this place and let me move on to wherever it was I was supposed to go, that was a nice bonus.

"Okay," I said quietly. "How does it work?"

He slid a pad and a piece of paper across the desk at me, along with a pencil. "You get to go to an address in Chicago," he said. "You write it there. Driver will drop you off."

I took the pad and paper and frowned at it, trying to work out where to go. I mean, it wasn't like I could show up just anywhere. If I was going in as a pure spirit, it would be futile to contact any of my usual allies. It takes some serious talent to see a spirit that hasn't manifested itself, the way a ghost can occasionally appear to the physical eye. My friends wouldn't even know I was there.

"Out of curiosity," I said, "what happens if

I don't catch the killer?"

His expression turned sober and his voice became quieter. "You'll be trapped there. Maybe forever. Unable to touch. Unable to speak. Watching things happen in the world, with no ability whatsoever to affect them."

"Hell," I said quietly.

"Hell."

"That's cheerful."

"You're dead, son," Jack said. "Cheer is contraindicated."

I nodded.

I was looking at one hell — *ba-dump-bump-ching* — of a risk. I mean, fitting in here in Chicago-tory might not be fun, but it probably wouldn't be torture, either. Judging from what Carmichael and Jack had said and from the way they went about their business, they were able to act in some fashion, maybe even do some good. They didn't look particularly thrilled to be doing what they were doing, but they carried that sense of professional purpose with them.

A ghost trapped on the mortal coil? That would be far worse. Always present, always watching, and always impotent.

I never really developed my Don't-Get-Involved skills. I'd go crazy in a year, and wind up one more pathetic, insane, trapped spirit haunting the town I'd spent my adult life protecting.

"Screw it," I said, and started writing on

the paper. "If my friends need me, I have to try."

Jack took the pad back with a nod of what might have been approval. Then he stood up and pulled on his suit coat. Car keys rattled in his hand. He was only medium height, but he moved with a confidence and a tightly leashed energy that once more made him seem familiar, somehow. "Let's go."

Several of the cops — because I was sure they were cops, or at least were doing something so similar that the word fit — nodded to Jack as he went by.

"Hey," called someone from behind us. "Murphy."

Jack stopped and turned around.

A guy wearing a suit that would have looked at home in the historic Pinkerton Detective Agency came over to Jack with a clipboard and held it out along with a pen. Jack scanned what was on it, signed off, and passed the clipboard back to the man.

Jack resumed his walking speed. I stuck my hands in my duster pockets and stalked along beside him.

"Captain Collin J. Murphy?" I asked quietly.

He grunted.

"You're Karrin's dad. Used to run the Black Cat case files."

He didn't say anything. We went down the elevator, past the guard angel, and out to the

31

street, where an old blue Buick Skylark, one with tail fins and a convertible roof, sat waiting by the curb. He went around to the driver's side and we both got in. The rain drummed on the roof of the car.

He sat behind the wheel for a moment, his eyes distant. Then he said, "Yeah."

"She's talked about you."

He nodded. "I hear you've looked out for my Karrie."

Karrie? I tried to imagine the person who would call Murphy that to her face. Rawlins had done it once, but *only* once, and not only was he her partner, but he'd also worked with her dad when she was a little girl. Rawlins was practically family.

Anyone else would need to be a Terminator. From Krypton.

"Sometimes," I said. "She doesn't need much in the way of protection."

"Everyone needs someone." Then he started the car, the engine coming to life with a satisfying, throaty purr. Jack ran his hand over the steering wheel thoughtfully and looked out at the rain. "You can back out of this if you want, son. Until you get out of this car. Once you do that, you've chosen your path — and whatever comes with it."

"Yep," I said, and nodded firmly. "The sooner I get started, the sooner I get done."

His mouth quirked up at one corner and he nodded, making a grunting sound of approval. He peered at the pad, read the address I'd written, and grunted. "Why here?"

"Because that's where I'll find the one person in Chicago I'm sure can help me," I said.

Captain Murphy nodded. "Okay," he said. "Let's go."

CHAPTER THREE

Captain Murphy's old Skylark stopped in a residential area up in Harwood Heights, a place that still looked as empty and hollow as the rest of the city. It was an odd home, for Chicago — a white stucco number with a red tile roof that looked like it had been transplanted from Southern California. In the steady rain and the mournful grey light of the streetlamps it stood, cold, lonely, and empty of purpose among the more traditional homes that surrounded it.

The Buick's windshield wipers thumped rhythmically.

"Once you get out," said Captain Murphy, "there's no coming back. You're on your own."

"Been there, done that," I said. I offered him my hand. "Thank you, Captain."

He traded grips with me. I didn't try to out-crush him. He didn't try to crush me. The men who can really handle themselves rarely do.

I wished Captain Murphy had lived long enough for me to meet him in the real world. I had a feeling he'd have made one hell of an ally.

"I might be in touch with Karrin," I said.

"No messages. I've done her enough harm," he said, almost before I had finished speaking. His voice carried a tone of unquestionable finality. He nodded toward the house. "But you can tell the big fellow over there that I sent you. It might help."

I nodded. Then I took a deep breath, opened the door of the car, and stepped out into —

I was more impressed with what I *hadn't* stepped into, for a moment. Because when my feet hit the ground and the car door shut behind me, I wasn't standing in Chicago's rainy, abandoned corpse. Instead, I was on a city street on a cold, clear evening. No rain fell. The stars and moon burned bright overhead, and the ambient city light combined with a fairly fresh and heavy snowfall to make it nearly as bright as daylight outside.

Sounds rushed all around me. Traffic, distant horns, the thumping beat of music from a large stereo. A jet's passage left a hollow roar behind it — I was standing only a few miles from O'Hare.

I turned to look behind me, but Captain Murphy's car had vanished, back into Chicago Between, presumably.

I stood there alone.

I sighed. Then I turned and walked onto the property of Mortimer Lindquist, ectomancer.

Once upon a time, Morty had covered his lawn with decorations meant to be intimidating and spooky. Headstones. A wrought-iron fence with a big metal gate. Eerie lighting. The overall impression could be scary if you were gullible enough and the lighting was low, but mostly it had looked like cheap Halloween decorations outside a crack house.

Times had changed.

Morty had gotten rid of all the cheap junk, except for the fence. He'd turned his front yard into a Japanese garden. There were a few hedges, and a koi pond complete with a little wooden bridge that spanned it. Raised planters everywhere contained bonsai, all of them trees native to North America. It was a little unnerving to see what looked like an adult oak tree — only fifteen inches high and complete with miniature leaves.

There weren't a lot of people in Chicago doing that for money, which implied that it was Morty's own handiwork. If so, it had taken him a lot of effort and patience to create those.

I walked forward calmly, reaching out to open the gate.

My hand went right through it.

Yeah, I know, I was essentially a ghost, but I'd never gotten much practice with intangibility. I was used to reaching out for objects and being able to touch them. Now my hand simply tingled, as if waking up after I'd taken a nap and used it as a pillow. I pushed my arm a little farther forward, leaning to one side, and saw my fingertips emerge from the metal of the gate. I waggled my fingers, just to be sure.

"Okay," I said. "No help for it, then." I took a deep breath and held it as if I were about to jump into deep water. Then I hunched my shoulders and rushed forward.

Anticlimax. As I went through the gate, I was subjected to a swift, intense tingling sensation. Then I was on the other side.

I walked up a little stone path leading to Morty's front door, but it wasn't until I had gone over the bridge that I saw the man standing in the shadows on the front porch.

He was huge. Not built like a weight lifter or anything, just a naturally big-boned, brawny man standing almost as tall as I. His dark hair was gathered at the nape of his neck with a bit of ribbon. A long, dark blue coat fell to his calves, its sleeves marked with gold braid. Beneath that, he wore a uniform — a tight-fitting blue jacket, white shirt, white pants, and high black boots. He carried some kind of long-handled ax over one shoulder, and as I came to a halt, he was already drawing a flintlock pistol from his belt with his free hand. He leveled it just a little bit to one side of me and called out, "Halt! Identify yourself, scoundrel, or begone!"

"Scoundrel?" I asked, putting my fingers on my chest as if distressed at the accusation. "That's a little unfair."

"Ye've the look of a scoundrel!" boomed the man. "And a dandysprat and a ragamuffin. Though I'll admit, for all that, ye could yet be a congressman." I could see the white flash of his teeth in the dark as he smiled. "Give me a name, man."

"Harry Dresden," I said in a clear tone.

The barrel of the gun wavered a few more degrees away from me. "The wizard?"

"The *late* wizard," I replied, then gestured down at myself. "The late Harry Dresden, really."

"Zounds," the man said. He frowned for a moment as if in thought.

It didn't look natural on him.

"If you lie," he said slowly, "I can see no veritable reason for doing so, and I am inclined to shoot you. Yet if you tell the truth, your presence here draws mischief to my friend's house, and I am inclined to shoot you repeatedly." He nodded firmly and settled the gun's barrel on me. "Either way . . ."

He was about to shoot. I didn't know if it would re-kill me or not, but given what I had experienced of the universe, it might. At the very least, I figured, it would probably hurt like a son of a bitch. I had to keep this bozo from bringing the hammer down. Assuming his period outfit was authentic, that might be simple.

"Little rude, isn't it, to shoot me?" I asked him. "I'm unarmed, and I've offered no violence or insult to you. Introduced myself, even. Whereas you haven't even told me your name."

The man in the blue coat looked suddenly abashed, and the pistol dropped slightly once more. "Ah yes. Um, please excuse me. Societal graces were imperfectly instilled in me in my youth, and that sad fact tends to be reflected in my more temperate afterlife." He straightened and literally clicked his heels together, without ever moving the gun far from me, and gave me a slight bow. "The late Captain Sir Stuart Winchester of the Colonial Marines."

I arched an eyebrow. "*Sir* Stuart of the *Colonial* Marines?"

He shrugged. "It is a protracted and complex tale."

"Well, Stu," I said, "with all due respect, my business here is not with you. It's with Mr. Lindquist."

"I hardly think so," Stu sniffed. "Have you an invitation?"

I gave him a blank look for a moment and

then said, "I'm new to the whole ghost thing, but I'm damned sure you don't just send out envelopes through the U.S. Ghostal Service."

"Ye'd be surprised how many postal workers leave a shade behind," Stu countered. "The routine, methinks, is what keeps them making their rounds. The poor things don't even realize anything's changed."

"Don't change the subject," I said. "I need to talk to Mort."

"I am sorry, sir," Stu said. "But the standing order regarding the visit of any uninvited ghosts is to deny them entry."

"And you have to follow Mort's orders?"

"It isn't as though you could cross his threshold uninvited in any case, man," he said.

"Right," I said. "You have to follow his orders."

"We are not compelled," Stu said at once, and severely. "We aid him out of friendship and respect and . . ." He sighed and added, "And boredom. Ye gods, but this city pales after but half a century, and I've lingered here more than four times that."

I found myself grinning at the ghost. "Stu, let me make you a promise. Maybe even an oath. I come to ask Mort's help, not to harm him — and I'm reasonably sure my presence will not contribute to your ongoing sense of ennui."

Stu let out a rolling belly laugh and began

40

to speak, but the sound died off, and he stared at me thoughtfully, tapping a fingertip against the pistol.

"If it makes any difference," I said, "Jack Murphy was the one who dropped me off here. Told me to mention his name."

Stu's eyebrows shot up. I could see the thoughts racing behind his eyes. They weren't going to win any sprints, but they seemed good for the long haul. "Aye?" He pursed his lips. "A good fellow. For an Irishman."

I snorted. "If he's ever around, you'd better smile when you say —"

A flood of intangible cold pressed against my back, as suddenly as if I'd been standing in front of an industrial freezer door when it opened.

I turned to see a humanoid, grey form floating just above the ground maybe five yards away from me and drifting closer. The details were obscure, the proportions slightly off, as if I were looking at a badly molded plastic doll. There were no real features on it, just hollow, gaping eye sockets within a sunken, nearly skull-like face, and a wide, empty mouth that hung open as if the tendons attaching the lower jaw had stretched out like old elastic bands.

It moved with a kind of shuffling grace, as if it had no real weight and needed only to touch the ground to propel itself forward with its toes. It made a sound as it came, a hollow, rattling, muted gasp. It was the sound of an agonized scream that had long since run out of breath to propel it — but tried to continue anyway.

It got closer to me, and I felt colder as it did.

"Get back," I snapped. "I mean it."

The creature came forward with another little touch of its toes to the earth, as mindless and graceful as a hungry jellyfish, and a hell of a lot creepier.

I took a pair of quick steps back and said, "Fine. Be that way." I lifted my right hand, drew in my will, and snarled, *"Fuego."*

And nothing — nothing at *all* — happened.

There was no stirring of forces deep inside me. There was no current of equal parts giddy excitement, vibrating tension, and raw lightning flashing through my thoughts. There was no flash of white-hot flame that would have incinerated the apparition coming toward me.

There was no magic.

There was no magic.

"Oh, crap," I choked and reeled back as the thing's fingers raked at me with deathly grace, the sound of its strangled scream growing higher pitched. Its fingers didn't end in nails. They just sort of trailed off into drifting shreds that were surrounded by deadly cold.

Behind me, there was a mechanical sound, *click-clack,* of a large, half-cocked trigger being pulled fully back and ready to fire.

I whirled my head around in time to see Stu's enormous old gun snap up to aim directly at the end of my nose. I'm sure its barrel wasn't actually as big as a train tunnel, but at the moment it sure as hell looked like it.

I felt the wave of cold intensify against my back, and by the time Stu shouted, "Get down!" I was already halfway to the ground.

I hit hard — apparently being insubstantial didn't free me from the laws of gravity or the discomfort of its unwavering enforcement — at the same time that Stu's pistol went off.

Everything happened in dreamtime, slowly enough for me to see every detail, but so swiftly that I felt that no matter how fast I moved, I would not be able to keep up. I was expecting the crack of a pistol round, or even the hollow *whump* of a large-bore black-powder weapon. What I got was a roar that sounded like it had been distorted by a dozen different DJs and a mile of train tunnel. The standard plume of black-powder smoke didn't emerge from the barrel. Instead, expanding concentric rings of pastel mist puffed out, swirling at their center as if pulled into following the contrail of the bullet.

The bullet itself was no lump of lead. It was a sphere of multicolored light that looked nearly big enough to be a golf ball. It went by a couple of feet over my head, and I swear it felt like I'd gotten a mild sunburn just from being close to it. A deep tone, like the thrumming of an amplified bass-guitar string, emanated from the sphere, vibrating through my flesh and against my bones.

I turned my head in time to see the sphere smash against the chest of the attacking apparition. The not-bullet plunged into its body, tearing a hole the size of my fist in its chest. A cloud of something that looked like steam poured out of the creature. Light kindled within it, almost like an old movie projector playing upon the vapor, and I suddenly saw a flicker of shadowy images, all of them dim, warped, twisted, as if someone had made a clips reel from the random strips of celluloid from the cutting-room floor.

The images grew steadily dimmer, until there was nothing left but a thinning cloud of mist. It wasn't until then that I saw that the grey form was gradually sagging, like a waterskin being slowly emptied.

The mists vanished. All that was left of the grey creature was an ugly, colorless lump on the ground.

Firm bootsteps came down the walkway from the porch, and Stu placed himself between me and the thing, whatever it had been. Though his hands were reloading the pistol, complete with powder horn and a short ramrod, his eyes swept up and down the street around us.

"What the hell was that?" I asked.

"Wraith," he said quietly, with a certain professional detachment in his voice. "A ghost, like you or me, who gave in to despair and gave up his sense of self-reason."

"Dangerous?"

"Extremely so," Stu said. He turned to look down at me. "Especially to someone like you."

"Like me?"

"A fresh shade. You've a paucity of experience in learning to defend yourself here. And it is all but impossible for a fresh shade such as yourself to hide: There is a sense of life that clings to you." He frowned. "To you especially."

"Because I'm a wizard, maybe."

Stu nodded. "Likely, likely."

"What would have happened if . . . ?" I gestured at the wraith's remains.

"It would have devoured your memories," Stu said calmly.

I considered that for a moment and studied the remains almost wistfully. "I don't know. I've got some I wouldn't mind losing."

Stu slid his readied pistol back into his belt. "For shades, memories are life, sustenance, and power. We *are* memories now, wizard."

"The images in the mist," I said. "When it was . . . was dying. They were its memories?"

"Aye. What was left of them." Stu moved forward and crouched over the remains. He

45

held out his hand, palm down over them, and took a deep breath. After a few heartbeats, glowing mist began to rise from the wraith's remains. It snaked through the air and into Stu's chest, flowing into him like water into a pool. When it was complete, he stood again and let out a sigh.

Whatever had struck the wraith, it had evidently been made of the same substance as Sir Stuart. If ghosts, then, were memories . . . "The bullet," I said. "You made it out of a memory?"

"Naturally," he said. His expression filled with a gentle, distant sorrow. "A strong one. I'll make it into another bullet at some point."

"Thank you," I said. "For helping me."

"I must admit, I did not put the poor brute down exclusively for your sake, wizard. You represent a feast for any wraith. Fresh from the world of the living, still with a touch of vitality upon you, and full to bursting with fresh, unfaded memories. The wraith that ate you would become powerful — a dire, fell creature indeed. One that could threaten the world of the living as easily as it could the world of spirit. I won't have that."

"Oh," I said. "Thanks anyway."

Stu nodded and offered me his hand. I took it, rose, and said, "I need to talk to Mort."

Even as I spoke, I saw two more wraiths appear from the darkness. I checked behind me and saw more coming, drifting with ef-

46

fortless motions and deceptive speed.

"If you get me inside Mort's threshold, I'll be safe from them," I said, nodding to the wraiths. "I don't know how to defend myself against them. They'll kill me. And if that happens, you'll have that monster wraith on your hands."

"Not if I kill you first," Stu said calmly, tapping a finger on the handle of his pistol.

I turned my head slightly to one side, eyeing him, studying his face. "Nah," I said. "Won't happen."

"How would you know, spook?" he asked in a flat voice. But he couldn't keep the smile out of his eyes.

"I'm a wizard," I said, infusing my voice with portentous undertones. "We have our ways."

He remained silent, expression stern, but his eyes danced.

I sobered. "And those wraiths are getting closer, man."

Stu snorted and said, "The wraiths are always getting closer." Then he drew his pistol and pointed it at my chest. "I hereby take you prisoner, late wizard. Keep your hands in plain sight, follow all my verbal instructions, and we'll do splendidly."

I showed him my hands. "Oh. Uh. Okay."

Stu nodded sharply. "About face, then. Let's go talk to the little bald man."

CHAPTER FOUR

I followed Stu through the front door (dammit, tingle, ouch), and paused on the other side to consider that fact for a moment. Only a member of the household's family could issue an invitation that would let an immaterial entity past the home's threshold.

So. Sir Stuart was practically family around Mort's place. Unless he was literal family. Hauntings, after all, have historically been known to remain with a specific family lineage. Could Stu be one of Mort's ancestors, here to watch out for his familial posterity? Or had the little ectomancer always possessed an odd sort of family, one I had never known about?

Interesting. It would be wise to keep my eyes open.

The house looked much different. What had been a cheesily staged séance room had become a living room with a sofa, love seat, and comfortable chairs. I'd seen only part of the rest of the house, but as I walked with Sir

Stuart, I could see that the dismal little den of a house had been renovated, redecorated, and otherwise made more beautiful. Stu guided me to a room that was part library, part office, with a fire crackling in the fireplace.

Mortimer Lindquist seemed to have finally given in to the inevitable. I'd seen him with a bad toupee, and with an even worse comb-over, but this was the first time I'd seen him sporting a full-on Charles Xavier. The unbroken shine of his pate looked a lot better than the partial coverage. He'd lost weight, too, since last I'd seen him. I mean, he wasn't going to be modeling for Abercrombie & Fitch or anything, but he'd definitely dropped from self-destructively obese down to merely stout. He was in his early fifties, under five and a half feet tall, and dressed in black slacks and a grey silk shirt, and he wore little square-rimmed spectacles.

He sat at his table, a deck of playing cards spread out in front of him in what could be either a fortune-telling through the cards or a game of solitaire — they tended to have about the same amount of significance, in my experience.

"Did I hear a shot, Sir Stuart?" Mort asked absently, staring intently at the cards. Then his hands froze in the act of dealing another, and he shot to his feet, whirling to face me. "Oh, *perfect*."

"Hiya, Morty," I said.

"This is not happening," Mort said, promptly getting up from the table and walking quickly toward another room. "This just can't be happening. No one is *this* unlucky."

I hurried forward, trying to keep up, and followed him into a hallway. "I need to talk to —"

"I don't *care*," Mort said, his arms crossing each other in a slashing, pushing-away gesture, never stopping. "I do *not* see you. I am *not* listening to you, Dresden. It's not enough that you have to keep dragging me into things in life. So now your stupid ghost shows up to do it, too? No. Whatever it is, no."

We entered a kitchen, where I found Sir Stuart already present, his arms folded, leaning back against a wall with a quiet smile as he watched. Mort went to a large cookie jar, opened it, and took out a single Oreo before replacing the lid.

"Morty, come on, it's never been like that," I said. "I've come to ask your help a couple of times because you're a capable professional and —"

"Bullshit," Mort snapped, spinning to face me, his eyes flashing. "Dresden came to me when he was so desperate he might as well try any old loser."

I winced. His summation of our relationship was partially true. But not entirely. "Morty, please."

"Morty, *what?*" he snapped back. "You've got to be kidding me. I am *not* getting involved in whatever international crisis you mean to perpetrate next."

"It's not like I've got a lot of choice in the matter, man. It's you or no one. Please. Just hear me out."

He barked out an incredulous little laugh. "No, you hear *me* out, shade. *No* means 'no.' It isn't happening. It isn't ever going to happen. I said *no!*" And then he slammed the door to the next room in my face.

"Dammit, Morty," I snarled, and braced myself for the plunge through his door after him.

"Dresden, st— !" Sir Stuart said.

Too late. I slammed my nose and face into the door and fell backward onto my ass like a perfect idiot. My face began to throb immediately, swelling with pain that felt precisely normal, identical to that of any dummy who walked into a solid oak door.

"—op," Sir Stuart finished. He sighed, and offered me a hand up. I took it and he hauled me to my feet. "Ghost dust mixed into the paint inside the room," he explained. "No spirit can pass through it."

"I'm familiar with it," I muttered, and felt annoyed that I hadn't thought of the idea before, as an additional protection against hostile spirits at my own apartment. To the beings of the immaterial, ghost dust was

51

incontrovertible solidity. Thrown directly at a ghost, it would cause tremendous pain and paralyze it for a little while, as if the spook had been suddenly loaded down with an incredible and unexpected weight. If I'd put it all over my walls, it would have turned them into a solid obstacle to ghosts and their ilk, shutting them out with obdurate immobility.

Of course, my recipe had used depleted uranium dust, which would have made it just a tad silly to spread around the interior of my apartment.

Not that it mattered. My apartment was gone, taken when a Molotov cocktail, hurled by a vampire assassin, had burned the boardinghouse to the ground along with most of my worldly possessions. Only a few had been left, hidden away. God knew where they were now.

I suppose I couldn't really count that as a loss, all things considered. Material possessions aren't much use to a dead man.

I lifted a hand to my nose, wincing and expecting to find it rebroken. No such thing had happened, though a glob of some kind of runny, transparent, gelatinous liquid smeared the back of my hand. "Hell's bells. I'm bleeding ectoplasm?"

That drew a smile from the late marine. "Ghosts generally do. You'll have to forgive him, Dresden. He can be very slow to understand things at times."

"I don't have time to wait for him to catch on," I said. "I need his help."

Sir Stuart grinned some more. "You aren't going to get it by standing there repeating yourself like a broken record. Repeating yourself like a broken record. Repeating yourself like a broken —"

"Ha-ha," I said without enthusiasm. "People who cared about me are going to get hurt if I can't act."

Sir Stuart pursed his lips. "It seems to me that if your demise was to leave someone vulnerable, something would have happened to them already. It's been six months, after all."

I felt my jaw drop open. "W-what? Six *months?*"

The ghost nodded. "Today is the ninth of May, to be precise."

I stared at him, flabbergasted. Then I turned, put my back against Morty's impenetrable door, and used it to stay upright as I sank to the ground. "Six *months?*"

"Yes."

"That's not . . ." I knew I was just gabbling my stream of thought, but I couldn't seem to stop myself from talking. "That's not right. It can't be right. I was *dead* for less than a freaking *hour.* What kind of Rip van Winkle bullshit is *this?*"

Sir Stuart watched me, his expression serious and untroubled. "Time has little meaning to us now, Dresden, and it's very easy to become unattached to it. I once lost five years listening to a Pink Floyd album."

"There is *snow* a foot and a half *deep* on the *ground*," I said, pointing in a random direction. "In *May?*"

His voice turned dry. "The television station Mortimer watches theorizes that it is due to person-made, global climate change."

I was going to say something insulting, maybe even offensive, but just then the rippling sound of metallic wind chimes tinkled through the air. They were joined seconds later by more and more of the same, until the noise was considerable.

"What's that?" I asked.

Sir Stuart turned and walked back the way we'd come, and I hurried to follow. In the next room over, a dozen sets of wind chimes hung from the ceiling. All of them were astir, whispering and singing even though there was no air moving through the room.

Sir Stuart's hand went to his ax, and I suddenly understood what I was looking at.

It was an alarm system.

"What's happening?" I asked him.

"Another assault," he said. "We have less than thirty seconds. Come with me."

CHAPTER FIVE

"To arms!" bellowed Sir Stuart. "They're coming at us again, lads!"

The ringing of the alarm chimes doubled as figures immediately exploded from the very walls and floor of the ectomancer's house, appearing as suddenly as . . . well, *as ghosts.* Duh.

One second, the only figures in sight were me and Sir Stuart. The next, we were striding at the head of a veritable armed mob. The figures didn't have the same kind of sharp-edged reality that Sir Stuart did. They were wispier, foggier. Though I could see Sir Stuart with simple clarity, viewing the others was like watching someone walk by on the opposite side of the street during a particularly heavy rain.

There was no specific theme to the spirits defending Mort's house. The appearance of each was eclectic, to such an extent that they looked like the assembled costumed staff from some kind of museum of American history.

Soldiers in the multicolored uniforms of regulars from the Revolutionary War walked beside buckskin-clad woodsmen, trappers, and Native Americans from the wars preceding the revolution. Farmers from the Civil War era stood with shopkeepers from the turn of the twentieth century. Men in suits, some armed with shotguns, others with tommy guns, moved toward the attack, the bitter divisions of the era of Prohibition apparently forgotten. Doughboys marched with a squad of buffalo soldiers, followed by half a dozen genuine, six-gun-toting cowboys in long canvas coats, and a group of grunts whose uniforms placed them as Vietnam-era U.S. Army infantry.

"Huh," I said. "Now, there's something you don't see every day."

Sir Stuart drew his gun from his belt as he strode forward, checking the old weapon. "I've seen a great many years in this city. Many, many nights. Until recently, I would have agreed with you."

I looked back at Sir Stuart's little army as we reached the front door and passed through it.

"I — glah, dammit, that feels strange — guess that means you're seeing a pattern."

"This is the fifth night running that they've come at us," Sir Stuart replied, as we went out onto the porch. "Stay behind me, Dresden. And well clear of my ax arm."

He came to a halt a step later, and I stood behind him a bit and on his left side. Sir Stuart, who had been a giant for his day, was only a couple of inches shorter than me. I had to strain to see over him.

The street was crowded with silent figures.

I just stared out at them for a moment, struggling to understand what I was looking at. Out on the road were scores, maybe even a couple of hundred wraiths like the one Sir Stuart had dispatched earlier. They were flabby, somehow hollow and squishy-looking, like balloons that hadn't been filled with enough gas — sad, frightening humanoid figures, their eyes and mouths gaping too large, too dark, and too empty to seem real. But instead of advancing toward us, they simply stood there in even ranks, leaning forward slightly, their arms held vaguely upward as if yearning toward the house, though their hands seemed limp and devoid of strength, their fingers trailing into shapeless shreds. The horrible sound of hundreds of nearly silent moans of pain emanated from the block of wraiths, along with a slowly building edge of tension.

"Tell me, wizard," Sir Stuart said. "What do you see?"

"A crap-ton of wraiths," I breathed quietly. "Which I do not know how to fight." None of them had the deadly, focused look of Sir Stuart and his crew, but there were a *lot* of them out there. "Something is getting them worked up."

"Ah," he said. He glanced back over his shoulder at me, his eyes narrowed. "I thought your folk had clear sight."

I frowned at him and then out at the small sea of wraiths. I stared and stared, bringing the focus of concentration I'd learned over endless hours of practice in my studies — and suddenly saw them. Dark, slithering shapes, moving up and down the ranks of wraiths at the backs of their lines. They looked vaguely like folk covered in dark, enveloping cloaks and robes, but they glided through the air with a silent, effortless grace that made me think of sharks who had scented blood in the water and were closing in to feed.

"Four . . . five, six of them," I said. "In the back ranks."

"Good," said Sir Stuart, nodding his approval. "That's the real foe, lad. These poor wraiths are just their dogs."

It had been a long, long time since I'd felt quite this lost. "Uh. What are they?"

"Lemurs," he said, with the Latin pronunciation: Lay-*moors*. "Shades who have set themselves against Providence and have given themselves over to malice and rage. They do not know pity, nor restraint, nor . . ."

"Fear?" I guessed. "They always never know fear."

Sir Stuart glanced over his shoulder and bounced his long-handled ax against his palm, his mouth turned up into an edged, wolfish grin. "Nay, lad. Perhaps they were innocent of it once. But they proved quick learners when they raised their hands against this house." He turned back to face the street and called out, "Positions!"

The spirits who had come along behind us flowed around and over us and — though I twitched when I saw it — beneath us. Within seconds, they were spread into a defensive line in the shape of a half dome between the house and the gathered wraiths and lemurs. Then those silent forms stood steady, whether their feet were planted on the ground or in thin air or somewhere just *below* the ground, and faced the small horde with their weapons in hand.

The tension continued to build, and the seething, agonized gasps of the wraiths grew louder.

"Um," I said, as my heart started picking up the pace. "What do I do?"

"Nothing," Sir Stuart replied, his attention now focused forward. "Just stay near me and out of my way."

"But —"

"I can see you were a fighter, boy," Stuart said, his voice harsh. "But now you're a child.

You've neither the knowledge nor the tools you need to survive." He turned and gave me a ferocious glare, and an unseen force literally pushed my feet back across five or six inches of porch. Holy crap. Stuart might not be a wizard, but obviously I had a thing or two to learn about how a formidable will translated to power on the spooky side of the street.

"Stay close to me," the marine said. "And shut it."

I swallowed, and Sir Stuart turned back to the front.

"You don't have to be a dick about it," I muttered. Very quietly.

It bothered me that he was right. Without Sir Stuart's intervention, I'd have been dead again already.

That's right — you heard me: dead again already.

I mean, come *on*. How screwed up is your life (after- or otherwise) when you find yourself needing phrases like *that?*

I indulged myself in half a second of disgust that once again the universe seemed to be making an extraspecial effort to align itself against me, but it was my pride that was in critical condition. I was accustomed to being the guy who did the fighting and protecting. Fear had been fuel for the fire, meat and potatoes, when I was the one calling the shots. But now . . .

This was terror of an alien vintage: I was helpless.

Without warning, the air filled with whistling and ear-slashing shrieks, and the horde of wraiths washed toward us in a flash flood of strangled moans.

"Give it to them, lads!" Sir Stuart bellowed, his voice rising above the cacophony of screams with the silvery clarity of a trumpet.

Spectral gunfire roared out at once from the weapons of the hovering defenders. Again, clouds of powder smoke were replaced with bursts of colored mist. Bullets had been switched out for streaking spheres of violent radiance. Instead of the explosions of propellant and projectiles breaking the sound barrier, hammering bass-note thrums filled the air and echoed on long after a gunshot would have faded.

A tide of destruction swept over the assaulting wraiths, distorted light and sound tearing great, ragged holes in them, filling the air with faded, warped shadow-images as their feeble memories bled into wisps of cloud that were swallowed by the night. They fell by the dozens — and there were still plenty more wraiths left to go around. Wraiths closed in with the Lindquist Historical Home Defense Society — and it still wasn't fair.

Sir Stuart's troops reacted like the fighting men they had once been. Swords and sabers appeared, along with stilettos and brass knuckles and bowie knives. The wraiths came at them with a slow, graceful, terrible momentum and were hacked, stabbed, punched, clubbed, and otherwise broken — but there were a *lot* of wraiths.

I heard a hollow scream that sounded as if it had come from a couple of blocks away, and lifted my eyes to see half a dozen wraiths who had all attacked together swarm over a phantom doughboy, a scrawny young man in a baggy uniform. Though one of the things was literally opened from one side to the other by a slash of the ghost soldier's bayonet, the other five just fastened onto him, first by a single fingertip, which was then blindly followed by others. Another wraith expired when the young soldier drew his knife. But then all those tattered fingers began winding and winding around him, lengthening impossibly, until within a few seconds he looked like nothing so much as a massive burn victim covered in heavy, dirty bandages.

The wraiths pressed closer and closer, their flabby bodies compressing until they hardly resembled human forms at all, and then with a sudden scream, they darted away in four different directions as more solid, lethal-looking shapes, leaving behind the translucent outline of a young man screaming in agony.

I watched, my stomach twisting, as even that image faded. Within seconds, it was gone.

"Damn their empty eyes," Sir Stuart said,

his teeth clenched. "Damn them."

"Hell's bells," I breathed. "Why didn't . . . Couldn't you have stopped them?"

"The lemurs," he spat. "I can't give them the chance to get by me into the house."

I blinked. "But . . . the threshold . . . They can't."

"They did the first night," he said. "Still don't know how. I can't leave the porch or they'll get through. Now be quiet." His fingers flexed and settled on the haft of his ax. "Here's where we come to it."

As the wraiths continued to assault and entangle the house's defenders, Sir Stuart moved to the top of the little stairs leading up to the porch and planted his feet. Out at the street, the shadowy forms of the lemurs had all gone still, each of them hunched down in a crouch, predators preparing to spring.

When it came, it came fast. Not fast like the rush of a mountain lion upon a deer, and not even fast like a runaway automobile. They were fast like bullets. One second, the lemurs were at the street, and the next they were in the air before the porch, seemingly without crossing the space between. I didn't have time to do more than yelp and go into a full-body twitch of pure, startled reaction.

But Sir Stuart was faster.

The first lemur to charge met the butt of Sir Stuart's ax, a blow that sent it into a fluttering, backward tailspin. The second and third lemurs charged at almost exactly the same moment, and Sir Stuart's ax swept out in a scything arc, slashing them both and sending them reeling with high-pitched, horrible screams. The fourth lemur drove a bony-wristed punch across Sir Stuart's jaw, staggering the marine and driving him to one knee. But when the lemur tried to follow up the attack, Stuart produced a gleaming knife from his belt, and it flashed in opalescent colors as he swept it in a treacherous diagonal slash over the thing's midsection.

The fifth lemur hesitated, seeming to abort its instantaneous rush about halfway across the yard. Stuart let out a bellow and threw the knife. It struck home, and the lemur frantically twisted in upon itself, howling like the others, until the knife tumbled free of its ghostly flesh and fell to the snowy ground.

Five wounded lemurs fled from Sir Stuart, screaming. The sixth crouched on the sidewalk, frozen in indecision.

"Coward," Stuart snarled. "If you can't finish, don't start."

All things considered, I thought Stuart might be being a little hard on the thing. It wasn't cowardly to *not* rush a juggernaut when you'd just seen your buddies get thrashed by it. Maybe the thing was just smarter than the others.

I never got a chance to find out. In the

space of an instant, *Sir Stuart* crossed the lawn to the final lemur, only his rush ended not in front of his foe, but six feet past it. The lemur jerked in the twisting, surprised reaction I had just engaged in a moment before.

Then its head fell from its shoulders, hood and all, dissolving into flickering memory embers as it went. Its headless body went mad, somehow letting out a scream, thrashing and kicking and falling to the ground, where grey-and-white fire poured from its truncated neck.

A shout of triumph went up from the home's defenders as they continued their own fight, and the suddenly listless wraiths began to be torn apart in earnest, the tide of battle shifting rapidly. Sir Stuart lifted his ax above his head in response and turned to almost casually step up behind a wraith and take its head from its shoulders with the ax.

Then, in the street, about ten feet behind him, a figure, one every bit as solid and real as Sir Stuart himself, appeared out of nowhere, a form shrouded in a nebulous grey cloak with eyes of green-white fire. It lifted what looked like a clawed hand, and sent a bolt of lightning sizzling into Sir Stuart's back.

Sir Stuart cried out in sudden agony, his body tightening helplessly, muscles convulsing just as they would on an electrocuted human being. The bolt of lightning seemed to attach itself to his spine, then burned a line down to his right hip bone, burning and searing and blowing bits of the tattered, flaming substance of his ghostly flesh into the air.

"No!" I screamed, as he fell. I started running toward him.

The marine rolled when he hit the ground and came up with that ridiculously huge old horse pistol in his hand. He leveled it at the Grey Ghost and fired, and once again his gun sent out a plume of ethereal color and a tiny, bright sun of destruction.

But the cloudy grey figure lifted its hand, and the bullet bounced off the air in front of it smoothly, catching a luckless, wounded wraith who had been attempting to retreat. The wraith immediately dissolved as the first one had — and Sir Stuart stared up at the Grey Ghost with his mouth open in shock.

Magic. The Grey Ghost was using magic. Even as I ran forward, I could feel the humming energy of it in the air, smell it on the cold breeze coming off the lake. I didn't move at ghostly superspeed. I mostly just ran across the hard ground, hurdled the little fence, went right through a car parked on the street (ow, grrrrrr!), and threw my best haymaker of a right cross at a point I nominated to be the Grey Ghost's chin.

My fist connected with what felt like solid flesh, a refreshingly familiar *smack-thump* of impact that immediately flashed red pain through my wrist to the elbow. The Grey Ghost reeled, and I didn't let up. I put a couple of left hooks into its midsection, gave it one hell of an uppercut with my right hand, and drove a hard reverse punch into its neck.

I am not a skilled martial artist. But I know a little, picked up in training with Murphy and some of the other SI cops over the years at Dough Joe's Hurricane Gym. Real fighting is only slightly about form and technique. Mostly it's about timing, and about being willing to hurt somebody. If you know more or less when to close the distance and throw the punch, you're most of the way there. But having the right mind-set is even more important. All the technique in the world isn't going to help you if you come to the fight without the will to wreak havoc on the other guy.

The Grey Ghost staggered back, and I kicked one leg out from under it as it went. It fell. I started kicking it as hard as I could, screaming, driving my toe into its ribs and back, then switching to move in and stomp at its head with the heel of my heavy hiking boot. I did not let up, not even for a second. If this thing could pull out more magic, it would deal with me as easily as it had Sir Stuart. So I focused on trying to crush the enemy's skull and kept kicking.

"Help me!" snarled the Grey Ghost.

There was a flash of blue light, and what

felt like a wrecking ball made from foam-rubber mattresses smashed into my chest. It threw me back completely through the car again (Hell's bells, *ow!*) and I landed on my back with stars in front of my eyes, unable to remember how to inhale.

A nearby wraith turned its empty-eyed head toward me, and a surge of fear sent me scrambling to my feet. I got up in time to see the Grey Ghost rising as well, and those burning green-white eyes met mine.

In the air behind the ghost floated . . . a skull.

A skull with cold blue flames flickering in its empty eye sockets.

"You've got to be kidding me," I whispered. "Bob?"

"You!" the ghost hissed. Its hands formed into arching clawlike shapes, and it hissed in rage — and in fear.

Click-clack, went the hammer of Sir Stuart's gun.

The Grey Ghost let out a scream of frustration and simply flew apart into thousands of tiny wisps of mist, taking the floating skull along with it. The wisps swarmed together into a vortex like a miniature tornado, and streaked down the road and out of sight, leaving a hundred voices screaming a hundred curses in its wake.

I looked around. The lasts of the wraiths were dying or had fled. The house's defenders, most of them wounded and bleeding pale ectoplasm and flickering memory, were still in their positions. Sir Stuart was holding one hand to his side, and with the other held the pistol pointed at the empty air where the Grey Ghost had been.

"Ahhhh," he said, sagging, once it became clear that the fight was over. "Bloody hell. That's going to leave a mark."

I moved to his side. "Are you okay, man?"

"Aye, lad. Aye. What the hell were you trying to do? Get yourself killed?"

I glowered at him and said, "You're welcome. Glad I could help."

"You nearly got yourself destroyed," he replied. "Another second and that creature would have blasted you to bits."

"Another second and you'd have put a bullet in its head," I said.

Sir Stuart idly pointed the gun at me and pulled the trigger. The hammer fell with a flash of sparks as flint struck steel . . . and nothing happened.

"You were *bluffing?*" I asked.

"Aye," Sir Stuart said. " 'Tis a muzzle-loading pistol, boy. You have to reload them like a proper weapon." Idly, he reached out a hand toward the last remnants of a deceased wraith, and flickers of light and memory flowed across the intervening space and into his fingertips. When he had it all back, Sir Stuart sighed and shook his head, seeming to recover a measure of strength. "Very well, then, lad. Help me up."

I did so. Sir Stuart's midsection on the right side was considerably more translucent than before, and he moved as if it pained him.

"When will they be back?" I asked him.

"Tomorrow night, by my reckoning," he said. "With more. Last night they had four lemurs along. Tonight it was six. And that seventh . . ." He shook his head and started reloading the pistol from the powder horn he carried on a baldric at his side. "I knew something stronger had to be gathering all those shades together, but I never considered a sorcerer." He finished reloading the weapon, put the ramrod back into its holder, and said, "Pass me my ax, boy."

I got it for him and handed it over. He slipped its handle through a ring on his belt and nodded. "Thank you."

A thumping sound made me turn my eyes back toward the house.

A man, burly, wearing a dark, hooded sweater and old jeans, was holding a long-handled crowbar in big, blocky hands. He shoved one hand into the space between the door and the frame, and with a practiced, powerful motion, popped the door from its frame and sent it swinging open.

Without an instant's hesitation, Sir Stuart fired. So did the house's spectral defenders. A hurricane of ghostly power hurtled down upon the man — and passed harmlessly through him. Hell, the guy looked like he hadn't noticed anything at all.

"A mortal," Sir Stuart breathed. He took a step forward, let out a sound of pain, and clutched at his side. His teeth were clenched, his jaw muscles standing out sharply. "Dresden," he gasped. "I cannot stop a mortal man. There is nothing I can do."

The hooded intruder took the crowbar into his left hand and drew a stubby revolver from his sweater with his right.

"Go," Stuart said. "Warn Mortimer. Help him!"

I blinked. Mortimer had made it clear that he didn't want to get involved with me — and some childish part of my nature wanted to snap that turnabout was fair play. But a wiser, more rational part of me reminded my inner child that without Mort, I might never be able to get in touch with anyone else in town. I might never find my own killer. I might never be able to protect my friends.

And besides. You don't just let people kick down other people's doors and murder them in their own home. You just don't.

I clapped Stuart on the shoulder and sprinted back toward the little house and its little owner.

CHAPTER SIX

The gunman had a big lead on me, but I had an advantage he didn't. I'd already been inside the house. I knew the layout, and I knew where Mort was holed up.

Oh. Plus I could *run through freaking walls.*

Granted, I think it would have been more fun to be Colossus than Shadowcat. But you take what you can get, and any day you've merely got the powers of an X-Man can't be all that bad. Right?

I gritted my teeth and plunged through the wall into Mort's kitchen and ran for the study, several steps ahead of the gunman.

"Mort!" I shouted. "Mort, they brought a hitter with them this time! There's a gunman running around your house!"

"What?" demanded Mort's voice from the far side of the ghost-dusted door. "Where's Stuart?"

"Dammit, Mort, he's hurt!" I called.

There was a brief pause, and then Mort said, as if baffled, "How did that happen?"

I was getting impatient. "Focus, Mort! Did you hear me? There's a frigging gunman loose in your house!"

Real alarm entered his voice for the first time. "A what?"

The gunman had heard Mort shouting at me. He came toward the door to the study, moving lightly for a big man. I got a better look at him, and noted that his clothing was ragged and unwashed, and so was he. He stank, enough that it carried through to me even given my condition, and his eyes were wide and wild, rolling around like those of a junkie who is hopped up on something that makes him pay too much attention to his surroundings. That didn't seem to have affected his gun hand, though. The semiautomatic he clutched in one big fist seemed steady enough to get the job done.

"Mort!" I called. "He's coming toward your study door right now! Look, just get your weapon and aim at the door and I'll tell you when to shoot!"

"I don't have one!" Mort screamed.

I blinked. "You don't *what?*"

"I am an ectomancer, not an action hero!" I heard him moving around in the office for a moment, and then he said, "Um. They cut the phone."

The gunman let out a low, rumbling chuckle. "You are wanted, little man." His voice sounded rotted, clotted, like something

73

that hadn't been alive in a long time. "It is commanded. You can come with me and it won't hurt. Or you can stay in there and it will."

"Dresden!" Mort called. "What do I do?"

"Oh, *now* you want to talk to me!" I said.

"You're the one who knows about this mayhem bullshit!" Mort shrieked.

"Gonna count, little man," said the gunman. "Five."

"Surviving mayhem is about being prepared!" I shouted back. "Little things like *having a gun!*"

"I'll get one in the morning!"

"Four!"

"Mort, there's gotta be something you can do," I said. "Hell's bells, every time I've run into a ghost it's tried to rip my lungs out! You're telling me none of your spooks can do something?"

"They're *sane,*" Mort shouted back. "It's crazy for a ghost to interact with the physical world. Sane ghosts don't go around acting *crazy!*"

"Three!" chanted the gunman.

"Go *away,*" Mort shouted at him.

"There's gotta be something I can do!" I yelled.

"I don't make the rules, okay?" Mort said. "The only way a ghost can manifest is if it's insane!"

"Two!" the gunman screamed, his voice rising to an excited pitch.

I jumped in front of the lunatic and shrieked, "Boo!" I flapped my hands in his face, as if trying to slap him left and right on the cheeks.

Nothing happened.

"Guess that was too much to hope for, huh?" Mort called lamely.

"One," the gunman purred. Then he leaned back and drove a heavy boot at the door. It took him three kicks to crack the frame and send the door flying inward.

Mort was waiting on the other side of the door, a golf club in hand. He swung it at the gunman's head without any preamble, a grimly practical motion. The gunman put an arm up, but the wooden head of the club got at least partly around it, and he reeled back a pace.

"This is your *fault,* Dresden," Mort snarled, swinging the club again as he spoke.

He hit the gunman full-on in the chest, and then again in one big arm. The gunman caught the next blow on his forearm, and swung wildly at Mort. He connected, and Mort got knocked on his can.

The gunman pressed one hand to a bleeding wound on his head and screamed, a howl of agony that was somehow completely out of proportion with the actual injury. His wild eyes rolled again and he lifted the gun to aim at the little man.

I moved on instinct, throwing myself uselessly between the weapon and the ectomancer. I tripped on a fragment of the ghost-dust-painted door and wound up falling in a heap on top of Mort and . . .

. . . sunk *into* him.

The world suddenly hit me in full Technicolor. It was so *dark* in here, the gunman an enormous, threatening shadow standing over me. His voice was hideous and so loud that my ears ached. The stench — unwashed body and worse things — was enough to turn my stomach, filling my nose like hideous packing peanuts. I saw the gunman's hand tighten on the trigger and I threw my arm up. . . .

My black-clad, thick, rather short arm.

"Defendarius!" I barked, faux Latin, the old defense spell I'd first learned from Justin DuMorne, my first teacher. I felt the magic surge into me, down through my arm, out into the air, just as the gun went off, over and over, as some kind of restraint in the gunman's head snapped.

Sparks flew up from a shimmering blue plane that formed in front of my outspread fingers, bullets and fragments of bullets shattering and bouncing around the room. One of them stayed more or less in one piece and smacked into the gunman's calf, and he pitched abruptly to one side, still jerking the trigger until the weapon was clicking on empty.

I felt my mouth move as Mort's voice — a voice that rang with a resonance and authority I had seldom encountered before, said, "Get *off* of me!"

If I'd been hurtled from a catapult, I don't think I'd have been thrown away any faster. I flew off at an upward angle — and slammed painfully into the ghost-dust-painted ceiling of the study. I bounced off it and fell to the equally hard floor. I lay there, stunned, for a second.

The gunman got to his feet, breathing hard and fast, slobber shooting out from slack lips as he did. He picked up the golf club that had fallen from Mort's fingers and took a step toward him.

Mort fixed hard eyes on the intruder and spoke, his voice ringing with that same unalterable authority. "To me!"

I felt the tug of some sudden force, as subtle and inarguable as gravity, and I had to lean against it to stop myself from sliding across the floor toward him.

Other spirits appeared, drawn in through the shattered door as if sucked into a tornado. Half a dozen Native American shades flew into Mort, and as the gunman swung the golf club, he let out a little yipping shout, ducked the swing more nimbly than any man his age and condition should have been able to, caught the gunman's wrist, and rolled backward, dragging the man with him. He planted his heels in the gunman's midsection and heaved, a classic fighting technique of the American tribes, and sent the man crashing into a wall.

The gunman rose, seething, eyes entirely wild, but not before Mort had crossed the room and taken an ancient, worn-looking ax down from a rack attached to one wall. It took my stunned brain a second to register that the weapon looked exactly like the one Sir Stuart had wielded, give or take a couple of centuries.

"Stuart," Mort called, and his voice rang in my chest as if it had come from a bass-amplified megaphone. There was a flicker of motion, and then Sir Stuart's form flew in through the doorway as if propelled by a vast wind, overlaying itself briefly onto Mort's far smaller body.

The gunman swung the club, but Mort caught it with a deft, twisting move of the ax's haft. The gunman leaned into it, using his far greater weight and strength in an attempt to simply overbear the smaller man and push him to the floor.

But he couldn't.

Mort held him off as if he'd had the strength of a much larger, much younger, much healthier man. Or maybe men. He held the startled intruder stone-still for the space of five or six seconds, then heaved, twisting with the full power of his shoulders, hips, and legs, and used the ax's head to rip the club from the intruder's paws. The gunman threw an enraged punch at his face, but Mort blocked it with the flat of the ax's head, and then snapped the blunt upper edge of the ax into the gunman's face with an almost contemptuous precision.

The intruder reeled back, stunned, and Mort followed up with the instincts and will of a dangerous, trained fighting man. He struck the intruder's knee with the weapon's haft, sending a sharp, crackling pop into the air, and swung the flat of the blade into the intruder's jaw as the bigger man began to fall. The blow struck home with a meaty *thunk* and another crackling noise of impact, and the gunman dropped like a proverbial stone.

Mortimer Lindquist, ectomancer, stood over the fallen madman in a wary crouch, his eyes focusing on nothing as he turned his head left and right, scanning the room around him.

Then he sighed and exhaled. The steel head of the weapon came down to thump gently against the floor. Shapes departed him, the guardian spirits easing free of him, most of them fading from view. Within a few seconds, the only shades present were me and an exhausted-looking Sir Stuart.

Mort sat down on the floor heavily, his head bowed, his chest heaving for breath. The veins on his bald pate stuck out.

"Hell's bells," I breathed.

He looked up at me, his expression weary, and gave me an exhausted shrug. "Don't have a gun," he panted. "Never really felt like I needed one."

"Been a while since you did that, Mortimer," Sir Stuart said from where he sat beside the wall, his body supported by the ghost-dusted paint. "Thought you'd forgotten how."

Mort gave the wounded spirit a faint smile. "I thought I had, too."

I frowned and shook my head. "Was that . . . was that a possession, just now? When the ghosts took over?"

Sir Stuart snorted. "Nay, lad. If anything, the opposite."

"Give me at least a little credit, Dresden," Mort said, his tone sour. "I'm an ectomancer. Sometimes I need to borrow from what a spirit knows or what it can do. But I control spirits — they don't control me."

"How'd you handle the gun?" Stuart asked, a certain, craftsmanlike professionalism entering his tone.

"I . . ." Mort shook his head and looked at me.

"Magic," I said quietly. My bell was still ringing a little, but I was able to form complete sentences. "I . . . sort of bumped into him and called up a shield."

Sir Stuart lifted his eyebrows and said, "Huh."

"I needed to borrow your skills for a moment," Mort said, somewhat stiffly. "Appreciate it."

"Think nothing of it," I said. "Just give me a few hours of your time. We'll be square."

Mort stared at me for a while. Then he said, "You're here twenty minutes and I nearly get killed, Dresden. Jesus, don't you get it?" He leaned forward. "I am not a crusader. I am not the sheriff of Chicago. I am not a goddamned death wish–embracing Don Quixote." He shook his head. "I'm a coward. And I'm very comfortable with that. It's served me well."

"I just saved your life, man," I said.

He sighed. "Yeah. But . . . like I said. Coward. I can't help you. Go find someone else to be your Panza."

I sat there for a moment, feeling very, very tired.

When I looked up, Sir Stuart was staring intently at me. Then he cleared his throat and said, in a diffident tone, "Far be it from me to bring up the past, but I can't help but note that your lot in life has improved significantly since Dresden first came to you."

Mort's bald head started turning red. *"What?"*

Sir Stuart spread his hands, his expression mild. "I only mean to say that you have grown in strength and character in that time. When you first interacted with Dresden, you were bilking people out of their money with — poorly — falsified séances, and you had lost your power to contact any spirit other than me."

Mort glowered ferociously at Sir Stuart. "Hey, Gramps. When I want your opinion, I'll give it to you."

Sir Stuart's smile widened. "Of course."

"I help spirits find peace," Mort said. "I don't do things that are going to get me taken to pieces. I'm a ghost whisperer. And that's all."

"Look, Mort," I said. "If you want to get technical, I'm not actually a ghost, per se. . . ."

He rolled his eyes again. "Oh, God. If I had a nickel for every ghost who had ever come to me, explaining to me how *he* wasn't really a ghost. How *his* case was special . . ."

"Well, sure," I said. "But —"

He rolled his eyes. "But if you aren't just a ghost, how come I could channel you like that? How come I could force you out of me? Huh?"

That hit me. My stomach may have been insubstantial, but it could still writhe uneasily.

Ghosts were *not* the people they resembled, any more than a footprint left in the ground was the being that made it. They had similar features, but ultimately a ghost was simply a remainder, a reminder, an impression of the person who died. They might share similar personalities, emotions, memories, but they weren't the same being. When a person died and left a ghost behind, it was as if some portion of his dying life energy was spun out, creating a new being entirely — though in the creator's exact mental and often physical image.

Of course, that also meant that they were subject to many of the same frailties as mortals. Obsession. Hatred. Madness. If what Mort said about ghosts interacting with the material world was true, then it was when some poor spirit snapped, or was simply created insane, that you got your really good ghost stories. By a vast majority, most ghosts were simply insubstantial and a bit sad, never really interacting with the material world.

But I couldn't be one of those self-deluded shades.

Could I?

I glanced at Sir Stuart.

He shrugged. "Most shades aren't willing to admit that they aren't actually the same being whose memories they possess," he said gently. "And that's assuming they can face the fact that they are ghosts at all. Self-deluded shades are, by an order of magnitude, more common than those that are not."

"So what you're saying is . . ." I pushed my fingers back through my hair. "You're saying that I only think I did the whole tunnel-of-light, sent-back-on-a-mission thing? That I'm in denial about being a ghost?"

The ghost marine waggled one hand in an ambivalent gesture, and his British accent rolled out mellow vowels and crisp consonants as he answered. "I'm simply saying that it is very much poss— *Mission? What* mission? What are you talking about?"

I eyed him for a moment, while he looked at me blankly. Then I said, "I'm gonna guess you've never seen *Star Wars.*"

Sir Stuart shrugged. "I find motion pictures to be grossly exaggerated and intrusive, leaving the audience little to consider or ponder for themselves."

"That's what I thought." I sighed. "You were about two words away from being called Threepio from here on out."

He blinked. "What?"

"God," I said. "Now we're transitioning into a Monty Python skit." I turned back to Morty. "Mort, Jack Murphy met me on the other side and sent me back to find out who murdered me. There was a lot of talk, but it mostly amounted to 'We aren't gonna tell you diddly, so just do it already.' "

Mort watched me warily for a moment, staring hard at my insubstantial form. Then he said, "You think you're telling the truth."

"No," I said, annoyed. "I *am* telling the truth."

"I'm sure you think that," Mort said.

I felt my temper flare. "If I didn't go right through you, I would totally pop you in the nose right now."

Mort bristled, his jaw muscles clenching. "Oh yeah? Bring it, Too-Tall. I'll kick your bodiless ass."

Sir Stuart coughed significantly, a long-suffering expression on his face. "Mortimer, Dresden just fought beside us to defend this home — and rushed in here to save your life."

Then it hit me, and I eyed Sir Stuart. "You could have come inside," I said. "You could have helped Mortimer against the shooter. But you wanted to see where I stood when I was under pressure. It was a test."

Sir Stuart smiled. "Somewhat, aye. I wouldn't have let you harm Mortimer, of course, and I was there to help him the instant he called. But it didn't hurt to know a little more about you." He turned to Mortimer. "I like this lad. And Jack Murphy sent him."

Both Mortimer and I glared at Sir Stuart and then settled slowly back from the confrontation.

"Head detective of the Black Cats a generation ago," Stuart continued. "Killed himself at his desk. Sometimes new shades show up claiming they've had a run-in with him, and that he brought them back from the hereafter. And you know that he is no deluded fool."

Mort didn't meet Sir Stuart's eyes. He grunted, a sound that wasn't exactly agreement.

"Or maybe Jack Murphy's shade is simply more deluded than most, and has a talent for nurturing the delusions of other new shades."

"Hell's bells, Morty," I said. "Next you'll be telling me that I didn't even meet his shade. That I deluded myself into deluding myself into deluding him into deluding me that I made the whole thing up."

Sir Stuart snorted through his nose. "A fair point."

"It doesn't matter," Mort said. "There's no real way to know."

"Incorrect," Sir Stuart interrupted. "Summon him. That shouldn't be difficult — if he is just one more deluded shade."

Mort didn't look up. But he said, very quietly, "I won't do that to Jack." He looked up and seemed to recover some of his composure. "But even if Captain Murphy is genuine, that doesn't mean Dresden's shade is legit. Or sane."

"Consider the possibility," Sir Stuart said. "There is something unusual about this one."

Mort perked up his metaphorical ears. "Unusual?"

"An energy. A vitality." Sir Stuart shrugged. "It might be nothing. But even if it is . . ."

Mort let out a long sigh and eyed the shade. "You won't let this rest, will you?"

"I have no plans for the next fifty or sixty years," Sir Stuart said affably. "It would give me something to do. Every half an hour or so."

Mort pinched the bridge of his nose and closed his eyes. "Oh, God."

Sir Stuart grinned. "There's another aspect to consider, too."

"Oh?"

"The attack was larger tonight. It cost us more defenders. And the creature behind it revealed itself." He gestured at his still-translucent midsection. "I can't keep holding them off forever, Mortimer. And the presence of a mortal pawn tells us two things."

I nodded. "One. The Grey Ghost is bad enough to have its way with mortals."

"Two," Sir Stuart said. "The creature is after *you*. Personally."

Mort swallowed.

I rose and shuffled over to look down at the still-unconscious intruder. The man let out a low groan.

"It is a good time to make friends," Stuart said, his expression serious. "Dresden's one reason you'll live the night. And he had allies in this city — people who could help you, if they had a reason to."

"You're fine," Mort said, his tone uncertain. "You've survived worse."

Sir Stuart sighed. "Perhaps. But the enemy isn't going to give me time to recover before he attacks again. You need Dresden's help. He's asking for yours." His expression hardened. "And so am I."

The intruder groaned again and stirred.

Mort's forehead broke out in a sudden sweat. He looked at the fallen man and then, rather hurriedly, heaved himself to his feet. He bowed his head. Then he turned to me and said, "Fine, Dresden. I'll help. And in return, I expect you to get your allies to look out for me."

"Deal," I said. I looked at Sir Stuart. "Thank you."

"One hour," Mort said. "You get one hour."

"Okay," I said.

"Okay," Mort echoed, evidently speaking mostly to himself. "I mean, it's not like I'm trying to join the Council or anything. It's one hour. Just one little hour. What could happen in one hour?"

And that's how I knew that Mort was telling the whole truth when he said he wasn't a hero.

Heroes know better than to hand the universe lines like that.

CHAPTER SEVEN

Mort drove one of those little hybrid cars that, when not running on gasoline, was fueled by idealism. It was made out of crepe paper and duct tape and boasted a computer system that looked like it could have run the NYSE and NORAD, with enough attention left over to play tic-tac-toe. Or possibly Global Thermonuclear War.

"Kinda glad I'm dead," I muttered, getting into the car by the simple expedient of stepping through the passenger's door as if it had been open. "If I were still breathing, I'd feel like I was taking my life into my hands here. This thing's an egg. And not one of those nice, safe, hard-boiled eggs. A crispy one."

"Says the guy who drove Herbie's trailer-park cousin around for more than ten years," Mort sniped back.

"Gentlemen," Stuart said, settling rather gingerly into the tiny backseat. "Is there a particular reason we should be disagreeable with one another, or do you both take some sort of infantile pleasure in being insufferably rude?"

Now that the fighting was done, Sir Stuart's mannerisms were reverting to something more formal. I made a mental note of the fact. The Colonial Marine hadn't started off a member of proper society, wherever he'd been. The rather staid, formal, archaic phrasing and patterns of speech were all something he'd acquired as a learned habit — one that apparently deserted him under the pressure of combat.

"Okay, Dresden," Mort said. "Where to?" He opened his garage door and peered out at the snow. It was coming down even more thickly than earlier in the night. Chicago is pretty good about keeping its streets cleared in winter weather, but it was freaking May.

From the deep piles of old snow that had apparently been there for a number of weeks, I deduced that the city must have become increasingly beleaguered by the unseasonable weather. The streets were covered in several inches of fresh powder. No plow had been by Mort's house in hours. If we hit a patch of ice, that heavy, crunchy little hybrid was going to skitter like a puppy on a tile floor.

Thinking, I referenced a mental map of the city. I felt a little bad making Mort come out into weather like this — I mean, given that he wasn't dead and all. I was going to feel like crap if something bad happened to him, and it wouldn't be a kindness to ask him to go farther than he absolutely had to. Besides, with the weather worsening, his one-hour time limit seemed to put further constraints on my options.

"Murphy's place," I said quietly. I gave him the address.

Mort grunted. "The ex-cop?"

I nodded. Murph had gotten herself fired by showing up to help me one too many times. She'd known what she was doing, and she'd made her own choices, but I still felt bad about it. Dying hadn't changed that. "She's a pretty sharp lady. Better able than most in this town to look out for you."

Mort grunted again and pulled out into the snow, driving slowly and carefully. He was careful to keep his expression blank as he did it.

"Mort," I said. "What aren't you telling me?"

"Driving over here," he said.

I made a rude sound. Then I looked back over my shoulder at Sir Stuart. "Well?"

Sir Stuart reached into his coat and drew out what looked like a briar pipe. He tapped something from a pouch into it, struck an old wooden match, and puffed it to life. The smoke rose until it touched the ceiling of the car, where it congealed into a thin coating of shining ectoplasm — the residue of the spiritual when it becomes the physical.

"To hear him tell it," he said, finally, indicating Mort, "the world's gone to hell the past few months. Though I've got to admit, it doesn't seem much different to me. Everything's been madness since those computers showed up."

I snorted. "What's changed?"

"The scuttlebutt says that you killed the whole Red Court of Vampires," said Sir Stuart. "Any truth to that?"

"They abducted my daughter," I said. I tried for a neutral tone, but it came out clipped and hard. I hadn't even known Maggie existed until Susan Rodriguez had shown up out of nowhere after years overseas and begged for my help in recovering our daughter. I'd set out to get her back by any means necessary.

I shivered. I'd . . . done things, to get the child away from the monstrous hands of the Red Court. Things I wasn't proud of. Things I would never have dreamed I would be willing to do.

I could still remember the hot flash of red from a cut throat beneath my fingers, and I had to bow my head for a moment in an effort to keep the memory from surging into my thoughts in all its hideous splendor. Maggie. Chichén Itzá. The Red King. Susan.

Susan's blood . . . everywhere.

I forced myself to speak to Sir Stuart. "I don't know what you heard. But I went and got my girl back and put her in good hands. Her mother and a whole lot of vampires died before it was over."

"All of them?" Sir Stuart pressed.

I was quiet for a moment before I nodded. "Maybe. Yeah. I mean, I couldn't exactly take a census. The spell could have missed some of the very youngest, depending on the details of how it was set up. But every single one of the bastards nearby me died. And the spell was meant to wipe the world clean of whoever it targeted."

Mort made a choking sound. "Couldn't . . . I mean, wouldn't the White Council get upset about that? Killing with magic, I mean?"

I shrugged. "The Red King was about to use the spell on an eight-year-old girl. If the Council doesn't like how I stopped that from happening, they can kiss my immaterial ass." I found myself chuckling. "Besides. I killed vampires, not mortals, with that magic. And what are they gonna do anyway? Chop my head off? I'm dead already."

I saw Mort trade a look with Sir Stuart in the rearview mirror.

"Why are you so angry at them, Harry?" Mort asked me.

I frowned at him and then at Stuart. "Why do I feel like I should be lying on a couch somewhere?"

"A shade is formed when something signifi-cant is left incomplete," Sir Stuart said. "Part of what we do is work out what's causing you to hold on to your life so hard. That means asking questions."

"What? So I can go on my way? Or something?"

"Otherwise known as leaving me alone," Mort muttered.

"Something like that," Sir Stuart said quickly, before I could fire back at Mort. "We just want to help."

I gave Sir Stuart the eye and then Mort. "That's what you do? Lay spirits to rest?"

Mort shrugged. "If someone didn't, this town would run out of cemetery space pretty fast."

I thought about that for a moment. Then I said, "So how come you haven't laid Sir Stuart to rest?"

Mort said nothing. His silence was a barbed, stony thing.

Sir Stuart leaned forward to put a hand on Mort's shoulder, seemed to squeeze it a little, and let go. Then he said to me, "Some things can't be mended, lad. Not by all the king's horses or all the king's men."

"You're trapped here," I said quietly.

"Were I trapped, it would indicate that I am the original Sir Stuart. I am not. I am but his shade. One could think of it that way nonetheless, I suppose," he said. "But I prefer to consider it differently: I regard myself as someone who was truly created with a specific purpose for his existence. I have a reason to be who and what and where I am. How many flesh-and-blood folk can say as much?"

I scowled as I watched the snowy road ahead of us. "And what's your purpose? Looking out after this loser?"

"Hey, I'm sitting right *here*," Mort complained.

"I help other lost spirits," Sir Stuart said. "Help them find some sort of resolution. Help teach them how to stay sane, if it is their destiny to become a mane. And if they become a lemur, I help introduce them to oblivion."

I turned to frown at Sir Stuart. "That's . . . kinda cut-and-dried."

"Some things assuredly are," he replied placidly.

"So you're a mane, eh? Like the old Roman ancestral ghost?"

"It isn't such a simple matter, Dresden. Your own White Council is a famous bunch of namers," he said. "Their history is, I have heard, rooted in old Rome."

"Yeah," I said.

He nodded. "And, like the Romans, they love to name and classify and outline facts to the smallest, permanently inflexible, set-in-stone detail. The truth, however, is that the world of remnant spirits is not easily cataloged or defined." He shrugged. "I dwell in Chicago. I defend Mortimer's home. I am what I am."

I grunted. After a few moments, I asked, "You teach new spirits?"

"Of course."

"Then can I ask you some questions?"

"By all means."

Mort muttered, "Here we go."

"Okay," I said. "I'm a ghost and all now. And I can go through just about anything — like I went through this car door to get inside."

"Yes," Sir Stuart said, a faint smile outlining his mouth.

"So how come my ass doesn't go through the *seat* when I sit down on —"

I was rudely interrupted by the tingling sensation of passing through solid matter, beginning at my butt and moving rapidly up my spine. Cold snow started slamming into my rear end, and I let out a yelp of pure surprise.

Sir Stuart had evidently known what was coming. He reached over, grabbed me by the front of my leather duster, and unceremoniously dragged me back up into the car and sat me on the seat beside him, back in the passenger compartment. I clutched at the door handle and the seat in front of me for stability, only to have my hands go right through them. I pitched forward, spinning as if I were floating in water, and this time it was my face plunging toward the icy street.

Sir Stuart hauled me back again and said, in a faintly annoyed tone, "Mortimer."

Mort didn't say anything, but when I was once again sitting down, I didn't fall right through the bottom of the car. He smirked at me in the rearview mirror.

"You don't fall through the bottom of the car because on some deep, instinctual level, you regard it as a given of existence here," Sir Stuart said. "You are entirely convinced that illusions such as gravity and solidity are real."

"There is no spoon," I said.

Sir Stuart looked at me blankly.

I sighed. "If I believe in an illusory reality so much, then how come I can walk through walls?" I asked.

"Because you are convinced, on the same level, that ghosts can do precisely that."

I felt my eyebrows trying to meet as I frowned. "So . . . you're saying I don't fall through the ground because I don't *think* I should?"

"Say instead that it is because you assume that you will not," he replied. "Which is why, once you actively considered the notion, you *did* fall through the floor."

I shook my head slowly. "How do I keep from doing it again?"

"Mortimer is preventing it, for the time being. My advice to you is not to think about too much," Sir Stuart said, his tone serious.

"Just go about your business."

"You can't *not* think about something," I said. "Quick, don't think about a purple elephant. I dare you."

Sir Stuart let out a broad laugh, but stopped and clutched at his wounded flank. I could tell it hurt him, but he still wore the smile the laugh had brought on. "It usually takes them longer to recognize that fact," he said. "You're right, of course. And there will be times when you feel like you have no control whatsoever over such things."

"Why?" I asked, feeling somewhat exasperated.

Sir Stuart wasn't rattled by my tone. "It's something every new shade goes through. It will pass."

"Huh," I said. I thought about it for a minute and said, "Well. It beats the hell out of acne."

From the front seat, Mort let out an explosive little snicker.

Stars and stones, I hate being the new guy.

Chapter Eight

Murphy inherited her house from her grand-mother, and it was at least a century old. Grandma Murphy had been a notorious rose gardener. Murphy didn't have a green thumb herself. She hired a service to take care of her grandmother's legacy. The flower garden in front would have fit a house four times as large, but it was a withered, dreary little place when covered in heavy snow. Bare, thorny branches, trimmed the previous fall, stood up from the blanket of white in skeletal silence.

The house itself was a compact colonial, single story, square, solid, and neat-looking. It had been built in a day when a ten-by-ten bedroom was considered a master suite, and when beds were routinely used by several children at a time. Murphy had upgraded it with vinyl siding, new windows, and a layer of modern insulation when she moved in, and the little house looked as if it could last another hundred years, no problem.

There was a sleek, expensive, black town

car parked on the street outside Murphy's home, its tires on the curbside resting in several inches of snow. It couldn't have looked more out of place in the middle-class neighborhood if it had been a Saint Patrick's Day Parade float, complete with prancing leprechauns.

Sir Stuart looked at me and then out at our surroundings, frowning. "What is it, Dresden?"

"That car shouldn't be there," I said.

Mort glanced at me and I pointed out the black town car. He studied it for a moment before he said, "Yeah. Kind of odd on a block like this."

"Why?" asked Sir Stuart. "It is an automatic coach, is it not?"

"An expensive one," I said. "You don't park those on the street in weather like this. The salt-and-plow truck comes by, and you're looking at damage to the finish and paint. Keep going by, Morty. Circle the block."

"Yeah, yeah," Mort said, his tone annoyed. "I'm not an idiot."

"Stay with him," I told Sir Stuart.

Then I took a deep breath, remembered that I was an incorporeal spirit, and put my feet down through the floorboards of the car. I dug in my heels on the snowy street as the solid matter of the vehicle passed through me in a cloud of uncomfortable tingles. I'd meant to simply remain behind, standing, when the car had passed completely through me. I hadn't thought about things like momentum and velocity, and instead I went into a tumble that ended with me making a *whump* sound as I hit a soft snowbank beside the home next to Murphy's. It hurt, and I pushed myself out of the snowbank, my teeth chattering, my body blanketed in cold.

"N-n-no, H-Harry," I told myself firmly, squeezing my eyes shut. "Th-that's an illusion. Your mind created it to match what it knows. But you didn't hit the snowbank. You can't. And you can't be covered in snow. And therefore you can't be wet and cold."

I focused on the words, putting my will behind them, in the same way I would have to attract the attention of a ghost or spirit. I opened my eyes.

The snow clinging to my body and clothes was gone. I was standing, dry and wrapped in my leather duster, beside the snowbank.

"Okay," I said. "That's bordering on cool."

I stuck my hands in my pockets, ignored the snow and the steady, gentle northern wind, and trudged across Grandma Murphy's rose garden to Murphy's door. I raised my hand and knocked as I'd done so often before.

A couple of things happened.

First, my hand stopped above the door, close enough that you could have slid one or two pieces of paper between my knuckles and the wood, but definitely not three. There was a dull, low *thud* of solid impact, even though I hadn't touched the door itself. Second, light flashed, and something like a current of electricity swarmed up my arm and down my spine, throwing my body into a convulsion that left me lying on the ground, stunned.

I just lay there on the snow for a moment. I tried the whole "there is no spoon" thing again, but apparently there was perception of reality and then there was hard-core, undeniable, real reality. It took me several seconds to recover and sit up again, and several more seconds to realize that I had been hit by something specifically engineered to stop intruding spirits.

Murphy's house had been warded, its natural defensive threshold used as a foundation for further, more aggressive defenses. And while I was only a shade of my former self, I was still wizard enough to recognize my own damned wards — or at least wards that were virtually identical to my own.

The door opened and Murphy appeared in it. She was a woman of well below average height, but built of spring steel. Her golden hair had been cut into a short brush over her scalp, and the stark style showed off the lines of muscles and tendons in her neck, and the pugnacious, stubborn set of her jawline. She wore jeans and a plaid shirt over a blue tee, and held her SIG in her right hand.

Something stabbed me in the guts and twisted upon seeing her.

A rush of memories flooded over me, starting with our first meeting, on a missing-persons case years ago, when I'd still been doing my time as an apprentice PI and Murphy had been a uniform cop working a beat. Every argument, every bit of banter and repartee, every moment of revelation and trust that had been built up between us, came hammering into me like a thousand major-league fastballs. The last memory, and the sharpest, was of facing each other in the hold of my brother's boat, trembling on the edge of a line we hadn't ever allowed ourselves to cross before.

"Karrin," I tried to say. It came out a whisper.

Murphy's brow furrowed and she stood still in the doorway, despite the cold wind and falling snow, her eyes scanning left and right.

Her eyes moved over me, past me, through me, without stopping. She didn't see me. She couldn't hear me. We weren't a part of the same world anymore.

It was a surprisingly painful moment of realization.

Before I could get my thoughts clear of it, Murphy, still frowning, closed the door. I heard her close several locks.

"Easy, lad," said Sir Stuart in a gentle, quiet voice. He hunkered down to put a hand on my shoulder. "There is no need to rush regaining your feet. It hurts. I know."

"Yeah," I said quietly. I swallowed and blinked away tears that couldn't really be real. "Why?"

"As I told you, lad. Memories are life here. Life and power. Seeing the people you care for most again is going to trigger memories much more strongly than they would in a mere mortal. It can take time to grow accustomed to it."

I wrapped my arms around my knees and rested my chin on my kneecap. "How long?"

"Generally," Sir Stuart said very softly, "until those loved ones pass on themselves."

I shuddered. "Yeah," I said. "Well. I don't have time for that."

"You have nothing but time, Dresden."

"But three of my people don't," I said, my voice harsh. "They're going to get hurt if I don't make things right. If I don't find my killer." I closed my eyes and took several deep breaths. I wasn't actually breathing air. I didn't need to breathe. Habit. "Where's Mort?"

"Waiting around the corner," Sir Stuart said. "He'll come in once we've given him the all clear."

"What? I'm the little chicken's personal Secret Service now?" I grumbled. I pushed myself up to my feet and eyed Murphy's house. "Do you see anything threatening around here?"

"Not at the moment," Sir Stuart said, "other than the allegedly suspicious auto coach."

"Well, the house is warded. I'm not sure if the defenses are purely against insubstantial intruders or if they might also attack a living intruder. Tell him not to touch the house with anything he wants to keep."

Sir Stuart nodded and said, "I'm going to circle the place. I'll return with Mortimer."

I grunted absently, reaching out a hand to feel the wards around the place again. They were powerful, but . . . flawed, somehow. My wards were all built into the same, solid barrier of energy. These wards had solidity, but it was a piecemeal thing. I felt like I was looking at a twelve-foot wall built from LEGO blocks. If someone with enough mystic muscle hit it right, the ward would shatter at its weakest seams.

Of course, that would probably punch a hole in the barrier, but not a catastrophic one. If one portion of my wards lost integrity, the whole thing would come down and whatever remained of the energy that had broken it would come through. If someone knocked out a bit of these wards, it would send a bunch of LEGOS flying — probably soaking up all of the energy by dividing it among lots of little pieces — but the rest of the barrier would stand.

That might offer several advantages on the minor-league end of the power scale. The modular wards would be easy to repair, compared to classic integral wards, so that even if something smashed through, the wards could be closed again in a brief time. God knows, the ingredients for the spell were probably a lot cheaper — and you wouldn't need a big-time White Council wizard to put them up.

But they had a downside, too. There were a lot of things that *could* smash through — and if you got killed after they came inside, the ease of repair wouldn't matter much to your cooling corpse.

Still. It was a hell of a lot better than nothing. The basic profile was my design, just implemented differently. Who the hell would have done this to Murphy's place? And *why?*

I turned and stepped off the porch to peer in a window, feeling vaguely voyeuristic as I did so. But I wasn't sure what else I was going to do until Mort got here to do some speaking for me.

"Are you quite all right?" asked a man's voice, from inside the house.

I blinked, scowled in concentration, and managed to stand up on some of the wispy shrubbery under the window, until I could see over the chair back that blocked my view from where I was standing.

There was a man sitting on the couch of

106

Murphy's living room. He was wearing a black suit with a crisp white shirt and a black tie with a single stripe of maroon. His skin was dark — more Mediterranean than African — but his short, neat sweep of hair was dyed peroxide blond. His eyes were an unsettling color, somewhere between dark honey and poison ivy, and the sharp angularity of his nose made me think of a bird of prey.

"Fine," said Murphy. She was on her feet, her gun tucked into the waist of her jeans in front. SIG made a fine, compact 9mm, but it looked big, dangerous, and clumsy on Murphy's scale. She folded her arms and stared at the man as if he'd been found at the side of the highway, gobbling up raw roadkill. "I told you not to show up early anymore, Childs."

"A lifetime of habit," Childs said in reply. "Honestly, it isn't something to which I give any thought."

"You know how things are out there," Murphy said, jerking her chin toward the front of the house. "Start thinking about it. You catch me on a nervous evening, and maybe I shoot you through the door."

Childs folded his fingers on one knee. He didn't look like a big guy. He wasn't heavy with muscle. Neither are cobras. There was plenty of room for a gun under that expensive suit jacket. "My relationship with my employer is relatively new. But I have a sense

107

that, should such a tragedy occur, the personal repercussions to you would be quite severe."

Murphy shrugged a shoulder. "Maybe. On the other hand, maybe we start killing his people until the price of doing business with us is too high and he breaks it off." She smiled. It was almost gleefully wintry. "I don't have a badge anymore, Childs. But I do have friends. Special, special friends."

Between them there was a low charge of tension in the room, the silent promise of violence. Murphy's fingers were dangling casually less than two inches from her gun. Childs's hands were still folded on his knee. He abruptly smiled and dropped back into a more relaxed pose on the sofa. "We've coexisted well enough for the past six months. I see no sense in letting frayed tempers put an end to that now."

Murphy's eyes narrowed to slits. "Marcone's top murderer —"

Childs lifted a hand. "Please. Troubleshooter."

Murphy continued as if he hadn't spoken. "— doesn't back down that quickly, regardless of how survival oriented he is. That's why you're here early, despite my request. You want something."

"So nice to know you eventually take note of the obvious," Childs replied. "Yes. My employer sent me with a question."

Murphy frowned. "He didn't want the others to hear it being asked."

Childs nodded. "He feared it might generate unintended negative consequences."

Murphy stared at him for a moment, then rolled her eyes. "Well?"

Childs showed his teeth in a smile for the first time. It made me think of skulls. "He wishes to know if you trust the Ragged Lady."

Murphy straightened at the question, her back going rigid. She waited to take a deep breath and exhale before responding. "What do you mean?"

"Odd things have begun happening near some of the locations she haunts. Things that no one can quite explain." Childs shrugged, leaving his hands in plain sight, resting comfortably on the sofa. "Which part of the question is too difficult for you?"

Murphy's shoulder twitched, as if her hand had been thinking about grabbing the gun from her waistband. But she took another breath before she spoke. "What's he offering for the answer?"

"Northerly Island. And before you ask, yes, including the beach."

I blinked at that. The island over by Burnham Park Harbor wasn't exactly prime criminal territory, being mostly parks, fields, and a beach a lot of families visited — but "Gentleman" John Marcone, kingpin of Chicago's rackets and the only plain-vanilla mortal to become a signatory of the Unseelie Accords, simply did not surrender territory. Not for anything.

Murphy's eyes widened, too, and I watched her going through the same line of thought I had. Though, to be perfectly fair, I think she got to the end of that line before I did.

"If I do agree to this," she said, her tone cautious, "it will have to pass our standard verification by Monday."

Childs's face was a bland mask. "Done."

Murphy nodded and looked down at the floor for a moment, evidently marshaling her thoughts. Then she said, "There isn't a simple answer."

"There rarely is," Childs noted.

Murphy passed a hand back over her brush cut and studied Childs. Then she said, "When she was working with Dresden, I'd have said yes, in a heartbeat, without reservation."

Childs nodded. "And now?"

"Now . . . Dresden's gone. And she came back from Chichén Itzá changed," Murphy said. "Maybe post-traumatic stress. Maybe something more than that. She's different."

Childs tilted his head. "Do you *dis*trust her?"

"I don't drop my guard around her," Murphy said. "And that's my answer."

The bleach-blond man considered her words for a few seconds and then nodded. "I will carry it to my employer. The island will be clear of his interests by Monday."

"Will you give me your word on that?"

"I already have." Childs stood up, the motion a portrait of grace. If he was a mortal, he was deadly fast. Or a ballet dancer. And somehow I didn't think he had some Danskins stuffed in his suit's pockets. "I will go. Please inform me if anything of relevance comes out of the meeting."

Murphy nodded, her hand near her gun, and watched Childs walk to the front door. Childs opened it and began to leave.

"You should know," Murphy said quietly, "that my trust issues don't change the fact that she's one of mine. If I think for a second that the outfit has done any harm to Molly Carpenter, the arrangement is over and we segue directly to the OK Corral. Starting with you."

Childs turned smoothly on a heel, smiling, and lifted an empty hand to mime shooting Murphy with his thumb and forefinger. He completed the turn and left the house.

Murphy came over to the window where I was standing and watched Childs walk to the black town car and get in. She didn't relax her vigilance until the car had pulled out into the snow and cruised slowly away.

Then she bowed her head, one hand against the window, and rubbed at her face with her other hand.

I stretched my arm to put my hand out to

111

mirror hers, being careful not to touch the wards humming quietly around the house's threshold. You could have fit two or three of Murphy's hand spans into one of mine. I saw her shoulders shake once.

Then she shook her head and straightened, blinked her eyes rapidly a few times, and schooled her expression into its usual cop mask of neutrality. She turned away from me, went to the room's love seat, and curled up on one side of it. She looked tiny, with her legs bunched up against her upper body, barely more than a child — if not for the care lines on her face.

There was a quiet motion, and then a tiny grey mountain lion with a notched ear and a stump of a tail appeared and leapt smoothly up onto the love seat with Murphy. She reached out a hand and gathered the cat's furry body against hers, her fingers stroking.

Tears blurred my eyes as I saw Mister. My cat. When the vampire couple, the Eebs, had burned my old apartment down, I knew Mister had escaped the flames — but I didn't know what had happened to him after that. I'd been killed before I could go round him up. I remembered meeting the cat as a kitten, scrambling in a trash bin, skinny and near starvation. He'd been my roommate, or possibly landlord, ever since I'd come to Chicago. He was thirty pounds of feline arrogance. He was always good about showing up when I was upset, giving me the chance to lower my blood pressure by paying attention to him. I'm sure he thought it a saintly gesture of generosity.

It's a cat thing.

I don't know how long I stood there staring through the window, but suddenly Sir Stuart was beside me.

"Dresden," he said quietly. "There are several creatures approaching from the southeast."

"You are not doing your lack of being named Threepio any good whatsoever, Sir Stuart."

He blinked at me several times, then shook his head and recovered. "There are half a dozen of them, as well as a number of cars."

"Okay. Keep Mort in his car until I can identify them," I said. "But I suspect he's in no danger."

"No?" the shade asked. "Know you these folk, then?"

"Dunno," I said. "Let's go see."

CHAPTER NINE

Ten minutes later, I was humming under my breath and watching the gathering in Murphy's living room. Sir Stuart stood beside me, his expression interested, curious.

"Beg pardon, wizard," he said, "but what is that tune you're trying to sing?"

I belted out the opening trumpet fanfare of the main theme and then said, in a deep and cheesy announcer's voice, "In the great Hall of the Justice League, there are assembled the world's four greatest heroes, created from the cosmic legends of the universe!"

Sir Stuart frowned at me. "Created from . . ."

"The cosmic legends of the universe," I repeated, in the same voice.

Sir Stuart narrowed his eyes and turned slightly away from me, his shoulders tight. "That makes no sense. None. At all."

"It did on Saturday mornings in the seventies, apparently," I said. I nodded at the room beyond the window. "And we've got something similar going on here. Though for a Hall of the Justice League, it looks pretty small. Real estate wasn't as expensive back then, I guess."

"The guests assembled inside," Sir Stuart asked. "Do you know them?"

"Most of them," I said. Then I felt obliged to add, "Or, at least, I knew them six months ago."

Things had changed. Murphy's buzz cut was just a start. I started introducing Sir Stuart to the faces I knew.

Will Borden leaned against one wall, slightly behind Murphy, his muscular arms folded. He was a man of below-average height and well-above-average build. All of it was muscle. I was used to seeing him mostly in after-work, business-casual clothing — whenever he wasn't transformed into a huge, dark wolf, I mean. Today, he was wearing sweats and a loose top, the better for getting out of in a hurry if he wanted to change. Generally a quiet, reliable, intelligent man, Will was the leader of a local band of college kids, now all grown-up, who had learned to take on the shape of wolves. They'd called themselves the Alphas for so long that the name had stopped sounding silly in my own head when I thought it.

I wasn't used to seeing Will playing the heavy, but he was clearly in that role. His expression was locked into something just shy of a scowl, and his dark eyes positively smoldered with pent-up aggression. He looked like a man who wanted a fight, and who would gladly jump on the first opportunity to get into one.

On the couch not far from Will, the other Alpha present was curled up into a ball in the corner, her legs up to her chest. She had straight hair the color of a mouse's fur that hung to her chin in an even sheet all the way around, and she looked as if a strong breeze might knock her to the floor. She peered owlishly out through a pair of large eyeglasses and a curtain of hair, and I got the impression that she saw the whole room at the same time.

I hadn't seen her in several years, but she'd been one of the original Alphas and had gotten her degree and toddled off into the vanilla world. Her name was . . . Margie? Mercy? Marci. Right. Her name was Marci.

Next to Marci sat a plump, cheerful-looking woman with blond, curly hair held sloppily in place with a couple of chopsticks, who looked a couple of years shy of qualifying to be a television grandmother. She wore a floral-print dress, and on her lap she held a dog the approximate size of a bratwurst — a Yorkshire terrier. The dog was clearly on alert, his bright, dark eyes moving from person to person around the room, but focused mostly on Marci. He was growling deep in his chest,

116

and obviously ready to defend his owner at an instant's notice.

"Abby," I told Sir Stuart. "Her name's Abby. The dog is Toto. She survived a White Court vampire who was hunting down her social circle. Small-time practitioners."

The little dog abruptly sprang out of Abby's arms to throw itself toward Will, but the woman moved in remarkably quick reaction and caught Toto. Except it hadn't been remarkably quick — it had simply begun a half second *before* the little dog had jumped. Abby was a prescient. She couldn't see far into the future — only a few seconds — but that was enough talent to make me bet there weren't many broken dishes in her kitchen.

Will looked at Toto as the little dog jumped, and smiled. Abby shushed the Yorkie and frowned at Will before turning to the table to pick up a cup of tea in one hand, still holding the dog with the other.

Next to Abby was a brawny young man in jeans, work boots, and a heavy flannel shirt. He had dark, untidy hair and intense grey eyes, and I could have opened a bottle cap with the dimple in his chin. It took me a second to recognize him, because he'd been a couple of inches shorter and maybe forty pounds lighter the last time I'd seen him — Daniel Carpenter, the eldest of my apprentice's younger brothers. He looked as though he were seated on a hot stove rather than a comfortable couch, like he might bounce up at any second, boldly to do something ill conceived. A large part of Will's attention was, I thought, focused on Daniel.

"Relax," Murphy told him. "Have some cake."

Daniel shook his head in a jerky negative. "No, thank you, Ms. Murphy," he said. "I just don't see the point in this. I should go find Molly. If I leave right now, I can be back before an hour's up."

"If Molly isn't here, we'll assume it's because she has a good reason for it," Murphy said, her tone calm and utterly implacable. "There's no sense in running all over town on a night like this."

"Besides," Will drawled, "we'd find her faster."

Daniel scowled from beneath his dark hair for a second, but quickly looked away. It gave me the sense that he'd run afoul of Will before and hadn't liked the outcome. The younger man kept his mouth shut.

An older man sat in the chair beside the couch, and he took the opportunity to lean over the table and pour hot tea from a china teapot into the cup in front of the young Carpenter. He added a lump of sugar to it, and smiled at Daniel. There was nothing hostile, impatient, or demanding in his eyes, which were the color of a robin's eggs — only complete certainty that the younger man

118

would accept the tea and settle down.

Daniel eyed the man, then dropped his eyes to the square of white cellulose at his collar and the crucifix hanging beneath it. He took a deep breath, then nodded and stirred his tea. He took the cup in both hands and settled back to wait. After a sip, he appeared to forget he was holding it — but he stayed quiet.

"And you, Ms. Murphy?" asked Father Forthill, holding up the teapot. "It's a cold night. I'm sure a cup would do you good."

"Why not?" she said. Forthill filled another cup for Murphy, took it to her, and pulled at his sweater vest, as if trying to coax more warmth from the garment. He turned and walked over to the window where Sir Stuart and I stood, and held out both hands. "Are you sure there isn't a draft? I could swear I feel it."

I blinked and eyed Sir Stuart, who shrugged and said, "He's one of the good ones."

"Good what?"

"Ministers. Priests. Shamans. Whatever." His expression seemed to be carefully neutral. "You spend your life caring for the souls of others, you get a real sense of them." Sir Stuart nodded at Father Forthill. "Ghosts like us aren't souls, as such, but we aren't much different. He feels us, even if he isn't fully aware of it."

Toto escaped Abby's lap and came scrambling over the hardwood floor to put his paws up on the walls beneath the windows. He yapped ferociously several times, staring right at me.

"And dogs," Sir Stuart added. "Maybe one in ten of them seem to have a talent for sensing us. Probably why they're always barking."

"What about cats?" I asked. Mister had fled the living room upon the arrival of other people and wasn't in sight.

"Of course cats," Sir Stuart said, his voice faintly amused. "As far as I can tell, all cats. But they aren't terribly impressed with the fact that we're dead and still present. One rarely gets a reaction from them."

Father Forthill gently scooped Toto from the floor. The little dog wiggled energetically, tail flailing in the air, and kissed Forthill's hands soundly before the old priest passed him carefully back to Abby, smiling and nodding to her before refilling his own cup of tea and sitting down again.

"Who are they waiting on?" Sir Stuart asked. "This Molly person?"

"Maybe," I said. There was one more chair in the room. It was closest to the door — and farthest from every other piece of furniture in the room. Practically every other seat in the room would have a clear line of fire to the last chair, if it came to shooting. Maybe that was a coincidence. "But I don't think so."

There was a quick chirping sound, and Murphy picked up a radio smaller than a deck of cards. "Murphy. Go."

"Ricemobile imminent," said a quiet voice. "Furry Knockers is running a sweep."

Will blew out a sudden snort of amused breath.

Murphy smiled and shook her head before she spoke into the radio. "Thanks, Eyes. Pull in as soon as she's done. Hot tea for you."

"Weather's just crazy, right? Only in Chicago. Eyes, out."

"That is just so wrong," said Daniel, as Murphy put the radio away. "That's a terrible radio handle. It could cause mixed messages in a tactical situation."

Murphy arched an eyebrow and spoke in a dry tone. "I'm trying to imagine the situation in which someone mistakenly being told to be alert for the enemy ends in disaster."

"If someone on the team was juggling glass vials of a deadly virus," Will supplied promptly. "Or nitroglycerin."

Murphy nodded. "Make a note: Discontinue use of radio in the event of a necessary nitro-viro juggling mission."

"Noted," Will drawled.

Daniel stiffened. "You've got a big mouth, Mr. Borden."

Will never moved. "It's not my mouth, kid. It's your skin. It's too thin."

Daniel narrowed his eyes, but Forthill put a

hand on the brawny youth's shoulder. The old man couldn't possibly restrain Daniel physically, but his touch might as well have been a steel chain attached to a battleship's anchor. His move to rise became an adjustment of himself in his seat, and he folded his arms, scowling.

"Pasty Face in five, four, three . . ." came from Murphy's radio.

Backs tightened. Faces became masks. Several hands vanished from sight. Someone's teacup clinked several times in rapid succession against a saucer before it settled.

I could see the front door from where I stood outside the window, and a couple of seconds after the radio stopped counting aloud, it opened upon a White Court vampire.

She was maybe five-two, with a dimpled smile and dark, curly hair that fell to her waist. She was wearing a white blouse with a long, full white skirt and bright scarlet ballet slippers. The first thought that went through my head was *Awww, she's tiny and adorable* — followed closely by the notion that she would be fastidious when blood was everywhere. I could just see her carefully lifting the hem of her pristine skirt so that only the scarlet slippers would touch it.

"Good evening, everyone," she said, breezing through the door without an invitation, speaking with a strong British accent. "I apologize for being a few moments late, but what's a lady to do with weather like this? Tea? Lovely." She minced over to the table and poured some hot tea into an empty cup. Her eyes fastened on Daniel as she did, and she bowed just low enough to draw the young man's eyes to her décolletage. He flushed and looked away sternly. After a second.

Tough to blame the kid. I've been a young man. Boobs are near the center of the universe, until you turn twenty-five or so. Which is also when young men's auto insurance rates go down. This is not a coincidence.

The vampire smirked, a surprisingly predatory expression on her cupid's-bow lips, and glided back to the empty chair by the door, seating herself in it like Shirley Temple on a movie set, sure that she held the attention of everyone there.

"Gutsy," I said quietly.

"Why do you say that?" Sir Stuart asked.

"She came in without an invitation," I said. "I thought vampires couldn't do that."

"The Reds ca— That is, they couldn't without being half-paralyzed. The Black Court vampires can't cross a threshold, period. The Whites can, but it cripples their abilities, makes it very difficult to draw on their Hunger for strength and speed."

Sir Stuart shook his head. "Ah yes. She's a succubus."

"Well . . . not exactly, but the differences

123

are academic."

The shade nodded. "I'm not exposing Mortimer to that creature."

"Probably not a bad idea," I agreed. "He's got access to way too much information. They'd love to get someone like Mort under their thumb."

"Hello, Felicia," Murphy said, her tone cool and professional. "All right, people. Mr. Childs won't be here tonight. I'm holding his proxy."

Felicia curled the fingers of both tiny hands around the teacup and sipped it. The tea had been scalding when the others had first sipped it. They'd been cautious. The vampire took a mouthful as if it had been room-temperature Kool-Aid and swallowed it down with a little shiver of apparent pleasure. "How convenient for you. Shall we ever see the dapper gentleman again?"

"That will be up to Marcone," Murphy replied. "Abby?"

Toto was staring at Felicia and standing with stiff legs on Abby's lap. If he'd been capable of a threatening growl, he'd have been doing it. Instead, there was just a steady squeaking sound coming from his general direction.

Abby took a firmer grip on Toto and looked down at a notebook in her lap. "The Paranet continues to operate at better than seventy-five percent of its original capacity. We actually regained contact with Minnesota, Massachusetts, and Alabama this week." She cleared her throat and blinked her eyes several times. "We lost contact with Oregon."

"Seattle or Tacoma?" Murphy asked.

"Yes," Abby said quietly. "No one has heard from a member in either place there for the past three days."

Forthill crossed himself and said something beneath his breath.

"Amen, Father," Felicia murmured.

"Someone got their roster," Daniel said, his voice harsh.

Will grunted and nodded. "Do we know who?"

"Um," Abby said, giving Will a brief, apologetic smile. "We haven't heard from anyone. So no. We'll have to send someone to investigate."

"Ugh," Murphy said, shaking her head. "No. If *that* many people have been taken, it means one of the larger powers is at work. If the Fomor have come to Oregon in strength, we'd just be throwing our scout into a snake pit."

"If we move quickly enough," Abby disagreed firmly, "we might be able to save some of them."

Murphy's expression turned introspective. "True. But there's nothing we can do from here." She looked at Forthill.

"I'll find out what I can through our channels," he promised. "But . . . I fear you will find little in the way of remedy there."

Murphy nodded. "We'll kick this one up to the Wardens."

Daniel snorted at exactly the same time I did. "Oh, sure, the White Council," the young man said. "They're the answer to this. Because they care so much about the little guy and the immediate future. They'll wander in right away — a mere year or two from now."

Will gave Daniel a flat look, and the muscles along his jaw twitched.

Murphy lifted a hand and said, "I'll call Ramirez and ask him to expedite. I'll ask Elaine Mallory to back me up."

Elaine Mallory. When Murphy said it, the name cracked something in my head and a geyser of memories erupted from it. Elaine had been my first. First friend. First crush. First lover. First victim — or so I had believed for years, at any rate. She somehow escaped the flames that consumed my old mentor, Justin DuMorne.

About a million sense-memories hit me all at once. It was like trying to watch a warehouse wall lined with televisions, all of them on different stations, all of them blaring at maximum volume. Sunshine on skin. Smooth curve of slender waist and leanly muscled back as Elaine dove into a moonlit swimming pool. The blindingly gentle sensation of our first kiss, slow and tentative and careful as it

126

had been.

Elaine. Who had been subverted into Justin's slave. Who hadn't been strong enough to defend herself when Justin came to claim her mind. Who I failed to protect.

Joy and pain came with those memories. It was deliriously intense, as disorienting and overwhelming as any drug.

Hell's bells, I *hate* being the new guy.

I managed to push the memories off after a few moments, in time to hear the vampire speak. Felicia cleared her throat and lifted a hand. "As it happens," she said, "I know that we have some assets in the area. It's possible they might be able to find something."

"It's also possible that they're responsible for the disappearances," Marci said mildly.

"Nonsense, child," Felicia responded with a little toss of her head. "We hardly need to capture our prey and corral them where their thick numbers will make hunting simple." She gave Marci a sweetly dimpled smile. "We already have such pens. They're called *cities*."

"We will be happy for any information the White Court is willing to provide, Felicia," Murphy said, her calm, professional, neutral tone expertly dulling the edges of the previous words. "What about Chicago, Abby?"

"We lost two this week," Abby said. "Nathan Simpson and Sunbeam Monroe."

"A ghoul took Simpson," Will supplied at once. "We settled his account."

Murphy glanced at Will in approval. "Have I met Sunbeam?"

Abby nodded. "The college student from San Jose."

Murphy winced. "Right. Tall girl? Hippie-esque parents."

"That's her. She was accompanied to the El station, and someone was waiting at her destination. She never arrived."

Murphy made a growling sound that more than made up for Toto's lack. "We know anything?"

Will looked at Marci. The stringy girl shook her head. "The snow is holding too many scents in place. I couldn't find anything solid." She looked down at her knees and added, "Sorry."

Murphy ignored that last bit. "She shouldn't have been traveling alone. We're going to have to stress the importance of partnering up."

"How?" Abby asked. "I mean, it's in every circular."

Murphy nodded. "Will?"

Will drummed his fingertips on his biceps and nodded. "I'll see to it."

"Thank you."

Abby blinked several times and then said, "Karrin . . . you can't possibly mean . . ."

"People are dying," Murphy said simply. "A good scare can do wonders to cure stupidity."

"Or we could try protecting them," said Daniel.

Forthill lifted a hand again, but the younger man ignored him, rising to his feet. Daniel's voice was a rich, strong baritone. "All over the world, dark things are rising up against mortals connected to the supernatural. Killing them or dragging them away into the dark. Creatures that haven't been seen by mankind in the past two *millennia* are reappearing. Fighting mortals. Fighting one another. The shadows are boiling over with death and terror, and no one is doing anything about it!

"The Wardens went from fighting the Vampire War to a new one, against an enemy without a face or an identity. The White Council doesn't have Wardens enough to handle everything that's happening anyway. If a cry for help is sent up anywhere but a major city, there's no chance at all of them showing up. Meanwhile, what are we doing?" Daniel's voice filled with quiet scorn. "Telling people to travel around in herds. Scaring them ourselves to make them do so, as if there wasn't terror enough in the world already."

Murphy stared steadily at him. Then she said, her tone hard, "That's enough."

Daniel ignored her, planting his feet and squaring his shoulders. "You know. You know what must be done, Ms. Murphy. You're holding two of the greatest weapons against darkness that the world has ever known. Bring forth the Swords."

A dead silence settled on the room, into which Sir Stuart asked me, conversationally, "Which swords?"

"The Swords of the Cross," I said quietly, out of habit — I could have sung it operatically without anyone there noticing. "The ones with the nails from the Crucifixion worked into them."

"Excalibur, Durendal, and Kusanagi, yes, yes," Sir Stuart said, his tone a little impatient. "Of course I know the Swords of the Cross. And the little blond woman has *two* of them?"

I just stared at the burly shade for a long second. I'd found what amounted to a rumor that *Amoracchius* was, in fact, the same sword given to King Arthur, but I hadn't ever heard anything about the other two — despite some fairly exhaustive research over the years. The shade had dropped their identities as if they were everyday knowledge.

Sir Stuart frowned at me and said, "What is it?"

"I just don't . . . Do you know how much research I . . ." I blew out an exasperated breath, scowled, and said, "I went to public school."

Back inside, Murphy didn't break the silence. She just stared at Daniel for maybe

130

two minutes. Then she directed a rather pointed glance at Felicia and eyed Daniel again.

The young man glanced at Felicia and closed his eyes as his cheeks got redder and his passion swiftly deflated. He muttered something under his breath and sat down again rather quickly.

The vampire sat in her chair, staring at Daniel over the rim of her teacup and smiling as if butter wouldn't melt in her mouth. For all I knew, it wouldn't. "I love young men," she purred. "I just love them."

"Mr. Carpenter," Murphy said. "I assume you have divulged secrets enough to the enemies of humanity for one evening?"

Daniel said nothing.

"Then perhaps you can join Eyes and Fuzz in keeping watch outside."

He rose at once, slipping into his heavy, fleece-lined, blue denim coat. It was an old, well-used garment. I'd seen his father wearing it, but it was a little big on Daniel. Without a word, he left the living room for the kitchen and went out the back door.

Silence was heavy when he left.

"Both swords," Felicia said, her tone light, her periwinkle eyes on Murphy. "My, my, my." She sipped at her tea and said, "Of course, you'll have to kill me, dear. If you can." The diminutive vampire looked casually at each person in the room. "I give you one chance in four."

"I can't let the White Court know about the Swords," Murphy agreed. Her fingers hung near the handle of her gun.

Will watched with sleepy eyes. But sometime in the past few seconds he had managed to center his weight over his feet. Marci still crouched with her legs curled up to the rest of her, but they were under her dress now. Within a heartbeat, she could have it off and clear it from impeding her shapeshifting.

Felicia was in exactly the same posture as several minutes before. She looked entirely unconcerned with any possible danger. I made a mental note never to play poker with her. "Well, darling. If you intended to dance, there would already be music. So perhaps we should talk." She smiled, and her eyes glittered, suddenly several shades lighter than before. "Just us girls. We can go for a walk."

Murphy snorted. She drew her gun from her belt and set it on the armrest of her chair. She rested her hand over it, not quite touching the trigger. "I'm not an idiot, Felicia. You'll stay right where you are. As will I. Everyone else, outside."

Abby had risen before Murphy finished speaking, holding Toto carefully as she left.

Will frowned at Murphy. "You sure?"

Father Forthill rose, frowning, and said, "These old legs want to go for a little walk, in any case. Good evening, Ms. Murphy. William?"

Will literally growled, and it came out sounding like no noise a human being ought to be able to make. But then he nodded to Murphy and turned toward the door. Marci hurried to her feet and went after him. Forthill stumped off after them. I heard everyone leave the house by the back door, probably to gather on the stone-paved patio just outside.

"I like this," Felicia said into the silence, smiling. "This charming little house feels so intimate. Don't you think?" She tilted her head. "Are the Swords on the premises?"

"I think you should name your price," Murphy responded.

Felicia arched an eyebrow, a sensual little smile bending one corner of her mouth into a smirk.

"F—" Murphy cleared her throat. "Forget that. It isn't happening."

The vampire turned her mouth down in a mocking little pout. "Such a Puritan work ethic. Business and pleasure can coexist, you know."

"This isn't business, Ms. Raith. It's blackmail."

"To-may-toe, to-mah-toe," Felicia said with a shrug. "The point is, Karrin, that you can hardly afford to be squeamish."

"No?"

"No. You're intelligent, skilled, and strong-

willed — quite formidable. . . ." She smiled.
"For a mortal. But, in the end, you *are* a lone
mortal. And you are no longer beneath the
aegis of city law enforcement or resident
members of the White Council."

Murphy moved nothing but her lips.
"Meaning?"

Felicia sighed and said in a practical,
dispassionate tone, "The Swords are valuable. They could be traded for a great deal of
influence. Should the White Court learn of
this and decide to take the Swords, they will
take you. They will ask you where they are.
They will force you to surrender them."

Murphy might have twitched one shoulder
in a shrug. Then she got up and walked
toward Felicia, gripping her gun loosely in
hand. "And . . . what? If I give you what you
want, you'll stay quiet?"

Felicia nodded, her eyelids lowering as she
watched Murphy approach. "For a few days,
at any rate. By which time, you will have been
able to take measures to prevent them from
being taken."

Murphy said, "You want to feed on me."

Felicia ran a very pink tongue over her upper lip, her eyes growing paler. "I do. Very
much."

Murphy frowned and nodded.

Then she whipped the pistol in a bone-
breaking stroke, smashing it into the vampire's jaw.

"Yes!" I hissed, clenching my hands into fists.

The vampire let out a short, stunned gasping sound and rocked beneath the blow. She slid out of the chair to her knees, feebly trying to move away from Murphy.

Murph wasn't having any of it. She grabbed Felicia by the hair, hauled her halfway to her feet, and then, with a furious shout and a contraction of her whole body, Murphy slammed the vampire's face down onto the coffee table. Felicia's head shattered the teapot and the platter beneath, and struck the oak table with such force that a crack erupted from end to end in the wood.

Murph slammed Felicia's head down with near-equal violence two more times. Then she turned and dragged Felicia over to the front door of her house by the hair. Murphy let her go with a contemptuous shove, stood over her, and pointed a gun at the vampire's head.

"This is what happens," Murphy said in a very quiet, hard voice. "You leave here alive. You keep your fucking mouth shut. And we never mention tonight ever again. If the White Court even blinks in the Swords' direction, I am going to come find you, Felicia. Whatever happens to me in the end, before I am taken, I *will* find you."

Felicia stared up at her, wobbling and shaking, clearly dazed. Murphy had broken the vampire's nose and knocked out at least two teeth. One of Felicia's high cheekbones was already swelling. The broken teapot had left multiple cuts on her face, and her skin had been scalded by the hot liquid still inside.

Murphy leaned a little closer and put the barrel of the gun against Felicia's forehead. Then she whispered, very quietly, "Bang."

The vampire shuddered.

"Do what you think best, Felicia," Murph whispered. Then she straightened again slowly, and spoke in a clear, calm voice as she walked back to her chair. "Now. Get out of my house."

Felicia managed to stagger to her feet, open the front door, and limp haltingly to the white limousine idling on the snowy street outside the house. Murphy went to the window to watch Felicia get into the limo and depart.

"Yeah," I said, deadpan. "The little blond woman has two of them."

"Oh, my," Sir Stuart said, his voice muted with respect. "I can see why you'd come to her for assistance."

"Damn skippy," I agreed. "Better go get Morty while she's still in a good mood."

CHAPTER TEN

I met Morty and Sir Stuart on Murphy's front porch. I guess it was a cold night. Morty stood with his entire body hunched against the wind, his hands stuffed into his coat pockets. His eyes darted around nervously. He was shivering.

"Hit the bell," I said. "And this is just my opinion, but if I were you, I'd keep my hands in plain sight."

"Thanks," Mort said sourly, jabbing the doorbell. "Have I told you how much brightness you bring to my world whenever you show up in it, Dresden?"

"All in a day's work when you're created from the cosmic legends of the universe," I replied.

"Be advised," Sir Stuart said, "that there are wolves to the left and right."

I looked. He was right. One was huge and dark-furred; the other smaller and lighter brown. They were sitting in the shadows, perfectly still, where a casual glance would simply pass over them. Their wary stares were intense. "Will and Marci," I said. "They're cool."

"They're violent vigilantes," Mort replied through clenched teeth.

"Buck up, little camper. They're not going to hurt you, and you know it."

Mort gave me a narrow-eyed glare, and then Murphy opened the door.

"Ms. Murphy," Morty said, nodding to her.

"Lindquist, isn't it?" Murph asked. "The medium?"

"Yes."

"What do you want?"

"Behind us," Sir Stuart murmured.

I checked. A slender male figure in heavy winter clothing was crossing the street toward us. A third wolf, this one's fur edged with auburn, walked beside him.

"I'm here to speak to you on behalf of someone you knew," Mort told Murphy.

Murphy's blue eyes became chips of glacial ice. "Who?"

"Harry Dresden," Mort said.

Murphy clenched her right hand into a fist. Her knuckles made small popping sounds.

Mort swallowed and took half a step back. "Look, I don't want to be here," he said, raising his hands and displaying his palms. "But you know how he was. His shade is no less stubborn or annoying than Dresden was in life."

"You're a goddamned liar," Murphy snarled. "You're a known con artist. And you are playing with fire."

Mort stared at her for a long moment. Then he winced and said, "You . . . you believed he was still alive?"

"He *is* alive," Murphy replied, clenching her jaw. "They never found a body."

Mort looked down, pressing his lips together, and ran his palm over his bald pate, smearing away a few clinging snowflakes. He blew out a long breath and said, "I'm sorry. I'm sorry that this is difficult."

"It isn't difficult," Murphy replied. "Just annoying. Because he's still alive."

Mort looked at me and spread his hands. "She's still in denial. There's not much I can do here. Look, I've done this a *lot*. She needs more time."

"No," I said. "We've got to make her see. Tonight."

Mort pinched the bridge of his nose between his thumb and forefinger. "It isn't like you're getting any older, Dresden."

Murphy fixed Morty with her cop glare. It hadn't lost any of its intensity. "This is neither believable nor amusing, Lindquist. I think you'd better go now."

Lindquist nodded, holding up his hands in a gesture of placation. "I know. I'm going. Please understand, I'm just trying to help."

"Wait!" I snapped. "There's got to be

139

something you can say."

Mort glanced at me as he began walking back toward his car and lifted both of his hands, palms up, in a little helpless gesture.

I ground my teeth, standing less than a foot away from Murphy. How the hell did I get her to believe it really was me?

"By having Morty talk about something only you could know, dummy," I said to myself. "Morty!"

He paused about halfway down the driveway and turned to look at me.

"Ask her this," I said, and spouted a question.

Mort sighed. Then he turned toward Murphy and said, "Before I go . . . Dresden wants me to ask you if you ever found that reasonably healthy male."

Murphy didn't move. Her face went white. After maybe a minute, she whispered, "What did you say?"

I prompted Mort. "Dresden wants me to tell you that he hadn't intended to do anything dramatic. It just sort of worked out that way."

The wolves and the man in the heavy coat had stepped closer, listening. Murphy clenched and unclenched her fist several times. Then she said, "How many vampires did Agent White and I have to kill before we escaped the FBI office last year?"

I felt another surge of fierce triumph. That

was Murph, always thinking. I told Mort the answer.

"He says he doesn't know who Agent White is, but that you and Tilly took out one of them in a stairwell on your way out of the building." Mort tilted his head, listening to me, and then said, "And he also wonders if you still feel that taking up the Sword of Faith would represent a . . . a rebound career."

Murphy's face by now was almost entirely bloodless. I could almost visibly see her eyes becoming more sunken, her features overtaken by a grey and weary sagging. She leaned against the doorway to her house, her arms sliding across her own stomach, as if she were trying to prevent her innards from spilling out.

"Ms. Murphy," Mort said gently. "I'm terribly sorry to be the one to bear this particular news. But Dresden's shade says that he needs to talk to you. That people are in danger."

"Yeah," Murphy said, her voice numb. "That's new." She looked up at Mort and said, "Bleed for me."

It was a common test among those savvy to the supernatural world but lacking any of its gifts. There are a lot of inhuman things that can pretend to be human — but relatively few of them have natural-looking blood. It wasn't a perfect test, by any means, but it was a lot better than nothing.

Mort nodded calmly and produced a

straight pin from his coat pocket. He hadn't even blinked at the request. Apparently, in the current climate, the test had become much more widely used. I wondered if Murphy had been responsible for it.

Morty pricked the tip of his left thumb with the pin, and it welled with a round drop of ruby blood. He showed it to Murphy, who nodded.

"It's cold out here. You'd better come inside, Mr. Lindquist."

"Thank you," Mort said with a heavy exhalation.

"Meeting time, kids," Murphy said to those outside. "I want this joker verified. Will, please send someone to invite Raggedy Ann over."

"I don't want to be any trouble . . ." Mort began.

Murphy gave him a chilly smile. "Get your ass inside and sit down. I'll tell you when you can go. And if you really are putting one over on us somehow, you should know that I am not going to be a good sport about it."

Mort swallowed. But he went inside.

Murphy, Will, and Father Forthill spent the next half hour grilling Morty, and, by extension, me, with Abby and Daniel looking on. Each of them asked a lot of questions, mostly about private conversations I'd had with them. Morty had to relay my answers:

"No, Father, I just hadn't ever heard a priest use the phrase *screw the pooch* before."

"Will, look. I offered to pay for that 'the door is ajar' thing."

"The chlorofiend? You killed it with a chain saw, Murph."

And so on and so forth, until my blood — or maybe ectoplasm — was practically boiling.

"This is getting ridiculous," I snapped, finally. "You're stalling. Why?"

Morty blinked at me in surprise. Sir Stuart burst out into a short bark of laughter from where he lounged against a wall in the corner.

Murphy looked at Mort closely, frowning. "What is it?"

"Dresden's getting impatient," Mort said, his tone of voice suggesting that it was something grossly inappropriate, if not outright impolite. "He, ah, suspects that you're stalling and wants to know why. I'm sorry. Spirits are almost never this . . ."

"Stubbornly willful?" Murphy suggested.

"Insistent," Mort finished, his expression neutral.

Murphy sat back in her chair and traded a look with Father Forthill. "Well," she said. "That . . . sounds a great deal like Dresden, doesn't it?"

"I'm quite sure that only Dresden knew several of those details he mentioned in passing," Forthill said gravely. "There are beings who could know such things regardless of whether or not they were actually present, however. Very, very dangerous beings."

Murphy looked at Mort and nodded. "So. Either he's both sincere *and* correct, in that Dresden's shade is there with him, or someone's been bamboozled and I've let something epic and nasty into my house."

"Essentially," Forthill agreed, with a small, tired smile. "For whatever it's worth, I sense no dark presence here. Just a draft."

"That's Dresden's shade, Father," Mort said respectfully. Mort, a good Catholic boy. Who knew?

"Where is Dresden now?" Murphy asked. She didn't exactly sound enthusiastic about the question.

Mort looked at me and sighed. "He's . . . sort of looming over you, a little to your left, Ms. Murphy. He's got his arms crossed and he's tapping one foot, and he's looking at his left wrist every few seconds, even though he doesn't wear a watch."

"Do you have to make me sound so . . . so childish?" I complained.

Murphy snorted. "That sounds like him."

"Hey!" I said.

There was a familiar soft pattering of paws on the floor, and Mister sprinted into the room. He went right across Murphy's hardwood floors and cannonballed into my shins.

Mister is a lot of cat, checking in at right

around thirty pounds. The impact staggered me, and I rocked back, and then quickly leaned down to run my hand over the cat's fur. He felt like he always did, and his rumbling purr was loud and happy.

It took me a second to realize that I could touch Mister. I could feel the softness of his fur and the warmth of his body.

More to the point, a large cat moving at a full run over a smooth hardwood floor had shoulder-blocked empty air and *had come to a complete halt doing it.*

Everyone was staring at Mister with their mouths open.

I mean, it's one thing to know that the supernatural world exists, and to interact with it on occasion in dark and spooky settings. But the weird factor of the supernatural hits you hardest at home, when you see it in simple, everyday things: a door standing open that shouldn't be; a shadow on the floor with no source to cast it; a cat purring and rubbing up against a favorite person — who isn't there.

"Oh," Murphy said, staring, her eyes welling up.

Will let out a low whistle.

Father Forthill crossed himself, a small smile lifting the corners of his mouth.

Mort looked at the cat and sighed. "Oh, sure. Professional ectomancer with a national reputation as a medium tells you what's go-

145

ing on, and nobody believes him. But let a stump-tailed, furry critter come in and everyone goes all Lifetime."

"Heh," said Sir Stuart, quietly amused. "What did I tell you? Cats."

Murphy turned to me, lifting her face toward mine. Her eyes were a little off, focused to one side of my face. I moved until I stood where she was looking, her blue eyes intent. "Harry?"

"I'm here," I said.

"God, I feel stupid," Murphy muttered, looking at Mort. "He can hear me, right?"

"And see you," Mort said.

She nodded and looked up again — at a slightly different place. I moved again.

I know. It wouldn't matter to her.

But it mattered to me.

"Harry," she said. "A lot of things have happened since . . . since the last time we talked. The big spell at Chichén Itzá didn't just destroy the Red Court who were there. It killed them all. Every Red Court vampire in the world."

"Yeah," I said, and my voice sounded hard, even to me. "That was the idea."

Murphy blew out a breath. "Butters says that maybe there were some it missed, but they would have had to have been the very youngest and least powerful members of the least powerful bloodlines, or else sheltered

146

away in some kind of protected location. But he says according to what he knows of magical theory, it makes sense."

I shrugged and nodded. "Yeah, I guess so. A lot depends on exactly how that rite was set up to work." But the Red Court was dead, the same way the Black Court was dead. Life would go on. They were footnotes now.

"When the Red Court fell," Murphy continued, "their territory was suddenly open. There was a power vacuum. Do you understand?"

Oh, God.

The Red Court had tried to murder my little girl and all that was left of my family, and I wouldn't lose any sleep over what had happened to them. (Assuming I would ever sleep again, which seemed to be a real question.) But I hadn't thought past that single moment, thought through the long-term consequences of wiping out the entire Red Court.

They were one of the major supernatural nations in the world. They controlled a continent and change — South and most of Central America — and had holdings all over the world. They owned property. Stocks. Corporations. Accounts. They as much as owned some governments. Assets of every kind.

The value of what the Red Court had controlled was almost literally incalculable.

And I had thrown it all up in the air and declared one giant game of finders, keepers.

"Oops," I said.

"Things . . . are bad," Murphy said. "Not so much here in Chicago. We've repulsed the worst incursions — mostly from some gang of arrogant freaks called the Fomor. And the Paranet has been a huge help. It's saved literally hundreds, if not thousands, of lives."

In my peripheral vision, I saw Abby's spine straighten and her eyes flash with a strength and surety I had never seen in her before.

"South America has the worst of it, by a long ways," Murphy said. "But every two-bit power and second-rate organization in the supernatural world sees a chance to found an empire. Old grudges and jealousies are getting dusted off. Things are killing one another as well as mortals, all over the world. When one big fish shifts its power base to South America, dozens of little fish left behind try to grow enough to fill the space. So there's fighting everywhere.

"The White Council, I hear, is running its tubby ass off, trying to hold things together and minimize the impact on regular folks. But we haven't seen them here, apart from a couple of times when Warden Ramirez came by, hunting for Molly."

"Molly," I said. "How is she?" I dimly heard Mort relaying my words. I noted that he was doing a credible job of mirroring my tone of voice. I guess he really had done a lot of this kind of thing before.

"She's still recovering from the wounds she took at Chichén Itzá," Murphy said. "She says they were as much psychic as physical. And that hit to her leg was pretty bad. I don't understand how your disappearance makes her a criminal to the White Council, but apparently it has. Ramirez has told us that the Wardens are looking to pass sentence on her — but he didn't seem to be working his ass off to find her, either. I know what it looks like when a cop is slacking."

"How is she?" I asked again. "Murph, it's me. How's she doing?"

She looked down and swallowed. "She . . . she isn't right, Harry."

"What do you mean?"

Murphy looked up at me again, her jaw set. "She talks to herself. She sees things that aren't there. She has headaches. She babbles."

"Sounds like me," I said, at approximately the same time Will said, "Sounds like Harry."

"This is different," Murphy said to Will, "and you know it. Dresden was in control of it. He used the weirdness to make him stronger. Were you ever afraid of him?" Murphy asked. "Outright afraid?"

Will frowned and looked down at his hands. "He could be scary. But no. I never thought he'd hurt me. By accident or otherwise."

"How do you feel about Molly coming

over?" Murphy asked.

"I would like to leave," Will replied frankly. "The girl ain't right."

"Apparently," Murphy continued, turning back to me, "the presence of a wizard in a city, any city, all around the world, is an enormous deterrent. Weird things are afraid of the Council. They know that the White Council can come get you fast, out of nowhere, with overwhelming force. Most of the scary-bad things around, the ones with any brains, at least, avoid White Council territory.

"Only with you gone and the White Council having its hands full . . ." Murphy shook her head. "God. Even the vanilla news is starting to notice the weirdness in town. So. Molly wouldn't stay with anyone. She's always moving. But she got it into her head that Chicago didn't need an actual White Council wizard to help calm things down — the bad guys just had to *think* one was here. So she started posting messages whenever she dealt with some wandering predator, and called herself the Ragged Lady, declaring Chicago protected territory."

"That's crazy," I said.

"What part of *she isn't right* didn't you understand?" Murphy replied to Morty, her voice sharp. She took a breath and calmed herself again. "The craziest part is that it worked. At least partly. A lot of bad things have decided to play elsewhere. College

150

towns out in the country are the worst. But . . . things have happened here." She shivered. "Violent things. Mostly to the bad guys. But sometimes to humans. Gangers, mostly. The Ragged Lady's calling card is a piece of cloth she tears off and leaves on her enemies. And there are lots and lots of pieces of cloth being found these days. A lot of them on corpses."

I swallowed. "You think it's Molly?"

"We don't know," Murphy replied in her professionally neutral voice. "Molly says she isn't going after anything but the supernatural threats, and I've got no reason to disbelieve her. But . . ." Murphy showed her hands.

"So when you said Raggedy Ann," I said, "you meant Molly."

"She's like this . . . battered, stained, torn-up doll," Murphy said. "Believe me. It fits."

"Battered, torn-up, *scary* doll," Will said quietly.

"And . . . you just let her be that way?" I demanded.

Murphy ground her teeth. "No. I talked to her half a dozen times. We tried an intervention to get her off the street."

"We shouldn't have," Will said.

"What happened?" Mort asked.

Will apparently assumed it had been my question. "She hammered us like a row of nails on balsa wood is what happened," he said. "Lights, sound, images. Jesus, I've got a picture in my head of being dragged off into the Nevernever by monsters that I *still* can't get rid of. When she gave it to me, all I could do was curl up into a ball and scream."

Will's description made me feel sick to my stomach. Which was ridiculous, because it wasn't like I ate food anymore — but my innards hadn't gotten the memo. I looked away, grimacing, tasting bitter bile in my mouth.

"Memories are weapons," Sir Stuart said quietly. "Sharp as knives."

Murphy held up her hand to cut Will off. "Whether or not she's going too far, she's the only one we have with a major-league talent. Not that the Ordo hasn't done well by us, Abby," she added, nodding toward the blond woman.

"Not at all," Abby replied, undisturbed. "We aren't all made the same size and shape, are we?" Abby looked at me, more or less, and said, "We built the wards around Karrin's house. Three hundred people from the Paranet, all working together." She put a hand on an exterior wall, where the power of the patchwork ward hummed steadily. "Took us less than a day."

"And two hundred pizzas," Murphy muttered. "And a citation."

"And well worth it," Abby said, arching an eyebrow that dared Murphy to disagree.

Murphy shook her head, but I could see

her holding off a smile. "The point is, we're waiting for Molly to confirm your bona fides, Harry."

"Um," Morty said. "Is . . . is that safe, Ms. Murphy? If the girl was his apprentice, won't her reaction to his shade likely be . . . somewhat emotional?"

Will snorted. "The way nitroglycerin is somewhat volatile." He took a breath and then said, "Karrin, you sure about this?"

Murphy looked around the room slowly. Abby's eyes were on the floor, but her usally rosy cheeks were pale, and Toto's ears drooped unhappily. Will's expression was steady, but his body language was that of a man who thinks he might need to dive through a closed window at any second. Forthill was watching the room at large, exuding calm confidence, but his brow was furrowed, and the set of his mouth was slightly tense.

With the exception of Forthill, I'd seen them all react to direct danger.

They were all scared of Molly.

Murphy faced them. She was the smallest person in the room. Her expression was as smooth and expressive as a sheet of ice, her body posture steady. She looked as though she felt she was ready for just about anything.

But I've been in more than one fur ball with Murph, and I saw through her outer shell to the fear that was driving her. She didn't know if I was real. For all she knew, I might be some kind of boogeyman from the nightmare side of the street, and that was unacceptable. She had to know.

The problem was that no matter what answer she got, it was going to hurt. If Molly pegged me as a bad guy, the knowledge that the real Harry Dresden was still missing and presumed dead, after the flash of contact Mort had provided, would be like a frozen blade in the guts. And if she learned that it really was my shade . . . it would be even worse.

"Molly will be fine," Murphy said. "We need her. She'll come through." She passed her hand over her brush of hair. Her voice turned into something much smaller, weighed down by pain. "No offense to Mr. Lindquist. No offense to Mister. But I . . . We have to know."

Paranoid? Probably.

But just because you're paranoid doesn't mean there isn't a wizard's ghost standing beside you with tears in his eyes.

CHAPTER ELEVEN

Not long after, something scratched at the front door, and Will opened it to admit a grey-brown-furred wolf. The wolf trotted over to where Marci's dress lay folded on the sofa, took it in her teeth, and vanished into the kitchen. Marci appeared a few seconds later, settling the dress around her slender form, and said, "She'll be here any moment. I already told Andi and Eyes."

"Thank you, Marci." Murph looked at everyone and said, "Settle down, people. You look like you're expecting Hannibal Lecter to come through the door."

"I could handle Hannibal," Will said. "This is different."

Murphy put a fist on her hip and said, "Will. Molly is one of us. And you aren't going to help her by looking nervous. If you can't settle down and relax, get out of here. I don't want you upsetting her."

Will grimaced. Then he went into the kitchen, and a moment later a large wolf with fur the same color as Will's hair padded back into the room. He went to a corner, turned around three times, and settled down on the floor. Toto let out a sharp little bark of greeting and hopped down to hurry over to Will. The little dog sniffed Will, then turned around three times and settled down next to him, their backs touching. The big wolf took a deep breath and exhaled it into a very human-sounding sigh of resignation.

"Thank you," Murphy said. She glanced at Mort. "There's a circle made out of copper wire in the kitchen. If it gets hot in here, you can run for it. You know how to empower a circle?"

"Yes, of course." He licked his lips and said, "Though I can't imagine running for my life and stopping in the kitchen. Meaning no offense to your protective ability, but I'll stop when I'm *home,* thank you."

"God," Murphy said. "If only more people had as much sense as you."

Murphy's radio chirped, and Eyes started to say something. His voice drowned an instant later in a burst of static.

That ratcheted more tension in everyone. Wizards and their major magical talent are tough on hardware. The more complex a machine is, the more disruptive a wizard's presence becomes, and electronics are nearly always the first to malfunction when a wizard is nearby. The wonky radio warned us of Molly's approach every bit as clearly as a sentry shouting, "Who goes there?"

"Huh," I said.

Mort glanced at me. "What?"

"The technology disruption a practitioner causes is relative to his — or her — strength."

"I knew that, actually," Mort said. "It's why I have to keep replacing my cell phone. So?"

"So Molly was not a heavyweight in terms of raw power. She had to be practically close enough to touch something to hex it down that fast." I narrowed my eyes. "She's gotten stronger. Either that or . . ."

"She's already in the room," Mort said.

Murphy looked up sharply at that. "What?"

The house lights flickered for a second and then went out.

They weren't gone long — the space of a heartbeat or two. But when they came back up, Murphy had her gun in hand, Marci had become a wolf with a sundress hanging around her neck, and a young woman wrapped in layers and layers of cast-off clothing sat on the sofa between Abby and Mort, not six inches away from either of them.

Molly was tall and built like a pinup model, with long, long legs and curves that not even the layers of clothing could hide. Her face was lovely and devoid of makeup, and her cheekbones pressed out harshly against her skin. Her hair was dirty, stringy, tangled, and colored a shade of purple so dark as to be

157

nearly indistinguishable from black. A wooden cane stained the same color of deep purple leaned against her knees, and an old military-issue canvas knapsack covered with buttons and drawings in Magic Marker rested between her hiking boots. From Abby's and Mort's reactions, it must have smelled like it had been at least several days since her last shower.

But it was her eyes that were the worst.

My apprentice's blue eyes were sunken, surrounded by shadows of stress and fatigue, and an odd light glittered there in the glassy shine I'd seen mostly in people recovering from anesthesia.

"It's interesting that you would notice me," Molly said to Mort, as if she'd been politely participating in the conversation all along.

The ectomancer twitched, and I saw him fight off the desire to get up and sprint for his car.

Molly nodded and looked around the rest of the room, person by person, until she got to Murphy. "I hope we're planning a civil discussion this time, Karrin."

Murph put her gun away, giving Molly a mild glance by way of reprimand. "We *were* being civil last time. We're your friends, Molly, and we're worried about you."

My apprentice shrugged. "I don't want anyone like friends anywhere near me. If you include yourself among them, you should leave me the hell alone." Her voice had turned into a snarl by the end of the sentence, and she paused to take a slow, deliberate breath and calm down. "I don't have the patience or the time for a group-therapy session. What do you want?"

Murphy seemed to consider her answer for a moment. She wound up going for brevity. "We need you to verify something for us."

"Do I look like a fact-checker to you, Karrin?"

"You look like a homeless scarecrow," Murphy said, her tone matter-of-fact. "You smell like a gutter."

"I thought you used to be a detective," Molly said, rolling her eyes. "See above, regarding not wanting anyone around me. It's not all that hard to understand."

"Miss Carpenter," said Father Forthill in a sudden tone of gentle authority. "You are a *guest* in this woman's home. A woman who has put her own life in danger to save others — including you."

Molly turned an absolutely arctic look onto Father Forthill. Then she said, in a quiet, flat monotone, "I don't particularly care to be spoken to as if I am still a child, Father."

"If you wish to be respected as an adult, you should comport yourself as one," Forthill replied, "which includes behaving with civility toward your peers and respect toward your elders."

Molly glowered for a moment more, but then turned back to Murphy. "All things considered, it's stupid for me to be here. And I'm a busy woman, Ms. Murphy — nothing but customers, customers, customers. So I'm out the door in five seconds unless you give me a good reason to stay."

"This is Mort Lindquist, ectomancer," Murphy said promptly. "He says he's here to speak to us on behalf of Harry's ghost, who is with him."

Molly absolutely froze in place. Her face blanched beneath the grime.

"I'd like it if you could verify for us whether or not it's true," Murphy said, her voice gentle. "I need to know if he's really . . . if it's really his ghost."

Molly stared at her for a second, then shivered and looked down at her hands. "Um."

Murphy leaned a little closer to Molly. "You could tell. Couldn't you?"

Molly shot her a wide-eyed glance and looked down again. She muttered something before she said, "Yes. But . . . not with so many people in the room."

"Why not?"

Molly's voice turned into a bitter snarl. "Do you want my help or not?"

Murphy folded her arms for a long moment. Then she said, "Time for another stroll in the evening air, people. Mr. Lindquist,

160

please stay. Everyone else, out."

Mort was trying very hard not to look like a man who wanted to run for the door, and getting mixed results. "I . . . Of course, Ms. Murphy."

Murphy had to urge the werewolves to leave and help Marci get untangled from her dress. Forthill and Abby looked at each other and left the room without a murmur. Molly sat completely still during this, staring down at her folded hands.

"You don't have clue one, do you?" she asked Murphy quietly. "You don't have any idea what you're asking me to go through."

"If I could do it myself, I would."

Molly looked up sharply at that. Her smile was unpleasant. Bordering on creepy.

"Easy words," she said. "Easy words. They leave little trails of slime on your lips when they pass them. But it doesn't make them go down any more smoothly."

"Molly . . ." Murphy sighed and sat down and spread her hands. "You won't let us help you. You won't talk to us. But this is something I literally cannot ask of anyone else."

"You always asked *him,*" Molly said, her tone spiteful.

"There's a boiler about to burst," Sir Stuart murmured to me.

"Shut your mouth," I said quietly, coming automatically to her defense. But he was right. The kid was teetering on a cliff as I sat there looking at her.

I stared at Molly and felt absolutely wretched. She was my apprentice. I was supposed to have taught her to survive without me. Granted, I hadn't planned on taking a bullet in the chest, but then, who does? Or was her condition simply symptomatic of the world she lived in?

Murphy regarded the younger woman for a long moment and then nodded. "Yes. I know enough to know when I'm out of my depth. My instincts say Mort isn't trying to con me, but we've got to have more than just my intuition. I need your help. Please."

Molly shook her head very slowly, shivering. She wiped at her face with her grimy gloves, and clean streaks appeared on her cheeks. "Fine." She lifted her head, looked at Mort, and said calmly, "If you're running a con, I will peel the skin off your brain."

The ectomancer spread his hands. "Look. Dresden's shade came to *me.* If it isn't him, that ain't my fault. I'm operating in good faith, here."

"You're a roach," Molly said pleasantly. "Runs and hides from any threat, but you survive, don't you?"

"Yes," Mort said frankly.

"Maybe I should have been a roach, too," Molly said. "It would be easier." She took a slow, deep breath and said, "Where is he?"

Mort pointed a finger at me. I took a few

steps until I stood in the mouth of the hallway that led down to Murphy's bedrooms. I gestured to Sir Stuart to stay back.

"Why?" he asked.

"She's going to use her Sight. The less she has to look at, the better."

Sir Stuart shrugged and stayed near Mort. He watched Molly through narrowed eyes, his fingertips on the handle of that monster pistol.

Molly grabbed her cane and rose to her feet, leaning on it, taking the weight off the leg that had been shot at Chichén Itzá. She straightened her back and shoulders, turned toward me, took a deep breath, and opened her Sight.

I'd never seen such a thing from this angle before. It was as if a sudden light, burning steady and unwavering, kindled just between and above her eyebrows. As it flooded out of her, I felt it as a tangible sensation on my immaterial flesh. It was blinding. I lifted a hand for a moment to shield my eyes against it before I looked up to meet Molly's gaze.

Her lips parted. She stared at me and tears blurred her vision. She tried twice to speak before she said, "How do I know it's you?"

I could answer her. It's called the Sight, but it embraces the entire spectrum of human perception, and then some. I met her gaze and composed my face. Then I said, in my very best Alec Guinness impersonation, "You will go to the Dagobah system. There you will learn from Yoda, the Jedi Master who instructed me."

Molly sat down abruptly, missed the couch, and hit the floor instead. "Ohmygod," she breathed. "Ohmygod, ohmygod, ohmygod. Harry."

I knelt to be on eye level with her. "Yeah, kid. It's me."

"Are . . . are you really . . . really gone?"

I shrugged. "I don't know. I guess I am. I'm sorta new at this, and they aren't in danger of winning any exposition awards around here."

She nodded as more tears came, but she didn't look away. "D-did you come to take me away?" she asked, her voice very small.

"No," I said quietly. "Molly . . . no. I was sent back here."

"W-why?" she whispered.

"To find my murderer," I said quietly. "People I care about are in danger if I don't get the job done."

Molly began rocking back and forth where she sat. "I . . . Oh. I've been trying. . . . The city has become so *dark,* and I knew what you would expect of me, but I'm not as *strong* as you. I can't just s-smash things like you could. . . ."

"Molly," I said in a calm, clear tone.

Her reddened, exhausted blue eyes looked up at me.

"You know who I want to know about, don't you? Who I wouldn't want you to talk about in front of anyone?"

I hadn't said my daughter's name since returning to Chicago. Hell, I'd barely dared to *think* it. As far as the rest of the world knew, Maggie had been engulfed in the conflagration that devoured the Red Court. Anyone who knew of her identity might well hold it against her. I didn't want that. Not if I wasn't going to be there to protect her.

My throat felt tight, because I thought it should, I suppose. "You know who I'm asking about?"

"Yes," she said. "Of course."

"Is that person safe and well?"

"As far as I know, yes," she said. A small smile made her, for an instant, resemble the girl I remembered. "Chewbacca is with her."

There was only one giant walking carpet to whom she could be referring — my dog, Mouse. The beast was smarter than a lot of people, and was probably the single best supernatural guardian any child *could* have had. And he was huge and warm and fuzzy, and perfectly content to be a blanket or pillow — or a furious incarnation of preternatural strength and speed, depending on which was needed at the moment. Hell, Maggie was only eight. He was probably spending half his time pretending to be a pony.

I exhaled slowly and felt a little dizzy. The

memories I had of Maggie — what few there were — were hammering their way across my consciousness. I mostly remembered holding her in the quiet after it was all over. I'm not sure how long I sat there with her. She had been a small, sleepy warmth in my arms, grateful for the comfort of being held.

"We can go see her," Molly suggested. "I mean . . . I know where she is."

I wanted to shout an agreement and leap at the chance. But I couldn't. So I didn't.

"Maybe after we take care of business," I said.

"All right," Molly said, nodding.

"Better button up your Sight, kid," I said quietly. "There's no reason to leave it open so long. Bad things could happen."

"But . . . I won't be able to see you. Or hear you. Which . . . seems odd, given that it's called the Sight . . ."

"It encompasses a lot," I said loftily. "Kid, you've got a gift. Trust your instincts. Which in this case should suggest to you that what you need is the spirit-viewing ointment we made off of Rashid's faerie-sight recipe, or something like it."

"Okay," she said. "Okay." She frowned and bowed her head, and I saw her Sight being withdrawn, the light at her forehead dwindling and finally winking out.

Murphy was sitting at the very edge of her chair, her back straight, her hands in her lap.

"Miss Carpenter?"

Molly turned to look at Murphy. It seemed to take her a second or two to focus her eyes. "Yes?"

"It's him?"

"He greeted me with a quote from *The Empire Strikes Back.*"

Murphy's mouth twitched at one corner. "Him."

My apprentice nodded and didn't meet Murphy's eyes.

"So," Murphy said. "He's really . . . really gone. That bullet killed him."

"He's gone," Molly said. "The shade is . . . It's Harry in every practical sense. It will have his memories, his personality."

"But it isn't *him.*"

Molly shook her head. "I asked him about that once. About what happens to a soul when a ghost is left behind."

"What did he say?"

"That he had no idea. And that he doubted anyone would ever get a straight answer."

"Molly," the older woman said. "I know you're tired. I would like it if you let me offer you some clothes. A meal. A shower. Some real sleep. My house is protected. I'd like to be able to tell your parents that I did at least that much for you, the next time they call me to ask about you."

Molly looked around the room for a moment, biting her lip. "Yes . . . it . . . ." She

167

shivered. "But . . . it's better if I don't."

"Better for who?"

"Everyone," Molly said. She gathered herself and rose, using the cane to get to her feet once again. She grimaced in the process. It was obvious that using her leg still caused her pain. "Honestly. I've been playing a lot of games, and I don't want any of them to splash onto you." She paused and then said tentatively, "I'm . . . sorry about the detective remark, Karrin. That was going too far."

Murphy shrugged. "Least said, soonest mended."

My apprentice sighed and began pulling her tattered layers about herself a little more securely. "Mr. Lindquist appears to be working in good faith. I'll come back tomorrow with something that might let you communicate with Harry's shade a little more easily."

"Thank you," Murphy said. "While you're at it, it might be smart to —"

There was the sudden blaring of a pocket-sized air horn from outside.

Mort hopped up from his seat into a crouch, ready either to run or to fling himself heroically to the floor. "What was that?"

"Trouble," Murphy said, unlimbering her gun. "Get d—"

She hadn't finished speaking when gunfire roared outside and bullets began ripping through the windows and the walls.

CHAPTER TWELVE

I did what any sane person would do in a situation like that. I threw myself to the ground.

"Oh, honestly, Dresden," Sir Stuart snapped. He sprinted toward the gunfire, out through the wall of the house. I actually saw the building's wards flare up with spectral, blue-white light around him as he went through unimpeded.

"Right, dummy," I growled at myself. "You're already dead." I got up and ran after the elder shade.

The living were all kissing hardwood floor as I plunged into the wall of the house. I wasn't worried about the wards keeping me in — no one ever designed their wards so that bad things couldn't *leave*, only so that they couldn't enter. Besides, I'd had an invitation to come in, which technically made me a friendly — but I found out that "friendly" wards operated on much the same principle as "friendly" fire. Going out through the warded wall didn't just tingle unpleasantly. I felt like I'd just plunged naked down a waterslide lined with steel wool.

"Aaaaaaaagh!" I screamed, emerging from the wards and onto Murphy's front lawn, chock-full of new insight as to why ghosts are always moaning or wailing when they come popping out of somebody's wall or floor. Not much mystery there — it freaking *hurts.*

I staggered for several steps and looked up in time to see the drive-by still in progress. They were in a pickup truck. Someone in the passenger's compartment had the barrel of a shotgun sticking out the window, and four figures in dark clothing crouched in the truck's cargo bed, pointing what looked like assault weapons and submachine guns at Murphy's house. They were cutting loose with them, too, flashes of thunder and lightning too bright and loud to be real, seemingly magnified by the quiet, still air between the snow and the streetlights.

These guys weren't real pros. I'd seen true professional gunmen in action, and these jokers didn't look anything like them. They just pointed the business end more or less in a general direction and sprayed bullets. It wasn't the disciplined fire of true professionals, but if you throw out enough bullets, you're bound to hit something.

Bullets went through me, half a dozen flashes of tingling discomfort too brief to be more than an annoyance, and I suddenly found myself sprinting toward the truck beside Sir Stuart, exhilarated. Being bulletproof is kind of a rush.

"What are we doing?" I shouted at him. "I mean, what are we accomplishing here? We can't do anything to them. Can we?"

"Watch and learn, lad!" Sir Stuart called, his teeth bared in a wolfish grin. "On three, be on the truck!"

"What!? Uh, I think —"

"Don't think," the shade shouted. "Just do it! Let your instincts guide you! *Be on the truck!* One, two . . ." The shade's feet struck the ground hard twice, like a long jumper at the end of his approach. I followed Sir Stuart's example on little more than reflex.

A sudden memory flashed into my head — a school playground from my childhood, where mock Olympic Games were being run, students competing against one another. The sun was hot above us, making the petroleum smell of warm asphalt rise from the surface of the playground. I had been competing in the running long jump, and it hadn't been going well. I forget exactly why I was so desperate to win, but I was fixated on it as only a child could be. I remembered willing myself to win, to run faster, to jump farther, as I sprinted down the lane toward the pink-chalk jump line.

It was the first time I used magic.

I had no idea at the time, naturally. But I remembered the feeling of utter elation that flooded through me, along with an invisible force that pushed against my back as I leapt, and for just an instant I thought I had spontaneously learned to fly like Superman.

Reality reasserted itself in rapid order. I fell, out of control, my arms spinning like a windmill. I went down on the blacktop and left generous patches of skin on its surface. I remember how much it hurt — and how I didn't care because I'd won.

I broke the Iowa state high school long-jump record by more than a foot. It didn't stick, though. They disqualified me. I hadn't even gotten serious about puberty yet. Clearly, something irregular had happened, mistakes had been made, and surely the best thing was to ignore the anomalous leap.

It was a vivid recollection, silly and a little sad — and it was my first time.

It was a powerful memory.

"Three!" Sir Stuart cried, and leapt.

So did I, my eyes and will locked on the retreating pickup full of gunmen.

There was a twisting, dizzying sensation that reminded me very strongly of a potion Bob had helped me mix up when I'd tangled with the Shadowman. It was that same experience: a feeling of flying apart into zillions of pieces, rushing forward at a speed too great to be measured, only to abruptly coalesce again.

There was a sudden cold wind against my face and I staggered, nearly falling off the roof of the pickup as it continued to slowly accelerate down the street.

"Holy crap!" I said, as a huge smile stretched my face. "That was *cool*. First Shadowcat, now Nightcrawler!"

I turned to find Sir Stuart standing on the bed of the truck, looking up at me with a disapproving eyebrow lifted. One of the shooters' backs was in the same space as the shade's right leg.

"Doesn't that hurt?" I asked him, nodding to his leg.

"Hmmm?" Sir Stuart said. He glanced down and saw what I was talking about. "Oh. I suppose, yes. I stopped noticing it after seventy or eighty years. Now. If you don't mind, Dresden, might we proceed?"

"To do what?" I asked.

"To teach you what are obviously badly needed lessons," Sir Stuart said, "and to stop these pirates." He spat the last word with a startling amount of venom.

I frowned and eyed the gunmen, who were all reloading, having emptied their weapons in sheer, nervous excitement. They weren't particularly good at reloading, either.

"Hell, one man with a handgun could take them all right now," I said. "Too bad neither of us has one."

"We cannot touch flesh," Sir Stuart said. "And while it is possible for a shade to, for example, move an object, it is impractical. With practice, you could push a penny across a table over the course of a couple of minutes."

"Too bad neither of us has a penny," I said.

He ignored me entirely. "That's because we can put forth only minuscule physical force. You couldn't lift the coin into the air against the pull of gravity."

I frowned. This sounded a lot like a basic lesson most young wizards received. Most of the time, when you wanted to move something around, you didn't have the kind of energy you needed stored inside you. That didn't mean you couldn't move it, though. It just meant you had to get the energy to do so from another source. "But . . . you can co-opt energy from elsewhere?"

The big man pointed an index finger at me, a smile stretching his mouth. "Excellent. We cannot interact with something being moved by a living creature. We can't even touch an object that is being carried too closely to a living body. But . . ." He glanced up at me, inviting me to finish the thought.

I blinked twice, mind racing, and said, "Machines. We can work with machines."

Sir Stuart nodded. "As long as they are in motion. And there is an enormous amount of energy and motion passing through a nonliving, mechanical engine."

Without another word, he paced forward, through the back wall of the cab, sat on the passenger's seat, and leaned to his left. I couldn't see what he was doing, so I dropped to all fours, took a deep breath, and stuck my face through the roof of the cab. It tingled and hurt, but I had literally spent a lifetime learning to cope with pain. I pushed it to the back of my mind, gritted my teeth, and watched.

Sir Stuart had pushed his hand into the steering wheel of the truck. He pushed the other forward, leaning partly through the dashboard to do it, and waited patiently, watching the road ahead of us. It didn't take long for the truck to hit a hummock in the ice coating the streets, and the truck bounced, shocks squealing. Just as it did, the shade's eyes fluttered closed, and he gave a peculiar jerking twist of his arm.

The truck's air bag exploded out of the steering wheel.

It struck the driver, smacking him back into the driver's seat, and the man panicked. His arms tightened in surprise as he was hit, and he turned the steering wheel several degrees to one side. Then he broke the cardinal rule of driving on ice and stomped his foot on the brake.

The slight turn and the sudden braking motion put the car into a slide. The driver was trying to push the air bag out of his face, and he didn't compensate and turn into the slide. The slide became a spin.

Sir Stuart watched in satisfaction, looked up at me, and said, "Not much different from spooking a horse, really."

The gunmen in the back were screaming in confusion as the car spun through three ponderous circles, somehow putting forth the illusion of grace. They bounced off the snow piled high on one side of the street, and then slid into an intersection, up over a sidewalk, and through the front windows of a small grocery store. The sounds of shattering glass and brick, screaming metal crumpling through its zones, and cracking snow and ice were shockingly loud.

The steadily ringing bell of the store's security alarm sounded like my old Mickey Mouse alarm clock, in comparison.

The gunmen sat there doing nothing for a moment, clearly stunned, but then they began cursing and scrambling to get gone before the cops showed up.

Sir Stuart vanished and reappeared across the street. I made the same effort of will I had while jumping to the truck, reaching back for that memory once more. Again I flew apart and came back together, reappearing standing next to Sir Stuart, facing a brick wall.

"Next time turn around on the way," he advised.

I snorted and looked back at the gunmen. "What about them?"

"What about them?"

"Can't we . . . I don't know, possess them and make them bang their heads into a wall or something?"

Sir Stuart barked out a harsh laugh. "We cannot enter unless the mortal is willing. That is the purview of demons, not shades."

I scowled. "So . . . what? We stand here and watch them walk?"

He shrugged. "I'm not willing to leave Mortimer alone for so much time. You may also wish to consider, Dresden, that dawn is not far away. It will destroy you if you are not within a sanctum such as Mortimer's residence."

I frowned, looking up at the sky. City light had wiped away all but the brightest stars, but the sky to the east held only a hint of blue, low on the horizon. Dawn was hard on spirits and shades and magical spells alike. Not because one is inherently good and one inherently evil, but because dawn is a time of new beginnings, and the light of a new day tends to sweep away the supernatural litter from the day before. For spirit beings to survive sunrise, they had to be in a protected place — a sanctum. My trusty lab assistant, Bob, had a sanctum; in his case, a specially

177

enchanted skull designed to protect him from dawn and daylight and to provide a home. A plain old threshold wouldn't get it done, although my old apartment had probably qualified as a sanctum, given how many layers and layers of defense I'd put up around it.

But I didn't have either of those things anymore.

"Go back to Mort," I said. "It was fun playing *Maximum Overdrive* with these chowderheads, but that isn't going to protect the people we care about. I'm going to follow the shooters back to their place and see what I can find out about them."

Sir Stuart frowned at me and said, "The dawn is not something to take chances with, man. I strongly advise against your doing so."

"So noted," I said, "but the only real weapon I have against them is knowledge. Someone needs to get it, and I'm the only one who isn't susceptible to lead poisoning. I'm the logical choice."

"Assume you get the information and manage to survive the dawn," the shade said. "Then what will you do?"

"I give it to Murphy, who uses it to rip the bad guys' tongues out through their belly buttons."

Sir Stuart blinked. "That . . . is certainly a vivid image."

"It's a gift," I said modestly.

He shook his head and sighed. "I admire your spirit, man, but this is foolish."

"Yeah. But I've gotta be me," I said.

Sir Stuart put both hands behind his back and tapped a toe on the ground a few times. Then he gave me a resigned nod. "Good hunting," he said. "If you have a problem with wraiths again, vanish. They won't be able to keep up."

"Thank you," I said, and offered him my hand.

We traded grips, and he turned on a heel and started marching back toward Murphy's place.

I watched him for a moment, then turned around and hurried after the snow-blurred forms of the gunmen, wondering exactly how much time I had left before the sunrise obliterated me.

CHAPTER THIRTEEN

The bad guys started hoofing it, and I followed them.

"Over here," said one of them. He was youthfully scrawny, his skin bronze enough to look Native American, though his tangled red hair and pug nose argued otherwise. His eyes were an odd shade of brown, so light as to be nearly golden.

"What, Fitz?" one of the other gunmen said.

"Shut up," Fitz said. "Give me your piece."

The other handed over his gun, and Fitz promptly removed the magazine, ejected a round from the chamber, and pitched it into the snowbank, along with the weapon he was carrying.

"What the fuck?" said the disarmed gunman, and struck Fitz lightly in the chest.

Fitz slammed a fist into the other man's face with speed and violence enough to impress even me — and I've seen some fast things in action. The other gunman went to his ass in the snow and sat there, hands lifted to cradle his freshly broken nose.

"No time for stupid," Fitz said. "Everyone, give me your guns. Or do you want to explain to *him* why you tried to get us all thrown in jail?"

The others didn't look happy about it, but they passed over the weapons. Fitz unloaded them and threw them all into the snowbank. Then, at his direction, they started patting snow into the hole the weapons had made, concealing them.

"Stupid, man," said one of the young men. "One of those wolves gets on our trail, we got nothing to defend ourselves."

"One of the wolves follows us back, we'll have the Rag Lady on our asses, and guns will be useless," Fitz snapped. "Pack it in tighter. Smooth it." Then he turned to the man he'd struck and piled some of the fresher snow into the man's hands. "Put that on your nose. Stop it from bleeding. You don't want to leave any blood behind if you have a choice."

The seated young man looked frightened, and did as Fitz told him.

"What are we doing?" asked another of the gunmen. He was smaller than the others, and his tone wasn't challenging — it was a question.

"The truck's stolen. They can't trace it to us," Fitz explained, dusting snow off his hands. "Even if the winter breaks tomorrow, it'll be days before this melts and they find the weapons. With luck, they'll never connect the two."

"That's long-term," the little one said. "I sort of want to survive the night."

Fitz almost smiled. "You want to walk down the streets of fucking Chicago with assault weapons in your hands? We could keep them out of sight in the truck. Not out here."

The little guy nodded. "I can keep the knife, right?"

"Out of sight," Fitz said, and lifted his head, listening and frowning. Sirens were a common sound in nighttime Chicago, but they had shifted from background noise to something louder, nearer. "Get moving, people."

Fitz jammed his hands into the pockets of his rather light coat and started walking. The others hurried to keep up with him.

I walked next to Fitz, studying him. I was more impressed with the young man in the lousy attack's aftermath than I had been during the drive-by. Any idiot can point a gun and squeeze a trigger. Not everyone can keep themselves calm and rational in the wake of an automobile collision, weigh the liabilities of the situation, and make — and enforce — their decisions in the face of opposition. Though the attack had been amateurish, it had not been stupid, and Fitz's actions in response to the sudden hitch Sir Stuart had thrown into his plans were probably as ideal as the situation allowed.

Fitz was smart under pressure, he was a natural leader, and I had a bad feeling that he was the sort of person who never made the same mistake twice. He had just done his best to kill several people I cared a great deal for. Brains plus resolve equals dangerous. I'd have to see to it that he was neutralized at the first opportunity.

I followed them through cold I no longer felt and practiced vanishing. I'd jump ahead of them, behind them, onto ledges above them — all the while trying not to notice that the sky was getting lighter.

Something bothered me about the red-headed kid.

With the cops on the way, the store alarm ringing, his associates bleeding and dazed around him . . . why take a few extra, vital seconds to empty the guns? It had cost him about half a minute of time he certainly couldn't afford to lose. Why do it?

I asked myself why I might do something similar. And the only answer I could come up with involved preventing whoever found the weapons from getting hurt. Fitz was willing to riddle a small Chicago house — and potentially the houses behind it, given the power of the weapons in question — with bullets, but he got all safety conscious when disposing of weapons? It was a contradiction.

Interesting.

Even more interesting was the fact that I'd cared enough to notice. Generally, if someone took a swing at my friends, I'd cheerfully designate him a target and proceed to make his world a noisy and dangerous place until he wasn't a threat anymore. I didn't lose a lot of sleep over it, either.

But I couldn't just throw myself into the fight now, dammit. And, unlike before, those who threatened my friends could *not* also threaten me. I was safe from Fitz and his crew, unless they planned to keep walking until sunrise, and I was similarly no danger to them. Normally, I'd be fuming at the presence of people who had tried to kill my friends. But now . . .

We were absolutely no threat to one another. That made it sort of hard to keep my inner kettle of outrage bubbling along at maximum boil.

Fitz kept them all moving through the snowbound streets, stopping only once to check on the bleeder's nose. Packing it in snow had stopped the blood loss, but the young man was disoriented from the wreck and the pain. There were other small injuries among his crew, and he stopped at a little convenience store, emerging with a bottle of water and an economy-sized bottle of pain-killers. He passed them off to the short, inquisitive kid, and told him to double-dose everyone — and to keep moving.

It took them most of an hour of steady trudging through the cold to clear Bucktown and head for the South Side. A lot of people think of the South Side as a sort of economic desert crossed with a gang-warfare demilitarized zone. It isn't like that — or at least, it isn't like that everywhere. There are neighborhoods you don't want to walk through wearing certain colors, or being a certain color, but they're more exception than rule. The rest of the South Side varies pretty widely, with plenty of it zoned for industry, and Fitz and his group of battered pedestrians headed into an area on the fringe of an industrial park to a manufacturing facility that had been closed and abandoned for several years.

It took up a block all by itself, a big building only a couple of stories high that covered acres of ground. The plows had piled snow higher and higher around it, like a fortress wall, with no need to create an opening for the unoccupied building. Fitz and his crew went over the wall of snow at a spot that had evidently been worked with shovels to form narrow, if slippery, stairs. There was a foot and a half of snow covering the building's parking lot, with a single pathway shoveled out of it. They followed it in single file, to doors that looked as if they'd been solidly chained shut — but Fitz rattled the chains and nudged one of the doors open wide enough for the crew of youngsters, all of them still skinny, to squeeze through.

I went through the doors ghost style and tried to ignore the discomfort, the way Sir Stuart did. It hurt anyway — not enough to make me howl in agony or anything, but way too much to simply lose track of. Maybe it just took time for your "skin" to toughen. At least there hadn't been a threshold, which would have stopped me cold. This place had never been meant to be anyone's home, and evidently nobody who lived there thought of it as anything special. The exact process that formed a threshold had never been fully explained or documented, but it might be a good idea for me to get a better idea of the exact why and how, given my circumstances.

"No, it is not a good idea. Focus, Dresden," I muttered. "The idea is for you to take care of business so you never have to learn all about the environmental factors of long-term ghostosity."

Fitz stopped long enough to do a head count, out loud, as the ragged troop of would-be gangsters moved deeper into the building. It was an industrial structure and it had been built for economy, not beauty. There weren't a lot of windows, and it was definitely on the shady side — even with dawn almost here and the lights of the city and sky reflecting from fresh snow. Cold, too, judging from the way the breath was congealing into fog every time the young men exhaled.

Fitz broke out a camping light and flicked it on. It was a red one, and didn't so much light the way as clarify the difference between utter darkness and not-quite darkness. It was enough for them to move by.

"I wonder," I mused aloud. After all, I was immaterial. Ghosts and the material universe didn't seem to have a completely one-way relationship, the way mortals and physics did. I didn't actually have pupils to dilate anymore. Hell, for that matter, light apparently passed right through me — how else was I invisible to everyone, otherwise? Which meant that, whatever it might seem like, I wasn't really *seeing* the world, in the traditional sense. My perceptions were something different, something more than light reflecting onto a chemically sensitive surface in my eyes.

"There's no real reason I should need the light to see, is there?" I asked myself.

"No," I said. "No, there isn't."

I closed my eyes for a few steps and focused on a simple memory — when, as a kid in a foster home, I'd first found myself in a dark room when a storm knocked out the power. It was a new place, and I had fumbled around blindly, searching for a flashlight or matches or a lighter, or any other source of light, for almost ten minutes before I found something — a decorative snow globe commemorating the Olympics at Lake Placid. A small switch turned on a light that made the red, white, and blue snowflakes drifting in the liquid gleam in sudden brilliance.

The panic in my chest had eased as the room became something I could navigate safely again, my fear fading. I could see.

And when I opened my ghostly eyes, I could see the hallway through which we walked with perfect clarity, as plainly as if the long-dead fluorescents overhead had been humming along at full glow.

A quick, pleased laugh escaped me. Now I could see in the dark. "Just like . . . uhhh . . . I can't think of an X-Man who I'm sure could see in the dark. Or was that a Nightcrawler thing . . . ? Whatever. It's still another superpower. There is no spoon. I am completely spoonless over here."

Fitz stopped in his tracks, turning suddenly, and lifted the camping light in my direction, his eyes wide. He suddenly sucked in a deep breath.

I stopped and blinked at him.

Everyone around Fitz had gone quiet and completely still, reacting to his obvious fear with the instant, instinctive stillness of someone who had good reason to fear predators. Fitz stared down the hall uncertainly, moving the light as if it might help him see a few inches farther.

"Hell's bells," I said. "Hey, kid. Can you

hear me?"

Fitz reacted, his body twitching a little, his head cocked to one side, then the other, as if trying to trace a faint whisper of sound.

"Fitz?" whispered the little kid with the knife.

"Quiet," Fitz said, still staring.

I cupped my hands over my mouth and shouted. "Hey! Kid! Can you hear me?"

The color had already drained out of his face, but the second call to him got another reaction. He licked his lips, turned away quickly, and said, "Thought I heard something, that's all. It's nothing. Come on."

Interestinger and interestinger. I stuck my hands in the pockets of my duster and paced along beside Fitz, studying him.

He was maybe an inch under six feet tall, but taller than all the others with him. He couldn't have been seventeen, but his eyes were decades older. He must have been surviving on his own for a while to have had so much composure at his age. And he'd known at least a little about the way a practitioner could use blood to send all kinds of mischief and mayhem at his enemies.

He had scars at the corner of his left eye, like a boxer — except boxers collected them on both eyes, and they were spread out, scattered around. These were all in a relatively tiny space. Someone right-handed had punched him in the same spot irregularly, repeatedly. I'd seen Fitz's speed. He hadn't tried to get out of the way.

Hell's bells. We'd just been hit by Oliver Twist.

It took Fitz and the gang about five minutes to make it to what had once been a shop floor. It was open to the thirty-foot ceiling. There were skylights — translucent panels on the roof, really — and the place looked like something out of an apocalypse movie.

Equipment sat neglected everywhere. The motorized assembly line was still. Cobwebs stretched out, covering everything, coated in dust. Empty racks and shelves gave no clue as to what was made there, but several steel half barrels were scattered around an open area halfway down the shop floor. They had been filled with flammable scraps, mostly doors, trim, and shelves that must have been scavenged from other parts of the building. Ragged old sleeping bags were scattered among the fire sources, along with trash sacks of what I guessed were meager personal belongings.

One of the low barrels had a metal grate over it — a makeshift grill. There was a man crouched over it. He was thin, practically skeletal, and wore only a pair of close-fitting jeans. His skin was pasty and white. His smooth head was covered with crude-looking tattoos — symbols of protection and concealment from multiple traditions of magical practice, completely encircling his skull. He needed to shave. His patchy beard was growing out in uneven lumps of brown and black and grey.

There were several cans of beans and chili sitting on the grill, presumably being prepared for Fitz's gang, who looked painfully interested in them. The bald man didn't give any indication that he knew Fitz had arrived until the group had been standing silently for a full five minutes. Then he asked, "Is it done?"

"No," Fitz said.

"And where are the guns?"

"We had to ditch them."

The bald man's shoulders clenched, suddenly stiff. "Excuse me?"

Fitz lifted a hand to touch his fingertips to his left eye, a gesture that struck me as unconscious, instinctive. He lowered it again quickly.

"There was an accident. The police were coming. We had to walk out and we couldn't carry the guns with us."

The bald man stood up and turned to face Fitz. His eyes were dark, deep-set, and burning. "You lost. The guns. The guns I paid so much for."

"The guns were already lost," Fitz said, his eyes on the floor. "There wasn't any sense in all of us going to jail, too."

The bald man's eyes blazed and a scream

exploded from his chest. There was a horrible, rushing, bass-thrumming sound in the air, and an invisible force struck Fitz full in the chest, knocking him back ten feet before he hit the concrete floor and tumbled another ten.

"Sense?!" the bald man screamed. "Sense? You don't *have* any sense! Do you know what the consequences of your idiocy could be? Do you know how many groups precisely like this one have been wiped out by the Fomor? By the Rag Lady? Idiot!"

Fitz lay on the floor, body curled defensively, and didn't even try to lift his head. He was staying down, hoping not to provoke Baldy any further, his expression resigned to the fact that he was probably going to suffer more pain in short order — and that there was nothing he could do about it.

"It was simple!" Baldy continued, stalking toward the young man. "I gave you a task that men with their veins and noses full of drugs execute routinely. And it proved too great a challenge? Is that what you are telling me?"

Fitz's voice was too steady to be sincere. He was used to hiding his fear, his vulnerability. "I'm sorry. The Rag Lady was there. We couldn't have gotten any closer. She'd have taken us. We had to hit them and run."

Baldy's rage vanished abruptly. He stared down at the young man with no expression on his face and spoke in a gentle voice. "If there is some reason you believe you should be allowed to keep breathing, you should share it with the class now, Fitz."

Fitz had a good poker face, but it had been a long night for him. He started breathing jerkily. "The idea wasn't to kill them, you told me. The idea was to make sure that no one pushes us. That we push back. We showed them that. We accomplished the mission."

Baldy stared at him and did not move. I saw a bead of sweat on his brow. "It isn't . . . It's not . . . Look, I can get the guns back. I can. I marked where we buried them. I can go get them."

Baldy glowered down at the young man and kicked him in the belly. The blow was offhand, absentminded, almost an afterthought. He seemed to reach a conclusion, and turned around to go back to the grill.

"Food's hot, boys," Baldy said. "Come eat up."

The gang moved forward nervously. After a moment, Fitz began to rise, being careful to make no sound.

There was a sudden, puffing sigh of displaced air. Baldy's shape blurred from the grill back over to Fitz, sending one of the young gunmen flying sideways. Baldy was suddenly slamming a hard right to Fitz's head, his fist moving almost too quickly to see.

The hit sent Fitz to the ground. I was close enough to see the scar tissue around his eye break open, blood trickling rapidly down the young man's cheek.

"Not you, Fitz," Baldy said, his voice gentle again. "I don't give food to dead men. Eat when you have corrected your error."

Fitz nodded, without looking up, his hand pressed to his head. "Yes, sir."

"Good lad," Baldy said. He wrinkled his nose as if there were a mild stench in the air, and spat, mostly on Fitz. Then he turned to walk away.

The kid looked up at Baldy with murder in his eye.

I don't mean that Fitz looked angry. You hear a lot about "if looks could kill" these days, but there just aren't many people who *really* know what it looks like. Killing — or, more accurately, making the choice to kill — isn't something we're good at lately. Ending the life of another living creature used to be part of the daily routine. Chickens were beheaded by the average farm wife for dinner. Fish were likewise caught, cleaned, and prepared for a meal. Slaughtering pigs or cattle was a regular event, part of the turning of the seasons. Most people on earth — farmers — worked and lived every single day with lives they knew they were going to choose to end, eventually.

Killing's messy. It's frequently ugly. And if

something goes wrong, it can be wretched, seeing another being in mortal agony, which means there's a certain amount of pressure involved in the act. It isn't easy, and that's just considering farm animals.

Killing another human being magnifies the worry, the ugliness, and the pressure by orders of magnitude. You don't make a choice like that lightly. There's calculation to it, consideration of the possible outcomes. Anyone can kill in a frenzy of fear or hatred — you aren't making the choice to kill that way. You're simply giving your emotions control of your actions.

I watched Fitz's eyes as he calculated, considered, and made his choice. His face went pale, but his jaw was clenched, his eyes steady.

I don't know what motivated me, exactly, but I leaned down near him and snapped, "Don't!"

The young man had begun to shift his weight, to get his feet beneath him. He froze in the act.

"He's expecting it, Fitz," I said in a harsh, forceful tone. "He spat on you to drive you to it. He's ready. He'll kill you before you've finished standing up."

Fitz looked around him, but his gaze went right through me. He couldn't see me, then. Huh.

"I've been where you are, kid. I know this

bald loser's type. Don't be a sucker. Don't give him what he wants."

Fitz closed his eyes very tightly for a moment. Then he exhaled slowly, and his body relaxed.

"Wise," Baldy said. "Make good on your claim, and we might still have a way to work together, Fitz."

Fitz swallowed, and grimaced as if at a bitter taste in his mouth, and said, "Yes, sir. I'm going to check the perimeter."

"An excellent idea," Baldy said. "I'd rather not see you for a while." Then he walked away from Fitz, leaning down to touch the shoulder of one of the young men, and muttered softly.

Fitz moved, quickly and quietly, getting off the shop floor and moving out into the hallway. There he hugged himself tightly, shivering, and began walking rapidly down a hallway.

"I'm not crazy," he said. "I'm not crazy. I'm not crazy."

"Well . . . kinda," I said, keeping pace. "What are you doing working for an asshole like that?"

"You aren't real," Fitz said.

"The hell I'm not," I replied. "I just can't figure out why it is that you can hear me talking."

"I'm *not* crazy," Fitz snarled, and put his hands over his ears.

"I'm pretty sure that won't help you," I

noted. "I mean, it's your mind that perceives me. I think you just happen to get it as, uh . . . one of those MV4 things, instead of as a movie."

"MP3," Fitz corrected me automatically. Then he jerked his hands from his ears and looked around him, eyes wide. "Uh . . . are you . . . you actually there?"

"I am," I confirmed. "Though any halfway decent hallucination would tell you that."

Fitz blinked. "Um. I don't want to piss you off or anything but . . . what are you?"

"I'm a guy who doesn't like to see his friends getting shot at, Fitz," I told him.

Fitz's steps slowed. He seemed to put his back against a wall out of reflex more than thought. He was very still for a long moment. Then he said, "You're . . . a, um . . . a spirit?"

"Technically," I said.

He swallowed. "You work for the Rag Lady."

Hell's bells. The kid was terrified of Molly. And I'd known plenty of kids like Fitz when I was growing up in the system. I met them in foster homes, in orphanages, in schools and summer camps. Tough kids, survivors, people who knew that no one was looking out for them except themselves. Not everyone had the same experience in the system, but portions of it were positively Darwinian. It created some hard cases. Fitz was one of them.

People like that aren't stupid, but they don't scare easily, either.

Fitz was terrified of Molly.

My stomach quivered in an unpleasant manner.

"No," I told him. "I don't work for her. I'm not a servitor."

He frowned. "Then . . . you work for the ex-cop bi . . . uh, lady?"

"Kid," I said, "you have no idea who you're screwing around with. You pointed weapons at the wrong people. I know where you live now. They will, too."

He went white. "No," he said. "Look . . . you don't know what it's like here. Zero and the others, they can't help it. He doesn't let them do anything but what he wants."

"Baldy, you mean?" I asked.

Fitz let out a strained, half-hysterical bark of laughter. "He calls himself Aristedes. He's got power."

"Power to push a bunch of kids around?"

"You don't know," Fitz said, speaking quietly. "He tells you to do something and . . . and you do it. It never even occurs to you to do anything else. And . . . and he moves so fast. I'm not . . . I think he might not even be human."

"He's human," I said. "He's just another asshole."

A faint, weary spark of humor showed in Fitz's face. Then he said, "If that's true, then how does he do it?"

"He's a sorcerer," I said. "Middleweight talent with a cult to make him feel bigger. He's got some form of kinetomancy I'm not familiar with, to move that fast. And some really minor mind mojo, if he's got to pick kids to do his dirty work for him."

"You make him sound like a small-time crook . . . like a car thief or something."

"In the greater scheme, yeah," I said. "He's a petty crook. He's Fagin."

Fitz frowned. "From . . . from that Dickens book? Uh . . . *Oliver Twist?*"

I lifted my eyebrows. The kid had read. Serious readers weren't common in the system. Those who did read mostly seemed to focus on, you know, kids' books. Not many of them rolled around to Dickens unless they got unlucky in high school English. I would have been willing to bet that Fitz hadn't made it past his freshman year of high school, at the very most.

He was someone who thought for himself, and he had at least a little bit of magical talent. That probably explained why he'd been put in charge of the other boys. Aside from his evident good sense, his company notwithstanding, the kid had some innate magical talent of his own. Fitz had probably been slowly learning to shake off whatever magic it was that Baldy — Aristedes — used on him. The bad guy operated in a cult-leader mind-set. Anyone who wasn't a slavish follower would be utilized as a handy lieutenant, until such time as they could be disposed of productively — or at least quietly.

I didn't like Fitz's chances at all.

"Something like that," I said.

Fitz leaned back against the wall and closed his eyes. "I didn't want to hurt anyone," he said. "I don't even know any of those people. But he ordered it. And they were all going to do it. And I couldn't let them just . . . just turn into murderers. They're the only . . . They're . . ."

"They're yours," I said quietly. "You look out for them."

"Someone has to," Fitz said. "Streets weren't ever easy. About six months ago, though . . . they got hard. Real hard. Things came out. You could see them at night sometimes — shapes. Shadows." He started shivering, and his voice became a whisper. "They'd take people. People who didn't have someone to protect them would just vanish. So . . ."

"Baldy," I said quietly.

"He killed one of them," Fitz whispered. "Right in front of me. I saw it. It looked human, but when he was done with it . . . It just *melted,* man." He shook his head. "Maybe I am crazy. God, it would almost be a relief."

"You aren't crazy," I said. "But you're in a bad place."

The light went completely out of the kid's

eyes. "What else is new?"

"Oy," I muttered. "Like I didn't have enough to do already."

"What?"

"Nothing. Look, kid. Go back to the guns at eleven tonight. That street will have gotten quieter by then. I'll meet you."

His dull eyes never flickered. "Why?"

"Because I'm going to help you."

"Crazy, imaginary, invisible-voice hallucination guy," Fitz said. "He's going to help me. Yeah, I've lost it."

There was the sudden, burring, metallic buzz of a bell, much like you'd hear in a high school or university hallway. It echoed through the entire building.

"Time for class?" I asked.

"No. Aristedes had us set it up on a timer. Says he needed the warning for his work. It goes off about five minutes before sunrise."

I felt my back stiffen. "Five minutes?"

Fitz shrugged. "Or seven. Or two. It's in there somewhere."

"Hell's bells," I said, turning it into a swearword. "Stu was right. Time *does* get away from you. Be at the guns at eleven, Fitz."

He grunted and said, in a tired monotone, "Sure, Harvey. Whatever."

Old books *and* old movies. I had to help this kid.

I turned away from him and plunged through several walls and out the side of the building, clenching my teeth over snarls of discomfort. The sky had grown almost fully light. Red was swiftly brightening to orange on the eastern horizon out over Lake Michigan. Once yellow got here, I was history.

Five minutes. Or seven. Or two. That was how long I had to find a safe spot. I consulted my mental map of Chicago, looking for the nearest probable shelter, and found the only spot I thought I could get to in a couple of minutes, Nightcrawler impersonation and all.

Maybe I could get there. And *maybe* it would protect me from the sunrise.

I gritted my teeth, consulted the images in my memory, and, metaphorically speaking, ran for it.

I just had to hope that it wasn't already too late.

Chapter Fourteen

One of the things a lot of people don't understand about magic is that the rules of how it works aren't hard-and-fast; they're fluid, changing with time, with the seasons, with location, and with the intent of a practitioner. Magic isn't alive in the sense of a corporeal, sentient being, but it does have a kind of anima all its own. It grows, swells, wanes, and changes.

Some facets of magic are relatively steady, like the way a person with a strong magical talent fouls up technology — but even that relative constant is one that has been slowly changing over the centuries. Three hundred years ago, magical talents screwed up other things — like causing candle flames to burn in strange colors and milk to instantly sour (which had to be hell on any wizard who wanted to bake anything). A couple of hundred years before that, exposure to magic often had odd effects on a person's skin, creating the famous blemishes that had become known as the devil's mark.

Centuries from now, who knows? Maybe magic will have the side effect of making you really good-looking and popular with the opposite sex — but I'm not holding my breath.

I mean, you know.

I wouldn't be. If I still had any.

Anyway, the point is that everyone thinks that the sunrise is all about abolishing evil. It's the light coming up out of the darkness, right?

Well, yeah. Sometimes. But mostly it's just sunrise. It's a part of every day, a steady mark of the passing of whirling objects in the void. Granted, there isn't much black magic associated with the sun coming over the horizon — in fact, I've never even heard of any. But it isn't a cleansing force of Good and Right.

It is, however, one hell of a cleansing force, generally speaking. Therein lay my problem.

A spirit isn't meant to be hanging around in the mortal world unless it's got a body to live in. It's supposed to be on Carmichael's El train, I guess, or in Paradise or Hell or Valhalla or something. Spirits are made of energy — they're made of 99.9 percent pure, delicious, nutritious magic. Accept no substitute.

Spirits and sunrise go together like germs and bleach, respectively. The renewing forces flowing through the world with the new day wash over the planet like a silent, invisible tsunami, a riptide of magic that will inevitably wear away at even the strongest of mortal spells, giving them an effective shelf life if they aren't maintained.

A wandering spirit, caught out beneath the sunrise, would be dissolved. It isn't a question of standing in a shady spot, any more than standing in your kitchen would protect you from an oncoming tsunami. You have to get to somewhere that is actually *safe,* that is somehow shielded, sheltered, or otherwise lifted above the renewing riptide of sunrise.

I was a ghost, after all. So I ran for the one place I thought might shelter me, and that I could reach the quickest.

I ran for my grave.

I have my own grave, headstone already in place, the darned thing all dug out and open, just ready to receive me. It was a present from an enemy who, in retrospect, didn't seem nearly as scary as she had been at the time. She'd been making a grand gesture in front of the seamier side of the supernatural community at large, delivering me a death threat while simultaneously demonstrating her ability to get me a grave in a boneyard with very exclusive access, convincing its management that it ought to break city ordinances and leave a gaping hole in the earth at the foot of my headstone. I don't know what she'd bribed or threatened them with, but it had stayed where it was, yawning open in Chicago's famous Graceland Cemetery, for years.

And maybe it would finally be useful as something other than a set piece for brooding.

I pulled Sir Stuart's vanishing trick and realized that I couldn't jump much farther than maybe three hundred yards at a hop. Still, I could do it a lot faster than running, and it didn't seem to wear me out the way I would expect such a thing to do. It became an exercise like running itself — repeating the same process over and over to go from Point A to Point B.

I blinked through the front gate of Graceland, took a couple more hops, trying to find the right spot by this big Greek temple–looking mausoleum, and arrived, in a baseball player's slide, at the gaping hole in the ground. My incorporeal body slid neatly over the white snow that ran right up to the edge of the grave, and I dropped into the cool, shady trench that had been prepared for me.

Sunlight washed over the world above a few heartbeats later. I heard it, felt it, the way I had once felt a minor earthquake through the soles of my shoes in Washington State. There was a harsh, clear, silvery note that hung in the air for a moment, like the aftertone of an enormous chime. I closed my eyes and scrunched up against the side of the grave that felt most likely to let me avoid obliteration.

I waited for several seconds.

Nothing happened.

It was dim and cool and quiet in my grave. It was . . . really quite restful. I mean, you see things on television and in movies about someone lying in a coffin or in a grave, and it's always this hideous, terrifying experience. I'd been to my grave before, and it had disturbed me every time. I guess maybe I was past all that.

Death is only frightening from the near side.

I sat back against the wall of my grave, stretching my legs out ahead of me, leaning my head back against it, and closed my eyes. There was no sound but for a bit of wind in the cemetery's trees, and the muted ambient music of the living, breathing city. Cars. Horns. Distant music. Sirens. Trains. Construction. A few birds that called Graceland home.

I couldn't remember the last time I'd felt so . . .

Peaceful. Content.

And free. Free to do nothing. Free to rest. Free to turn away from horrible, black things in my memory, to let go of burdens for a while.

I left my eyes closed for a time, and let the contentment and the quiet fill me.

"You're new," said a quiet, calm voice.

I opened my eyes, vaguely annoyed that my

rest had been interrupted after only a few moments — and looked up at a sky with only a hint of blue still in it. Violet twilight was coming on with the night.

I sat up, away from the wall of my grave, startled. What the hell? I'd been resting for only a minute or two. Hadn't I? I blinked up at the sky several times and pushed myself slowly to my feet. I felt heavy, and it was harder to rise than it should have been, as if I'd been covered in wet, heavy blankets or one of those lead-lined aprons they use around X-ray machines.

"I always like seeing new things being born," said the voice — a child's voice. "You can guess what they're going to become, and then watch and see if it happens."

My grave was about six feet deep. I'm considerably over six feet tall. As I stood, my eyes were a few inches above the top of half a foot of snow that covered the ground at that spot. So it wasn't hard to see the little girl.

She might have been six years old and looked small, even for her age. She wore a nineteenth-century outfit, an almost ridiculously frilly, ornate dress for a child who would probably have it splattered with dirt or food within the hour. Her shoes looked handmade and had little buckles on them. Over one shoulder she was carrying a tiny, lacy parasol that matched her dress. She was pretty — like most children — and had blond hair and bright green eyes.

"Hi," I said.

"Hello," she said, with a little Shirley Temple curtsy. "It is a pleasure to meet you, the late Mr. Harry Dresden."

I decided to be careful. What were the odds she was really a little girl, as she appeared? "How did you know my name?"

She folded the little parasol closed and tapped it against the headstone. It was made of white marble. Letters had been inscribed upon it in gold, or at least something gold-like, and it still gleamed despite about a decade of exposure. It had a pentacle inscribed beneath its simple legend: HERE LIES HARRY DRESDEN. Beneath the pentacle, it continued: HE DIED DOING THE RIGHT THING.

For a moment, there was a strange, sweet taste in my mouth, and the scent of pine needles and fresh greenery filled my nose. A frisson rippled up and down my spine, and I shivered. Then the taste and scent were both gone.

"Do you know me?" she asked. "I'm famous."

I squinted at her for a moment. Then I made an effort of will and vanished from the bottom of the grave, reappearing beside the child. I was facing the wrong direction again, and I sighed as I turned to face her and then glanced around me. In Graceland there's a statue of a small girl, a child known as Inez. It's been there for going on two centuries, and every few years stories circulate about how the statue will go missing — and how visitors to the graveyard have reported encounters with a little girl in a period dress.

The statue was gone from its case.

"You're Inez," I said. "Famous ghost of Graceland."

The little girl laughed and clapped her hands. "I have been called so."

"I heard they debunked you a couple of years ago. That the statue was just there as advertising for some sculptor or something."

She opened the parasol again and put it over a shoulder, spinning it idly. "Goodness. People confused about things that happened hundreds of years before they were born. Who would have imagined." She looked me up and down and said, "I like your coat."

"Thank you," I said. "I like your parasol."

She beamed. "You're so courteous. Sometimes I think I shall never again meet anyone who is properly polite." She looked at me intently and then said, "I think . . . you shall be" — she pursed her lips, narrowed her eyes, and nodded slowly — "a monster."

I frowned. "What?"

"All newborn things become something," said Inez.

"I'm not a newborn."

"But you are," she said. She nodded down

at my grave. "You have entered a new world. Your old life is no more. You cannot be a part of it any longer. The wide universe stretches before you." She looked around the cemetery calmly. "I have seen many, many newborns, Mr. Dresden. And I can see what they are going to become. You, young shade, are quite simply a monster."

"Am not," I said.

"Not at the moment, perhaps," she said. "But . . . as time goes by, as those you care about grow old and pass on, as you stand helpless while greater events unfold . . . you will be. Patience."

"You're wrong."

Her dimples deepened. "Why are you so upset, young shade? I really don't see anything wrong with being a monster."

"I do," I said. "The monster part?"

"Oh," the girl said, shaking her head. "Don't be so simple. People adore monsters. They fill their songs and stories with them. They define themselves in relation to them. Do you know what a monster is, young shade? Power. Power and choice. Monsters make choices. Monsters shape the world. Monsters force us to become stronger, smarter, better. They sift the weak from the strong and provide a forge for the steeling of souls. Even as we curse monsters, we admire them. Seek to become them, in some ways." Her eyes became distant. "There are far, far worse things to be than a monster."

"Monsters hurt people. I don't."

Inez burst out in girlish giggles. She turned in a circle, parasol whirling, and in a singsong voice said, "Harry Dresden, hung upon a tree. Afraid to embrace his des-tin-y." She looked me up and down again, her eyes dancing, and nodded firmly. "Monster. They'll write books about you."

I opened my mouth, but no words came out. I didn't know what to say.

"This little world is so small," she continued. "So dull. So dreary." She gave me a warm smile. "You aren't shackled here, Mr. Dresden. Why remain?"

I shivered. A cold feeling swelled up in the pit of my stomach. It began to spread. I said nothing.

"Ahh," Inez murmured — a sound of satisfaction. Her eyes went to my gravestone and she tilted her head to one side. "Did you?" she asked brightly.

I shook my head. "Did I what?"

"Did you die doing the right thing?"

I thought about it for a moment. And for a moment more. Then I said, quietly, "I . . . No. I didn't."

She tilted her head the other way. "Oh?"

"They had . . . a little girl," I said quietly. It took me a moment to realize that I was speaking the words out loud and not just hearing them in my head. "They were going to hurt her. And I pulled out all the stops. To get her back. I . . ."

I suddenly felt sick again. My mind flashed back to the image of Susan's death as her body fought to change into a monstrous form, locking her away forever as a prisoner of her own blood thirst. I felt her fever-hot skin beneath my lips where I had kissed her forehead. And I felt her blood spray as I cut her throat, triggering the spell that wiped out every murdering Red Court son of a bitch on the same planet with my little girl.

It had been the only way. I had no choice.

Didn't I?

Maybe not at that point. But it was the choices I'd made up until that moment that had shaped the event. I could have done things differently. It might have changed everything. It might have saved Susan's life.

I shuddered as another memory struck me. Complete, lifeless numbness in my legs. Aching pains of the body. The helpless fury I'd felt when I realized that a fall from a ladder had broken my spine — that I was paralyzed and helpless to do anything for my daughter. I remembered realizing that I was going to have to do something I would never have considered before that point.

"I crossed a line," I said quietly. "Lines, plural. I did things I shouldn't have done. It wasn't right. And I knew it. But . . . I wanted to help the little girl. And I . . ."

"Sinned?" she suggested, her large eyes eerily serene. "Chose the left-hand path? Fell from grace? Cast the world into madness?"

"Whatever," I said.

"And you think you aren't a monster." Calmly, she folded the parasol again and trailed its tip in the snow, humming a quiet little song.

That cold, sick feeling swelled and began to spread even more. I found myself shivering. Dear God, she was right. She was exactly right. I hadn't meant any of it to hurt anyone, but did that really matter? I had made a decision to do something I knew was wrong. I bargained my life away to Queen Mab, promised her my service and loyalty, though I knew that the darkness of the mantle of the Winter Knight would swallow me, that my talents and strengths could be subsumed into wicked service for the Queen of Air and Darkness.

My little girl's life had been on the line when I made that choice, when I had acquired power beyond the ken of most mortals.

I thought of the desperation in the eyes of Fitz and his gang. I thought of the petty malice of Baldy and those like him. Of the violence in the streets.

How many other men's daughters had died because of my choice?

That thought, that truth, hit me like a landslide, a flash of clarity and insight that erased every other thought, the frantic and blurry activity of my recent efforts.

Like it or not, I had embraced the darkness. The fact that I had died before I could have found myself used for destructive purposes meant nothing. I had picked up a red lightsaber. I had joined the Brotherhood of Evil Mutants.

I had become what I always fought.

There was no denying it. No chance to correct my mistake. I suddenly wanted, desperately, to simply drop back into the grave and seek out the quiet and peace I had found there. Dammit, but I wanted to rest.

I folded my arms and stared at Inez. My voice came out ragged and harsh. "You aren't the ghost of a little girl."

Her little face lit up with another smile. "If I am no ghost, why do you look so haunted?"

And then she was gone. No sound, no flash, no nothing. Just gone.

If I were living, then the headache I felt coming on would be typical of this kind of situation. Cryptic supernatural entities go with the territory in my line of work.

But, man, I hate it when they get in the last word.

"An insufferable entity," murmured a slow, deep, redolent basso voice behind me. "Her soul is made of crooked lines."

I stiffened. I hadn't sensed any kind of presence the way I had with Inez, and I knew exactly what could happen when you let someone sneak up behind you. Even though rule number one for dealing with supernatural beings — never show fear — is simple, it sure as hell isn't easy. I know the kinds of things that are out there.

I turned, very calmly and slowly, reminding myself that I didn't have a heart to pound wildly, and that there wasn't really any sweat on my palms. I didn't need to shiver from fear any more than I needed to shiver from cold.

My self apparently found its own assurances unreliable. Stupid self.

There was a tall and menacing figure floating in the air behind me, maybe three feet off the ground. It was swathed entirely in a rich cloak of patina, its hood lifted, creating an area of completely black shadow within. You could see the dim suggestion of a face in the blackness. It looked like the old images of the Shadow, who clouded the minds of men. The cloak wavered and billowed slowly in a breeze with the approximate viscosity of a lava lamp.

"Um," I said. "Hi."

The figure drifted downward until its feet were resting atop the snow. "Is this preferable?"

"Aren't we literal?" I said. "Uh, yes. That's fine." I peered at it. "You're . . . Eternal Silence. The statue on Dexter Graves's monument."

Eternal Silence just stood there in silence.

"I'll take that as a yes," I said. "I guess you aren't really just a local statue. Are you?"

"Your assumption is correct," Eternal Silence replied.

I nodded. "What do you want?"

It drifted slowly closer. The deep voice — and this guy made James Earl Jones sound like Mickey Mouse — rumbled out. "You must understand your path."

"My path."

"That before you. That behind."

I sighed. "That's less than helpful."

"It is more than necessary," Eternal Silence said. "It is essential to survival."

"Survival?" I asked, and I couldn't help myself. I chuckled. When you've faced off with enough Grim Reaper wannabes, it gets kinda routine. "I'm already dead."

It said nothing.

"Okay," I said, after a minute. "Survival. Of who?"

It didn't answer for a long moment, and I shook my head. I began to think that I could probably spend all night talking to every lunatic spirit in this freaking place and never make sense of any of them. And I didn't have all night to waste.

I had begun to focus my thoughts on another series of Nightcrawler hops, when that deep voice spoke — and this time, it wasn't something I heard. It just resonated in my head, in my thoughts, a burst of pure meaning that slammed into my head as if inscribed on the front of a cruise missile:

EVERYONE.

I staggered and clutched at my skull with my hands. "Agh!" I stammered. "Hell's bells! Is it too much to ask you to turn down the volume?"

UNINTENTIONAL. MORTAL FRAILTY. IN-SUFFICIENT UNDERSTANDING OF VOCAL-IZATION. PRECONSIDERED VOCABULARY EXHAUSTED.

I actually discorporated at this full-on assault of thought. My freaking spirit body spread out into a giant, puffy cloud of vaguely Dresden-colored mist. And it hurt. I mean, that's the only word I can think of that really applies. It wasn't like any kind of pain I'd felt before, and I'm a connoisseur when it comes to pain. It wasn't pain of the body, the way I had known it. It was more like . . . like the way your head feels when you hear or see an image or concept that flabbergasts you so hard that the only thing you can say about it is, "That is *so* wrong."

That. Times a million. And not just in my head, but full body.

It took a full minute for that feeling to fade, and it was only then that I could see myself coming back together again.

"Don't explain!" I said, almost desperately, when I looked up to see Eternal Silence hovering a little closer to me. "Don't! That hurt!"

It waited.

"We have to keep this simple," I stuttered, thinking out loud. "Or you're going to kill me. Again." I pressed the heel of my hand against my forehead and said, "I'm going to ask yes or no questions," I said. "For yes, stay silent. For no, indicate otherwise. Agreed?"

Nothing. Eternal Silence might not have even been there, except that his cloak kept rolling and billowing, lava-lamp fashion.

"Is your cloak red?"

The hood of the cloak twitched left and right, once.

"Fantastic," I muttered. "Communication." I mopped at my face with my hands and said, "Okay. When you say everyone, are you talking, like, everyone I know?"

Twitch.

"More than that?"

Silence.

"Um. The whole city?"

Twitch.

"What — more?"

Silence.

"So . . . you mean . . . like . . . everyone-everyone. Everyone. The whole planet."

Silence.

"And me understanding my freaking path saves them?"

Silence. Twitch.

"Great," I muttered. "Next you'll want me to take a pebble out of your hand."

Twitch.

"I wasn't being *literal.* . . . Okay, yeah, you and I aren't going to communicate well this way."

Silence. Somehow . . . emphatic.

I stopped and pondered for a moment. Then I said, "Wait. This is connected, isn't it? With what Captain Murphy sent me to do."

Silence.

"Find my killer?" I asked him. "I don't get it. How does finding my killer save the world?"

The deep voice repeated earlier phrases. "You must understand your path. It is more than necessary. It is essential to survival."

"There's a little irony in Eternal Silence being stuck on a looping sound bite." I sighed.

A wraith's moan drifted into the air, and I tensed, looking around.

One of those ragged-scarecrow shapes was rising from the earth of a grave, like something being hauled up out of deep mud. It moaned in mindless hunger, its eyes vacant.

Then there was another moan. And another. And another.

Wraiths were coming up out of graves all around me.

I started breathing harder, though I didn't

need to. "Yeah, okay, brilliant idea for a safe house, Harry. *It's a freaking graveyard.* Where else are ghosts going to be?"

Eternal Silence only stared at me. There was an amused quality to its silence.

"I have to go," I said. "Is that all you had for me? Understand my path?"

Silence. It lifted a green-shrouded limb in a gesture of farewell.

The first wraith finished with what was evidently its nightly routine of slogging out of the earth and moaning. Its empty eyes turned toward me and it began to drift my way, immaterial toes dangling down through the snow.

"Screw this," I said, and vanished. One, two, three hops, and I was to the nearest brick wall of the cemetery. I gritted my teeth and plunged into it.

And slammed my face into cold stone.

Pain lanced through my nose, and I snarled at my own stupidity. *Dammit, Harry.* Walls are built to keep things out — but walls around graveyards are built to keep things *in.* I'd known that since I was a freaking kid.

I checked behind me. The wraiths were drifting after me in a slow, graceful horde, adding members as they went. They weren't fast, but there were dozens and dozens of them. Again I was reminded of documentaries I'd seen showing giant clouds of jellyfish.

I gritted my teeth and thought fast. When

221

walls are built, they are intended as physical barriers. As a result of that intention, invested by dozens or scores of builders, they took on a similar solidity when it came to the spiritual, as well. It's why they held most ghosts inside graveyards — and it probably had something to do with the way a threshold formed around a home, too.

But where human intention had created a barrier, that same intention had also created an access point.

I turned and began vanishing in a line, straight for the gates of the boneyard.

I don't know what I would have done if they had been closed. Shut gates and shut doors carry their own investment of intention, just as the walls do. But *open* gates are another matter entirely, and the gates of Graceland stood wide-open. As I went through them, I looked back at what seemed like a modest-sized army of wraiths heading for the opening.

I had a lightbulb moment.

The gates of the cemetery were being left open.

And hordes of wraiths haunted the streets of Chicago by night lately.

"Aha, Morty," I said. "And now we know where they're coming from."

Someone, someone *alive,* was opening those gates at night. That meant that we had a place to begin, a trail we could attempt to follow to find out who was stirring up the city's spooks to use against Morty — and why.

I had information. I had something to trade Mort for his ongoing help.

I suddenly felt like an investigator again.

"Hot diggity dog," I said, grinning. "The game's a-freaking-foot!"

CHAPTER FIFTEEN

I revved up the memory and started jumping. It was a quick way to travel in the city — the ability to go over buildings and ignore traffic signals, one-way streets, and cars was a real plus. It didn't take me long to get to Mortimer's house.

It was on fire.

There were fire trucks there, lights blazing. The firemen were moving quickly, professionally, but though the house was well ablaze, they had only one hose up and running. As I stood there, staring, two more started up, but I knew it was a lost cause. Morty's place was burning even more swiftly and brightly than mine had. Or maybe the dark was just making it look that way.

A cop or two showed up as the firemen kept the blaze from spreading to the houses around it — not hard, given the snow on the ground. Blue lights from the bubbles on the cop cars joined the red and yellow of the CFD. People stood around watching the fire

— in my experience, they often do.

Of course . . . they didn't usually do it out in the cold. And they didn't usually do it in six inches of snow. And they tended to wander off when the fire began to subside. And talk. And blink. And their clothing is generally from the current century.

The crowd of onlooking Chicago civilians were ghosts.

I walked among them, looking at faces. They were much like any other group of folks, apart from the period outfits. I recognized a few from Sir Stuart's home-defense brigade — but only a few, and they were the more recent shades. The rest were just . . . people. Men, women, and children.

A boy maybe ten years old was the only shade who seemed to notice me. Beside him stood a girl, who must have been about seven when she died. They were holding hands. He looked up at me as I passed by, and I stopped to stare down at him.

"Where do we go now?" he asked. "I don't know another place to go."

"Um," I said. "I don't know, either. Hey, did you see what happened?"

"It came back again tonight. Then men came with fire. They burned the house. They took the little man away."

I stiffened. "The Grey Ghost took Mort?"

"No, men took him," the boy said.

The girl said, in a soft little voice, "We used

to play with other children by the river. But he brought us here. He was always nice to us." Her facial expression never changed. It was flat, empty.

The boy sighed, touched the little girl's shoulder, and turned back to stare at the dwindling flames. I stood there watching them for a moment, and could see them growing more visibly transparent. I checked the other shades. It was happening to them, too, to a greater or lesser degree.

"Hey," I said, to the boy. "Do you know Sir Stuart?"

"The big man. The soldier," the boy said, nodding. "He's in the garden. Behind the house."

"Thank you," I said, and went to look, vanishing to the side of Mort's house and then jumping again, to the garden.

Mort's backyard was like his front — sculpted, carefully maintained, decorated with Japanese sensibilities, spare and elegant. There was what looked like a koi pond, now filled with snow. There were trees, and more of the little bonsai pieces, delicate and somehow vulnerable. The fire had been close enough and hot enough to melt any coating of snow from their little branches.

What was left of Sir Stuart lay in a circle in the snow.

They'd used fire.

A perfect circle was melted in the show, out

toward the back of the yard. They'd used gasoline, it looked like — the snow was melted down all the way to the scorched grass. Alcohol burns about three times as hot as gas, and faster, and it melts the snow fast enough for water to drown the flame. Someone had used the fire as part of a circle trap — pretty standard for dealing with spirits and other heavily supernatural entities. Once trapped in a circle, a spirit was effectively helpless; unable to leave, and unable to exercise power through its barrier.

The devilish part of the trap was the fire. Fire's real, even to spirits, and brings pain to the immaterial as fast as it does to flesh-and-blood creatures. That's one huge reason I always used fire in my mortal career. Fire burns, period. Even practically invulnerable things don't like dealing with fire.

There was maybe half of Sir Stuart left. Most of his upper body was there and part of his right arm. His legs were mostly gone. There wasn't any blood. What was left of him looked like a roll of papers rescued from a fire. The edges were blackened and crumbling slowly away.

The horrible part was that I knew he was still alive, or what passed for being alive among ghosts. Otherwise, he would simply be gone.

Did he feel pain? I knew that if I were in his condition, I would. Sure, maybe I knew that there was no spoon, but when it came down to it, I wasn't sure I could deny that much apparent reality. Or maybe the memory of pain wasn't an issue. Maybe the weird form of pain Eternal Silence had showed me had some sort of spiritual analogue. Or maybe, fire being fire, he was just in very real, very familiar agony.

I shuddered. Not that I could do anything about it. The circle that trapped him would keep me out as easily as it kept him in. In theory, I could take it down, but only if I could physically move something across it to break its continuity. I looked around quickly and spotted a twig standing out of the snow a few feet away. All I would need to do was move it about three feet.

It was like trying to eat broth with a fork. I just couldn't get hold of the stick. My hand went through it time and time again, no matter what I tried. I couldn't even get the damned thing to wiggle.

I wasn't ghost enough to help Sir Stuart. Not like that, anyway.

"Sir Stuart?" I asked quietly.

I could see only one of his eyes. It half opened. "Hmmmm?"

I squatted down on my heels next to the circle. "It's Harry Dresden."

"Dresden," he slurred, and his mouth turned up in a faint smile. "Pardon me if I don't rise. Perhaps it was something I ate."

"Of course," I said. "What happened?"

"I was a fool," he said. "Our attacker came at the same time every night. I made the mistake of assuming that was true because it was as soon as the attacker could assemble his forces."

"The Grey Ghost," I said.

Sir Stuart grunted. "Arrived at dusk, sooner than I would have dared the open air. No mob of spirits this time. It came with half a dozen mortals and they set the house on fire. I was able to get Mortimer out of the house in time, but they'd set a trap for me in the backyard." One hand gestured at the circle within which he lay. "He was taken at the command of the Grey Ghost."

I frowned. "These mortals. They could hear the Grey Ghost?"

"Aye," Sir Stuart said.

"Stars and stones," I growled. "I could barely get two people in Chicago to hear me. This joker has half a dozen? How?"

Sir Stuart shook his head faintly. "Would that I knew."

"We'll find Morty," I said. "Let me figure out how to get you out of there, and then we'll go find him."

He opened his eyes fully and focused on me for the first time. "No," he said in a gentle voice. "I won't."

"Come on," I said. "Don't talk like that. We'll get you patched up."

Sir Stuart let out a small laugh. "Nay, wizard. Too much of me has been lost. I've only held together this long so that I could speak to you."

"What happened to our world being mutable in time with our expectations? Isn't that still true?"

"To a degree," Sir Stuart said affably, weakly. "I've been injured before. Small hurts are restored simply enough." He gestured at his broken body. "But this? I'll be like the others when I restore myself."

"The others?"

"The warriors who defended Mortimer's home," he said. "They faded over time. Forgetting, little by little, about their mortal lives."

I thought about the soldiers I'd seen battling the enemy shades and wraiths — silent, severe, seemingly disconnected from the world around them. They'd fought loyally and ably enough. But I was willing to bet that they couldn't remember why they did so or who they were fighting.

I imagined Sir Stuart like the rest of them — a translucent outline, his empty eyes focused on something else entirely. Always faithful. Always silent.

I shivered.

It could happen to me, too.

"Listen to me, boy," Sir Stuart said. "We didn't trust you. We assumed you were mixed up in whatever it is the Grey Ghost wanted."

"Like hell," I said.

"You don't know that," Sir Stuart said flatly. "For all we knew, you could have been directed by that creature without your own knowledge. For that matter, you don't have the feel of a normal ghost. It could have created you whole from the spirit world."

I scowled and began to argue — and couldn't. I've been faced with the odd and unusual and had drawn incorrect conclusions too many times. When people are scared, they don't think straight. Mort had been terrified.

"Do you still think that?" I asked.

"No reason for you to be here if you were," Sir Stuart said. "The worst has happened. Were you a plant, you would not have come. Though I suppose you might still be a dupe."

"Thanks," I said wryly.

He softened the words with another smile. "But dupe or not, it may be that ye can help Mortimer. And it is critical that you do so. Without his influence, this city will be in terrible danger."

"Yeah, you aren't exactly increasing the tension by telling me that," I said. "We're already sort of playing for maximum stakes."

"I know not what you mean," Sir Stuart replied. "But I tell you this: Those shades standing around the house, one and all, are murderers."

I blinked and looked back at the still-

231

smoldering house and at the enormous circle of spirits around it.

"Each and every one of them," Sir Stuart said. "Mortimer gave them something they needed to turn aside from their madness: a home. If you do not restore him to freedom so that he may care for these poor souls, they will kill again. As sure as the sun rises, they won't be able to help themselves." He exhaled wearily and closed his eyes. "Fifty years of maddened shades unleashed upon the city all at once. Preying on mortals. Blood will run in buckets."

I stared at him for a moment. Then I said, "How am I supposed to do that?"

"I've not the foggiest," Sir Stuart replied. He fumbled at his belt and drew that monster pistol. He paused for a moment, grimacing. Then he tossed it weakly at my feet. It tumbled through the circle with a flicker of energies and landed atop the snow without sinking into it — the apparition of a weapon.

I stared for a second. A spirit couldn't project its power across a circle — and I was sure that power was exactly what the gun represented. So if it had crossed the circle's barrier, it meant that it was power that no longer belonged to Sir Stuart. On several levels, what he had just done was a violent act of self-mutilation — like chopping off your own hand.

He gestured weakly toward the gun, and

said, "Take it."

I picked it up gingerly. It weighed a ton. "What am I going to do with this?"

"Help Mortimer," he replied. His shape began to flicker and fade at the edges. "I'm sorry. That I couldn't do more. Couldn't teach you more." He opened his eyes again and leaned toward me, his expression intent. "Memories, Dresden. They're power. They're weapons. Make from your memory a weapon against them." His voice lost its strength and his eyes sagged closed. "Three centuries of playing guardian . . . but I've failed my trust. Redeem my promise. Please. Help Mortimer."

"Yes," I said quietly. "I will."

That faint smile appeared again, and Sir Stuart nodded once. Then he let out his breath in a sigh. He faded even more, and as I watched, his limbs simply renewed themselves, appearing as his shape became more translucent. The damage reversed itself before my eyes.

A moment later, he sat up. He looked around, his gaze passing right through me. Then he paused and stared at the ruined house, his brow furrowed in puzzled concentration — an expression mirrored on the faces of most of the spirits present.

Sir Stuart was nowhere to be seen in the shade's hollow eyes.

I bowed my head and clenched my teeth,

cursing. I had *liked* the guy. Just like I had liked Morty, whatever insults I may have offered him. I was angry about what had happened to him. And I was angry about the position he had put me in. Now I was the one responsible for somehow finding and helping Morty, when I could barely communicate with anyone without him. All while the bad guy, whatever the hell it was, apparently got to chat it up with its own flunkies at will.

I couldn't touch anything. I couldn't make anything happen. My magic was gone. And now not only was I to track down my own murderer, but I had to rescue Mort Lindquist, as well.

Fabulous. Maybe I should make it my new slogan: *Harry Dresden — I take responsibility for more impossible situations in the first twenty-four hours of being dead than most people do all day.*

More snow was beginning to fall. Eventually, it would break the circle that had trapped what was left of Sir Stuart. Though I didn't know where he would go to take shelter from the sunrise. Maybe he would just know, the way I had seemed to — some kind of post-death survival instinct. Or maybe he wouldn't.

Either way, it didn't seem like there was much I could do about it, and I hated that fact with a burning passion. Sir Stuart and the other spirits needed Morty Lindquist. Before I died, I might have been Harry Dresden, wizard at large. Now I was Harry Dresden, immaterial messenger boy, persuader, and wheedler.

I desperately wanted to blow something into tiny, tiny pieces — and then disintegrate the pieces.

All things considered, it was probably not the best frame of mind in which to handle a confrontation in a rational, diplomatic manner.

"Ah," said a whispery, oily voice behind me. "She was right. The tall one returns."

"Look at him," said another voice, higher-pitched and inhuman. "He will make *such* a meal."

"Our orders are —"

"Orders," said a third voice, filled with scorn. "She is not here. We shall share him, the three of us, and none shall be the wiser."

"Agreed," said the second voice eagerly.

After a pause, the first voice said, "Agreed."

I turned and saw three of the dark-robed forms from the night before during the attack on Casa Lindquist. Lemurs. Their clothing stirred with lazy, aquatic fluidity at the touch of an immaterial wind. From this close, I could see the faint images of pale faces inside their hoods, and the sheen of gleaming, hungry eyes.

"Take him!" said the first lemur.

And three of the hungriest old ghosts of Chicago blurred toward the new guy.

CHAPTER SIXTEEN

The lemurs pounced, and I vanished, straight up.

I stood in empty air a hundred feet above them, furious, and called down, "You mooks picked a really lousy time to start up with me!"

Hooded heads searched upward, but I was an indistinct shape in a darkened sky already blurred by snow, while they were sharp outlines against a field of white.

I started throwing a punch, vanished again, and reappeared right behind lemur number one. My fist drove into the base of his neck just as I shouted, "BAMF!"

There isn't much honor in a rabbit punch, but it's a pretty darned good way to down an opponent. Whatever rules governed the world of spirit, there must have been some kind of analogue to a human nervous system. The lemur let out a choking gasp and fell to the ground as the other two panicked at the sudden assault and vanished. I kicked the downed guy in the head and neck a few times to help him on his way to Analogue-Concussion Land, screaming in pure and incoherent rage all the while.

I had a fraction of a second's warning, a cold breath on the back of my neck, a rippling wave of ethereal pressure against my back. I vanished, to reappear five feet behind my original position — and this time, I *meant* to be facing the same way when I arrived.

I got there in time to see one of the other lemurs swing a freaking hatchet at the space my skull had recently vacated. He stumbled, off balance from the miss, and I kicked his ass — literally. I leaned my upper body back a bit and pretended I was using my heel to stomp an aluminum can flat. It's a powerful kick, especially with my full body weight behind it, and the lemur flew forward and into the snow.

"Who's the man?!" I screamed at the sprawled lemurs, fear and anger and excitement pitching my voice about an octave higher than usual. "Who's the man?!"

The hood had fallen from the face of the second, and an unremarkable man of middle age goggled at me in complete incomprehension — which made sense. Who knew how many decades of pop culture the lemurs had missed out on. They'd probably never even heard of Will Smith.

"I am completely unappreciated in my

time," I muttered.

I am also, apparently, no wizard when it comes to simple mathematics: While I was Will Smithing, lemur number three appeared out of nowhere and smashed a baseball bat against the side of my neck.

The pain was something incredible — more than merely the reaction of physical trauma that I would have expected from such a blow. It also encompassed an almost Olympian sense of nausea combined with a force-five storm of whirling confusion. I felt myself note idly that I guessed egos literally *could* be bruised. It took me another second or two after that to realize that I was floating, drifting sideways and slightly upward, my body at a forty-five-degree diagonal to the ground. There was a roaring sound in my head. An eerie cry of triumph and hunger pealed through the night.

Then the lemurs came for me.

I felt bitterly cold fingers seize me, clamping down like steel claws. I was hauled out to horizontal by frigid, steely hands. I was still disoriented — I was barely able to turn my head enough to see the third lemur approach.

Her hood had fallen back. She was a young woman of unexceptional appearance, neither beautiful nor displeasing. Her eyes, though, were dark and hollow, and a hideous emptiness lay behind them. She stared intently at me for a long beat, her body quivering in some kind of dark rapture.

Then she let out a slow hiss, sank her fingers into the flesh of my left biceps, and ripped off a handful of meat.

Ectoplasmic blood flew. My blood. It scattered through the air in lazy globules that, once they were a few feet from me, fell like raindrops to the surface of the snow.

It hurt. I screamed.

All three lemurs screamed with me, as if triggered into a response by my own cries. The female lemur lifted the gobbet of flesh aloft in triumph, then held it over her open mouth and squeezed. More blood pattered out onto her lips and tongue, and she let out a gasp of unadulterated ecstasy before shoving the raw flesh into her mouth as though she hadn't eaten in weeks.

Her eyes rolled back into her head. She shuddered. "Oh," she breathed. "Pain. He's felt so much *pain.* And rage. And joy. Oh, this one *lived.*"

"Here," said the second lemur. "Come take his legs. My turn."

The female bared her bloodied teeth at him and tore another, smaller piece from my arm. She snapped it up and then leaned on my legs, pinning them. The second lemur looked me over like a man perusing a side of beef. Then he ripped a handful of flesh from my right thigh.

It went like that for several minutes, with

the three of them taking turns ripping meat from my body.

I won't bore you with the details. I don't like to think about it. They were stronger than me, better than me, more experienced than me when it came to spiritual conflict.

They got me. The monsters got me. And it hurt.

Until footsteps crunched toward us through the snow.

The lemurs never took notice. I was in too much agony to care very much, but I wasn't exactly busy, either. I looked up and saw a lone figure slogging my way through the thick snow. He wasn't very big, and he was dressed in a white parka and white ski pants, with one of those ninja cap-mask things, also white, covering his face. In his right hand he carried a big, old-style, heavy, portable spotlight, the kind with a plastic carrying handle on top. Its twin incandescent bulbs shone a garish orange over the snow.

I sniggered to myself. He was a person. He sank into the snow with every step. He wouldn't be able to see what was happening right in front of him. No wonder the lemurs paid him no mind.

But ten feet away from me, he abruptly froze in his tracks and blurted, "Holy crap!"

He reached up and ripped off the ninja hood, revealing the thin, fine features of a man of somewhere near forty. His hair was

dark, curly, and mussed from the hood; he
had glasses perched askew on his beak of a
nose; and his dark eyes were wide with shock.
"Harry!"

I stared at him and said, through the blood,
"Butters?"

"Stop them," Butters hissed. "Save him! I
release you for this task!"

"On it, sahib!" shouted another voice.

A cloud of campfire sparks poured out of
the two sources of light in the spotlight, rushing out by the millions, and congealed into a
massive, manlike shape. It let out a lion's roar
and blurred toward the lemurs.

Two of them were sharp enough to realize
something dangerous was coming, and they
promptly vanished. The third, the young
woman, was in the middle of another bite —
and she didn't look up until it was too late.

The light form hit the lemur and simply
disintegrated it. As I watched, skin and clothing and flesh were ripped away from the evil
spirit, as swiftly and savagely as if peeled off
with a sandblaster. A heartbeat later, there
was nothing left but a gently drifting cloud of
sparks, speckled here and there with the floating shapes of somewhat larger, prismatic gem-
stones.

The light being looked up and then
promptly split into two parts, each one
becoming a comet that hurtled into the night
sky. There was an explosion almost at once

— and the raining bits and pieces of a second lemur came drifting lazily down through the night air, along with more multicolored gems.

There was a terrible howling sound in the night sky above. I heard the flap of heavy robes snapping with rapid motion. The second comet of light darted back and forth, evidently engaged in some kind of aerial combat, and then lemur and comet both came hurtling back down. They struck earth with a thunder that shook the ground while leaving the snow untouched.

The orange lights flowed together into a manlike shape again, this time straddling the lemur's prone form. The being of light rained blows down on the lemur's head, over and over, striking with the speed and power of a motor's pistons. Within ten or twelve seconds, the head of the lemur had been crushed into ectoplasmic guck, and his sparkles of light — his memories — and the same odd, tiny gems began to well up from his broken form.

The light being rose from the form of the fallen lemur and scanned the area around us, his featureless face turning in a slow, alert scan.

"What the hell!" Butters said, his eyes wide. "I mean, what the hell was that, man?"

"Relax, sahib," said a young man's voice. It was coming from the fiery figure, which nodded and made hand-dusting motions of unmistakable satisfaction. "Just taking out the trash. Scum like that are all over these old mortal cities. Part of the posthuman condition, you might say."

I just watched. I didn't feel like doing anything else.

"Yeah, yeah," Butters said. "But he's safe now?"

"For now," the being said, "and as far as I know."

Butters crunched through the snow and stared down at me. The little guy was one of Chicago's small number of medical examiners, a forensic investigator who analyzed corpses and found out all sorts of details about them. A few years ago, he'd analyzed corpses of vampires that had burned to death in a big fire someone started. He'd asserted that they obviously were not human. He'd been packed off to an institution for half a year in response. Now he treaded carefully in his career — or at least he had when I was last alive.

"Is it really him?" Butters asked.

The being of light scanned me with unseen eyes. "I can't spot anything that would suggest he was anything else," he said cautiously. "Which ain't the same as saying it's Harry's ghost. It has . . . more something than other ghosts I've encountered."

Butters frowned. "More what?"

"Something," the being said. "Meaning I'm

not sure what. Something I'm not expert in, clearly."

"The, uh, the ghost," Butters said. "It's hurt?"

"Quite severely," the being said. "But it's easily mended — if you wish to do it."

Butters blinked at him. "What? Yes, yes, of *course* I wish it."

"Very good, sahib," the being said. And then it whipped and darted through the night air, gathering up all the floating, glittering gems from the vanishing remains of the lemurs. It brought them together into a single mass and then knelt down next to my head.

"Bob," I said quietly.

Bob the Skull, formerly my personal assistant and confidant, hesitated beside me as I said his name. Once again, I became aware of his intense regard, but if he saw anything, it didn't register on his featureless face.

"Harry," he said. "Open up. You need to restore these memories to your essence."

"Restore what?" I asked.

"Eat 'em," Bob said firmly. "Open your mouth."

I was tired and confused, so it was easier to just do as he said. I closed my eyes as he dropped the mass of gems into my open mouth. But instead of feeling hard gems, fresh, cool water flowed into my mouth, swirling over my parched tongue and throat as I eagerly swallowed it down.

Pain vanished instantly. The disorientation began to fade and disappear. My confusion and weariness followed those others within a moment, and a deep breath later, I was sitting up in place, feeling more or less as sane and together as I had been when I had woken up that evening.

Bob offered me a hand and I took it. He pulled me to my feet as if I'd weighed less than nothing. "Well," he said. "At least you don't seem to be a bad copy. I was half-afraid you'd be some kind of demented Winter Knight wannabe with an eye patch and a goatee or something."

"Um," I said. "Thank you?"

"De nada," Bob said.

"Bob," Butters said in a firm voice. "You've fulfilled your task."

Bob the Skull sighed and turned to bow in a florid gesture of courtesy toward Butters, before dissolving into a cloud of orange sparks again and flowing back toward the flashlight. I saw then that the spotlight casing hadn't contained lightbulbs and batteries and such — just Bob's skull, a human-bone artifact of a long-dead enchanter who had built it as a haven that could harbor the essence of a spiritual being.

"Hey, Bob," I said. "Could you relay my voice to Butters?"

"Don't have to, former boss," Bob said cheerfully. "On account of the fact that Butters is a whole heck of a lot more talented at magical theory than you."

I frowned. "What?"

"Oh, he doesn't have a lick of magical talent," Bob assured me. "But he's got a *brain,* which, let's face it, hasn't always been your most salient feature."

"Bob," Butters said in a scolding tone. Then he fumbled in his parka's pocket and produced a small, old radio. "Here, see? I had Bob go over your notes from the Nightmare case, Harry. Bob said you created a radio that he could communicate through. So . . ."

I refrained from hitting my own head with the heel of my hand, but just barely. "So it wasn't much of a trick to turn it into a baby monitor. You just needed an old crystal radio."

Butters listened with his head tilted toward the radio and nodded. "I explained the concept to Molly this morning and she put it together in an hour." He waved the spotlight housing Bob's skull. "And I can see spooks by the light of the spirit's form. So I can see and hear you. Hi!"

I stared at the skinny man and didn't know if I wanted to break out into laughter or wild sobs. "Butters . . . you . . . you figured this all out on your own?"

"Well . . . no. I mean, I had a tutor." He bobbled the spotlight meaningfully.

"Ack! Don't make me puke," Bob warned

him. "You won't like me when I puke."

"Hush, Bob," said Butters and I in exactly the same tone at exactly the same time.

We both turned to eye each other for a moment. He might have tucked the skull close to his side in a protective gesture of possession.

"You shouldn't stay here, with all the official types around," I said.

"Just thinking the same thing," Butters said. "Come with me?"

"Sure," I said. "Uh. Where?"

"Headquarters," he said.

From Butters's other pocket, there was a hiss and a squawk from what proved to be a long-range walkie-talkie. He picked it up, looked at something on its little display, and said, "Eyes here."

"We've got nothing at his old place," said Murphy's tired voice. "What about you, Eyes?"

"He's standing right here talking to me," Butters said, and not without a trace of pride.

It looked good on him.

"Outstanding, Eyes," Murphy said, her voice brightening with genuine pleasure. "I'm sending you some shadows. Bring him in right away."

"Wilco," Butters said. "Out." He put the radio away, beaming to himself.

"Eyes?" I asked him.

"Daniel kind of gave me the nickname," he

said. "They kept putting me on watch, and he wanted to know why they kept making the four-eyed guy our lookout. It stuck as my handle."

"Except we have six eyes," Bob the Skull said. "I tried to get him to get me a pair of glasses, and then we'd have *eight.* Like spiders."

I nodded, suddenly understanding. "You still work for the morgue."

Butters smiled. "There are plenty of people listening to our transmissions. Murphy wouldn't let me use my name."

"Murphy is smart," I said.

"Extremely," Butters said, nodding agreement.

"She gave Bob to you?"

"She did," he said. "You being dead and all. She wanted to keep it need-to-know."

"It doesn't upset me," I said, even though it sort of did. "I entrusted those things to her judgment."

"Oh, hey, great segue. Speaking of judgment, you'd better come with me."

"I can do that," I said, and fell into pace beside him. "Where are we going?"

"The Batcave," he said. "Headquarters."

"Headquarters of what?" I asked.

He blinked at me. "The Alliance, of course. The Chicago Alliance."

I lifted my eyebrows. "What Chicago Alliance?"

"The one he organized to help defend the city from the Fomor," Butters replied.

"He?" I asked. "Fomor? What he? He who?"

"I'm sorry, Harry," he said. He bit his lip and looked down. "I figured you knew . . . Marcone. Baron John Marcone."

CHAPTER SEVENTEEN

I found Stu's pistol on the ground where I'd dropped it during the struggle. Then I followed Butters to his car — an old Plymouth Road Runner. It looked almost worse than my old VW Beetle had the last time I'd seen it. Dents and dings covered its all-steel frame, and some of them looked suspiciously like they'd been raked into the metal with a two-pronged claw — but its engine throbbed with impressive, harmonious power. Its license plates read: MEEPMEEP.

"I kinda traded in my old one," Butters told me as I got in, going straight through the door. I didn't make any noise about the discomfort. Not in front of Butters. It would totally blow my ghostly cool.

"For another old one," I said. My voice issued out of the radio he slipped into a clip attached to the car's sun visor.

"I like steel better than fiberglass," he said. "The Fomor and the faeries are apparently related. Neither one of them likes the touch of any metal with iron in it."

Bob's skull rested in a container that had been custom mounted on the Road Runner's dash — a wooden frame set on a plate that made the skull wobble back and forth like a bobblehead doll. "Lot of interbreeding there," Bob said. "Back in the old, old, *old* days. Before the Sidhe Wars."

I lifted my eyebrows. "I haven't heard much about it."

"Crazy stuff," Bob said with tremendous enthusiasm. "Even before my time, but I've heard all kinds of stories. The Daoine Sidhe, the Tuatha, the Fomor, the Tylwyth Teg, the Shen. Epic alliances, epic betrayals, epic battles, epic weddings, epic sex —"

"Epic sex?" I sputtered. "By what standards, precisely, is *sex* judged to be epic?"

"And tons and tons of mortal simps like you used as pawns." Bob sighed happily, ignoring my question. "There are no words. It was like *The Lord of the Rings* and *All My Children* made a baby with the Macho Man Randy Savage and a Whac-A-Mole machine."

Butters sputtered at that image.

But . . . I mean, Hell's bells. Who wouldn't?

"Anyway," he choked out a moment later, "the Fomor have a lot of faerie blood in their makeup. I like having Detroit steel around me when I drive."

"Murphy said something about the Fomor last night," I said. "I take it they've been moving in on the town?"

His face grew more remote. "Big-time. I've been busy." He exhaled a slow breath. "Um. Look, man. It's really you?"

"What's left of me," I said tiredly. "Yeah."

He nodded. "Um. There's a problem with Molly."

"I saw," I said.

"You didn't see," he said. "I mean, I heard that Murphy told you she was a couple bubbles off plumb last night, but there's more than that."

"Like what?" I asked.

"Seventeen people murdered in the past three months," he replied in a steady voice.

I didn't say anything for a couple of blocks. Then I said, "Who?"

"Scum," he said candidly. "Mostly. A cop who was maybe raping a prostitute. Petty criminals. Muggers. She doesn't even try to avoid being seen. She's gone totally Dark Knight. Witnesses left and right have reported a tall woman dressed in layers and layers of ragged, cast-off clothing. Took the papers about two weeks to name her the Rag Lady. People call her various versions, to make fun, to show her they aren't afraid, but . . ."

"A lot of people get killed in this town," I said. "Doesn't mean it's Molly."

"Harry . . ." Butters stopped at a light and gave me a direct look. "I've examined twelve of the victims. Different manner of death for

253

each of them, but I found them all with a scrap of torn cloth stuffed in their mouths."

"So?" I demanded.

"I matched the cloth. It's the same as what was left of the clothes you wore to Chichén Itzá. They had some of it in evidence when they investigated the scene of your . . . your murder. Only someone got in there without being seen by anyone or any camera, and took it right out."

Memory flashed at me, hard. The silent stone ziggurats in the night. The hiss and rasp of inhuman voices. The stale, reptilian scent of vampires. My faerie godmother (yes, I'm serious. I have one, and she is freaking terrifying) had transformed my clothes into protective armor that had probably saved my life half a dozen times that night without my even being aware of it. When they had turned back into my coat, my shirt, and my jeans, there had been little left of them but tatters and scraps.

Sort of like me.

Someone who had major issues with my death was killing people in my town.

Could it be my apprentice?

She had a thing for me, according to practically every woman I knew. I didn't have a thing back. Yes, she was gorgeous, intelligent, quick-witted, brave, thoughtful, and competent. But I'd known her when her bra had been a formality, back when I'd begun working with her father, one of the very few men in the world I hold in genuine respect.

There was darkness in Molly. I'd soulgazed her. I'd seen it in more than one of her possible futures. I'd felt it in the black magic she had worked, with the best of intentions, on fragile mortal minds.

But though she'd fought tooth and nail at Chichén Itzá, beside the rest of us . . . she wasn't a killer. Not Molly.

Was she?

People could be driven to extremes by the right events, the right stakes. I'd bargained away my future and my soul when I had needed to do it to save my daughter.

And I was Molly's teacher. Her mentor. Her example.

Had she let herself be driven to extremes at my loss, the way I had been to the potential loss of my daughter? Had she turned aside from everything I'd tried to teach her and let herself slide down into the violent exercise of power?

Why shouldn't she have done so, moron? I heard my own voice say in the dark of my thoughts. *You showed her how it worked. She's always been an able student.*

Worse, Molly was a sensitive, a wizard whose supernatural senses were so acute that surges of powerful magic or the emotions that accompanied life-and-death situations were something that caused her psychic and physical pain. It was something I had barely even considered when I dragged her along to Chichén Itzá with me for the largest, most savage, and deadliest brawl I had ever personally participated in.

Had the pain of participating in the battle done something to my apprentice? Had it left her with permanent mental damage, just as the gunshot wound she'd received must have left her a permanent scar? Hell, it didn't require any supernatural elements at all for war — and that was what Chichén Itzá was, make no mistake — to screw up young soldiers who found themselves struggling to stay alive. Throw in all the mystic menace on top of it, and it started to seem a little bit miraculous that I'd gotten as far as I had while remaining mostly sane.

I didn't want to admit it or think about it, but I couldn't deny that it was possible that my apprentice hadn't been as lucky as I had.

"Hey," Butters said quietly. "Harry? You all right?"

"That's . . . kinda subjective, all things considered," I answered.

He nodded. "No one wanted to be the one to tell you the details. But Murphy's pretty sure. She says that if she was still working as a cop, she'd be convinced and digging as hard as she could to turn up enough evidence to let her put the perp away."

"Yeah," I said quietly. "I get what she means

by that." I swallowed. "Why hasn't she?"

"We need Molly," Butters said. "She's made the difference between happily ever after and everyone dying in two raids against the Fomor."

I rubbed my eyes. "Okay. It's . . . something I'll start processing. But I'm not saying that I believe it. Not until I talk to her about it. See her reaction with my own eyes."

"Right," Butters said, his voice gentle.

I eyed him. "Murphy wouldn't want you telling me this."

He shrugged. "Murphy's not full all the way to the brim herself some days. What she's been doing . . . It's been hard on her. She's gotten more and more guarded."

"I can imagine."

Butters nodded. "But . . . I've always been kind of a trust-my-instincts guy. And I think you need to know this stuff."

"Thanks," I said. "We've got some other problems, too."

His tired, worried face lifted into a sudden grin. "Of course we do. Harry Dresden is in town. What's that?"

I put Sir Stuart's pistol into the voluminous pocket of my duster and said, "A cannon. Someone gave it to me."

"Huh." His voice turned casual. "Could something like that hurt me?"

I grinned and shook my head. "Nah. Ghost-on-ghost action only. Assuming I'm able to make it work in the first place."

The snow had stopped falling, and Butters turned off his windshield wipers. "What's it like?"

"What is what like?"

"Being . . . you know."

"Dead?"

He shrugged a shoulder, betraying his discomfort. "A ghost."

I thought about my answer for a moment. "Everything in my body that used to hurt all the time got better. I don't feel hungry or thirsty. Other than that, it feels a lot like being alive, except . . . my magic is gone. And, you know, hardly anyone can see me or hear me."

"So . . . so the world is the same?" he asked.

I shivered. "No. It's chock-full of all sorts of weird stuff. You wouldn't believe how many ghosts are running around this place."

Even as I spoke, I turned my head to watch two wraiths glide down the sidewalk as the car passed them. I frowned. "Including one of you, Bob."

Bob the Skull snorted. "I'm not mortal. I don't have a soul. The only thing waiting for me when I cease to be is entropy. I can't leave a ghost."

"Then how come I saw a floating skull with blue eyelights helping attack Mort Lindquist's place last night?"

The skull just stared for a moment. Then

258

he suggested lamely, "You were high?"

I snorted. "Can't be many things like that running around," I said. "What do you know?"

"I have to think about this," Bob said in a rushed tone, and his orange eyelights winked out.

Butters and I both stared at the skull.

"Huh," Butters said. "I've never seen anyone make him shut up before."

I grunted. Then I said quietly, "Scared the hell out of me, seeing that. Thought something had happened to him."

"He's fine," Butters said. "Best roommate I ever had."

"I'm glad you're taking care of him," I said. "He wouldn't do well alone."

"It's not a big deal, right?"

"What isn't a big deal?"

"If there's an Evil Bob out there," he said. "I mean . . . it'll just be another nerd like this one, right? Only with a black hat?"

The orange eyelights winked back on, and Bob said, "Hey!"

"Butters . . . Bob is spooky strong," I said quietly. "Knowledge is power, man. Bob has a lot of it. When I accidentally flipped his switch to black hat a few years ago, he nearly killed me in the first sixty seconds."

Butters blinked several times. He tried to talk for a few seconds, swallowed, and then said in a small voice, "Oh." He eyed Bob sideways.

"I don't like to make a big thing of it, sahib," Bob said easily. "Not really my bag to do that kind of thing anyway."

I nodded. "He was created to be an assistant and counselor," I said. "It's unprofessional to treat him as anything else."

"Which sahib doesn't," Bob noted. "Due to complete ignorance, but he doesn't."

"Oh," Butters said again. Then he asked, "How do I . . . make sure not to set him on black hat?"

"You can't," Bob said. "Harry ordered me to forget that part of me and never to bring it out again. So I lopped it off."

It was my turn to blink. "You *what?*"

"Hey," Bob said, "you told me never to bring it out again. You said *never.* As long as I was with you, that wouldn't be an issue — but the next guy could order me to do it and it would still happen. So I made sure it couldn't happen again. No big whoop, Dresden. Oy, but you are such a little girl sometimes."

I blinked several more times. "Oy?"

"My mother calls me twice a week," Butters explained. "He listens in."

"She's right, you know, sahib," Bob said brightly. "If you'd just do something with your hair and wear nicer clothes, you'd find a woman. You're a doctor, after all. What woman doesn't want to marry a doctor?"

"Did he just get a little Yiddish accent?" I asked Butters.

"I get it twice a week already, Bob," Butters growled. "I don't need it from you, too."

"Well, you need it from somewhere," Bob said. "I mean, look at your hair."

Butters ground his teeth.

"Anyway, Harry," Bob began.

"I know," I said. "The thing I saw with the Grey Ghost must be the piece that you cut off."

"Right," he said. "Got it in one."

"Your offspring, one might say."

The skull shuddered, which added a lot of motion to the bobblehead thing. "If one was coming from a dementedly limited mortal viewpoint, I guess."

"So it's a part of you, but not all of you. It's less powerful."

Bob's eyelights narrowed in thought. "Maybe, but . . . the whole of any given being is not always equal to the sum of its parts. Case in point: you. You aren't working with a lot of horsepower in the brains department, yet you manage to get to the bottom of things sooner than most."

I gave the skull a flat look. "Is it stronger than you or not?"

"I don't know," Bob said. "I don't know what it knows. I don't know what it can do. That was sort of the whole point in amputating it. There's a big hole where it used to be."

I grunted. "How big?"

Bob rolled his eyes. "Do you want me to tell you in archaic measurements or metric?"

"Ballpark it."

"Um. A hundred years' worth of knowledge, maybe?"

"Damn," I said quietly. I knew that Bob had once been owned by a necromancer named Kemmler. Kemmler had fought the entire White Council in an all-out war. Twice. They killed him seven times over the course of both wars, but it didn't take until number seven. Generally remembered as the most powerful renegade wizard of the second millennium, Kemmler had at some point acquired a skull inhabited by a spirit of intellect, which had served as his assistant.

Eventually, when Kemmler was finally thrown down, the skull had been smuggled away from the scene by a Warden named Justin DuMorne — the same Justin who had adopted me and trained me to grow up into a monster, and who had eventually decided I wasn't tractable enough and attempted to kill me. It didn't go as he planned. I killed him and burned down his house around his smoldering corpse instead. And I'd taken the same skull, hidden it away from the Wardens and company, and named it Bob.

"Is that bad?" Butters asked.

"A bad guy had the skull for a while," I said. "Big-time dark mojo. So those memories

Bob lost are probably everything he learned serving as the assistant to a guy who was almost certainly the strongest wizard on the planet — strong enough to openly defy the White Council for decades."

"Meaning . . . he learned a lot there," Butters said.

"Probably," Bob said cheerfully. "But it's probably limited to pretty much destructive, poisonous, dangerous stuff. Nothing important."

"That's not important?" Butters squeaked.

"Destroying things is easy," Bob said. "Hell, all you really have to do to destroy something is wait. Creation, now. *That's* hard."

"Bob, would you be willing to take on Evil Bob?"

Bob's eyes darted nervously. "I'd . . . prefer not to. I'd really, *really* prefer not to. You have no idea. That me was crazy. And buff. He worked out."

I sighed. "One more thing to worry about, then. And meanwhile, I still don't know a damned thing about my murder."

Butters brought the Road Runner to a stop and set the parking break. "You don't," he said. "But we do. We're here. Come on."

CHAPTER EIGHTEEN

I gritted my teeth and got out of Butters's car, then paused to look at my surroundings. The piled snow was deep, and the mounds on either side of the street were like giant-sized versions of the snow ramparts that appeared every year in the Carpenters' backyard. They changed the outlines of everything — but something was familiar.

I stopped and took at least half a minute to turn in a slow circle. As I did, I noticed a pair of fleeting shadows moving easily over the snow — wolves. Murphy's comment about sending shadows to escort Butters home made more sense in context. I watched one of the wolves vanish into the darkness between a pair of half-familiar pines, and only then did I recognize where we stood. By then, Butters had taken Bob from his holder in the car and was carrying him in the handheld spotlight case again. He shone the light around for a moment until he spotted me, then asked, "Harry?"

"This is my house," I said after a moment. "I mean . . . where my house was."

Things had changed.

A new building had been put up where my old boardinghouse — my home — had been. The new place was four stories tall and oddly cubical in appearance. The walls fell even farther out onto the lawn than those in the old building had, encasing it in a strip of yard only slightly wider than my stride.

I moved close enough to touch the wall and pushed my hand inside. It hurt, but the hurt never varied as I pushed in farther. This was no facade. It was made of stone. I'm not kidding. Freaking stone. Basalt, maybe? I'm no stonemason. It was dark grey with veins and threads of green and silver running through it, but I could only see them from up close.

The windows were narrow — maybe nine inches wide — and deep. There were bars on the outside. I could see more bars on the inside, and there was at least a foot between them. The roof was lined with a staggered row of blocks — real by-God crenellation. As the pièce de résistance, gargoyles crouched at the corners and at the midpoint of each wall, starting up at the second floor and moving in three rows of increasingly ugly statuary toward the roof.

Someone had turned the ruin of my home into a freaking fortress.

A plaque hung over what had to be the

main entrance. It read, simply, BRIGHTER
FUTURE SOCIETY.

Butters followed my gaze to the plaque.
"Ah," he said. "Yeah. We named it that
because if we didn't do something, there
wasn't going to *be* much of a future for this
town. I wanted Brighter Future Group, actually, for the initialism, but I got voted down."

"Hell's bells," I said. I did some math. To
build on the ruins of the boardinghouse,
construction would have had to start practically the same day that I died. Actual stone is
expensive to build with because it's difficult
and time-consuming. This place was as big as
a small castle. It should have taken months
and months and months to build. It had gone
up in six. Probably significantly less, given
the weather. "This place cost a damned fortune."

"Meh," Butters said, and walked to the
front door. "Hang around a bit and you'll
take it for granted like the rest of us." He
entered a sequence of numbers on the keypad
beside the door. They made a little mechanical clicking sound that reminded me of a
manual typewriter. He put his hands back
into his pockets and waited.

A moment later, a heavily accented basso
voice emerged from a crackling speaker box.
"Who goes there?"

"Butters," he said. "With Dresden's shade.
Hi, Sven."

The speaker made a rumbling sound. "Waldo," it said, pronouncing it Valdo. "The night is dangerous. One day you will stumble across a fox and it will eat you."

Roars of laughter erupted from the speakers — evidently, several other men were with the door guard.

Butters didn't laugh, but he did grin. "I'll just get stuck in his throat until you can haul your walrus ass over to him and save me, Sven."

Louder laughter erupted from the speaker, and a voice half-choked with it said something in a language that had come from somewhere in northern Europe. There was a click, and Butters opened the door. I started to follow him in — and remembered, in time, to put my hand out and check the doorway first. My hand moved smoothly past the twelve inches of stone, but then hit something as solid as a brick wall where the doorway opened up into the entry hall.

"Uh, Butters," I said.

He smacked the heel of his hand against his forehead. "Right, sorry. Please come in."

The invisible wall vanished, and I shook my head. "It's got a threshold. People live here?"

"Bunch of 'em," Butters confirmed, and we went inside. "Lot of Paranetters come through for a little while when they don't have a safe place to sleep. Uh, visiting Netters who are passing through town. Venatori, when they meet with us. That kind of thing."

I felt anger stirring in me, irrational but no less real. "My home . . . is a supernatural flophouse?"

"And armory! And jail!" Bob said enthusiastically.

Ghosts can sputter in outrage. "Jail?"

"And day care!" Bob continued.

I stopped in my tracks and threw my hands up. "Day care? *Day care?!*"

"People have kids, man. And they have jobs," Butters said in a gentle voice. "The Fomor aren't above using children to get what they want. High-risk kids come here on workdays. Now, shut up, Bob. And get off your high horse, Harry. People need this place."

I turned my gaze to Butters and studied him for a minute. The little guy had come a long way from the somewhat timid, insecure man I'd first met years before. That Butters would never have said anything like that to me.

Or maybe he was the same guy. Butters went right to the wall for the sake of the truth, even when it cost him his job and got him locked up in a nuthouse. He was a man of principles.

And he was probably right. This wasn't my home anymore.

We passed the guard station after we got buzzed through a security gate. Four of the biggest, toughest-looking men I'd ever seen were stationed there. They wore biker leathers — and swords. Their muscles swelled tight against their skin, their beards bristled, and their uniformly pale eyes watched us pass with calm attention.

"Einherjaren," Butters said quietly. "Soldiers of Valhalla, if they're telling the truth."

"They are," I replied just as quietly. "Where did we get them?"

"Marcone. They aren't cheap."

"Him again."

Butters shrugged. "I don't like the guy, either, Harry. But he's smart enough to realize that if the Fomor take control of the streets, they're going to get rid of him as a matter of course."

"Too simple," I said. "Too easy. He's running some kind of game on you."

We went through another door and then up some stairs, which opened onto the second floor.

The place was one enormous chamber almost entirely free of interior walls. There was a small gym, complete with shower rooms and a boxing ring. Inside the ring, Murphy, wearing her street clothes, stood facing a man who had inherited a portion of his DNA from a rhinoceros — and not many generations ago. He was huge and heavily muscled, his dark hair and beard in long braids. He wore an old pair of jeans and nothing else. His upper body was coated with more dark hair.

(Not like a werewolf or circus freak or anything. Just at the top end of the hirsute bell curve. A real hair ball.)

Butters froze in place, waiting.

Murphy stared steadily at the big man for several moments, her body relaxed, her eyes never blinking. He returned a blank stare of his own. Then they both moved.

I couldn't tell who went first, but Murphy's fist streaked toward the big guy's groin. He twisted his hip, deflecting the blow, and when he returned it to balance, his leg scythed up in an arc that clipped the tip of Murphy's chin. She spun away and went down.

Hair Ball did not hesitate for so much as a second. He moved toward her, fast for someone so large, and stomped his heel down toward her head.

Murphy rolled and dodged the blow, but he followed up and she had to keep rolling to stay ahead of his sledgehammer heels. She hit the edge of the boxing ring, then abruptly reversed her roll, moving toward him instead of away.

She slipped the next stomp, scissored his knee with her legs, twisted her whole body, and brought him down. Hair Ball fell like a tree, huge and slow. The boxing ring ropes shook when he landed.

Murphy came up onto all fours, scrambled

a bit to one side, and then swept her foot at Hair Ball's head. He dodged, but her kick shifted direction, her leg moving up, then straight down, bringing her heel down like a hatchet onto the hand Hair Ball was using to support his weight. Bones snapped.

Hair Ball howled, scrambled to his feet, and started swinging wildly at her. Murphy dodged and slipped one blow after another, and at one point abruptly turned and drove her heel into Hair Ball's solar plexus.

The blow rocked him back a step, but Murphy followed it too closely, too recklessly. Hair Ball recovered from the kick almost instantly, slapped a blow aside, and seized her arm. He turned and flung her, one-handed, over the top rope of the ring and into the nearest wall. She hit it with a yell and bounced off onto the floor.

"Dead," I snarled, my fists clenched. I started forward and took three or four whole steps before I realized that I wasn't going to be able to hit the guy. Or blow him up. Or send him on a vacation to another reality. Hell, I couldn't even sneak up on him and shout, "Boo!"

"Harry, wait," Butters hissed. "It's okay."

Murphy picked herself up from the floor, moving slowly. As she did, the giant Hair Ball came over to the nearest side of the ring, holding his right hand in his left. Murphy brushed some dust from her clothing and turned to face him. Her blue eyes were steady and cold, her mouth set in a small smile. Her teeth were white, and rich red blood quivered on her lower lip where the impact had split it open. She wiped the blood off on her sleeve without looking away from Hair Ball. "Three?" she asked.

"Broke all four," he said, moving his right hand a little by way of demonstration. "Took out my best sword hand. Good. If you hadn't gotten greedy for the kill, maybe you'd have taken this round."

Murphy snorted. "You've been drinking bad mead, Skaldi Skjeldson."

That made Hair Ball smile. "Sword tomorrow?"

Murphy nodded. The two of them stared at each other for a moment, as if each expected the other to suddenly charge the second the other turned his back. Then, with no detectable signal passing between them, they simultaneously nodded again and turned away from each other, relaxing.

"Butters," rumbled Skaldi Hair Ball. If he really had broken fingers, it didn't look like they were bothering him much. "When are you going to get in this ring and train like a man?"

"About five minutes after I get a functional lightsaber," Butters replied easily, much to Hair Ball's amusement. Then the little medical examiner nodded to Murphy and said,

"Can we talk in the conference room?"

"Sure," she said. She walked by the ring and bumped (left) fists with Skaldi. Then she led Butters and me out of the gym, down another hallway, and into a long, narrow conference room. She shut the door behind us, and Butters popped Bob's flashlight onto the table. His eyelights winked on again, and I saw Murphy react visibly when that light revealed my presence.

She stiffened a little, looking at me, and her eyes showed a sudden weariness and pain. She took a deep breath through her nose and closed her eyes for a second. Then she took off her jacket, moving gingerly, and said, "Hi, Harry."

Butters put the radio on the table and I said, "Hi, Murph."

She was wearing thin, light padding under the jacket — like the stuff I'd seen on stuntmen on a case I'd done not long after I'd gone into business. So her full-contact practice hadn't been as vicious as it had looked. She'd be covered in bruises, but the impact with the wall hadn't actually been likely to break her back. Her skull, maybe, but not her back.

"You okay?"

She rolled one shoulder with a grimace of discomfort. "I will be."

"Big guy like that going to town on you," I

growled. "Someone needs to push his face in."

Her eyes glittered as she gave me a sharp look. "Dresden . . . when, exactly, am I going to fight someone my size and strength?"

"Um."

"If you want to wrestle hostile mooses —"

"Moose," Butters corrected absently. "Singular and plural, same word."

"Gorillas," Murphy continued, hardly breaking stride, "then the best way to train for it is by wrestling slightly less hostile gorillas. Skaldi's two hundred pounds heavier than me, almost two feet taller, and he has going on two millennium —"

"Millennia," Butters said. "*Millennium* is the singular."

Murphy pushed a breath out through her nose and said, "Millennia of experience in breaking the backs of annoying little doctors with annoying little grammar fetishes."

Butters grinned.

"I'm not going to beat him, Harry. Ever. That isn't the point." She looked away and her voice became quiet. "The point is that the world isn't getting any kinder. A girl's got to take care of herself."

The expression on her face? It hurt. Hearing the words that went with it felt like a knife peeling back layers of skin. I didn't say anything. I didn't let it show. Murphy would have been offended at the notion that she needed my protection, and if she thought I felt guilty for not being there to protect her, to help her, she'd be downright angry.

Don't get me wrong. I didn't think Murphy was a princess in a tower. But at the end of the day, she was just one person, standing in defiance of powers that would regard her with the same indifference as might an oncoming tsunami, volcanic eruption, or earthquake. Life is precious, fragile, fleeting — and Murphy's life was one of my favorites.

"Okay, Harry," Murphy said. "Where do we get started?"

I felt awkward standing there while she and Butters sat at the table, but it wasn't like I could pull out a chair. "Um. Maybe we get started with what you know about my . . . my shooting."

She nodded and pulled on her cop face — her expression professionally calm, detached, analytical. "We don't have much, officially speaking," she said. "I came to pick you up and found the blood and a single bullet hole. There wasn't quite enough to declare it a murder scene. Because the vic . . . because you were on the boat and it was in motion, there was no way to extrapolate precisely where the bullet came from. Probably a nearby rooftop. Because the bullet apparently began to tumble as it passed through your body, it left asymmetric holes in the walls of the boat. But forensics thinks it was something between a .223 assault-rifle round and a .338 magnum-rifle round; more likely the latter than the former."

"I never got into rifles. What does that mean?"

"It means a sniper rifle or a deer rifle," Butters clarified. "Not necessarily military. There are plenty of civilian weapons that fire rounds in those calibers."

"We never found the bullet," Murphy said. She took a deep breath. "Or the body."

I noticed that both Murph and Butters were staring at me very intently.

"Uh," I said. "I . . . sort of did that whole tunnel-of-light thing — which is a crock, by the way." I bit down on a mention of Murphy's father. "Um, I was sent back to solve the murder. Which . . . sort of implies a death. And they said my body wasn't available, so . . ."

Murphy looked down and nodded.

"Huh," Butters said, frowning. "Why send you back?"

I shrugged. "Said what came next wasn't for whiners or rubberneckers."

Murphy snorted. "Sounds like something my father would say."

"Yeah," I said. "Heh."

Butters arched an eyebrow. His dark eyes flickered between me and Murphy, and thoughtful lines appeared on his face.

"Anyway," I said. "That's what you know

276

officially, right? So . . . what else do you know?"

"I know it wasn't Marcone," Murphy said. "All of his troubleshooters have alibis that check out. So do he and Gard and Hendricks. I know which building the shot probably came from, and it wasn't an easy one."

"Four hundred and fifty yards," Butters said. "Which means it was probably a professional gunman."

"There are amateurs who can shoot that well," Murphy said.

"As a rule, they don't do it from buildings at their fellow Americans," Butters replied. "Look, if we assume it's an amateur, it could be anyone. But if we assume it was a professional — which is way more likely, in any case — then it gives us the beginning of an identity, and could lead us back to whomever he works for."

"Even if we do assume that," Murphy said, "I don't have the access to information that I used to. We'd need to review TSA video records, security cameras — all kinds of things I can't get to anymore."

"Your brother-in-law can," I said. "Dick can."

"Richard," she corrected me. "He hates that nickname."

"Dick who?" Butters asked, looking between us.

I said, "Her brother-in-law," at the same

277

time she said, "My ex-husband."

Butters's brow arched even farther and he shook his head. "Man. Catholics."

Murphy gave him a gimlet look. "Richard runs by the book. He won't help a civilian."

"Come on, Murph," I said. "You were married to the guy. You've got to have some dirt on him."

She shook her head. "It isn't a crime to be an asshole, Harry. If it was, I'd have put him away for life."

Butters cleared his throat. "We could ask —"

"No," Murphy and I said at the same time, and continued speaking over each other.

"The day I ask for that bastard's help will be the day I —"

"— told you before, over and over, that just because he's reasonable doesn't mean he's —"

"— a murderer and a drug dealer and a pimp, and just because Chicago's corrupt government can't put him away doesn't mean —"

"— you were smarter than that," Murphy finished.

Butters lifted his hands mildly. "Okay, okay. I was on board at *no*. No going to Marcone for help." He paused and looked around the room as if he'd never seen it before. "Because that would be . . . unprecedented."

"Wally," Murphy said, one eyebrow arching

dangerously.

He held up his hands again. "Uncle. I don't understand your reasoning, but okay."

"You think Marcone was behind it, Harry?" Murphy asked.

I shrugged. "Last time I saw him, he said he didn't need to kill me. That I'd get myself killed without any help from him."

Murphy frowned. It made her lip hurt and she winced, reaching up. The wince made it hurt worse, apparently, because fresh blood appeared. "Dammit. Well. You can take that a couple of different ways, can't you?"

"Like how?"

Murphy looked at me. "Like maybe Marcone knew something was happening already, and that's why he said he didn't need to kill you. It wasn't him, but it was still something he was aware of."

I grunted. Marcone ran Chicago like his own personal clubhouse. He had legions of employees, allies, and flunkies. His awareness of what happened in his city wasn't supernatural; it was better than that. He was rational, intelligent, and more prepared for a crisis than any man I'd ever seen. If the Eagle Scouts had some sort of Sith equivalent, Marcone was it.

If someone's wet-work specialist had come to town, Marcone was very likely to have learned of it. He and his underworld network missed little.

"Dammit," Murphy said, evidently coming to the same conclusions I had. "Now I have to talk to the scum." She got out her little notepad and scribbled on it. "Butters, you said that Lindquist's house had burned down?"

"Big-time," said Butters.

I nodded. "According to the ghosts hanging around it, the Grey Ghost showed up — I didn't tell you about the Grey Ghost, did I?"

"Mr. Lindquist filled us in after the shooting," Butters said.

"Oh, right. Anyway, it showed up with several mortals and snatched him. We've got to get him back."

Murphy nodded, still writing. "What happens if we don't?"

"A bunch of serial killer–type ghosts start wandering around Chicago, looking for a good time. Ghosts like that can manifest — make themselves the next-best thing to real, Murph. Like the Nightmare. People will get hurt. A lot of them."

Murphy's mouth thinned into a line. She wrote on her notepad. "We'll do triage in a minute. What else?"

"I found the gang who shot up your house last night," I said.

The tip of Murphy's pencil snapped against the notepad. She looked up at me, and her eyes were cold, furious. She spoke in a very quiet voice. "Oh?"

"Yeah," I said. I paused for a moment to think about what I was going to say: Murphy's temper was not a force to be invoked lightly. "I don't think you're going to have to worry about them anymore."

"Why?" she asked, in her cop voice. "Did you kill them?"

There'd been a little too much intensity in that question. Wow. Murphy was clearly only too ready to go after these guys the minute she knew where they were.

I glanced at Butters, who looked like someone sitting near an armed explosive.

"No," I said, working out my words carefully. If Murphy's fuse was really as short as it seemed, I didn't want her charging off to deal with Fitz and his poor crew in true Viking tradition. "But they don't have the resources they had before. I don't think they're going to hurt anybody in the immediate future."

"That's your professional opinion, is it?"

"Yes."

She stared at me for a minute, then said, "Abby was standing on my patio last night when they came by. She took a round in the belly during that attack. She didn't get down fast enough. They don't know if she's going to live or not."

I thought of the plump, cheerful little woman, and swallowed. "I . . . I didn't know,

Murph. I'm sorry."

She continued speaking as if I hadn't said anything. "There was a retiree living in the house behind mine. He used to give me tomatoes he grew in his garden every summer. He wasn't as lucky as Abby. The bullet hit him in the neck while he was sleeping in bed. He had enough time to wake up, terrified, and knock the handset of his phone out of its cradle before he bled out."

Hell's bells. That put a different spin on things. I mean, I had been hoping to go for a no-harm, no-foul argument with Murphy. But if blood had been spilled and lives lost . . . Well. I knew Murphy. Whether or not she was a cop anymore, she wasn't going to back away.

"Where are they?" she asked.

"This is not a time to kick down doors," I told her. "Please hear me out."

Her hand tightened into a fist, but she visibly took control of her anger, took a deep breath, and then nodded. "Go ahead."

I told her about Fitz and his gang. I told her about Aristedes.

"I notice, Harry," she said, "that you didn't tell me where they are."

"Yeah," I said. "I, uh. I sorta told the kid I would help him. That you would help him."

Murphy narrowed her eyes. "You did what?"

"They're *kids,* Murph," I said. "In over their

heads. They need help."

"They've killed at least one person, maybe more," Murphy said. "There are still laws in this town, Dresden."

"Send the cops in and it'll get ugly. I'm not sure how much juice their boss has, but even if he can't shoot, he'd be a nightmare for the police — even SI."

Murphy frowned. "How sure are you about that?"

"Guys like him use fear and violence as daily tools. He won't think twice about hurting a cop."

Murphy nodded. "Then I'll deal with him."

"Murph, I know you can handle yourself, but —"

"Dresden, I've dealt with two men since you . . . since the shooting, who were skilled enough for Carlos to call them the next-best thing to full Council-quality warlocks. I've handled several lesser talents, too. The Fomor like to use them as officers and commanders. I know what I'm doing."

"You've killed them," I said quietly. "That's what you mean, isn't it?"

She looked away. It was a moment before she answered. "With someone that powerful . . . there's not really a choice. If you try to take them alive, they have plenty of time to kill you."

I winced in sympathy for her. She might not be a cop anymore, but it was where her heart lay — with the law. She believed in it, truly believed that the law was meant to serve and protect the people of Chicago. When she was a cop, it had always been her job to make sure that those laws worked toward that purpose, in whatever way she could manage.

She loved serving her city under the rule of law, and that meant judges and juries got to do their job before the executioner stepped in. If Murphy had dispensed with that belief, regardless of how practical and necessary it had been, regardless if doing so had saved lives . . .

Butters had said that she was under stress. I now knew the nature of that stress: guilt. It would be ripping away steadily at her insides, at her conscience, scraping them both raw.

"They were all killers," she said, though I don't think she was talking to me. "Killers and kidnappers. And the law couldn't touch them. Someone had to do something."

"Yeah," I said. "Someone always does."

"The point is," she continued, "that the way you deal with this kind of problem is to hit it with absolutely everything you've got, and to do it immediately. Before those spell-casting yahoos have enough time to fort up, bend people's minds into defending them, or to start coming after you or someone you care about." She looked up at me. "I need the address."

"You don't," I said. "I'll bring the kids to

you. Once you get them away from Aristedes, he's out of help and vulnerable. Then you can help Fitz and company."

"Fitz and company," she said in a flat tone, "are murderers."

"But —"

"No, Harry. Don't give me any rap about how they didn't mean it. They opened fire with deadly weapons in a residential neighborhood. In the eyes of the law and anyone the least bit reasonable, *It was an accident* is unconvincing. They knew what could happen. Their intentions are irrelevant."

"I know," I said. "But these aren't bad kids. They're just scared. It drove them to a bad choice."

"You've just described most of the gang members in this town, Harry. They don't join the gang because they're bad kids. They do it because they're frightened. They want to feel like they belong somewhere. Safe." She shook her head. "It doesn't matter if they started out as good kids. Life changes them. Makes them something they weren't."

"What do you want to do?"

"Take a team to their hideout. Deal with the sorcerer. We'll make every effort to avoid harming the others."

"You're going to open fire with deadly weapons on their home. Maybe you don't want to hurt the kids, but you know what could happen. If you wind up with bodies on the floor, your intentions would be irrelevant. Is that what you're telling me?"

Her eyes flashed with sudden anger. "You haven't been here the past six months. You don't know what it's been like. You —" She pressed her lips together. Then she looked at me and stared, clearly waiting.

I said, very quietly, "No."

She shook her head several times. Then she said, "The real Dresden wouldn't hesitate."

"The real Dresden would never have gotten a chance to see them. To talk to them. He'd just skip to the fight."

She flipped her notepad closed with a snap of her wrist and stood. "Then we've covered what needs doing. There's nothing more to discuss."

Murphy got up and left the room without a word, her steps smooth and purposeful.

Butters rose and collected Bob and the little spirit radio. "I, uh . . . I usually follow along after her when she's setting up something. Take care of the details. Excuse me."

"Sure," I said quietly. "Thanks for your help, Butters."

"Anytime," he said.

"You, too, Bob," I said.

"De nada," the skull replied.

Butters hurried out.

I was left standing in the conference room alone.

Chapter Nineteen

I stood there for several minutes, doing nothing. Not even breathing.

Doing nothing is difficult. Once you aren't busy, your head starts chewing things over. Dark, bleak thoughts appear. You start to think about what your life means. If you're a ghost, you start to think about what your death means.

Murphy was being slowly devoured from within by a guilty conscience. I had known her a long time. I knew how she thought. I knew what she held dear. I knew what it looked like when she was in pain. I had no doubt that I made the right call on that one.

But I also knew that she was a woman who wouldn't kill another human, even if he were over-the-hill-and-around-the-bend crazy, unless it was absolutely necessary. No killing is easy for anyone of conscience — but Murphy had been facing that demon for a long time. Granted, she'd been hurt by my death (and let me tell you how furiously frustrated it made me that I was powerless to have changed that). But why would her conscience start catching up to her now? Why develop a sudden case of the damsels when I'd asked her to get more information from her ex-husband? Brick walls didn't stop the woman when she had a mind to walk somewhere.

I noticed something, too, when we had been talking about the shot that had killed me and the shooter's location, and gathering more information about potential assassins. Murphy hadn't said much — but she'd *not* said a whole hell of a lot more.

She had never, not once, mentioned Kincaid.

Kincaid was a partially inhuman mercenary who worked for the scariest little girl on God's green earth. He was centuries old and he was a phenomenon in a fight. He had somehow overcome the negative aspects of the human nervous system, at least as it applied to firing a weapon under pressure. I'd never seen him miss. Not once.

And it was he who had told me that if he wanted to kill me, he'd do it from at least half a mile away, with a heavy-duty rifle round.

Murphy knew as well as I did that the opinion of an assassin with centuries of experience would be invaluable in the investigation. Initially, I hadn't suggested it, because Murph had kinda been dating the guy for a while, and seemed to care for him. So it seemed more appropriate to let her bring it up.

But she hadn't.

She'd never mentioned him at all.

She'd run the meeting too rapidly, and was ready to fight with me over something, anything. The entire argument about Fitz and his crew had been a smoke screen.

The only question was for whose benefit it had been. Mine, so that a possibly crazy ghost wouldn't go storming off for vengeance of some kind? Or had it been a veil of fog for her own benefit, because she couldn't reconcile her view of Kincaid with that of the faceless person who had killed me?

That felt right. That she knew it in her heart and, without realizing it, was frantically scrambling to find a less painful truth with her head.

My reasoning was based on my knowledge of human nature and of Murphy's personality, and on my intuition — but I'd spent a lifetime trusting my instincts.

I thought they were probably right.

I played through the possibilities in my head. I imagined Murphy, distraught and falling to pieces on the inside, in the days after my murder. We never got to find out if we'd be anything together. We'd missed it by moments. I knew that when there had been enough time for her rage to abate, the sorrow would begin to pile up. I imagined her in the next month or so, no longer a cop, her world in shambles.

Word of my death would have gotten around fast — not only among the wizards of the White Council, but among the remaining vampire Court, over the Paranet, and from there to the rest of the supernatural world.

Kincaid probably heard about it within a day or two. As soon as someone filed a report about me, the Archive, the supernatural recorder of all written knowledge that dwelled within a child named Ivy, would have known. And I was probably one of the only people in the world she thought of as a friend. She was what? Twelve? Thirteen?

News of my death would shatter Ivy.

Kincaid would, I think, have gone to Murphy to offer what comfort he could. Not the hot-chocolate-and-fluffy-robe brand of comfort. He was more likely to bring bottles of whiskey and a sex-music CD.

Especially if he was already right here in town, a dark, nasty part of me whispered in my head.

I imagined Murphy taking shelter where she could and bidding him farewell when he left — and then, over the next few weeks, slowly lining up facts and reaching conclusions, all the while repeating to herself that she was probably wrong. That it couldn't be what it looked like.

Frustration. Pain. Denial. Yeah, that would be enough to draw rage out of anybody. Rage she would be carrying with her like a slowly growing tumor, becoming more and more of a burden. It was the sort of thing that might push someone to kill another person, even when maybe it wasn't necessary.

That death would cause more guilt, more frustration, which would cause more rage, which would cause more violence, which would add to guilt again; a literal vicious cycle.

Murphy didn't want to get shots from airport and train-station security cameras because she didn't want to find out that the man she'd been sleeping with had killed one of her friends. When drawn close to that plausibility, she reacted in anger, pushing away the source of illumination about to fall on what she didn't want to see.

She probably wasn't even aware of the clash of needs in her head. When you're grief-stricken, all kinds of irrational stuff flies around in there.

Detective work isn't always about logic — not when you're dealing with people. People are likely to do the most ridiculously illogical things for the most incomprehensible of reasons. I had no logic to aim at Kincaid. But the theory fit a whole lot of pieces together. If it was correct, it explained a lot.

It was only a theory. But it was enough to

make me want to start digging for more evidence where I might not otherwise have looked.

But how? How was I going to start digging into Jared Kincaid, the Hellhound, the closest thing to a father Ivy had ever had — and do it without Murphy's help? For that matter, I'd have to find some way to do it without her knowledge, and that seemed like something that would be more than a little slimy to do to a friend. *Augh.* Better, maybe, to focus on the immediate problems first.

I had to find Morty, whose plight had clearly been low on Murph's priority list.

I had to help Fitz and the rest of his clueless, teenage pals.

And for all of it, I needed the help of someone I could trust.

I took a deep breath and nodded.

Then I walked until I had passed through an exterior wall of the Bright Future house, and set off to find my apprentice before the night got any deeper.

CHAPTER TWENTY

I always considered myself a loner.

I mean, not like a poor-me, Byron-esque, I-should-have-brought-a-swimming-buddy loner. I mean the sort of person who doesn't feel too upset about the prospect of a weekend spent seeing no one, and reading good books on the couch. It wasn't like I was a people hater or anything. I enjoyed activities and the company of friends. But they were a side dish. I always thought I would also be happy without them.

I walked the streets of a city of nearly three million people and, for the first time, there was nothing that connected me to any of them. I couldn't speak to them. I couldn't touch them. I couldn't get in an argument over a parking space, or flip the bird to a careless driver who ran a light while I was crossing. I couldn't buy anything in one of the stores, making polite chitchat with the clerk while paying. Couldn't pick up a newspaper. Couldn't recommend a good book to someone browsing the shelves.

Three million souls went about their lives around me, and I was alone.

Now I understood Captain Murphy's shadow Chicago. The actual town had already begun to *feel* like the shadow version. With enough time, would the real city look that way to me, too? Dark? Empty? Devoid of purpose and vaguely threatening? I'd been here for barely a day.

What would I be like if I was here for a year? Ten years? A hundred years?

I was starting to get why so many ghosts seemed to be a couple of French fries short of a Happy Meal.

I had to wonder, too, if maybe Sir Stuart and Morty were right about me. What if I really was the deluded spirit they thought I was? Not the true Harry Dresden, just his image in death, doing what the lunatic had always done: setting out to help his friends and get the bad guy.

I didn't feel like a deluded spirit, but then, I wouldn't. Would I? The mad rarely know that they are mad. It's the rest of the world, I think, that seems insane to them. God knew it had always seemed fairly insane to me. Was there any way I could be sure I was anything other than what Sir Stuart and Mort thought?

More to the point, Mort was the freaking expert on ghosts. I mean, I knew my way around the block, but Mort had been a specialist. Normally, on purely technical matters regarding spirits and shades, I would give his opinion significant weight, probably a little more than I would my own. Morty had never been a paragon of courage and strength, but he *was* smart, and clearly tough enough to survive a long career that had been a lot more dangerous than I thought.

Hell. For all I knew, while I had been busy saving Chicago from things no one knew were there, Mort might have been saving me from things *I* never knew were there. Funny world, isn't it?

I stopped in my tracks and shook my head as if to clear water from my eyes. "Dresden, have your personal existential crisis later. The bad guys are obviously working hard. Get your ass in gear."

Good advice, that.

The question was, How?

Normally, I would have tracked Molly down with a fairly simple piece of thaumaturgy I'd done a thousand times. After her unplanned vacation to Arctis Tor, in Faerie, I had always been sure to keep a fairly recent lock of her hair handy. And more recently, I'd found I could get a fix on all the energy patterns she used to make her first few independent magical tools — like the hair, they were something specific and unique to her and her alone. A signature. I could be pretty sure to find her when I needed to do so. Hell, for that matter, I'd spent so much time around her that she had become almost like family. I could generally tell by pure intuition when she was nearby, as long as she wasn't actively trying to hide herself.

That, of course, had all been when I had magic. Now I didn't.

Which was, upon thinking about it, probably another bit of evidence in favor of Stuart and Mort's theory, and against mine. You can't take magic away from a person. It's a part of who and what they are. They can abandon it, if they work at it hard enough, but you can't strip it out of them. If my ghost had truly been me, it would have had power, just as that bastard Leonid Kravos's ghost had.

Right?

Or . . . maybe not. Maybe I'd been making more assumptions without ever questioning them. I had already assumed that matter was solid when it wasn't; that I could get cold, which I couldn't; and that I was still beholden to the laws of gravity, which I wasn't.

Maybe I'd made the same assumptions about magic. I mean, after all, I had thrown a solid shield spell during the first attack on Mort's place, when I had been sharing space with the ectomancer. *That* would seem to show that my talent was still there, still real.

I just had to figure out how to access it.

Memories are power.

I dug into my duster's pocket and drew out the massive pistol Sir Stuart had given me. Black-powder weaponry isn't my thing, but I made sure there was nothing in the priming pan before turning it barrel down and shaking it. I had to give it several hard thumps with the heel of my hand to get the ball, wad, and powder to spill out into my palm.

The ball, the bullet, gleamed as if newly molded. Upon closer look, fine swirls on the surface of the metal took on the shapes of a simple, pastoral scene: a colonial-style home in the middle of a little green valley surrounded by apple trees; clean, neat cropland; and a pasture dotted with white sheep. Just looking at it seemed to give the scene life. Wind stirred the crops. Apples stood out like specks of bright green against the darker leaves. Lambs gamboled among adult members of the flock, playing for the pure joy of it. The door to the house opened, and a tall, straight-backed woman with hair blacker than a raven's wing emerged from the house, trailing a small cloud of children, clearly giving calm instructions.

With the sight, a flood of emotions coursed through me. A fierce and jealous pride of possession — not pride that I owned such a beautiful home, but that the home was beautiful *because* I owned it, because I had made it so. Mixed with that was an ocean-deep surge of love for the woman and her

children, raw happiness at seeing them —
and a heavy, entirely pleasurable surge of
desire for the woman, whom I had not held
in far too long —

I suddenly felt that I had intruded upon
something personal and intimate. I closed my
eyes and looked away from the scene.

Memories, I realized. These were all things
from Sir Stuart's mortal memories. This
memory was what he had cast forth against
that wraith the first time I met him. He
hadn't used memories of destruction as his
weapon, but those of identity, of the *reasons*
he was willing to fight.

That was why as a ghost he still used that
ax, this pistol. Far more modern weapons
were available to copy, but *his* memories were
of himself using those weapons, and so they
were the source of his power, the embodi-
ment of his will to change what was around
him.

They were Sir Stuart's identity. They were
also his magic.

Memories equaled power.

For a moment, I thought it couldn't be that
simple. But a lot of magic is actually disgust-
ingly simple — which is not to be confused
with easy.

There was only one way to find out.

The first spell I'd ever done had been during that long-ago class Olympics — but that
was spontaneous, accidental magic, hardly

worthy of the term. The first conscious spell I'd knowingly worked, fully planned, fully visualized, fully realized, had been calling forth a burst of fire.

Justin DuMorne had shown me how it worked.

I plunged into the memory.

"I don't understand," I complained, rubbing at my aching temples. "It didn't work the first fifty times. It isn't going to work now."

"Forty-six times," Justin corrected me, his voice very precise, like always. He had an accent, but I couldn't figure out which kind it was. I hadn't heard one like it on TV. Not that Justin had a TV. I had to sneak out on Friday nights to watch it in the store at the mall, or else face the real risk that I'd miss *Knight Rider* altogether.

"Harry," Justin said.

"Okay," I sighed. "My head hurts."

"It's natural. You're blazing new trails in your mind. Once more, please."

"Couldn't I blaze the trails somewhere else?"

Justin looked up at me from where he sat at his desk. We were in his office, which was what he called the spare bedroom in the little house about twenty miles outside Des Moines. He was dressed in black pants and a dark grey shirt, like on most days. His beard was short, precisely trimmed. He had very long, slender fingers, but his hands could make fists that were hard as rocks. He was taller than me, which most grown-ups were, and he never called me anything mean when he got mad, which most of the foster parents I'd been with did.

If I angered Justin, he just went from saying *please* to using his fists. He never swung at me while screaming or shook me, which other caretakers had done. When he hit me, it was really quick and precise, and then it was over. Like when Bruce Lee hit a guy. Only Justin never made the silly noises.

I ducked my head, looking away from him, and then stared at the empty fireplace. I was sitting in front of it with my legs crossed. There were logs and tinder ready to go. There was a faint smell of smoke, and a bit of wadded-up newspaper had turned black at one corner, but otherwise there was no evidence of a fire.

In my peripheral vision, I saw Justin turn back to his book. "Once more, if you please."

I sighed. Then I closed my eyes and started focusing again. You started with steadying your breathing. Then once you were relaxed and ready, you gathered energy. Justin had told me to picture it as a ball of light at the center of my chest, slowly growing brighter and brighter, but that was a load of crap. When the Silver Surfer did it, energy gathered around his hands and his eyes. Green Lantern gathered it around his ring. Iron Fist had glowing fists, which was pretty much as cool as you could get. I guess Iron Man had the glowing thing in the middle of his chest, but he was, like, the only one, and he didn't really have superpowers anyway.

I pictured gathering my energy together around my right hand. So there.

I pictured it glowing brighter and brighter, surrounded by a red aura like Iron Fist's. I felt the power making tingling sensations up and down my arms, making my hairs stand up on end. And when I was ready, I leaned forward, thrusting my hand into the fireplace, released the energy, and said clearly, *"Sedjet."*

And as I spoke, I flicked the starter on the Bic lighter I had palmed in my right hand. The little lighter immediately set the newspaper alight.

From right next to me, Justin said, "Put it out."

I twitched and dropped the lighter in pure surprise. My heart started beating about a zillion times a minute.

His fingers closed into a fist. "I don't like to repeat myself."

I swallowed and reached into the fireplace to drag the burning paper out from under the wood. It singed me a little, but not enough to cry about or anything. I slapped the fire out with my hands, my cheeks turning bright red as I did.

"Give me the lighter," Justin said, his voice calm.

I bit my lip and did.

He took the lighter and bounced it a couple of times in his palm. A faint smile was on his lips. "Harry, I believe you will find that such ingenuity may be of great service to you as an adult." The smile vanished. "But you are not an adult, boy. You are a student. This sort of underhanded behavior will not do. At all."

He closed his fist and hissed, *"Sedjet."*

His hand exploded into a sphere of scarlet-and-blue flame — which pretty much made Iron Fist's powers look a little bit pastel. I stared and swallowed. My heart beat even faster.

Justin rotated his hand a few times, contemplating it, and making sure that I saw his whole fist and arm — that I could see it wasn't sleight of hand. It was completely surrounded in fire.

And it wasn't burning.

Justin held his fist right next to my face, until the heat was beginning to make me uncomfortable, but he never flinched and his flesh remained unharmed.

"If you choose it, this is what you may one day manage," he said calmly. "Mastery of the elements. And, more important, mastery of yourself."

"Um," I said. "What?"

"Humans are inherently weak, boy," he

continued in that same steady voice. "That weakness expresses itself in a great many ways. For instance, right now you wish to stop practicing and go outside. Even though you know that what you learn here is absolutely critical, still your impulse is to put play first, study later." He opened his hand suddenly and dropped the lighter in my lap.

I flinched away as it struck my leg, and let out a little yell. But the red plastic lighter simply lay on the floor, unmarked by any heat. I touched it with a nervous fingertip, but the lighter was quite cool.

"Right now," Justin said, "you are making a choice. It may not seem like a large and terrible choice, but in the long term, it may well be. You are choosing whether you will be the master of your own fate, with the power to create what you will from the world — or whether you will simply flick your Bic and get by. Unremarkable. Complacent." His mouth twisted and his voice turned bitter. "Mediocre. Mediocrity is a terrible fate, Harry."

My hand hovered over the lighter, but I didn't pick it up. I thought about what he had said. Then I said, "What you mean is that if I can't do it . . . you'll send me back."

"Success or failure of the spell is not the issue," he said. "What matters is the success or failure of your will. Your will to overcome human weakness. Your will to work. To learn. I will have no shirkers here, boy." He settled down onto the floor next to me and nodded toward the fireplace. "Again, if you please."

I stared at him for a moment, then down at my hand, at the discarded lighter.

No one had ever told me I was special before. But Justin had. No one had ever taken so much time to do anything with me. Ever. Justin had.

I thought of going back into the state system — to the homes, the shelters, the orphanages. And suddenly, I truly wanted to succeed. I wanted it more than I wanted dinner, more even than I wanted to watch *Knight Rider.* I wanted Justin to be proud of me.

I left the lighter where it was and focused on my breathing.

I built up the spell again, slowly, slowly, focusing on it more intently than on anything I'd ever done in my life. And I was nearly thirteen, so that was really saying something.

The energy swelled until I felt like someone had started a trash fire in my belly, and then I willed it out, through my empty, outstretched right hand, and as I did, instead of using the Egyptian phrase, I said, *"Flickum bicus!"*

And the remaining tinder under the logs burst into bright little flames. I didn't think I'd ever seen anything more beautiful.

I sagged and almost fell over, even though I

was already sitting on the floor. My body suddenly ached with hunger and weariness, like this one time when all us orphans had gotten to go to a water park. I wanted to eat a bucket of macaroni and cheese and then go to sleep.

A strong, long-fingered hand caught my shoulder and steadied me. I looked up to see Justin regarding me, his dark eyes flickering with warmth that wasn't wholly the reflection of the small but growing fire in the hearth.

"*Flickum bicus?*" he asked.

I nodded and felt myself blushing again. "You know. 'Cause . . . the mediocrity."

He tilted his head back and let out a rolling laugh. He ruffled my hair with one hand and said, "Well-done, Harry. Well-done."

My chest swelled up so much I thought I was going to bounce off the ceiling.

Justin held up a finger, went to his desk, and returned with a brown paper package. He offered it to me.

"What's this?" I asked.

"Yours," he said. "You've done the work after all."

I blinked and then tore the package open. Inside was a Wilson baseball mitt.

I stared for several seconds. No one had ever given me a present before — not one that was meant for me, and not just some random, charity-donated Christmas package with a label that said: FOR: BOY. And it was an excellent glove. George Brett had one just

305

like it. I'd been to two Kansas City Royals baseball games on field trips when I was little, and they were awesome. So was Brett.

"Thank you," I said quietly. Oh, come on. *Now* I was gonna cry? Sometimes I thought I was kinda goofy.

Justin produced a baseball, a brand-new one that was still all white, and held it up, smiling. "If you're up for it, we can go outside right now."

I felt really tired and hungry, but I had a brand-new glove! I shoved my hand into it until I figured out where all my fingers were supposed to go. "Yes," I said, pushing myself up. "Let's do it."

Justin bounced the ball up and down in his hand a couple of times and grinned at me. "Good. When all is done, I think you'll find baseball a rewarding experience."

I followed him outside. It didn't matter that I was tired. I was practically floating.

I opened my eyes, standing on a random Chicago sidewalk, immaterial and unseen. I turned my right hand palm up and focused upon that sudden kindling of light and hope, crystallized by the memory of that moment of triumph and joy.

"*Flickum bicus,*" I whispered.

The fire was every bit as beautiful as I remembered.

CHAPTER TWENTY-ONE

It took me a couple of hours to work out how to make my trusty tracking spell function. I easily found several memories that I could use to power the spell; it was figuring out how to create the link to Molly that was hard. Usually, I would use one of the trusty traditional methods for directing thaumaturgy — a lock of hair, a fresh drop of blood, fingernail clippings, et cetera. That wasn't going to work, obviously. I couldn't touch them, even if I had them.

So instead of tracking Molly with physical links, I tried using *memories* of her in their place. It worked — sort of. The first tracking spell led me to the hotel that had once hosted a horror convention known as SplatterCon! It was closed now, and deserted. I guess maybe all the deaths at SplatterCon! had taken a toll on the hotel in the civil-court cases that followed the phobophage attacks. I took a quick spin through the place, hardly even flinching before I stomped through one wall after another. Except for a few transients who had broken into the building and were squatting there, I found nothing.

I went back over my work. The memory I'd used was one that had stuck in my head for some reason, of Molly here in this building. That must have thrown off the spell. It had homed in on this place because it had been part of the memory I used to create the link.

I tried again, this time omitting the background and picturing only Molly against an empty field of black. This second attempt took me to a police station from which I had once posted bail for Molly's boyfriend. I figured I'd bungled the spell somehow, but took a quick look around anyway, just in case. No Molly.

"Okay, smart guy," I said to myself. "So what if the memory-image you're using is too old? You're tracking her memory-self to a memory-location. Which means you have to think of her *as* she is now to find *where* she is now. Right?

"Theoretically," I said to myself.

"Right. So test the theory."

Well, obviously. Although discussing a problem with yourself is almost never a good way to secure a divergent viewpoint.

"In fact, talking to yourself is often considered a sign of impending insanity," I noted aloud.

Which hardly seemed encouraging.

I shook off the unsettling thought and worked the tracking spell again. This time, instead of using one of my earlier memories of Molly, I used my most recent one. I pictured her in her cast-off clothing and rags, as she'd been at Murphy's place.

Forming a memory into an image that would support the energy required for a spell isn't as simple as closing your eyes and daydreaming. You have to produce it in exact, even fanatical, detail, until it is as real in your mind as any actual object. It takes a lot of practice and energy to do that — and it is why people use props when they set out to do magic. A prop can be used as an anchor, saving the spellcaster the effort of creating not just one, but multiple, mental constructs, and supporting them all in a state of perfect focus and concentration.

I had learned how to do magic the hard way first — all of it in my head. Only after I'd proved I could do it without the aid of props did Justin tell me that it was even possible to use them. Over the years, I'd practiced fairly complex thaumaturgic spells without props maybe once a season, keeping my concentration and imagination sharp. It was a damned good thing I had. Working magic as a ghost was all about doing it au naturel.

I reached into my memory to produce the construct I'd need to stand in for Molly in the tracking spell. At the time, I'd been handed a lot to process, and I hadn't really taken stock of exactly what kind of shape Molly was in. I'd seen that she was under strain, but upon closely reviewing the memory, I was somewhat shocked at how gaunt and weary she looked. Molly had always been the sort of young person who almost glowed with good health. After six months on her own, she looked like an escapee from a gulag: scrawny, tough, and beaten down, if not broken.

I added more than that to the image. I imagined her cheery goodwill, the self-loathing she still sometimes felt for the pain she'd caused her friends in the days before I agreed to teach her. I thought of her precise, orderly approach to her studies, so much different from my own, her diligence, and the occasional arrogance that pretty much every young wizard has until they've walked into enough walls to know better. I thought of the most powerful force in her life, a deep and abiding love for her family, and added in the desolation she must be feeling to be separated from them. Eager, beautiful, dangerous Molly.

I held that image of my apprentice in mind, drew together my will, and tapped into the recollection of one of my more memorable tracking spells, all at the same time. I established the pattern of the modified version of the spell I'd had to cobble together, walked, chewed bubble gum, and released the spell with a murmured word.

The power surged out through me, and a precise, powerful force spun me into a pirouette. I extended my left arm, index finger pointing, and felt a sharp tug against it each time it passed an easterly point of the compass. Within a couple of seconds I stopped spinning, rotated a little past the point, and then settled back slightly in the opposite direction. My index finger pointed straight at the heart of the city.

"Crombie," I said, "eat your heart out."

I followed the spell to Molly.

I pulled my vanishing act and went zipping downtown a few hundred yards at a time. I paused to check the spell twice more and correct my course, though by the third check, I was starting to feel like a human weather vane. I had to stop more frequently as I got closer to make sure I was moving in the right direction, and the trail took me down into the great towers within the Loop, where the buildings rose high enough to form what felt like the walls of a deep ravine, a man-made canyon of glass, steel, and stone.

I wasn't terribly surprised when the spell led me to the lower streets. Some of the streets downtown have two or even three levels. One is up on the surface, with the others stacked below it. A lot of the buildings have upper and lower entrances and parking as well, doubling the amount of access to the buildings within those blocks.

There were also plenty of empty spaces, pseudo-alleyways, walkways, and crawl spaces. Here and there, abandoned chambers in the basements and subbasements of the buildings above sat in silent darkness, waiting to be remade into something new. The commuter tunnels could connect down there, and there were several entrances to the insane, deadly labyrinth beneath the city known as Undertown.

Chicago cops patrolled the lower streets on a regular basis. Things came slinking out of Undertown to prowl the darkness. Traffic would blaze through on the actual streets, which were occasionally only separated from the sidewalks by a stripe of faded paint.

All in all, it's not the sort of place a sane person will casually wander through.

I found Molly standing in one of the narrow alleyways. Snow had fallen through a grate twenty feet overhead and covered the ground. She was dressed in the same rags I'd seen the night before, with her arms clenched around her stomach, shivering in the cold. There was a fresh, purpling bruise on her cheek. She was breathing heavily.

"Again," said a cool, calm woman's voice from farther down the alley, out of sight.

"I'm t-t-tired," Molly said. "I haven't e-eaten in a day and a half."

"Poor darling. I'm sure Death will understand and agree to return another time."

There was a sharp hissing sound, and Molly threw up her left hand, fingers spread. She spat out a word or two, and flickering sparkles of defensive energy spread from her fingertips into a flat plane.

Molly simply didn't have a talent for defensive magic — but this was the best shield I'd ever seen the grasshopper pull off.

A hurtling white sphere hit the shield. It should have bounced off, but instead it zipped through the shield, its course barely bent. The sphere struck Molly in the left shoulder and exploded into diamond-glitter shards of ice. She let out a short, harsh grunt of pain and staggered.

"Focus," said the calm woman's voice. "Use the pain. Make the shield real with your will. *Know* that it will protect you. Again."

Molly looked up with her teeth clenched. But instead of talking, she raised her left hand once more, and another ball of ice flew at her. This one hit the shield and went through — but its path was attenuated more significantly than the last. It flew past her, barely clipping one arm.

She gasped and sank to one knee, panting. Magic taxes the endurance of anyone who uses it — and if you use magic you aren't particularly skilled with, you get worn down even faster.

I shivered to see Molly like that. I knew how she felt. When Justin began teaching me how to create protective shields, he threw baseballs at me at top speed. When I failed, I was hit with a fastball moving at more than eighty miles an hour. Justin said pain was an excellent motivator, and that the activity was good training.

When I had been teaching Molly how to shield, I hadn't used anything more painful than fluffy snowballs and rotten fruit.

"That will do for now," said the woman's voice. "Tomorrow we will move up to knives."

Molly shuddered and looked down.

The speaker came walking calmly down the alley to stand over Molly.

It was my faerie godmother, the Leanansidhe.

Lea was beautiful beyond the loveliness of mere humanity, but it was a stark, hungry, dangerous beauty that always reminded me of a hunting cat. She was tall and pale, her hair the color of autumn leaves at sunset. Her ears were very slightly pointed, though I wasn't sure she hadn't done that to herself in order to conform to mortal expectations. She wore a long gown of green silk, wholly unsuitable to the task of protecting a mortal from the weather, but as she was one of the most powerful Sidhe of the Winter Court, I doubted she even noticed the cold.

She reached out a hand and touched Molly's hair with her fingertips.

"Why?" Molly asked, her voice barely more than a whisper. "Why are you doing this to me?"

"Obligation, child," Lea replied. "Favors owed and loyalties given."

"You owed it to Harry to do this to me?" Molly asked.

"Nay, child, not me. But my queen is committed to him through ancient law and custom. She dispatched me to continue your training in the Art — and pain is an excellent teaching tool."

"Harry didn't believe that," Molly said, her voice brittle. "He never hurt me."

The Leanansidhe stooped and seized Molly's chin, jerking my apprentice's face up to meet her inhuman gaze. "Then he wronged you badly, child," Lea replied, enunciating each word sharply. "He cheated you of the legacy he lived — and suffered to acquire. I am not teaching you how to tie knots in rope or to bake pastries. I am making you ready to face battle and emerge alive."

"I *have* faced battle," Molly said.

"In which you were shot, of all things, by a mere mortal foot soldier," Lea said, contempt flavoring her words. "You nearly died, which would have been greatly humiliating to your mentor and by extension to my queen."

"What does it matter to Mab?" Molly said, her voice bitter. "He's dead."

Lea sighed. "Mortals can be so obsessed with useless detail. It grows tiresome."

"I don't understand," Molly said.

"Your mentor took an oath of fealty to my queen. Such oaths are not to be made lightly — and they place mutual obligations on both parties. Minor details do not excuse either party from its responsibilities."

"His *death* is a *minor* detail?"

"As these things go," Lea said, "of course it is. You're all mortals. Even the life length of a wizard is something brief and transitory to an immortal. Similarly, extending her hand to the assistance of those her vassal knew in life is a minor detail. If you live another three centuries, it is little more than a long season to the Queen of Air and Darkness."

Molly closed her eyes. "He made her promise to take care of me?"

Lea blinked at her, politely baffled. "No, of course not, child. He took an oath of fealty. She is one of the Sidhe. The oath binds her as tightly as it does him. Just as when I was" — Lea shivered — "unable to perform my duties to young Dresden, Mab assumed those responsibilities until I could be restored to them. Thus does she now do for you, through me."

Molly wiped a hand over her eyes. She shook her head and rose to her feet, moving slowly. "Did he know? I mean . . . did he know Mab would do this?"

"I should have," I said quietly. "If I'd stopped to think about it for two minutes. I should have known." But neither of them heard me.

"I knew the boy well," Lea said. "Better than ever he realized. Many a night did I watch over him, protecting him, and he none the wiser. But I was not privy to his mind or his heart."

Molly nodded slowly. She looked at Lea for a long moment. My godmother simply watched her, waiting until Molly nodded to herself and said, "His shade is in town, looking for the person who killed him."

The Leanansidhe's pale red-gold eyebrows flew up. It was one of the most drastic reactions I'd ever seen from her. "That . . . seems unlikely."

Molly shrugged. "I used my Sight. It's his ghost, all right. A construct couldn't have hidden from me."

"Six months after his death?" the Leanansidhe murmured. "It is rare for a shade to arise after the season in which it was made — and he was slain last autumn. . . ." Her eyes narrowed. "Interesting." She tilted her head, studying Molly. "What is your condition?"

Molly blinked dully once before she said, "I need to curl into a ball and sleep for a week.

I'm starving. I'm cold. I think I'm *getting* a cold. I hurt everywhere. I would —" Molly paused and eyed Lea. "Why do you ask?"

The Sidhe only smiled in answer.

Bootsteps sounded, heavy and quick, and a small crowd appeared at the far end of the alley. They were all rough-looking men, carrying an assortment of guns, blades, clubs, and axes. They dressed exclusively in black, to the extent that it looked like they all shopped in the same store. They were also wearing turtlenecks — every single one of them. Talk about weird.

Molly let out a hiss. "Servitors. How did they find me here?"

"I told them where to look," Lea said calmly.

Molly whirled to her. "You *what?*"

"I didn't share your location with the Fomor themselves, child. Just with some of their guard dogs. They think that if they catch you and return you to the Fomor, they will gain great honor — and I did not give them enough time to contact their masters for instructions." She smiled, showing daintily pointed canines. "Initiative in an underling can be such a troubling thing."

Molly made a disgusted sound. "I don't believe this."

Twenty armed thugs kept striding forward, exuding the calm that comes only from professionals who are not hurrying, keeping their spacing smooth. They were all glaring at Molly.

Lea smirked, already fading out of sight. "It is good training, child." She vanished Cheshire Cat style, only she left her voice behind instead of her smile. "Let us see what you have learned."

CHAPTER TWENTY-TWO

"What I've learned," Molly muttered, mostly under her breath. "So help me, one of these days, I'll *show* you what I've learned, you skinny bitch."

Then she focused on the enemy, took a breath, just as I'd taught her to do under stress, and calmed herself. She began to withdraw, calmly, slowly, one pace at a time. That was smart. Had she turned and sprinted, it would have provoked immediate pursuit. Instead, the guys in turtlenecks kept their professional cool, moving steadily forward in a solid block of muscles and weapons. All of them ready to kill a lone, exhausted young woman.

Scum. No way in hell that was happening to my apprentice.

I hadn't yet tried any true evocation magic, the fast-and-dirty side of violent wizardry, but I thought I had the basic concept down. So I tuned in to a memory of a particularly powerful evocation, when I had blown a rampaging loup-garou straight through the brick wall of one building and *entirely* through the building across the street. I left out all the details except for the energy blast itself, vanished, and reappeared in front of the oncoming servitors, and snarled, *"Fuego!"*

A blast of flame and raw kinetic force exploded from my outflung right hand. It hit the front of the enemy formation like a blazing locomotive —

— and washed completely through them, having no effect whatsoever. I didn't even ruffle their clothes.

"Oh, come *on!*" I shouted. "That is just not fair!"

I still couldn't act, couldn't touch, couldn't help.

Molly faced the men alone.

She kept walking back until she emerged from the alley into a small parking lot contained within concrete walls and open to the sky. There were only a handful of cars in it, along with a motorcycle and a couple of mounds of piled snow. There were doors fitted with those magnetic card-swipe locks on two of the lot's walls — employee or executive parking, obviously. The fourth opening led out to the lower avenue, where dull yellow lights cast a feeble gleam.

Molly walked to the middle of the little lot, looked around her, and nodded. "Well, boys," she said aloud. "I don't suppose there's any chance we could talk about this over a cup of coffee at Denny's? I'm starving."

One of the turtlenecks, presumably their leader, said, "Submit yourself to the will of the masters. Your pain will be much shortened."

"Right," Molly said. She rolled her neck as if to loosen it up and nodded at the speaker. "You're my huckleberry."

The turtleneck tilted his head to one side, frowning.

Molly blew him a kiss.

A gust of wind, channeled through the lower street, rushed by, tugging at her ragged clothes, pulling her long coattails out like a flag beside her — and then she exploded.

It happened so fast that I could barely understand what was happening, much less anticipate what would come next. Where my apprentice had been standing suddenly became half a dozen identical, leanly ragged figures darting in every direction.

One Molly flew sideways, both arms extended in front of her, firing a pair of 1911 Colts, their hammering *wham-wham-wham* as recognizable as familiar music. Another flipped into a cartwheel and tumbled out of sight behind a parked car. Two more ran to each door, virtually mirror images of each other, swiping a card key and slamming into the buildings. A *fifth* Molly ducked behind a mound of snow and emerged with a shotgun, which she began emptying at the turtlenecks. The sixth ran to the motorcycle, picked it up as if it had been a plastic toy, and flung it toward her attackers.

My jaw dropped open. I mean, I had known the kid was good with illusions, but Hell's bells. I might have been able to do *one* of the illusions Molly had just wrought. Once, I had managed two, under all kinds of mortal pressure. She had just thrown out *six. Simultaneously.* And at the drop of a hat, to boot.

My gast was pretty well flabbered.

The turtlenecks clearly didn't know how to react, either. The ones with guns returned fire, and they all scattered for cover. The motorcycle didn't hit anyone as it tumbled past the group, though the crashing sound it made when it landed was so convincing that it made me doubt my such-as-they-were senses. The guns barked several times as the illusionary Mollys all sought cover behind the snow mounds and cars.

I gritted my teeth. "You aren't one of the rubes, Dresden. You've got a backstage pass." I bent my head, touched my fingers to my forehead for a moment, and opened up my own Sight.

The scene changed colors wildly, going from a dull winter monochrome to an abstract done in smearing, interweaving watercolor. The blurs of magic in the air were responsible for all the tinting — Molly had unleashed a hell of a lot of energy in very little time, and she'd done so from the point of exhaustion. I'd been there enough times to know the look.

Now I could see the illusions for what they were — which was the single largest reason why the wizards of the White Council didn't put much stock in illusion magic: It could be easily nullified by anyone with the Sight, which was the same thing as saying "anyone on the Council."

But against this band of hipster, emo, mooklosers? It worked just fine.

Molly, behind an almost perfect magical veil, was standing precisely where she had been at the beginning of the altercation. She hadn't moved a muscle. Her hands were extended at her sides, fingers twitching, and her face was still and expressionless, her eyes shifted out of focus. She was running a puppet show, and the illusions were her marionettes, dancing on strings of thought and will.

The illusionary versions of Molly were very slightly transparent and grainy, like I remembered movies being when I was a kid. The motorcycle had never moved from where it was parked — an illusion had flown through the air, and a short-term veil was now hiding the bike.

The turtlenecks, though, weren't going to be shut down by half a dozen young women, even if they had just appeared out of nowhere and apparently were possessed of weapons and superhuman strength. At barked orders from their leader, they came bounding over parked cars and mounds of snow in teams of five, moving with the light, lithe grace rarely seen outside of the Olympics and martial arts movies. They advanced with the kind of frighteningly focused purpose you see only in veterans. These men knew how to survive a battle: Kill before you are killed.

If even one of them closed in on Molly, it was over.

I thought of what it might be like to watch my apprentice die with my Sight open, and almost started gibbering. If that happened, if I saw that horror with eyes that would make sure I could never, ever forget it or distance myself from it, there wouldn't be anything left of me. Except guilt. And rage.

I shut away my Sight.

"It must be difficult," said my godmother, standing suddenly beside me, "to watch something like this without being able to affect the outcome."

"Glah!" I said, or something close to it, jumping a few inches to one side out of sheer nerves. "Stars and stones, Lea," I said between my gritted teeth a moment later. "You can see me?"

"But of course, Sir Knight," she replied, green eyes sparkling. "My duty to oversee my godson's spiritual growth and development would be entirely futile could I not perceive and speak to a spirit such as thee."

"You knew I was there a moment ago. Didn't you?"

Her laugh was a bright, wicked sound. "Your grasp of the obvious remains substantial — even though you do not."

A curtain of green-blue fire about seven feet high sprang up and swept rapidly across the width of the parking lot, between the position of the various Mollys and the turtlenecks. The flames emitted eerie shrieking sounds, and the faces of hideous beings danced about inside them.

I just blinked. Holy crap.

I hadn't taught the kid *that*.

"Tsk," Lea said, watching the scene. "She has an able mind, but she is filled with the passions of youth. She rushes to her finale without building anything like the tension required for something so . . . overt . . . to prove effective."

I wasn't sure what my godmother was talking about, but I didn't have time to try to pry an explanation out of her. . . .

Except that I did.

I mean, what else was I going to do, right?

"Whatever do you mean?" I replied in a polite tone. I almost managed not to grit my teeth.

"Such an" — her mouth twisted in distaste

— "overt and vulgar display as that wall of fire is worthy only of frightening children or appearing in something produced by Hollywood. It might yield a short-lived panic reaction, if built up and timed properly, but it is otherwise useless. And, of course, in very bad taste." She shook her head in disapproval. "True terror is much more subtle."

I gave my godmother a sharp look. "What?"

"Veils are of limited utility with snow upon the ground," she explained. "The footprints, you see. It's quite difficult to hide so many individual disruptions of the environment. Thus, she must work in another medium to survive."

"Stop this. You're going to get her killed," I said.

"Oh, child," the Leanansidhe said, smiling. "I've been doing this for a very long time. All teaching involves an element of risk."

"Yeah," I said, "and look at what happened to your last student."

Her eyes glinted. "Yes. From nothing more than a terrified child, in a mere score of years he grew into a weapon that all but utterly destroyed a world power. The Red Court lies in ruins because of my student. And it was, in part, my hand that shaped him."

I clenched my teeth harder. "And you want to do the same thing to Molly."

"Potentially. She has a talent for verisimilomancy —"

"Versa what?"

"Illusion, child," Lea clarified. "She has a talent, but I despair of her ever truly understanding what it is to cause terror."

"That's what she's learning from you? Fear?"

"In essence."

"You aren't teaching her, Godmother. Teachers don't do that."

"What is teaching but the art of planting and nurturing power?" Lea replied. "Mortals prattle on about lonely impulses of delight and the gift of knowledge, and think that teaching is a trade like metalsmithing or healing or telling lies on television. It is not. It is the dissemination of power unto a new generation and nothing less. For her, as for you, lessons demand real risk in order to attain their true rewards."

"I won't let you turn her into a weapon, Godmother."

Lea arched a red-gold eyebrow, showing her teeth again. "You should have thought of that before dying, child. What, precisely, will you do to stop me?"

I closed my hands into impotent fists.

The turtlenecks had been briefly stymied, but not stopped, by the wall of flame. It wasn't high enough. I saw three of them moving together. Two of them linked their hands while a third backed off, then sprinted toward the other two. The runner planted his foot on the linked hands of his supporters, and then both men lifted while the runner leapt. They flung him a good twenty feet up and over the wall of flame.

The runner flipped neatly at the top of his arc and landed in a crouch, holding a machete in his right hand, a pistol in his left. He calmly put two rounds directly into the shotgun-wielding Molly, and two more into the pistol-packing version. Before the last shot rang out, a second turtleneck had gone over the wall and landed beside the first — the leader, I noted. He carried no obvious weaponry, though his belt had been hung with several seashells in a manner that suggested they were dangerous equipment. He remained in a crouch when he landed, looking around with sharp, steady eyes, while his partner covered him.

Shotgun Molly crumpled slowly to the ground, still fumbling at a pocket for more shells for the weapon, while scarlet blood stained the fresh layer of thin snow. Two-Gun Molly's head snapped back as a dark hole appeared in her forehead, and her body dropped to the snow like a rag doll. Motorcycle-Chucking Molly screamed and snatched up her fallen sister's guns.

The turtleneck on lookout raised his weapon, but Captain Turtleneck moved his hand in a sharp, negative gesture, and the man lowered the weapon again. Both did nothing as the newly armed Molly aimed the guns and began to fire. Puffs of snow flitted up from the ground a couple of times, but neither was hit.

Captain Turtleneck nodded to himself and smiled.

Crap. He'd figured it out. Coordinated squads of bad guys are one thing. Coordinated squads of bad guys being led by someone who remained observant and cool in the middle of combat chaos were far, far worse.

"Ah, disbelief," Lea murmured. "Once the mark begins to suspect illusion is at work, there's little point in continuing."

"Stop them," I said, to Lea. "Godmother, please. Stop this."

She turned to blink at me. "And why should I?"

Captain Turtleneck scanned the ground, and I saw his eyes trace the line of footsteps Molly had made when she had backed into the center of parking lot, when the confrontation had begun. His eyes flicked around and I could practically see the thoughts going through his head. A trail of messy, backward tracks suddenly ended in two clear boot prints. The only Molly in sight had proven to be an illusion — and therefore the real Molly must be nearby, supporting the still-active illusions around him. Where would she be standing?

That last set of boot prints seemed a logical

place to look.

Captain Turtleneck drew one of the sea-shells from his belt, murmured something to it, and gave it an expert, effortless flick. It sailed through the air and landed only inches from my invisible apprentice's toes.

"Oh," Lea said, setting her mouth into a pouting moue. "Pity. She had such potential."

I gave my godmother my most furious glare and sprinted forward.

The shell began to glow with a urine-colored light.

It had worked for Morty. Maybe it would work again.

I flung myself at Molly, focusing on protecting her, and I felt myself slide into her, merging and mingling from the soles of my feet to the crown of my head. (Which hardly made sense, given how much taller I was than she — one more example of the way physics doesn't necessarily apply to spirits.)

I suddenly felt utterly exhausted, frightened, and at the same time in a state of euphoric exultation. I could feel the various illusions dancing upon threads of my will, demanding complete focus and concentration. My legs and feet ached. My ribs ached. My face and shoulder hurt.

And then I felt myself choke, then wonder what the hell was happening to me.

It's me, kid, I thought, as loudly as I could. *Don't fight me.*

I didn't know what the seashell would do, but there wasn't much time to get particular. I extended my left hand along with my will, and murmured, *"Defendarius."*

Blue energy suddenly blazed up around Molly and me in a sparkling sphere.

The seashell shone brighter and exploded into a sphere of pure white fire, as hot and fierce as a microscopic nuclear warhead. It lashed against the blue sphere like a bat hitting a baseball. The sphere went flying, taking us with it. I braced my arms and legs against the sides of the sphere, straining to hold it together. Without my shield bracelet, I wasn't sure how long I could keep it up.

The sphere struck a car and bounded off it into the wall of the building. Its path had us careening tail over teakettle, but our braced arms and legs kept us from smashing our head against the sphere's interior. We wobbled and rolled into a corner of the lot, and I realized dully as I looked around that Molly's illusions had vanished. My bad. The strength of the shield had cut her off from them and ended her ability to keep them going.

I looked up to find the turtlenecks advancing on us in a crowd, and I dismissed the sphere, landing in a crouch. I gathered more of my will together and swept my arm from left to right with a murmured word, and a second curtain of blue fire sprang up between me and the oncoming bad guys.

One of them gave the wall of flame a disdainful snort and calmly walked into it.

Like I said, I'm not much when it comes to illusions.

I am, however, reasonably good with fire.

The turtleneck didn't scream. He didn't have time. When fire is hot enough, you never really feel the heat. Your nerves get fried away and all you feel is the lack of signal from them — you feel cold.

He died in the fire, and he died cold. The cinder that fell backward out of the fire could never have been casually identified as human.

Now, *that* got their attention.

I stood there holding the fire against the remaining turtlenecks, the heat scorching away the thin layer of snow on the asphalt, then making it bubble and quiver, changing it into my own personal moat of boiling-hot tar. It was hard work to keep it going, but I've never been afraid of that.

Harry, I need some room, came a thought from Molly, hardly able to be heard over the blaze of concentration necessary for maintaining the fire.

I gritted my teeth. It was like trying to hold an immensely heavy door open while half a dozen friends squeezed in around me. I felt an odd sensation and increased weariness and blocked them both away. I needed to focus, to hold the turtlenecks away from Molly.

Once again, the bad guys impressed me. They knew that an intense magical effort could be sustained for only a limited amount of time. They didn't risk losing more men to the fire. Instead, they played it smart.

They just waited.

The fire blazed for another minute, then two, and as my control over it began to get shaky, something attracted my attention.

Flashing blue lights, out on the lower avenue.

A CPD prowler had stopped across the entrance to the parking lot, and a pair of cops, guys I'd seen before, got out and walked quickly into the lot, flashlights up. It took them about half a second to see that something odd was going on, and then they had both guns *and* flashlights up.

Before the turtlenecks could turn their guns on the police, the officers had retreated to the cover offered by their car, out of direct line of sight from the parking lot. I could clearly hear one of them calling for backup, SWAT, and firefighters, his voice tense and tight with fear.

I felt myself giggling with exhaustion and amusement as I grinned at Captain Turtleneck. "Bad boys, bad boys," I sang, off-key. "Whatcha gonna do?"

That made Molly cough up a chittering belly laugh, which shouldered my awareness aside and came bubbling out of our mouth.

Captain Turtleneck stared at me without expression for a moment. He looked at the fire, the moat, and then at the police. Then he grimaced and made a single gesture. The turtlenecks began to move as a single body, retreating rapidly back the way they had come.

Once I was sure they were gone, I dropped the wall and slumped to the ground. I sat there for a second, dazzled by the discomfort and the weariness, which I had rapidly grown accustomed to missing, apparently. The smell of hot asphalt, a strangely summertime smell, mingled with the scent of charred turtleneck.

I shivered. Then I made a gentle effort and withdrew from the same space Molly occupied. The weariness and pain vanished again. So did the vibrant scents.

The grasshopper looked up and around, sensing the change. Then she said, "Hold on, Harry," and fumbled at her pockets. She produced a small silver tuning fork, struck it once against the ground, and then said, "I can hear you with this."

"You can?"

"Yeah, no big deal," she said, her voice slurred with fatigue. "See you, too, if I line it up right. And it's easier to carry around than a bunch of enchanted Vaseline."

"We've got to get out of here," I said. "Before the cops show up. They'd try to lock you up for a long time."

Molly shook her head.

"Kid, I know you're tired. But we have to move."

"No," she said. "No cops."

I arched an eyebrow at her. "What?"

"Never were any cops," Molly said.

I blinked, looked at the empty entrance to the parking lot, and then found myself slowly smiling. "They were another illusion. And you sold it to the turtlenecks because they thought you'd already blown your wad on the flashy stuff."

"Excellent," purred Lea, appearing at my side again.

I flinched. Again. Man, I hate that sudden-appearance stuff.

"An unorthodox but effective improvisation, Miss Carpenter," she continued. "Adding complexity on the meta level of the deception was inspired — especially against well-informed adversaries."

"Uh-huh, I'm a rock star," Molly said, her voice listless. "Lesson over?"

The Leanansidhe glanced at me and then back to Molly, still smiling. "Indeed. Both of them."

CHAPTER TWENTY-THREE

Which only goes to prove that you're never too old, too jaded, too wise — or too *dead* — to be hoodwinked by one of the fae.

"You set her up," I snarled, "for *my* benefit? As a lesson for *me?*"

"Child," Lea said, "of course not. It was entwined with her own lesson as well."

Molly smiled very slightly. "Oh yes. I feel I have grown tremendously from my experience of nearly being incinerated."

"You saw that your survival depended on the protection of another," my godmother responded, her voice sharp. "Without help from my godson's spirit, you would have died."

"There are a lot of people who can say something like that," Molly said. "There's no shame in being one of them."

Lea looked from Molly to me and then said, "Children. So emotional — and so rarely grateful. I will leave you to consider the value of what I have this evening shown unto you both."

"Hold it," I said. "You aren't going yet."

Lea looked at me with a flat expression. "Oh?"

"No. You're giving Molly money first."

"Why would I do such a thing?"

"Because she's hungry, she's tired, she survived your lesson, and she needs to eat."

Lea shrugged a shoulder. "What is that to me?"

I scowled. "If you're her mentor, your support of her physical needs while she learns is implicit in the relationship. And since you're filling in for me anyway, and since my choice right now would be to get food into her, if you don't do it, you'll be failing in your duty."

The Leanansidhe rolled her eyes and murmured, with a trace of amusement, "*Now* is when you choose to begin paying attention to proper protocol, child?"

"Apparently," I said. "Stop being cheap. Cough up the dough."

Her green eyes narrowed dangerously. "I do not care for your tone, child."

"I'm through being intimidated by you," I replied, and to my surprise, it came out in a calm and reasonable tone, rather than a defiant one. "You're the one with an obligation. I'm not being unreasonable. Pay up."

The Leanansidhe turned to face me fully, those feline eyes all but glowing with either anger or pleasure. Or maybe both.

■ ■ ■ ■

Molly ordered the Moons Over My Hammy. And hot chocolate.

I sat across the table from her at Denny's, my elbow on its surface, my chin resting on the heel of my hand. The table could support my elbow because I had decided it should. Her tuning fork sat upright on the table, humming slightly, directly between us. She'd said she could see me if I didn't move too far to the left or right.

Molly tore into the food with a voracious appetite.

"Weren't you the one always trying to get me to eat healthier?" I mused.

"Bite me," she mumbled through a mouthful of food. "Freaking ice age out there. Gotta have fats, proteins, carbs, just to get my furnace going, keep my body temperature up."

"You know what else would keep it up?" I asked her. "Being indoors."

She snorted and ignored me for several minutes, venting a ravenous appetite onto the food. I watched her and found it oddly fulfilling. I'd been looking out for the grasshopper for a while. It made me feel good to see her hunger being satisfied because of something I had done.

I guess ghosts have to take pleasure in the

little victories — just like everyone else.

I waited until she was cleaning up the remains to ask, "So. What's with the Ophelia act in front of Murphy and company?"

She froze for a second, then continued moving bits and pieces around her plate with somewhat less enthusiasm. "It isn't . . ." She exhaled slowly, and her eyes moved around the room restlessly. "There's more than one reason."

"I'm listening," I said.

"Well. Who says it's an act?" She flipped a couple of bits of hash brown onto her fork and then into her mouth. "Look at me. I'm sitting here talking to my dead mentor. And half the restaurant is worried about it."

I looked around. She was getting covert stares, all right. "Yeah, but there's hardly anyone here."

She laughed a bit harshly. "That makes me feel better." She put her cup of hot chocolate to her lips and just held it there, trails of steam curling up around her blue eyes. "So. You've finally been inside me. I feel like I should be offering you a cigarette."

I choked and had to clear my throat. "Um. It wasn't like that, kid."

"Of course it wasn't," she said, an edge in her voice. "It never was. Not for you."

I rubbed at the back of my neck. "Molly. When I met you . . ."

"I was a child who didn't need a bra," she said.

"It's about your father, too," I said. "Michael —"

"Is the uncle you never had," she said, her voice still calm but crisp. "You've always wanted his approval. Because he's a good man, and if he approves of you, you can't be a total wreck."

I scowled at her. "I've never said that," I said.

She looked at me through wisps of steam and said, "But it's true all the same. I had that worked out by the time I was about seventeen. You were afraid that if you touched me, you'd be losing his approval. That it would make you some kind of monster."

"I was afraid that I'd be losing *my* approval of me," I responded. "And not a monster, Molly. Just an asshole."

"When I was a child," she said, still speaking very quietly, "you'd have been right. I'm in my mid-twenties, Harry. I'm not a child."

"Don't remind —" I paused. Then I said, "I was going to make an old-age joke." I looked down at my immaterial self. "But all things considered . . ."

She let out enough of a snort to stir the steam. She took a slow drink of hot chocolate. "Little inappropriate. Even if you were still alive."

"But funnier," I said.

"You're not the one who is going to watch her entire family grow old and die, Harry." She said it without malice. "Not just my parents. My brothers and sisters. All of them. I'm going to be beginning to get respect from other wizards about the same time Hope and Little Harry are dying of old age."

"Maybe you'll get lucky and someone will kill you first."

She shrugged. "Lea's been doing what she could about that. If it happens, it happens. As long as there's a reason for it, that kind of death wouldn't bother me."

I shivered, just from the emotionless tone of her voice. "Except for the dead part?"

"Everyone dies, Harry," she said. "There's no use whining about it."

I waited for a couple of beats and then said, "Here's where you talk about how what you do with your life is what's truly important."

Her head fell back and she let out a belly laugh. It sounded warm and natural. Her eyes were just too wide, though, her smile too strained.

"Yeah. Exactly." She shook her head and looked at me intently. "Is that what it's always like for you? Throwing fire that way?"

I blinked and tried to change mental gears. I didn't do it as smoothly as she had. Someone uncharitable or unbiased might note that it could be because Molly had stripped said gears. "Um. Oh, back at the fight with the

Fomor guys?"

"They weren't the Fomor," Molly corrected me. "They were humans the Fomor have altered. They're called —"

"Turtlenecks," I said.

She arched an eyebrow. "You and Murphy both. No, they're known as servitors. The Fomor muck around with them. Install things. Gills, extra muscles, organs for sonar, night-vision eyes . . ."

I whistled. "All kinds of fun."

She nodded. "The odd bits kind of turn to jelly when they die. Police are calling them transients."

I nodded, and tried to keep the conversation casual. "A lot of them dying around here?"

"It's Chicago," she said. "There's always someone dying around here. And you should see what these . . . these animals do, Harry. They take people right out of their beds. Grab children waiting for the school bus. They've tortured people to death for fun."

As she spoke, the calm in her voice had begun to fracture. It wasn't dramatic. Just a break of her voice, an inhalation between sentences that was a little too harsh.

"You can't stand around doing nothing," I said, nodding.

"No," she said. "They'll come and scream at you in your sleep if you try. So . . ."

"So?"

Molly was silent. I didn't push. Five minutes went by before she closed her eyes and whispered, "It's easy. It shouldn't be so easy."

Technically, I didn't have a heart anymore. It couldn't twist. It couldn't break.

It did anyway.

"The first one was paying off a cop. Gold coins. He stood there with a little girl in a gym bag and paid the cop to look the other way." She swallowed. "God, if I could be like you. Have so much power to pour out. Like water from a hydrant. But I've just got a squirt gun. Not even a Super Soaker. Just one of the little ones." She opened her eyes and met mine. "But it was enough. They didn't even know I was there."

"Molly," I said gently, "what did you do?"

"An illusion. A simple one. I made the bag of gold look like a gun. The cop drew his weapon and shot him. But the servitor lived long enough to break the cop's neck." She held up a pair of fingers. "Twofer. For one little illusion."

I swallowed. I couldn't speak.

Her voice slowly gained volume. "There have been others like that. I mean, God, they make it simple. You just need an opportunity and the right little nudge at the right time. Green traffic light instead of a red one. Put a knife in someone's hand. Or a wedding ring on one finger. Add a spot of blood to someone's collar. They're animals. They tear into one another like animals."

"Molly," I said gently.

"I started leaving the bits of rag on them," she said. "It hurt at first. Being near that kind of . . . experience. It still hurts. But I have to do it. You don't know, Harry. What you did for this town."

"What do you mean?"

"You don't know how many things just *didn't come here* before, because they were afraid."

"Afraid of what?"

She looked at me as if her heart was breaking. "Of *you,* Harry. You could find anything in this town, but you never even noticed the shadow you cast." Her eyes overflowed and she slashed at them angrily with one hand. "Every time you defied someone, every time you came out on top against things you couldn't possibly have beaten, your name grew. And they feared that name. There were other cities to prey on — cities that didn't have the mad wizard Dresden defending them. They *feared* you."

I finally understood. "The Rag Lady."

"Sometimes me," Molly said. "Sometimes it's Lea. She's like a kid on recess when she takes a shift. I'm building a new name. Creating something else for them to fear. I can't do what you did, Harry." Her eyes, red and blue, flashed with something dangerous, deadly, and she slammed the heel of her hand onto the table as she leaned toward me. "But I can do that. I can kill them. I can make the fuckers afraid."

She stared at me, her breathing heavy. It took her several seconds to look slowly around the room.

Every eye in the place was locked on Molly. A waitress stood with wide eyes and a telephone against her ear.

Molly looked around at them for a moment and then said, "God, you people have it good. You don't know. You wouldn't know if one of them walked up to you and tore the thoughts out of your skull."

She rose, grabbed the tuning fork, and left a pile of wadded bills on the table. She pointed at the waitress and said, "Put the phone down. Or you won't get a tip."

The telephone dropped from the woman's fingers and clattered on the floor.

"See?" she said, glancing back in my general direction. "It's what I do. It's what I'm good for."

I sat there, stunned and heartbroken, unable to think of anything to say or do to help Molly.

I watched my mad apprentice stalk out of the silent restaurant and into the frozen night.

CHAPTER TWENTY-FOUR

I walked the shadowy streets, thinking. Or, at least, trying to think.

When I'd been alive, walking was something I did when I needed to chew something over. Engage the body in effort and activity and the purely physical manifestations of a mental problem stop being distractions. I didn't have a body anymore, but I didn't know how else to cope with so many overwhelming troubles.

So I walked, silent and invisible, my head down, and I thought furiously as I went.

A single fact glared out at me, blazing in front of my mind's eye in stark reality illuminated by all the lives that were on fire around me:

In the end, when it had mattered most, I'd blown it.

I grew up an orphan with nothing but a few vague memories of my father before he'd died. My childhood hadn't been the kind of thing I'd wish on anyone. I had run into some bad people. Justin was the worst — a true monster.

When I was sixteen or seventeen, still agonized by his betrayal, and certain that I would never know anything like a home, friends, or family, I made myself a promise: I would never allow a child of mine to grow up as I had — driven from home to home, an easy victim with no protector, never stable, never certain.

Never.

When Susan had asked me to help her recover Maggie, I went all-in without a second thought. The child was my daughter. It didn't matter that I hadn't known about her or that I had never seen her with my own eyes. There was a child of my blood who needed my help and protection. I was her father. I would die to protect her if need be.

End of story.

I may have had good reasons. I may have had the best of intentions.

But intentions aren't enough, no matter how good they are. Intentions can lead you to a place where you're able to make a choice.

It's the choice that counts.

To get my daughter back, I'd crossed a line. Not just crossed it; I'd sprinted at it and taken a flying freaking leap over it. I made a pact with the Queen of Air and Darkness, giving away my free will, my very self, to Mab in exchange for power enough to challenge the Red King and his monstrous Court. That was stupid.

I'd had excuses at the time. My back had been against the wall. Actually, it had been *broken* and against a wall. All the help I'd been able to call upon, all the allies and tricks and techniques in my arsenal, had not been enough. My home had been destroyed. So had my car. I couldn't even get up and walk, much less fight. And the forces arrayed against me had been great — so great that even the White Council of Wizards was terrified of confronting them.

In that bleak hour, I had chosen to sell my soul. And after that, I had led my closest friends and allies out on what I knew was practically a suicide mission. I'd known that such a battle would put a savage strain on Molly's psychic senses, and that even if she did manage to survive, she might never be the same. I'd risked the two irreplaceable Swords of the Cross in my keeping, sending them into the battle even though I knew that if we fell, some of the world's mightiest weapons for good would be captured and lost.

And when I saw that the sacrificial blood rite the Red King had intended to destroy me could be turned back on the Red Court, I had used it without hesitation.

I murdered Susan Rodriguez on a stone altar in Chichén Itzá and wiped out the Red Court. I saved my little girl.

I created a perfect situation for chaos to

engulf the supernatural world. The sudden absence of the Red Court might have removed thousands of monsters from the world, but it meant only that *tens* of thousands of other monsters were suddenly free to rise, to expand into the vacuum I'd created. I shuddered as I wondered how many other men's little girls had been hurt and killed as a result.

And, God help me . . . I would do it again. It wasn't right. It wasn't noble. It wasn't good. I'd spent less than three hours in the company of my daughter — and so help me, if it meant keeping her safe, I would do it again.

Maybe the White Council needed an Eighth Law of Magic: the law of unintended consequences.

How do you measure one life against another? Can thousands of deaths be balanced by a single life? Even if Mab had not had time to fully take possession of me, how could I be sure that the very act of choosing to cross that line had not changed me into something monstrous?

I found myself stopped, standing on the Michigan Avenue bridge over the Chicago River. The mounded snow filled the night with light. Only the waters below me were dark, a black and whispering shadow, the Lethe and the Styx in one.

I looked up at the towers nearby. NBC.

Trump's place. The Sheraton. They stood tall and straight and clean in the night. Lights winked golden in windows.

I turned and stared south of me at the Loop, at the skyline I knew so well. There was a rare moment of stillness down Michigan Avenue. Streetlights. Traffic lights. A scattering of fresh snowflakes, enough to keep everything pretty and white instead of slushy and brown.

God, my town is beautiful.

Chicago. It's insane and violent and corrupt and vital and artistic and noble and cruel and wonderful. It's full of greed and hope and hate and desire and excitement and pain and happiness. The air sings with screams and laughter, with sirens, with angry shouts, with gunshots, with music. It's an impossible city, at war with itself, every horrible and wonderful thing blending together to create something terrifying and lovely and utterly unique.

I had spent my adult life here fighting, bleeding, to protect its people from threats they thought were purely imaginary.

And because of what I'd done, the lines I crossed, the city had gone mad. Fomor and their turtlenecks. Freakish ghost riots. Huddled groups of terrified folks of the supernatural community.

I hadn't meant for that to happen, but that

didn't matter. I was the guy who made the choice.

This was all on me.

I stared down at the quiet blackness of the river. I could go down there, I realized. Running water would disrupt supernatural energy, disperse it, destroy the pattern in which it flowed.

And I was made out of energy now.

The black, whispering river could make everything go away.

Styx. Lethe. Oblivion.

My apprentice was bitter, damaged. My friends were fighting a war, and it was tearing at their souls. The one guy who I was sure could help me out had been snatched, and there wasn't a whole lot I could do about it. Hell's bells, I was doing well just to find someone who could hear me talk.

What could I do?

What do you do to make up for failing everyone in your life? How do you make it right? How do you apologize for hideous things you never intended to happen?

I don't remember when I fell to my knees. Memories, stirred by my rumination, flooded over me, almost as sharp and real as life. Those memories stirred others and brought them along, like pebbles triggering a landslide. My life in Chicago rolled over me, crushed me, all the black pain and bright joy doubling me over, ripping tears out of my eyes.

Later, it was quiet.

It was difficult. A tremendous, slow inertia resisted my desire. But I pushed myself to my feet again.

I turned away from the river.

This city was more than concrete and steel. It was more than hotels and businesses and bars. It was more than pubs and libraries and concerts. It was more than a car and a basement apartment.

It was home.

My home.

Sweet home Chicago.

The people here were my family. They were in danger, and I was part of the reason why. That made things pretty clear.

It didn't matter that I was dead. It didn't matter that I was literally a shadow of my former self. It didn't matter that my murderer was still running around somewhere out there, vague prophecies of Captain Murphy notwithstanding.

My job hadn't changed: When demons and horrors and creatures of the night prey on this city, I'm the guy who does something about it.

"Time to start doing," I whispered.

I closed my hands into fists, straightened my back, and vanished.

CHAPTER TWENTY-FIVE

I was ten minutes late to the meeting with Fitz, but he was still there, lurking at a nearby storefront, looking about as innocent as an only child near a fresh Kool-Aid stain. He had a huge, empty sports-equipment bag hanging over one shoulder. For the love of God. The kid might as well have been wearing a stocking cap and a black mask, with a giant dollar sign printed on the outside of his bag to boot.

I appeared next to him and said, "You look so relaxed and calm. I'll bet any cop that rolls by will ask you for tips on self-control."

Fitz twitched, clearly controlling an instant instinct to flee. Then he spat on the frozen ground and said, "You're late, Harvey."

"Forgot to wind my watch," I said.

"And I was starting to think my brain had thrown a rod after all." Fitz looked up and down the street and shook his head. "But nothing's ever that easy."

"Life can be a bitch that way," I said.

"So, you're real."

"I'm real."

Fitz nodded. "You said you would help. Were you serious about that?"

"Yes," I said.

A gust of wind pulled his longish, curly red hair out to one side. It matched his lopsided smirk. "Fine. Help."

"Okay," I said. "Turn left and start walking."

Fitz put a fist on his hip and said, "You were going to help me with the guns."

"Never said that," I said. "You need help, kid, not tools. Guns aren't gonna cut it." I waited for him to begin to speak before I interrupted him. "Besides. If you don't play along, I've arranged for word to get to Murphy about where you and your band of artful dodgers are crashing."

"Oh," he snarled. "You . . . you son of a bitch."

"Excuse me?" I said.

"You can go fuck yourself."

"You need help. I've got it to give. But there ain't no free lunch, kid," I said in a calm and heartless tone. "You know that."

"You can kiss my ass is what you can do," he said, and turned away.

"Go ahead and walk," I said. "But you're throwing away your only chance to get your crew out from under Baldy."

He stopped in the middle of taking a step.

"If you bug out now, where are you going to go — back to Baldy? He'll kill you for failing to get the guns. And after that, Murphy's crew and the Rag Lady will take out the whole building. Baldy will probably skate out on your buddies, and do the same thing to some other batch of kids."

Fitz turned his head in my general direction, his eyes murderous. But he was listening.

"Look, kid. Doesn't have to be the end of the world. If you work with me, everything's peachy."

I was lying, of course. The last thing I wanted was to hand Murphy a convenient target in her present frame of mind. And I really did want to help the kid — but I've been where he was mentally. He wouldn't have believed in a rescuer on a white horse. In his world, no one just gave anyone anything, except maybe pain. The best you could hope for was an exchange, something for something, and generally you got screwed even then. I needed his cooperation. Handing him a familiar problem was the best way to get it.

"I'm not a monster, Fitz. And honestly, I don't care about you and your goons or what happens to you. But I think you can help me — and I'm willing to help you in return if you do."

The young man grimaced and bowed his

head. "It's not as though I have a lot of choice, is it?"

"We've all got choices," I said calmly. "At the moment, yours are limited. You gonna play ball?"

"Fine," Fitz spat. "Fine. Whatever."

"Groovy," I said. "Hang a left and get going. We've got some ground to cover."

He shoved his hands into his pockets, his eyes sullen, and started walking. "I don't even know who the hell you are."

"My name is Harry Dresden," I said.

Fitz stumbled. "Holy shit," he said. "Like . . . *that* Harry Dresden? The professional wizard?"

"The one and only."

He recovered his pace and shook his head. "I heard you were dead."

"Well, yeah," I said, "but I'm taking it in stride."

"They say you're a lunatic," Fitz said.

"Oh yeah?"

Fitz nodded. "They also . . ." He frowned. I could see the wheels spinning. "They also say you help people."

"So?"

"So which is it?"

"You've got half a clue, Fitz," I said. "You know that talk is cheap. There's only one way to find out."

Fitz tilted his head to one side and then nodded. "Yeah. So. Where we going?"

"To visit an old friend."

We went to a street toward the north end of the South Side. *Seedy* wasn't a fair description for the place, because *seeds* imply eventual regrowth and renewal. Parts of Chicago are wondrous fair, and parts of Chicago look postapocalyptic. *This* block had seen the apocalypse come, grunted, and said, "Meh." There were no glass windows on the block — just solid boards, mostly protected by iron bars, and gaping holes.

Buildings had security fences outside their entrances, literally topped with razor wire. You'd need a blowtorch to get through them. At least one of the fences in my line of sight had been sliced open with a blowtorch. Metal cages covered the streetlights, too — but they were all out anyway. Tough to make a cheap metal cage that stops rounds from a handgun.

Every flat, open space had been covered in spray-painted graffiti, which I guess we're supposed to call *urban art* now. Except art is about creating beauty. These paintings were territorial markers, the visual parallel to peeing on a tree. I've seen some gorgeous "outlaw" art, but that wasn't in play here. The *thump-thud* of a ridiculously overpowered woofer sent a rumbling rhythm all up and down the block, loud enough to make the freshly fallen snow quiver and pack in a little tighter.

There was no one in sight. No one. Granted, it was getting late, but that's still an oddity in Chicago.

I watched as Fitz took in the whole place and came to the same conclusion I had the first time I'd seen it — the obvious squalor, the heavy security, the criminally loud music with no one attempting to stop it.

"This is territory," he said, coming to an abrupt halt. "I'm alone, I'm unarmed, and I'm not going there."

"Vice Lords," I said. "Or they were a few years ago. They're a long-term gang, so I assume they still are."

"Still not going there," said Fitz.

"Come on, Fitz," I said. "They aren't so bad. For a gang. They almost always have a good reason to kill the people they kill. And they keep the peace on this street, if you aren't too far behind on your payments."

"Yeah. They sound swell."

I shrugged, though he couldn't see it. "Police response time for this place is way the hell after everything has already happened. People here are more likely to get help from a gang member than a cop if they're in trouble."

"You're a fan?"

"No," I said. "It shouldn't be like this. The gangs are dangerous criminals. They rule through force and fear. But at least they don't pretend to be anything else."

Fitz grimaced and looked down to stare at his open palms for a moment. Then he said, "Guess I'm not in a place where I can throw stones."

"You couldn't break anything if you did," I said. "You're of no use to me dead, kid. We're not going down the block. First place on the right. If you don't walk past there, you won't be crossing any lines."

Fitz frowned. "The place with the metal shutters?"

"Yeah. You remember what I told you to say?"

"Yeah, yeah, I remember the script," Fitz said, scowling. "Can we get this over with?"

"I'm not the one who can knock on the door."

He scowled more deeply and started walking.

The building he went to was part of a larger building that had once held four small businesses. One had been a clinic, one a lawyer, and one a small grocery. They were gutted and empty now. Only the fourth one remained. The metal shutter over the doorway held the only thing that looked like actual art: a nearly life-sized portrait of a rather dumpy angel, the hem of his robe dirty and frayed, his messy hair doing nothing to conceal his oncoming baldness. He held a doughnut in one hand and had a sawed-off shotgun pointing straight toward the viewer in the other.

"Heh," I said. "That's new."

Fitz regarded the painting warily. "What is this place again?"

"A detective agency," I said. "Ragged Angel Investigations."

"Looks kinda closed," Fitz said.

"Nick can't afford an apartment," I said. "He sleeps here. He drinks sometimes. You might have to be loud."

Fitz eyed the block and then the door. "Yeah. Great." He rapped on the metal shutter. Nothing happened. He repeated it, knocking slightly louder and longer. Still nothing.

"Ticktock, kid."

He glowered in my direction. Then he started pounding on the shutter in a heavy, steady rhythm.

Maybe five minutes later, there was the click of a speaker, evidently small enough to be concealed virtually in plain sight. "What?" said a cranky, whiskey-roughened voice.

"Um," Fitz said. "Are you Nick Christian?"

"Who wants to know?"

"My name is Fitz," the kid said. He'd pitched his voice slightly higher than usual. It made him sound a hell of a lot younger. "Harry Dresden said that if I was ever in trouble, I could come to you."

There was a long silence. Then Nick's voice said heavily, "Dresden is history."

"That's why I'm here," Fitz said. "I don't have anywhere else to go."

Nick sounded annoyed. "Dammit. He told you to say that, didn't he?"

Fitz looked slightly bemused. "Well. Yes, actually."

"I am getting too old for this crap," he growled. Then there were several loud clicks and a short, heavy screech of metal, and the shutter rolled up.

Nick Christian hadn't changed much since I'd last seen him. He was short, out of shape, well past his fiftieth birthday, and had sharp, quick, dark eyes that seemed to notice everything. His bald spot was larger. So was his stomach. He was dressed in a white undershirt and boxer shorts, and he held an old wooden baseball bat in his right hand. He shivered and glared at Fitz.

"Well, boy. Get in out of the cold. And keep your hands in sight, or I'll brain you."

Fitz held his hands up in plain sight and went in. I followed. There was a threshold at the doorway, but it was flimsy as hell, and felt more like a sheet of Saran Wrap than a wall. The muddling of business and home life in the same space was probably responsible. I pushed through it, following Fitz.

"Right," Nick said. "Close the shutter and the door. Turn all the locks."

Fitz eyed Nick for a moment. Streetwise and cynical, the kid didn't like the idea of

362

locking himself into a strange building with a strange old man.

"It's all right, Fitz," I said. "He might kick your ass out his door if you give him trouble, but he won't do anything to hurt you."

Fitz glowered in my general direction again, but he turned and followed Nick's instructions.

We stood in his one-room office. It looked . . . Hell, it looked almost exactly like mine had, though I'd never compared the two in my head before. Old filing cabinets, a coffee machine, a desk, and a couple of chairs that had been pushed all the way to one wall to make room for a simple folding cot on an aluminum frame. Nick also had a computer and a television set, features my office never had. Nick was no wizard — just an old detective with a set of iron principles and a self-appointed mandate to help people find their lost children.

There were also seven pictures on his wall, every one of them an eight-by-ten school photo of a child between the ages of six and thirteen. The first few were faded, the hair and clothing styles in them clearly aged.

Nick went around to the back of his desk, sat down, pulled a bottle of rye from the top drawer, and slugged back a swallow. He capped it, put it back, and eyed Fitz warily. "I don't get involved in Dresden's line of work," he said. "I know my limits."

"The magic stuff," Fitz said.

Nick shuddered and glanced at his top drawer. "Yeah. That. So if you came here for that, you're out of luck."

"No," Fitz said. "It's about gangs. Dresden said you knew them."

Nick shrugged one shoulder. "Some."

"A man I know was abducted," Fitz said. "There's a description of the guy we think did it." Fitz dished out what I remembered about the thug who had broken into Morty's house.

Nick listened to it all without saying a word. Then he nodded once. Then he asked, "Who is this man to you?"

"No idea," Fitz said. "You're the expert."

"Not the kidnapper." Nick sighed. "The victim."

Fitz hardly hesitated. "My uncle."

Nick mused over that. Then he said, "I am too old to get up in the middle of the night and get conned. Get out."

"Wait," Fitz said, holding out a hand. "Wait, please."

Nick opened the top drawer again, but this time he came out with an old 1911. He didn't point it at Fitz. "Good try, kid. But I've been in this town a while. Walk back to the door and let yourself out."

"Dammit," I muttered. "Fitz, listen to me. Tell him this, word for word."

Fitz listened, nodded, and then said, "I

364

can't tell you everything for a reason, Mr. Christian. Dresden said you and he had an understanding. That you wanted nothing to do with his side of the street."

"I don't," he said. "Get out."

I fed Fitz his next line.

"He also said that you owed him a favor."

Nick narrowed his eyes to slits. "What favor?"

Fitz listened to me, then said, "All the money and fame the Astor case brought you."

Nick arched an eyebrow. "All the . . ." He looked away and shook his head. He couldn't keep the smile off his mouth, until he finally snorted. When he spoke, there was laughter under his words. "That sounds like Harry."

The Astor case had been about a little girl lost. Her parents cared more about the fame of having an abducted daughter than they did about her, and when she ran off one day, they hired the child-recovery specialist Nick Christian and his apprentice, Harry Dresden, to find her. We did. She hadn't been kidnapped, but the Astors had reported her so, and, in the absence of an actual perpetrator, fingered Nick and me. It had been a trick and a half to get her safely back into her parents' custody without going to jail. There was a lawsuit afterward. The judge threw it out. But, all in all, finding that little girl had cost Nick about two thousand bucks.

Nick hadn't wanted to take the case. I had

talked him into it. He had wanted to cut and run the moment I confirmed the kid was at liberty. I had talked him into seeing it through, being sure she was safe. When I'd completed my apprenticeship, Nick's graduation present had been to forgive me the two grand I owed him.

"You were tight with him?" Nick asked.

"He was sort of my adviser," Fitz said. "Sometimes it's almost like he's right there next to me, still."

Nick grunted. "Investigation apprentice or the other kind?"

Fitz put on a sober face. "I'm not at liberty to say."

"Hngh," Nick said, nodding. "Heard he'd picked up an apprentice. You're holding back to keep me distanced from the situation."

"Yes."

"And you just want the information? You don't want me to work the field on it?"

"That's right."

"Awwww," Nick said. He scratched at his ear and said, "Yeah. I guess. What else can you tell me about this guy?"

I fed Fitz his lines. "He was crazy."

Nick snorted. "Whole hell of a lot of gangers are crazy, kid. Or the next best thing."

"Less money-drugs-sex-violence crazy," Fitz said. "More creepy-cult crazy."

"Hngh," Nick said. Lines appeared on his brow. "There's one, where they all wear the hoodies with the hoods up all the time. Got rolling maybe three or four years back. They don't call themselves anything, but the gangs call them the Big Hoods. No one knows much about them."

"Perfect," I said to Fitz. "Sounds like the assholes we're looking for. Ask him where they're set up."

"A tunnel under the Eisenhower Expressway, on the south end of the Meatpacking District. The other gangs think they're crazy to be where the cops move so freely, but the Big Hoods never seem to attract any police attention." He scrunched up his eyes. "Don't think they even claim any territory. That's all I got."

"Because they aren't a gang, per se," I said. "Excellent, Fitz. Let's move."

"Thank you," Fitz said to Nick.

"Thank Dresden. Wouldn't have said that much to anyone else."

"I'll do that." Fitz stared intently at Nick for a moment and then said, "What do you do here?"

"As a private cop?" Nick asked. "Take some cruddy work to keep the lights on — divorces and so on. But mostly I look for lost kids."

"Doing it a while?" Fitz asked.

"Thirty years."

"Find any?"

"Plenty."

"Find any in one piece?"

367

Nick stared hard at Fitz for a long time. Then he pointed a finger up and behind him, to the row of portraits on the wall.

"Seven?" Fitz asked.

"Seven," Nick said.

"In thirty *years?* You live like this and . . . *Seven? That's it? That's all?*"

Nick leaned back in his chair and gave Fitz a small smile. "That's enough."

Outside, Fitz said, to me, "He's crazy."

"Yeah," I said. "And he helps people."

Fitz frowned and moved hurriedly back out of the Vice Lords' domain. He was silent for several blocks, seemingly content to walk beside me and think. Eventually, he looked up and asked, "You still there?"

"Yeah."

"All right. I helped you. Pay up."

"Okay," I said. "Take a right at the next corner."

"Why?"

"So I can introduce you to someone who will help."

Fitz made a rude sound. "You really love not telling people things, don't you?"

"I don't love it, so much as I'm just really good at it."

Fitz snorted. "Does this guy drink, too?"

"Nah. Sober as a priest."

"Fine," Fitz sighed, and kept trudging.

CHAPTER TWENTY-SIX

"You've got to be kidding me," said Fitz.

We were standing outside Saint Mary of the Angels. Calling the place a church is like calling Lake Michigan a swimming hole. It's huge, literally taking up an entire city block, and an architectural landmark of Chicago. Gorgeously built, a true piece of gothic art, both inside and out, St. Mary's had often served as a refuge for people with the kind of trouble Fitz was facing.

The kid was not in good shape. We'd done a considerable bit of hiking that evening, and despite what might have been the beginnings of a thaw, it was still below freezing, and the slight lack of bitter cold in the wind wasn't stopping it from cutting through Fitz's layers of mismatched clothing and his old jacket. Those lean, gangly kids have the worst of it when winter sets in. They lose their body heat fast. He'd been making up for it in exercise, but he was getting tired, and I remembered that he probably hadn't eaten since I'd seen him before the previous day's sunrise.

He stood clutching his arms around his body, shivering and trying to look like nothing was wrong. His teeth were chattering.

"I know a guy here," I said. "Go around to the back door and knock until someone answers. Ask for Father Forthill."

Fitz looked skeptical. "What's he gonna do for me?"

"Give you a blanket and some hot food, for starters," I said. "Look, kid, I'm giving you my A game here. Forthill's a decent guy. This is what he does."

Fitz clenched his jaws. "This isn't getting me the guns back. I can't go back without them. If I can't go back, I can't get my crew out."

"Go inside," I told him. "Talk to Forthill. Get some food in you. If you decide you want to go back and try to sneak the guns out of that drift on your own, you'll have plenty of time before dawn."

Fitz set his jaw stubbornly.

"Your choice, man," I said. "But going hungry in cold like this is hard on the body. You had, what — seven weapons? Most of them submachine guns? Comes out to maybe forty pounds. Call it fifty if you bring back all the clips and ammo. Think you can burrow into a half-frozen snowbank, get all those guns out, load them up, and walk for most of an hour in the coldest part of the night? On an empty stomach? Without a cop spotting you and wondering what a guy your age is doing on the dark streets so late, carrying a really heavy bag?"

He grunted.

"At least have a damned sandwich."

Fitz's stomach gurgled audibly, and he sighed. "Yeah. Okay."

It took Fitz five minutes to get anyone to answer the door, and when it finally opened, a dour, sour-looking elderly man in a heavy brown bathrobe vaguely reminiscent of a monk's habit opened the door. His name was Father Paolo, and he took himself very seriously.

Fitz told him that he needed to see Father Forthill, that it was a matter of life and death. Only after several minutes of emphasizing his original statement did Father Paolo sigh and invite Fitz in.

"Stay there," Paolo said, pointing a stern finger at Fitz.

Fitz pointed at the ground, questioningly, and then nodded. "Got it." Then he deliberately took a small shuffle-step to one side as the priest began to turn away, drawing a scowl worthy of at least a cardinal.

I probably shouldn't have undermined Paolo's authority by chuckling like that, but come on. That's comedy.

Forthill came down the hall from his chambers a few moments later, dressed in flannel pajamas and a heavy, black terry-cloth robe. He had thick, fuzzy house shoes on his feet, and his fringe of hair was standing up every which way. His bright blue eyes were a little watery and squinty without the aid of his glasses. He blinked at Fitz for a moment and then said, "Can I help you, my son?"

"Harry Dresden said you could," Fitz said.

Forthill raised his eyebrows. "Ah. Perhaps you should come with me."

Fitz looked around and then nodded. "I guess."

Forthill beckoned and led Fitz back down some hallways to the neat, modest chamber where he slept and lived. It was maybe ten feet square and contained a bed, a desk, a chair, and a couple of lamps. Forthill let Fitz in, then closed the door behind the young man. "Please have a seat, my son."

Fitz looked around for a moment, then sat down on the chair. Forthill nodded and sat on the edge of his bed. "First things first," he said, his eyes twinkling. "Should I give you a good set-up line for you to make a pithy comment about Catholic priests and sexual abuse of young men, or would you prefer to find your own opening during the conversation?"

Fitz blinked a couple of times and said, "What?"

"Such remarks are apparently quite popular. I wouldn't want to deny you the enjoyment."

"Oh, uh. No, that's all right, Father."

Forthill nodded gravely. "As you wish. Shall we talk about your problems now?"

"All right."

"Well, then," the priest said, "perhaps you should start by telling me when Dresden told you to come to me for help."

"Uh . . ." Fitz said. He glanced around, as if looking for me.

"Go ahead," I told him. "Just tell him the truth. It's all right."

Fitz took a deep breath and said, "About thirty minutes ago, Father."

Forthill's eyebrows tried to turn themselves into a toupee. "Oh?"

"Yeah," Fitz said, his eyes restless. "I, uh. I hear dead people."

"That must be disconcerting."

"I'm not crazy," Fitz said quickly.

"I never thought you were, my son," Forthill said.

Fitz gave him a suspicious scowl. "You believe me?"

The old man gave him an imp's grin. "I'm well aware of the supernatural facets of our city — and that the streets have been particularly dangerous for the past six months or so."

"That's . . . putting it sort of lightly, Father," Fitz said.

He nodded. "I'm sure your experience has not been a gentle one," he said. "I won't add to it with my own disbelief."

Fitz bit his lower lip for a moment. "Okay."

"I am also aware," Forthill continued, "that Dresden's shade is apparently taking a hand in things. I assume that's who you've spoken to?"

"Yeah."

Forthill nodded and looked around the room. "He's . . . he's here with you, isn't he?"

"Wow," I said. "Points for Forthill."

"Yeah," Fitz sighed. "He . . . kinda doesn't shut up."

Forthill chuckled. "He is — he was — a very determined young man."

"Hasn't changed," Fitz said.

"I see," the priest said. "My son, I am sure you understand that these are perilous times. I am afraid that I must ask for some kind of confirmation that this entity is who he says he is."

Fitz looked at the priest blankly. Then around the room. "You hear that?"

"Yeah," I said. I walked over to the far wall of the room and stuck my head through it. On the other side was a dark space, a hidden storage compartment just large enough to contain a couple of small file cabinets. The concealed compartment had been unknown to anyone but Forthill until I worked a case for an archangel a while back. Michael

Carpenter and I had seen him open the hidden cabinet.

"Come over here," I said. "Knock on the wall, right here. Forthill will know what it means."

"Uh, dude," Fitz said. "I can't see where you are."

I sighed. "Can you hear my voice?"

"Yeah," he said, "but it's just . . . like, this disembodied thing. There's not much direction to it."

Which made sense. He was not actually, physically, hearing me speak. Fitz's gift to sense spirits simply expressed itself as something his mind could interpret — in this case, auditory stimulus.

"Uh, okay," I said. "Walk over to the back wall of the room, the one you were facing when you came through the door."

Fitz said to Forthill, "He's trying to tell me how to prove he isn't full of crap." Then he stood up and walked across the room.

"Okay," I said. "Put your hand out on the wall. Now move to your right. Little more. Little more. Too far. Okay, now about nine inches down, and rap on it with your knuckles."

Fitz did all of that and finally knocked on the wall. Then he turned to Forthill and said, "Mean anything to you?"

The old priest pursed his lips and nodded. "Indeed. Indeed it does."

"Man," Fitz said, shaking his head. "Old people."

Forthill smiled at that. "Well, my son. Are you as cold and hungry as you look?"

Fitz tried to look nonchalant. "I could eat, I guess."

"How long has it been since you've had a hot shower?"

Fitz rolled his eyes and said, "Now, if that isn't a straight line, I don't know what is."

Forthill chuckled and spoke to the air. "Dresden, I'm sure that you're in a hurry and that there is some kind of dire deadline, but I'm not talking business with you until the young man is seen to." He said to Fitz, "That door leads to my bathroom. There's a shower. There's a cardboard box under the sink with several items of clothing in it. I keep them on hand for events such as this. Feel free to take any of them."

Fitz just stared, frowning. "Uh. Okay."

"Get cleaned up," Forthill replied, his tone firm. "I'll go round up something to eat while you do. Do you prefer tea or cocoa?"

"Um," Fitz said. "I guess cocoa."

"Excellent taste," Forthill said. "If you will excuse me." He left the room quietly.

Fitz started looking around the room immediately.

"I doubt there's much to steal," I said. "Forthill isn't really into material things."

"You kidding? Look at this place. Pillows,

blankets." He looked under the bed. "Three pairs of shoes. It's a hell of a lot more than my crew has. Zero rolls in four pairs of socks and some old moccasin house slippers."

"Guy's offering you clothes and food," I said. "You're not seriously going to steal his stuff, are you?"

Fitz shrugged. "You do what you have to do to live, man. I do. Everyone does. Nothing personal." He looked in Forthill's closet, at maybe half a dozen outfits' worth of clothing, and shook his head. "Ah. He'll notice if I try to take any of this stuff." He looked toward the bathroom.

"Go ahead," I said. "You can lock the door behind you. I'm telling you, kid, Forthill is one of the good guys."

"That's make-believe. There ain't no good guys," Fitz said. "Or bad guys. There's just guys."

"You're wrong about that," I said.

"Heard that one before. People who want to use you always say they're the good guys," Fitz said. "You're one of them, right?"

"Heh," I said. "No. I'm an arrogant ass. But I know what a good guy looks like, and Forthill is one of them."

"Whatever, man," Fitz said. "I haven't had a shower in two weeks. If I tell you to buzz off, will you do it? Or do I have to keep hearing you yammer?"

"Sorry, Fitz. You aren't my type."

He snorted, went into the bathroom, and locked the door behind him. I heard the water start up a moment later.

I stood in the priest's empty chamber for a moment, looking around it. Everything there was plain, modest, functional, and cheap. The quilt covering the bed looked like it might have been made for Forthill by his mother when he went to seminary. There was a King James Bible next to the bed. It, too, looked worn and old.

I shook my head. Granted, my life hadn't exactly been featured on an MTV series covering the excesses of the rich and famous, but even I'd had more than Forthill did. How could a man go through life with so little? Nothing of permanence, nothing built up to leave behind him. Nothing to testify to his existence at all.

The kind of man who isn't focused on his own existence, I guess. The kind of man who cares more about others than he does himself — to the point of spending the whole of his life, a life as fleeting and precious as anyone else's, in service to his faith and to humanity. There was no glamour in it, no fame.

Forthill and men like him lived within their communities, where they could never escape reminders of exactly what they had missed out on. Yet he never called attention to himself over it, never sought sympathy or pity. How hard must it be for him to visit the expansive, loving Carpenter family, knowing the whole time that he could have had a family of his own? Did he ever spend time dreaming of what his wife would have been like? His children? He would never know.

I guess that's why they call it sacrifice.

I found Forthill in the church's kitchen, assembling a meal from leftovers. When I'd been the one taking shelter in the church, it had been sandwiches. Fitz was rating a larger meal. Hot soup; a couple of sandwiches, turkey and tuna, respectively; a baked potato; an ear of corn on the cob; and a small salad.

A few seconds after I walked into the kitchen, Forthill paused, aimed a vague smile at the room, and said, "Hello, Harry. Assuming that's you, of course."

"It's me, Father," I replied. I mean, he couldn't hear me and I knew it, but . . . it just seemed sort of rude not to say anything.

"I had a difficult conversation with Karrin this evening," Forthill said. "She told me that you had found the persons who shot at her home last night. And that you want us to help them."

"I know," I sighed. "It sounds insane, but . . ."

"I think that to Karrin, you must have sounded quite insane," he continued. "But I consider your reaction to be remarkable for its compassion. I can only presume that the

379

boy is one of these gang members."

He finished off the food preparations and turned to face me, more or less. "Don't worry. I have no intention of bringing Ms. Murphy into this situation — at least not for the time being. Her judgment has been clouded since your death, and grows more so as the fighting goes on."

I felt myself relax a little. "I hoped you wouldn't."

"I will grant the boy sanctuary here for now. I'll talk with him. I'm sure he will tell me the particulars of his situation. After that, I will have to act in accordance with my conscience."

"Can't ask a man for more than that, Father," I said. "Thank you."

He picked up the simple wooden tray laden with Fitz's meal and stood there for a moment. "It's a shame we can't converse. I would love to hear about your experience. I should think it would be fascinating, a chronicle of one of the most enigmatic functions of Creation — Death itself."

"Nah," I said. "The mystery doesn't stop even after you get to the other side. There's just a lot more paperwork."

"Also, I find it interesting that you are here on holy ground," Forthill said. "If I remember correctly, the last ghost who attempted to enter this church couldn't even touch the building, much less wander freely around it.

What does it mean?" He shook his head, bemused. "I suppose you'd be the one to ask, eh?" He tipped his head in a polite, if badly aimed, nod, and left the room.

It was an excellent question, the thing about ghosts and holy ground. When Leonid Kravos, aka the Nightmare, had come to kill one of my clients I'd stashed at the church, he hadn't been able to get in. He'd torn up several thousand dollars' worth of landscaping and flower beds in sheer frustration.

The Nightmare had been a more powerful shade than I was at the moment. So why could I make myself at home, when he'd been stopped as cold as the Big Bad Wolf at the third Little Pig's house?

"Note to self," I said. "Look into apparent mystic anomaly later. Help your friends now."

I sometimes give myself excellent advice. Occasionally, I even listen to it.

It was time to pay a visit to the Grey Ghost and the Big Hoods.

CHAPTER TWENTY-SEVEN

I headed for the Big Hoods' hideout with several important facts in mind.

Fact one: The Big Hoods themselves could not do me harm.

Fact two: There wasn't diddly I could do to the Big Hoods.

Fact three: The Big Hoods were apparently led by this Grey Ghost, a spirit that had been tossing lightning around with impunity during the attack on Morty's house. That meant that the Grey Ghost was the shade of someone with at least a sorcerer's level of talent, and while I felt sure I could defend myself against such an assault if I was ready for it, if I got blindsided, I might end up like Sir Stuart quicker than you could say *ka-zot.*

Fact four: The Grey Ghost had a bunch of lemurs hanging around. While my own spectral evocations might not be able to affect the living, they would sure as hell work on lemurs and the like. I could handle them easily one-on-one, but it seemed likely that they would come at me in waves, or maybe try to wear me down by throwing a horde of wraiths at me first.

Fact five: If the Grey Ghost was giving the orders to mortal cultists, they might have taken measures of their own to deal with ghosts. There might be circle traps prepared. There might be wards or other magical barriers. There might be dangerous substances like ghost dust. If I went in all fat and happy and confident, I could wander right into serious trouble.

Fact six: There were all kinds of spiritual beings in the wide universe, and ghosts were only a tiny cross section of them. I had to be ready for anything. Another entity of some sort might well wander in, drawn by the conflict. Or, hell, for all I knew, one might already be taking a hand.

"No closed minds, Dresden," I ordered myself. "Don't get suckered into thinking this is one limited, small-scale problem. There's every chance it might be part of a much, much larger problem."

If my afterlife went anything like my life had, that seemed a safe bet.

Fact seven: Sooner or later, dammit, I was going to start laying out a little chastisement where it was long overdue.

I flashed back to several vivid memories of when I had done exactly that. Images of violence and flame and hideous foes flickered through my head, sharp and nearly real. The emotions that accompanied those memories came along for the ride, but they were one step removed, distant enough to let me process them, identify them.

Rage, of course. Rage at the creatures who were trying to harm the innocent or my friends or me. That rage had been both a weapon and armor to me in moments of mortal peril. It was always there, and I always welcomed its arrival — being filled with anger was infinitely preferable to being filled with terror. But seeing it in my heightened memories, it made me feel a little sick. *Rage* was a word we used for *anger* when it was being used in the cause of right — but that didn't sanctify it or make it somehow laudable. It was still anger. Violent, dangerous anger, as deadly as a flying bullet. It just happened to be a bullet that was aimed in a convenient direction.

Fear next: always fear. It doesn't matter how personally courageous you are. When something is trying to kill you and you know it, you're afraid. It's a mindless, lizard-brain emotion. There's no way to stop it. Courage is about learning how to function despite the fear, to put aside your instincts to run or give in completely to the anger born from fear. Courage is about using your brain and your heart when every cell of your body is screaming at you to fight or flee — and then follow-

ing through on what you believe is the right thing to do.

The White Council blamed me for causing trouble with various supernatural evils, and while I'm not quite arrogant enough to blame all the world's problems on my mistakes, they probably had a point. I have issues with bullies and authority figures. And I refuse to stand by and do nothing when those too weak to defend themselves become victims.

But how much of that had been courage, and how much of it had been me embracing my probably righteous anger so that I wouldn't feel the fear? As the memories flipped by, I saw myself again and again throwing myself into the fire — sometimes literally — to help someone who needed it or to kill something that needed killing. The tidal surges of my emotion had propelled me, fueled my magic, and many times they had made it possible to survive when I wouldn't have otherwise.

But when I'd been running on adrenaline, I'd rarely stopped to consider the extended consequences of my actions. By saving Susan from Bianca of the Red Court, I had offered a high-profile insult to the entire vampire nation. When Duke Ortega had shown up to challenge me to a duel, to restore the honor of the Red Court and forestall a war, it had ended in a bloodbath — and it had never occurred to me to attempt to ensure any other

outcome. As a result of the disastrous duel, a wizard named Ebenezar McCoy, my grandfather, had brought an old Soviet satellite down from its orbit, right on top of Ortega's stronghold. No one survived. Then Arianna, Ortega's wife, the daughter of the Red King, had sought her own vengeance even as the Red Court launched a full-scale war.

Arianna's vengeance had materialized in the form of murdering my daughter's foster family and abducting her. Once Susan heard about it, she got in touch. And again I flung myself into fire without a thought.

None of those things *had* to happen. I mean, I wasn't the only guy in the world who had driven that course of events. I knew that. But I had been the guy who had been standing at the tipping point between possible outcomes with depressing regularity. Could I have done something differently? Was it even possible to know?

In my memories, I murdered Susan Rodriguez again.

Time heals all wounds, they say, but I somehow knew I wouldn't be able to escape this one. Granted, only a few days' subjective time had passed since the events of tha' evening, so the memory was still fresh in n painfully clear recollection. But time wa' going to help much with what I had d And it probably shouldn't.

I wanted to hurt the Grey Ghost

merry band of shades. I wanted to hurt them badly, make them feel the vitriol burning inside my belly. I wanted to take them on and smash them to flinders upon my will.

But . . .

Maybe I should pause for a moment. Maybe I should think. Maybe I should reject both anger and fear and strive for an outcome beyond kicking down the door and smashing everything in my way. Play it smart. Play it responsible.

"Little late for you to be learning that lesson now. Isn't it, dummy?" I asked.

No. It was never too late to learn something. The past is unalterable in any event. The future is the only thing we can change. Learning the lessons of the past is the only way to shape the present and the future.

Why did I want this fight so badly?

"Here's a thought, genius," I said to me. "Maybe it's got something to do with Maggie."

Maggie. My little girl. I would never see her grow up. I would never get to watch for any signs of manifesting talent, so that I could teach her and give her the choice of how to live her life. I would never get to hear her sing a song, or go trick-or-treating, or send her a present for Christmas. I would never . . .

At some point during that dark thunderstorm of regret, fire had erupted from seemingly every surface of my body, a furious red-gold flame. It wasn't hot at first, but after a few seconds it got uncomfortable and rapidly progressed to actual pain. I ground my teeth, closed my eyes, and forced order upon my thoughts, tried to replace the outrage with cool, steady logic.

Several seconds later, the fire died away. I opened my eyes slowly, eyeing the scorch marks on my coat and a blister or two on my exposed skin. Clear bubbles of ectoplasm dribbled from the blisters.

"So, yeah," I said. "You may have anger issues where Maggie is concerned, Harry."

Heh. You think?

"Got a rocket," I sang, "in your pocket. Turn off the juice, boy."

Show tunes? Really? It wasn't bad enough that you've started talking to yourself, man. Now you're doing performing art.

But the musically inclined me had a point.

"Play it cool, boy," I whispered. "Real cool."

I approached the Big Hoods' lair obliquely and cautiously. One might even accuse me of being overly cautious. I circled the lair from all angles, including up above, in a slow, spiral-shaped pattern that only gradually drew closer. I held a veil over myself the entire time, too. It wasn't any easier as a ghost than it had been in the flesh, and I still couldn't throw the greatest veil in the world, but I managed to make myself if not invisible, at least difficult to see.

I wasn't there to fight. I was there to learn. Mort needed my help, but maybe the best way to give it to him wasn't to go charging in like a rogue rhinoceros. Knowledge is power. I needed all the power I could get if I was going to help Morty.

The problem was that the Grey Ghost had apparently marshaled supporters of both the spirit and the flesh — and I couldn't fight the damned crazy thugs who just happened to be made of solid matter. I'd need help. Maybe I could hop into Morty again and toss out enough power to let him run away — but that assumed Morty would let me step in at all. He sure as hell didn't seem to like it the first time. It also assumed that he would be free and able to physically escape, and that I could neutralize his material captors. There was no guarantee either of those things would be the case.

I thought that the tip from Nick was a good one. I think he had identified the right bunch of yahoos, and I had faith in his knowledge of Chicago streets. After a lifetime walking them — and surviving — Nick was an expert. Chicago PD's gang unit sometimes went to him for advice. Sometimes he even gave it to them.

But any expert could be wrong. If the Grey Ghost was wily enough to have a hideout separate from its material mooks' living quarters and had stashed Mort there, I was about to waste a whole lot of time. But how would it *get* a setup of its own without physical help to establish it? If it was strong enough, I supposed, it could have a demesne of its own in the Nevernever — the spirit world. I'd dealt with a ghost named Agatha Hagglethorn once, and she'd had her own little pocket dimension filled with a Victorian-era copy of Chicago.

(It burned down.)

(I was not responsible.)

Anyway, I had to wonder if the Grey Ghost didn't have a similar resource. It would make one fine hidey-hole to avoid annoying things like sunrise, daylight, and recently deceased wizards.

I paused for a moment to consider a notion. I wondered if I could establish a demesne of my own. I mean, theoretically, I knew how it would work. Granted, there's as much space between theory and practice in magic as there is in physics, but it isn't an unbridgeable gap. I was reasonably sure that it could be done. Maybe I could get Butters to let me talk shop with Bob for a few minutes. He'd know what I needed to make it happen, I was sure.

But what would I make it look like? I mean . . . in theory, I could make it practically anything I wanted. I'm sure there would be some kind of energy-to-area requirement that would limit it in absolute terms, but if I wanted, I could make it look like the Taj Mahal or the old Aladdin's arcade where I used to play video games, back before my magic made it all but impossible. I could have a mansion. I could probably make some kind of simulacrum of a butler, if I wanted.

I sighed. Bob would, I was certain, suggest simulacrum French maids tottering around in stiletto heels as his first and most conservative contribution. It would only get more depraved from there.

In the end, there was really only one of a couple of things my demesne could possibly be: a Burger King restaurant or my old apartment. The one that had burned with the rest of my life.

Suddenly, there was no appeal in considering my own demesne anymore.

"Stop wasting time," I told myself.

I shook off the thoughts and continued my stalk of the Big Hoods' clubhouse, sniffing around for possible magical defenses; alarm spells seemed most likely, but I had to assume that a ghostly sorcerer could create as much destructive mayhem as a mortal one. I could run into anything from ill-tempered guardian entities to a magical equivalent of claymore antipersonnel mines.

Hell, I'd seen a vampire's nest that used *actual* AP mines. Nasty toys. I would be keeping an eye out for any physical defenses as well, in the event I needed to warn Murphy or her crew about them when I showed up for the actual rescue operation.

"For the op," I corrected myself. "Sounds cooler if you call it the op." I moved closer, veil in place, senses tuned to the possibility of danger. "Definitely. Murphy would call it the op."

The entrance to the hideout was just where Nick had said it would be, beneath an overpass where a steel door had once led to an old city-works storage area. I found no suspect magic in the immediate area around the bridge, which made sense. If I had been spreading detection spells around my own hideout, I wouldn't have gone to the trouble to set them up where the sunrise would obliterate them every morning.

To make something that lasted longer than a day or two at most, considerable effort was required. At the very least, you'd have to use some kind of physical object to harbor the spell's energy. Technically, you could use any object, though it was not unheard-of for wizards to utilize whatever they happened to have in their pockets at the time. It's probably where all the old stories of enchanted spindles, combs, brushes, and mirrors come from.

Most often, the magical energy was channeled into carvings or painted symbols. I'd once set up a rental storage unit as a short-term haven in case things ever went to hell. I'd laid up about a hundred small protective spells on the walls, floor, and ceiling of the place in various colors of paint. The energy inside them was stored in the paint, safe from the sunrise and ready to project a shield whenever the symbols felt the touch of hostile magic.

But a monitoring spell wouldn't be the kind of thing that could lie dormant. It had to actually be "looking" around all the time. That meant a constant, modest expenditure of energy, which would in turn be exposed and vulnerable to sunrise. Land mine–type spells were a lot easier, like my protective spells, only with more kaboom in them. I wasn't surprised that I didn't find any of those outside the hideout. Few people would host a picnic underneath the overpass, but it *was* Chicago, and all sorts of folks would be through this area during the day. Random people being horribly incinerated would certainly draw the attention of the local authorities, and possibly that of the White Council. The Grey Ghost didn't seem to be an idiot. No death traps were left lying around where some schoolkid or bum might stumble into them.

I wouldn't have set up like that, either. It made far more sense for such sentry spells to be laid down underground, deep enough for the steady presence of the earth to shield the spell energy from disruption.

The Grey Ghost was smart. Things would get interesting about fifteen or twenty feet down.

I finished my last circuit of the site and moved to the door. I reached out a hand and stopped with my palm about an inch away from the metal. I sensed something subtle but there, like the attractive field around an old, weak magnet. I frowned and focused on it, finding a spell of a composition unlike anything I'd ever seen before.

It was something subliminal, sending out a kind of beckoning energy that I wouldn't have noticed had I not been specifically looking for something like it. It would otherwise have been buried in the background energy of the city and its inhabitants. I stretched out a hand to touch the stream of energy flowing steadily outward. It oozed over the surface of my skin, a crawling sensation that made me shudder.

It's smarter not to play around with unfamiliar magic. Besides, I had other things to do. I lowered my hand and stepped toward the source of the music I'd begun hearing in my head at some point. There was little sense wasting more time up on the surface. And I hadn't heard that song in forever, but I could still sing along. I started humming and —

— and stopped myself with my nose about half an inch from the steel door.

I broke out into a cold sweat.

Hell's bells. That magic hadn't been heavy-duty, but it had been puissant. A few seconds after touching it, I had almost walked blindly and mindlessly through the door and into whatever reception was prepared for intruders on the other side. I couldn't know exactly what was over there without getting a look, but it sure as hell wasn't a gift basket and a bottle of wine.

I stepped back from the door and the siren spell with what I felt was a properly Darwinian appreciation of the danger it represented. Oh, it might not blow you up like the defensive wards I'd had on my apartment, but a scalpel can open up your arteries just as readily as a sword. In some cases, more so. I shivered and clutched my arms to my belly.

That spell wasn't the work of a novice or marauding sorcerer experimenting with magic he'd found in the metaphysical section of a bookstore. Whoever had put that thing together had been a true professional, one with centuries of experience.

One who was probably more capable than I when it came to magic.

Don't get me wrong: I'm hoss. When the spells start flying, mine are some of the flashiest, most violent on the planet. I'm like the Andre the Giant of the supernatural world. I've got a lot of power and mass to throw around.

Andre would be a great person to have on

your side in a brawl against a rowdy tavern crowd. But in a more focused situation, he would be at the mercy of professionals who, while lacking his raw power, could nonetheless apply their own strength more efficiently and effectively. Murphy was an excellent example of that kind of fighter. She wasn't much bigger than a bread box, but I'd seen her toss around guys weighing most of three hundred pounds like they were unruly puppies.

If the Grey Ghost was responsible for that spell, then I was lucky to have survived our first meeting. The smart move would be to scamper. If it came to a fair fight, I might find myself completely outclassed.

I felt a shivering, cold presence on the back of my neck, and turned to find wraiths nearby. They drifted toward the hideout from all directions, coming in a slow, steady procession and moving in perfectly straight lines. The siren spell made sense to me now. It wasn't a guard spell, though it could certainly have that purpose. It was also a beacon, a dinner bell being rung to signal the mindless horde now approaching.

They never sped up, never slowed. They just kept floating forward until they began to pass through the closed steel door in groups of two and three as they converged upon it.

I pursed my lips, thinking. The Grey Ghost wasn't killing wraiths. It was using them. For the moment, at least, there wouldn't be any kind of guard spell on the other side of the door. There couldn't be, or the Grey Ghost would be slaughtering its own troops and wasting its own investment of time and energy to boot.

I might have an opportunity here. The inbound wraiths would almost certainly be routed by what amounted to a cattle chute. That route would most likely be clear of supernatural booby traps. It might be possible to gain entry, find a vulnerable point along the chute, and then duck out of it to run a quick reconnaissance of the Grey Ghost's headquarters and find Mort.

It took half an hour for the procession to be complete, and the flow of wraith traffic never let up. I stopped counting them at 450 and swallowed. That wasn't a herd of wraiths. That was a bloody *horde.* If one of the wraiths decided it wanted to eat me, it would have to perform a miracle to divide me into enough pieces to feed all of its dinner company.

My veil seemed to have prevented me from being noticed as they approached, but that could just as easily be the effect of the beacon spell. For all I knew, once the beacon shut off, they'd all turn around and come at me like greyhounds leaving the gate. It would require a singularly stupid man to go hang around in narrow tunnels and cramped spaces alongside a threat like *that.*

"And I, Harry Dresden, am that man," I stated.

I waited for the last wraith to go in and counted to twenty. My mouth felt dry. Fear boiled in my belly and made my knees feel unsteady. My fingers trembled.

I told them all that they were just preconceived residual memories anyway and that I would tolerate no guff from them.

Then I ground my teeth and followed the horde.

CHAPTER TWENTY-EIGHT

I slipped through the steel door and into the blackness on the other side. I ignored the darkness until it went away, and then began to move stealthily forward.

I stopped with the Scooby-Doo action a couple of feet later and just started walking. I mean, honestly, sneaking. It wasn't as though I could step on a twig or accidentally kick an old can and make a sound, right? Being a ghost, the problem wasn't being sneaky — it was getting noticed in the first place.

Besides. Nobody who was concerned about detecting my presence would be using their ears to sense me coming.

I began extending my wizard's senses out in front of me.

When I say *wizard senses,* I mean it in a similar fashion to *spider sense.* Spidey's enhanced senses detect when he's in danger and warn him that he's got incoming. A wizard's senses don't do that (though I suppose with enough work, someone could come close). What they do sense is the presence of magic, in both its natural state and its worked forms. You don't have to be concentrating to make it happen — it's natural in every practitioner.

The theory I've heard espoused most often is that the ability to sense such energies makes it possible for a regular person to become a wizard, providing the kind of sensory feedback he needs to gradually work with more and more energy. So while a regular person who lacked the sense could, technically, learn how to use magic without it, it would be a process as difficult as someone who was born blind teaching himself to paint.

I focused on that sense in me, partially blocking out my less important, physical senses to give greater attention to the presence of magic in my surroundings. It was pretty thick in here. The door led to a concrete stairway going down into the earth, and each step bore lit candles and thickly painted magical symbols. The latent energy in the paint was almost devoid of arcane power, barely detectable, but it was there and I saw it as faint phosphorescence. The energy of the beacon spell was still going strong. Somewhere in my head I had evidently decided to interpret it as a sound, because I could hear its slow throb like a bass beat on a big woofer.

I went down the stairs, my senses attuned to the ground at my feet. What looked like one more bit of barely magical scribbling could be concealing something far more potent and dangerous — but it didn't. I went down two flights of stairs unmolested.

The bottom of the stairway opened onto a rectangular room that had once been some sort of electrical junction. It obviously wasn't in service anymore. Large steel boxes and glass-faced readouts were spotted with rust and dust. There was more of the occult writing down here — all of it disjointed and fantastically disconnected, as if someone had composed a poem in a foreign language by randomly stringing together words from a dictionary.

It all bore the same trace amounts of magical energy as the writing on the stairs. The Big Hoods evidently had a certain amount of latent talent, which seemed to fit together with the idea of the Grey Ghost recruiting some mortal flunkies to assist it in . . .

. . . In whatever the hell he or she was trying to do.

What *was* he or she trying to do?

I mean, I knew the Grey Ghost had attacked Mort's place. But why? Why take Mort to begin with? Granted, the little ectomancer could probably be a pain in the ass to any ghost who got too ambitious in Chicago, but the Grey Ghost's ambitions seemed

to have been limited to gunning for Morty.
What could he possibly have to offer as a
target?

At the far end of the junction room, there
was a gaping, ragged hole in the wall that
looked like it had been made with sledgeham-
mers. It opened onto a rough tunnel beyond
— the beginnings of Undertown proper.

A man's anguished scream came from the
opening.

I nearly burst into a sprint but stopped
myself. Unthinking sprints were a good way
to get killed. Re-killed. Instead, I moved
forward into the rough-hewn corridor. It was
cold and damp, and slime and mold were
everywhere. I unimagined the strong, musty
smell that would otherwise have filled my
nose and paced forward, watching for traps
and working hard not to move my feet in time
with the bass-drum rhythm of the beacon
spell.

I passed a number of alcoves that joined
the corridor. They were individual quarters
for the Big Hoods, apparently. Each contained a mattress or an air mattress and
something resembling bedding, only covered
with mildew and mold. Each had a box or a
couple of bags, containing what I presumed
to be personal belongings. More arcane gibberish covered the walls, along with slogans
such as THE LIZARD FOLK ARE ALREADY
HERE! WATCH FOR THEIR EYES! A couple of

them looked occupied, with large, bulky forms snoring under the disgusting blankets.

A minute or two later, the passage opened up into a torch-lit room about the size of a hockey rink. The entrance was high up on one wall, so that my head was level with the larger room's ceiling. There were stairs cut into the wall beneath my feet, so that I could walk down them into the large room — which I didn't, as it was packed full of bad guys. I swallowed and made sure my veil was still running strong.

The bass beat of the beacon hammered loudly here, coming from a pit that had been cut into the floor. It must have been at least ten feet across, and I couldn't tell how deep it was. It was surrounded by written formulae that were far less nonsensical than the others, and they sent out flashes of dim red light in time with each pulse of the beacon.

The pit was full of wraiths.

They swirled round and round in steady, mindless motion, each of them overlapping with dozens of others, so that it looked less like a group of beings moving in a circle than some bizarre stew with the occasional recognizable portion of human anatomy appearing above the mix. The hollow not-scream of the empty-eyed wraiths was a huge and hideous sound, one that surged in time with the beacon.

Maybe two dozen lemurs were scattered

around the room. They'd lowered their hoods, and without their faceless menace to back them up, they just looked like people. Some were standing. Some were sitting. Another group was playing cards. Still others just stared at nothing, bemused.

A group of Big Hoods was gathered around the pit, all but two of them on their knees and chanting. They bowed at regular intervals and clapped their hands together at others. A gallows that looked like it had been constructed out of a driveway basketball goal hung over the pit, with a pair of Big Hoods holding one end of the rope.

Morty dangled from the other end, trussed up from his hips to his neck. He was swinging back and forth on the end of the line and slowly spinning. Gasps and broken sobbing sounds came from him.

Standing in empty air directly before him, moving as he did, was the Grey Ghost. The figure looked at least as menacing as it had the first time around. When it spoke, its voice was liquid, calm — and feminine.

"You need not do this to yourself, Mortimer," the Grey Ghost said. "I take no pleasure in inflicting pain. Yield. You will do it in the end. Save yourself the agony."

Mort opened his eyes. He licked his lips and said in a cracked, thick voice, "G-g-go fuck yourself."

The Grey Ghost murmured, "Tsk." Then

nodded and said, "Again."

"N-no," Morty choked out, beginning to twist against his bonds. He accomplished nothing other than to start spinning more rapidly. "No!"

The two Big Hoods holding the rope calmly lowered Mort down into the swirling pit of insanely hungry wraiths. They collapsed in on Morty, as if the surf could choose where it wished to crash — and it all wished to crash on the little ectomancer. The cauldron of mad ghosts boiled and congealed onto him, all but hiding him from sight.

Mort began to scream again, a horrible, humiliated sound.

"One," counted the Grey Ghost. "Two. Three. Four."

At the last number, the flunkies hauled him up out of the pool of wraiths, and Morty hung there, swinging back and forth and sobbing again, gasping for breath.

"Each time you refuse me, Mortimer, I will add another second to the count," said the Grey Ghost. "I know what you're thinking. How many seconds will it take to drive you mad?"

Mort tried to regain control of his breathing, but it was a futile effort. Tears marked his face. His nose had begun to run. He opened his eyes, his jaw clenched, his bald pate scarlet, and said, his voice cracking, "Go watch the sunrise."

"Again," said the Grey Ghost.

The Big Hoods lowered Morty into the pit once more. I didn't know what happened to a living mortal attacked by a wraith, but if Morty's reaction was any indicator, it wasn't good. Again he screamed. It was higher pitched than a moment before, more raw. The screams all but drowned out the calm, monotonous count of the Grey Ghost. She went to five, and then the Big Hoods hauled him up again. He twitched in spasmodic motion, as if he'd developed a simultaneous charley horse in every muscle and sinew. It took his screams at least ten seconds to die away.

"It's more art than science," the Grey Ghost continued, as if nothing had happened. "In my experience, most minds break before seven. Granted, most do not have your particular gifts. Whatever happens, I'm sure I will find it fascinating. I ask again: Will you help me?"

"Go jump in a river, bitch," Morty gasped.

There was a moment of silence. "Again," the Grey Ghost snarled. "Slowly."

The obedient Big Hoods began to lower Mort slowly toward the wraith pit again.

Mort shook his head vainly and twisted his obviously battered body, trying to curl up and away from the swirling tide of hungry ghosts. He managed to forestall his fate by a few seconds, but in the end, he went down among the devouring spirits once more. He screamed again, and only after the scream had well and truly begun did the Grey Ghost start counting.

I'd never really had the highest opinion of Morty. I had hated the way he'd neglected his talents and abused his clients for so long, back when I'd first met him. He'd gone up in my estimation since then, and especially in the past day. So maybe he wasn't a paragon of virtue, but he was still a decent guy in his own way. He was professional, and it looked like he'd had more juice all along than I thought he had.

That said a lot about Morty, that he'd kept quiet about the extent of his ability. It said even more about him that he was standing in the lion's den with no way out and was still spitting his defiance into the face of his captor.

Dammit, I thought. *I like the guy.*

And the Grey Ghost was destroying him, right in front of my eyes.

Even as I watched, Morty screamed again as the wraiths surged against him, raking at him with their pale, gaunt fingers. The Grey Ghost's calm voice counted numbers. It felt like a minor infinity stretched between each.

I couldn't get Mort out of this place. No way. Even if I went all-out on the room and defeated every single hostile spirit in it, Mort would still be tied up and the Big Hoods would still be looming. There was no percentage in an attack.

Yet standing around with my thumb up my ghostly ass wasn't an option, either. I didn't know what the Grey Ghost was doing to Morty, but it was clearly hurting him, and judging from her dialogue (straight out of Cheesy Villain General Casting, though it might be), exposure to the wraiths would inflict permanent harm if Morty continued to refuse her. And there were the murderous spirits back at the ruins of Mort's house to think about, too.

And as if all that wasn't enough, sunrise was on the way.

Dammit. I needed an edge, an advantage.

The fingers of my right hand touched the solid wooden handle of Sir Stuart's pistol, and I was suddenly keenly aware of its power, of the sheer, tightly leashed potency of the weapon. Its energy hummed silently against my right palm. I remembered the fight at Morty's place and the havoc Sir Stuart's weapon had wreaked among the enemy — or, rather, upon a single enemy.

The Grey Ghost had feared Sir Stuart's gun, and I couldn't imagine she'd done so for no reason. If I could take her out, the other spirits who followed her would almost certainly scatter — the kind of jackals who followed megalomaniacs around rarely had the stomach for a confrontation without their leader to stiffen their spines. Right?

Sure. Just because the lemurs still outnumber you more than a dozen to one doesn't mean they'll see you as an easy victim, Dresden. You'll be fine.

There should be a rule against your own inner monologue throwing around that much sarcasm.

But there was still merit in the idea: Kill the Grey Ghost and then run like hell. Even if the lemurs came after me, at least the main voice who appeared to be guiding the Big Hoods would be silenced. It might even get all the malevolent spiritual attention entirely off of Morty.

All I had to do was make one shot with Sir Stuart's pistol. No problem. If I missed, I probably wouldn't survive the experience, sure, but other than that it should be a piece of cake.

I gritted my teeth and began to move slowly toward the Grey Ghost. I didn't know how close I could get before my half-assed veil became useless, but I had to do everything I could to maximize the chances of a hit. I wasn't a marksman, and the pistols of the eighteenth century weren't exactly precision instruments, but I couldn't afford to miss. Of course, if the Grey Ghost sensed me coming, she would have time to run, to dodge, or to pull some sort of defense together.

I had to kill her before she knew she was under attack. There was some irony there, considering the way I'd died.

The Grey Ghost finished her count, and the Big Hoods hauled a sobbing Morty out of the pit again. He hung there, twitching, suffering, making involuntary sounds as he gasped for breath. The Grey Ghost stood in front of him, motionless and, I felt certain, gloating.

Ten feet. I knew my veil was shoddy and my aim only middling, but if I could close to ten feet, I figured I had a fairly good chance of hitting the target. That would put me on the near edge of the wraith pit, shooting across it to hit the Grey Ghost. Of course, if I missed, the Grey Ghost wouldn't need to kill me. All she'd have to do was freaking *trip* me. The wraiths, once they sensed my presence, would be all over me.

Then I'd get what Morty was getting. Except that as a ghost myself, they'd be tearing me into tiny, ectoplasm-soaked shreds. And eating them.

What fun, I thought.

I tried to move steadily, to keep myself calm. I didn't have any adrenaline anymore to make my hands shake, but they shook anyway. Dammit. I guess even a ghost is still, on some level, fundamentally human. Nothing for it but to keep moving.

Thirty feet.

I passed within a few yards of a lemur who was apparently staring into nothingness —

though his eyes were lined up directly with me. Perhaps he was lost in a ghostly memory. He never blinked as I went by.

Twenty-five.

The wraiths wheezed out their starving, strangled howls in the pit a few feet ahead of me.

Twenty.

Why do I keep winding up in these situations? Even after I'm *dead?*

For the fun, I thought to myself. *For the fun, fun, fun-fun, fun.*

CHAPTER TWENTY-NINE

Then the floor near the Grey Ghost's feet rippled, and a human skull floated up out of it, its eye sockets burning with a cold blue flame.

The Grey Ghost turned to look at the skull, and something about her body language soured. "What?"

"A Fomor messenger is at the outer perimeter," the skull said. It sounded creepily like Bob, but there was a complete absence of anything but a vague contempt in its voice. "He bears word from his lord."

I got the impression that the Grey Ghost tilted her head beneath its hood. "A servitor? Arriving from the Nevernever?"

"The outer perimeter is the Nevernever side, of which I am custodian," the skull replied. "The inner perimeter is the mortal world. You established that more than a year ago."

The Grey Ghost made a disgusted sound. "Have a care, spirit. You are not indispensible." She looked at the suspended Morty and sighed. "Of course the Fomor disturb me with sunrise near. Why must my most important work continually be interrupted?"

The skull inclined itself in a nod of acknowledgment. "Shall I kill him and send back the body, along with a note suggesting that next time they call ahead?"

"No," snapped the Grey Ghost. "Of course not. Curb your tongue, spirit, lest I tear it out for you."

"If it pleases you to do so. I am but a servant," the skull said with another nod. The contempt in its tone held steady, though. "Shall I allow him to pass?"

"And be quick about it," the Grey Ghost snarled.

"As it pleases you," the skull replied, speaking noticeably more slowly than a moment before. It vanished into the floor.

I held very, very still. Motion was the hardest thing for a veil to hide, and I suddenly realized that the one-shot, one-kill plan had a serious flaw in it: I had forgotten to account for Evil Bob. The spirit was powerful, intelligent, dangerous — and apparently incapable of anything resembling fear or respect. I suppose that after a few decades of working with Kemmler, the most dangerous necromancer since the fall of the Roman Empire, it was difficult to take a lesser talent seriously.

Not that regular Bob was exactly overflow-

413

ing with respect and courtesy. Heh. Take that, bad guy.

In any case, I had a chance to find out more about the enemy. You can't ever get too much dirt on these cloaked lunatics. Frequently, learning more about them exposes some kind of gaping hole in their armor, metaphorical or otherwise. I've never had cause to regret knowing more about an enemy before commencing a fight.

Besides. If the Grey Ghost was a part of some kind of partnership, instead of operating alone, I had to know about it. Bad-guy alliances were never good news.

The Grey Ghost stepped away from the pit. In fewer than thirty seconds, the ground rippled again and a man appeared, arising from the ground a bit at a time, as if he were walking up a stairway. The skull came with him, floating along behind, just above the level of his head.

I recognized him at once: the leader of the Fomor servitors who had come after Molly. He was still dressed in the black turtleneck, but had added a weapons belt with a holstered pistol beneath his left hand and a short sword at his right. It was one of those Japanese blades, but shorter than the full katana. Wakazashi, then, or maybe it was a ninja-to. If it was, minus points for carrying it around out in the open like that.

Oh, there was something else odd about

him: His eyes had changed color. I remembered them as a clear grey. Now they were a deep, deep purple. I don't mean purple like the dark violet eyes that lots of Bob's romance-novel heroines always seem to have. They were purple like a bruised corpse, or like the last colors of a twilit sky.

He faced the Grey Ghost calmly and bowed from the waist, the gesture slow and fluid. "Greetings, Lady Shade, from my master, Cantrev Lord Omogh."

"Hello. Listen," the Grey Ghost replied, her tone sour, "what does Omogh want from me now?"

Listen bowed again, purple eyes gleaming. "My master desires to know whether or not your campaign is complete."

The Grey Ghost's voice came out from between clenched teeth. "Obviously not."

Listen bowed. "He would know, then, why you have escalated your search to a seizure of a second-tier asset." The servitor paused to glance at Morty and then back to the robed figure. "This action runs counter to your arrangement."

The eye sockets of the skull flickered more brightly. "We could still send the Fomor the message about calling ahead."

"No," the Grey Ghost said severely.

"It would be simple and direct. . . ."

"No, spirit," the Grey Ghost snarled. "I forbid it."

The skull's eyes flickered rapidly for a moment, agitated. Then it bowed lower and said, "As you wish."

The Grey Ghost turned to Listen and said, "My servant believes it would be logical to murder you and send your corpse back to your master in order to express my displeasure."

Listen bowed again. "I am one of many, easily replaced. My death would be but a brief annoyance to my lord, and, I think, a somewhat anemic symbolic gesture."

The Grey Ghost stared at him and then said, "If you weren't speaking the literal truth, I think I should be satisfied with letting the skull have you. But you really have no sense of self-preservation at all, do you?"

"Of course I do, Lady Shade. I would never throw away my life carelessly. It would make it impossible for me to ensure that my death is of maximum advantage to my lord."

The Grey Ghost shook her head within the hood. "You are a fool."

"I will not contest the statement," Listen said. "However, Lady Shade, I must ask you for an answer to return to my lord." He added mildly, "Whatever form that answer may take."

"Inform him," said the Grey Ghost, voice annoyed, "that I will do as I see fit to acquire an appropriate body."

Whoa.

The Lady Shade was looking for a meat suit.

Which meant . . .

I shook off the line of logic to be examined later. I focused on the conversation at hand.

"You made no mention of requiring such a valuable specimen for your ends," Listen said.

"Look at what I have to work with," Lady Shade snarled, gesturing at the Big Hoods gathered around the pit. "Scraps that cannot support the weight of my talent. Tell Omogh that if he wishes an ally who can face the Wardens, he must be tolerant. This specimen is of the least value to his purposes, and the greatest to mine."

Listen considered that for a moment and then nodded. "And the Rag Lady?"

"Once I am seated within a mortal form, I will deal with her," Lady Shade said. Her voice became detectably smug. "Assuming, of course, you have not already removed her yourself. Is that a burn on your cheek, Listen? I hope it does not pain you."

"Very kind, Lady," Listen said with another bow. "I am in no discomfort worth noting. May I tell my lord that you will make him a gift of these fourth-tier creatures, once you are restored?"

Lady Shade seemed to consider that for a moment. She tilted her head and looked around at the Big Hoods. "Yes, I suppose so. I'll have little need for such baubles."

"Excellent," Listen said. He sounded genuinely pleased.

Lady Shade shook her head again. "Is he so enamored of such minor talents?"

"A moment ago," Listen said, "I was preparing to inform him of the potential loss of a second-tier. Now I may inform him of the probable gain of a dozen lesser acquisitions. It pleases me to draw positive gains for my lord from negative situations."

From his place dangling over the pit, Morty said, in a slurred voice, "Tell him he ain't getting squat. Bitch can't have me."

Listen lifted both eyebrows and looked at Lady Shade.

"I require his consent," the Lady Shade said, her voice tight. "I will have it. Had you not interrupted me, I would have it already. Now dawn nears. It may be several hours after sundown before I complete the transfer."

"Ah," Listen said. Nothing in his tone made him sound overtly skeptical, but I got the impression that he was nonetheless. "Then with your leave, I will depart to carry word to my lord and trouble you no more."

Evil Bob popped up into sight over Listen's shoulder again. "Are you sure you do not wish this creature to be *departed,* my lady?"

"Go in peace, Listen," Lady Shade said without so much as glancing at Evil Bob. "Inform your lord that I anticipate that we will be able to move against the Rag Lady

and her allies in the fortress sometime tomorrow evening."

Listen bowed at the waist again; then he
turned and, followed by the floating skull,
stepped down into the floor, vanishing from
mortal reality and into the spirit world.

The moment Listen was gone, Lady Shade
waved a hand, and with reedy howls of
protest, the wraiths in the pit were unceremoniously scattered from it, the heavy bass beat
of the beacon spell coming to an abrupt halt.
The will of Lady Shade pressed against them
like the current of a river, and they were
driven from the chamber, carried out through
the walls and the floor by an unseen force.

I could feel it myself, the force of her will,
simultaneously banishing the wraiths and
commanding the attention of the lemurs in
the chamber. I fought to hold still before it,
to let it slide away from me around my veil,
to use it to help me hide rather than being
revealed by it.

"Children," she said, her tone full of contempt, "beware: The dawn approaches. To
your sanctums, all." She turned to the Big
Hoods. "Mortal dears. Mother is pleased with
you. Keep safe the prisoner until nightfall.
His life is worth the world to me. Guard him
with your own."

The Big Hoods shivered, as if they'd heard
the voice of a god whispering in their minds,
and bowed their heads as one. They mur-

mured words of some kind of ritual devotion, though they were too mush-mouthed for me to clearly understand them. The lemurs began clearing out at once, rising from their activities (or lack thereof) and departing, moving silently from the chamber.

I got lucky. None of them actually plowed into me by mistake.

"Well," murmured Lady Shade to Morty. "We shall continue our discussion in several hours. You will have no food, no water. You will not be untied. I'm sure that sooner or later, you will see things my way."

"I would rather die than let you in," Morty replied, his voice a croak.

"You can't always have what you want, dear child," Lady Shade said. Her voice was matter-of-fact, calm, and practical. "I will continue to hurt you. And eventually, you will be willing to do anything to stop the pain. It is an unfortunate limit of mortality."

Morty said nothing. I couldn't tell whether he shivered at the cold-blooded confidence in her voice, but I did.

And I realized, finally, who I was dealing with.

The Grey Ghost turned and sank into the floor, evidently moving into a demesne in the Nevernever. I waited until I was sure she was gone, then simply vanished, straight up, appearing over the streets of Chicago above. Dawn was a golden promise over the eastern horizon. I headed toward my grave as fast as I could possibly travel.

The Grey Ghost was a shade; that I knew. But where had the shade come from? From someone with a knowledge of possessing others' bodies. From someone who seemed confident she could confront the Wardens of the White Council, the cops of the wizarding world, and come out on top. From someone who had been known to this Omogh person, whoever he was, and who needed a body with enough of an innate gift for magic to support what was apparently a much greater talent.

Only so many people with a wizard's level of ability had perished in Chicago. Most of them had been foes of mine. I hadn't been the one to gack all of them, but I'd killed this one. With a gun, no less, from about ten feet away.

I reached the shelter of my grave and sank into it gratefully, still shivering.

Morty was in the hands of the Corpsetaker, one of the heirs of that lunatic Kemmler, a body-hopping wizard with a serious case of the long-term crazies and maybe three or four times my own ability with magic. If she got into Morty, I was guessing that, like me, she would have access to her full abilities once more. She would be able to start hopping bodies again, and pick up her career right where she left off.

And she'd start by killing Molly.

I'd survived my original encounter with her thanks only to the intervention of "Gentleman" John Marcone, a little bit of good luck and better guesswork, and some truly epic paranoia. She was an absolute, first-class threat, one I would prefer to avoid confronting at all, much less alone.

Sunrise came roaring over the land, and I felt grateful to have it between the Corpsetaker and me. I was glad to have a chance to rest while I could.

Things had gotten considerably more urgent.

Come nightfall, I knew, I was going to have to find a way to take her on.

CHAPTER THIRTY

I huddled in my grave as the sun rose. I would have thought I'd be more nervous about a personally lethal, fiery cataclysm sweeping over the world, but I wasn't. When dawn came, it was like listening to a big truck roll by outside — dangerous if you were in front of it, but nothing but background noise if you weren't. My grave was peaceful.

I tried to track that feeling, to identify that sense of contentment I enjoyed down in the ground. It took me a few moments, but then I understood: It was like being in my basement apartment during a winter storm. Outside, the wind howled and the snow and sleet fell, but I was home with Mouse and Mister piled onto the couch for warmth, sipping a cup of hot chicken soup in front of a big fire in the fireplace, and reading a good book.

It was the same thing, resting in my grave. Peace. I wasn't going anywhere and it made me happy. If only I'd brought a book, my day would have been perfect.

Instead, I just leaned back against the earthen wall of the grave and closed my eyes, soaking in the quiet. I would be trapped here until sundown. There was no sense in chewing my own guts out worrying about what would happen that evening.

I drifted through my memories, sad and joyous and just plain ridiculous.

I thought about Elaine and me in high school. We had lived like superheroes: two young people with incredible powers who must hide themselves from those around them, lest they be isolated and persecuted for their different-ness.

I hadn't really been interested in girls yet when I met Elaine. We'd both been twelve, bright, and stubborn, which meant that we generally drove each other crazy. We had also been best friends. Talking about our dreams of the future. Sharing tears or a shoulder, whichever was needed. At school, we both found the subject matter to be tedious beyond bearing — in comparison to the complexity of Justin's lessons, acquitting ourselves well in the public-school curriculum had been only nominally more difficult than sharpening a pencil.

It was difficult to relate to the other kids, in many ways. We just weren't interested in the same things. Our magic talents increasingly made television a difficulty, and video games had been downright impossible. Elaine and I wound up playing a lot of card and board games, or spending long, quiet hours in the same room, reading.

Justin had manipulated us both masterfully. He wanted us to bond. He wanted us to feel isolated from everyone else and loyal to him. Though he put up a facade about it that fooled me at the time, he wanted us to work through our nascent sexuality with each other and save him the bother of explaining anything — or the risk of either Elaine or me forming attachments with someone outside our little circle.

I never suspected a thing about what he really wanted, until the day Elaine stayed home sick. Concerned about her, I skipped my last class and came home early. The house seemed too quiet, and an energy I had never sensed before hung in the air like cloying, oily perfume. The second I walked in the door, I found myself tensing up.

It was my first encounter with black magic, the power of Creation itself twisted to maim and destroy everything it touched.

Elaine sat on the couch, her expression calm, her spine locked rigidly into perfect posture. I now know that Justin had put the mental whammy on her while I was gone, but at the time I knew only that my instincts were screaming that something was wrong. A wrongness so fundamental it made me want to run away screaming filled the room.

And besides. Elaine only sat like that when she was making a statement — generally, a sarcastic one.

I still remembered it, plain as day.

Justin appeared in the kitchen doorway, on the other side of Elaine, and stood there for a moment, looking at me, his expression calm. "You skipped class again." He sighed. "I probably should have seen that coming."

"What's going on here?" I demanded, my voice high and squeaky with fear. "What have you done?"

Justin walked to the couch to stand over Elaine. Both of them stared at me for a long moment. I couldn't read their expressions at all. "I'm making plans, Harry," he said in a steady, quiet voice. "I need people I can trust."

"Trust?" I asked. His words didn't make sense. I couldn't see how they applied to the current situation. I couldn't see how they would make sense at all. I looked from Elaine back to Justin again, searching for some kind of explanation. Their expressions gave me nothing. That was when my eyes fell to the coffee table and to the object lying quietly next to my well-mauled paperback copy of *The Hobbit*.

A straitjacket.

There was something quietly, calmly sinister

in the congruence. I just stared for a moment, and the bottom fell out of my stomach as I finally realized, for the first, awful time, what my instinct had been screaming at me: I was in danger. That my rescuer, teacher, my guardian meant to do me harm.

Tears blurred my vision as I asked him, in a very quiet, very confused voice, "Why?"

Justin remained calm. "You don't have the knowledge you need to understand, boy. Not yet. But you will in time."

"Y-you can't do this," I whispered. "N-not you. You saved me. You saved us."

"And I still am," Justin said. "Sit down next to Elaine, Harry."

From the couch, Elaine said in a quiet, dreamy monotone, "Sit down next to me, Harry."

I stared at her in shock and took a step back. "Elaine . . ."

Justin threw kinetomancy at me when I looked away.

Some instinct warned me in the last fraction of a second, but instead of trying to block the strike, I moved with it, toward the front picture window, weaving my own spell as I went. Instead of interposing my shield, I spread it wide in front of me like a sail, catching the force of Justin's blast and harnessing it.

Me, my shield, Justin's energy, and that picture window exploded onto the front lawn.

I remembered the enormous sound of the shattering glass and wood, and the hot sting of a dozen tiny cuts from bits of flying glass and wood. I remember being furious and terrified.

I went through the open space where the window had been, fell onto the lawn, took it in a roll, and came up sprinting.

"Boy!" Justin said, projecting his voice loudly. I looked over my shoulder at him as I ran. His eyes were more coldly furious than I had ever seen them. "You are here with me — with Elaine. Or you are *nowhere.* If you don't come back right now, you are dead to me."

I lopped the last two words off the sentence to get his real meaning and poured on more speed. If I stayed, he meant to render me helpless, and from that beginning there could be no good endings. If I went back angry, I could fight him, but I couldn't win — not against the man who taught me everything I knew. I couldn't call the cops and tell them Justin was a mad wizard — they'd write me off as a nutcase or prankster without thinking twice. It wasn't like I could run to Oz and ask a more powerful wizard for help.

He'd never told me about the White Council or the rest of the supernatural world. Abusers like to isolate their victims. People who feel that they are completely alone tend not to fight back.

"Boy!" Justin's voice roared, now openly filled with rage. "Boy!"

He didn't need to say anything more. That rage said it all. The man who had given me a home was going to kill me.

It hurt so much, I wondered if he already had.

I put my head down and ran faster, my tears making the world a blur, with only one thought burning in my head:

This wasn't over. I knew that Justin could find me, no matter where I ran, no matter how well I hid. I hadn't escaped that strait-jacket. I had only delayed it for a little while.

I didn't have any choice.

I had to fight back.

"What happened next?" asked a fascinated voice.

I shook my head and snapped out of the reverie, looking up to the sunlit sky outside my grave. Winter's hold was definitely weakening. The sky was grey clouds interspersed with streaks of summer blue sky. There was a lot of water dripping down the edges of my grave, though the snow at the bottom was still holding its chill.

The Leanansidhe sat at the edge of my grave, her bare, dirty feet swinging back and forth. Her bright red hair had been bound back in a long tail, and she was dressed in the shreds of five or six different outfits. Her head was wrapped in a scarf that had been knitted from yarn duplicating various colors of dirty snow, and the tattered ends of it hung down on either side of her head. It gave her a sort of lunatic-coquette charm, especially considering the flecks of what looked like dried blood on the pale skin of her face. She looked as happy as a kid on Christmas morning.

I just stared up for a moment and then shook my head faintly. "You saw that? What I was thinking?"

"I see you," she said, as though that explained it. "Not what you were thinking. What you were remembering."

"Interesting," I said. It made a certain amount of sense that Lea could discern the spirit world better than I could. She was a creature who was at least partly native to the Nevernever. I probably looked like some kind of pale, white, ghostly version of myself to her, while the memories that were my substance played across the surface.

I thought about the wraiths and lemurs that Sir Stuart had put down on my first night as a ghost, and how they had seemed to bleed images as they faded away.

"Yes," she said, her tone pleased. "Precisely like that. My, but the Colonial Knight put on a display for you."

"You knew Sir Stuart?"

"I have seen him in battle on several occa-

430

sions," Lea said, her eyes somewhat dreamy. "He is a worthy gentleman, in his fashion. Quite dangerous."

"Not more dangerous than the Corpsetaker," I said. "She destroyed him."

Lea thrust out her lower lip and her brow furrowed in annoyance. "Did she? What a contemptible waste of a perfectly doughty spirit." She rolled her eyes. "At least, my godchild, you have discerned your foe's identity — and that of her pet."

I shivered. "Her and Evil Bob."

She waved a hand. "Evil is mainly an aesthetic choice. Only the spirit's power is significant, for your purposes."

"Not true," I said mildly. "Though I know you don't agree."

Her expression was pensive for a moment before she said, "You have your mother's Sight, you know."

"Not her eyes?"

"I've always thought you favored Malcolm." The serious expression vanished and she kicked her feet again. "So, young shade. What happened next?"

"You know. You were there."

"How do the mortals say it?" she murmured. "I missed that episode."

I coughed out a surprised little laugh.

She looked faintly miffed. "I do not know what happened between the time you left Justin and the time you came to me."

"I see." I grinned at her. "Do you think I just give away stories for free? To one of the Sidhe?"

She tilted back her head and laughed, and her eyes twinkled. Like, literally, with little flashes of light. "You have learned much. I began to despair of it, but it seems you may have acquired wisdom enough, and in time."

"In time to be dead," I said. "But, yeah. I've worked out by now that the Sidhe don't give anything away. Or take anything for free. And after however long, I realized why that might be: because you can't."

"Indeed," she said, beaming at me. "There must be balance, sweet godchild. Always balance. Never take a thing without giving such a thing in return; never give a favor without collecting one in kind. All of reality depends on balance."

I squinted at her. "That's why you gave Bianca *Amoracchius* years ago. So that you could accept that knife from her. The one Mab took from you."

She leaned toward me, her eyes all but glowing with intensity and her teeth showing in a sudden, carnivorous smile. "Indeed. And such a *treacherous* gift it was, child. Oh, but if that deceitful creature had survived you, such a vengeance I would have wreaked that the world would have spoken of it in whispers for a thousand years."

I squinted at her. "But . . . I killed Bianca

before you could balance the scales."

"Indeed, simple boy. Why else, think you, that I gifted you with the most potent powers of faerie to protect you and your companions when we battled Bianca's ultimate progenitors?"

"I thought you did it because Mab ordered you to."

"Tsk. In all of Winter, I am second in power only to Mab — which she has allowed because I have incurred with it proportionate obligation to her. She is my dearest enemy, but even I do not owe Mab so much. I helped you as much as I did, sweet child, because I owed you for collecting a portion of my due justice from Bianca," the Leanansidhe said. Her eyes grew wider, wilder. "The rest I took from the little whore's masters. Though I admit, I hadn't expected the collection to be quite so *thorough.*"

Memories flashed in my head. Susan. An obsidian knife. I felt sick.

I'll get over it, I told myself. Eventually. It hadn't been much more than a day from my point of view. I was probably still in shock or trauma or something — if ghosts could get that, I mean.

I looked up and realized that Lea was staring at me, at my memories, with undisguised glee. She let out a contented sigh and said, "You do not settle things by half measures, do you, my godson?"

I could get mad at her for being callous about calling those memories to my mind, or I could revile her for taking such joy in so much destruction and pain, but there wasn't a point in doing so. My godmother was what she was — a being of violence, deceit, and the thirst for power. She wasn't human. Her attitudes and reactions could not fairly be called inhumane.

Besides. I had gotten to know Lea's sovereign, Queen Mab, in a fashion so hideously intimate that I could not possibly describe it. And believe me. If Lea had been the high priestess of murder, bloodlust, scheming, and manipulation, then Mab was the goddess my godmother worshipped.

Come to think of it, that was probably an apt description of their relationship.

Six of one, a half dozen of another. My godmother wasn't going to change. There was no sense in holding what she was against her. So I just gave her a tired, whimsical smile instead.

"Saves time," I told her. "Do it thoroughly once, and you don't have to fool around with it again later."

She dropped back her head and let out a deep-throated laugh. Then she tilted her head and looked at me. "You didn't realize what would happen to mortal kind when you struck down the Red King and his brood. Did you?"

"I saw the opportunity," I said, after a moment. "If I'd stopped to think about the trouble it would create . . . I don't know if I'd have done it any differently. They had my girl."

Her eyes gleamed. "Spoken as someone worthy to wield power."

"Coming from you," I said, "that's . . . a little bit unsettling, actually."

She kicked both feet, girlishly pleased, and smiled down at me. "How sweet of you to say so."

The best thing about my faerie godmother is that the creepy just keeps on coming.

"I'll trade you," I said. "The rest of the tale for information."

She nodded her head in a businesslike fashion. "The tale for questions three?"

"Done."

"Done, done, and done," she replied.

So I told her.

CHAPTER THIRTY-ONE

I ran and ran for a good long while. I wasn't on the cross-country team at school, but I often went running with Elaine. It was how we'd hidden sneaking off to make out — and stuff — from Justin. He was a thorough sort of guy, so we made sure to actually do the running, too, in order to make our deception flawless. And the whole time, we thought we were getting away with it.

As an adult, I could see that our efforts were about as obvious as they could possibly be. Justin had known, I was certain — now. But back then, Elaine and I had been sure that we were masters of deceit.

That scheme's trappings were sure as hell turning out to be handy that day. My strides slowed but turned longer, steadier, machine-like. I was sixteen. I didn't wind down for almost an hour.

When I finally stopped, the terror had faded, if not the heartache, and I found myself in an entirely unexpected position.

I didn't know what was coming next. I didn't know what was expected of me.

I had to think. All by myself.

I ducked off the road and into a large culvert, huddling there while I got my breath back and flailed at the wet paper bag my brain was trapped within.

Mostly, I just kept thinking that I should have known. No one in my life had gone an inch out of their way to look out for me once my parents were gone. Justin's generosity, even seasoned with the demands of studying magic, had been too good to be true. I should have known it.

And Elaine. She'd just sat there while he'd been doing whatever he was going to do. She hadn't tried to warn me, hadn't tried to stop him. I had never known anyone in my life I had loved as much as Elaine.

I should have known she was too good to be true, too.

I wept for a while. I was tired and cold and my chest ached with the pain of loss. In a single moment, my home had been destroyed. My life had been destroyed.

But I shook my head ferociously, wiping my eyes and my nose on the leather sleeves of my jacket, heedless of what it did to them. I was still in danger. I had to think.

I had no means of travel, no money, and no idea of where to go. Hell's bells, I was lucky I had my shiny new driver's license in my pocket. It was mid-November, and my school letter jacket wasn't going to be enough to keep me warm once it got dark. My stomach made a cavernous noise, and I added starving hunger to my list of problems.

I needed shelter. I needed food. I needed to find someplace safe to hide from my mentor until I could figure out how to take him on — and to get all of that, I needed money. And I needed it fast.

So, once it got dark, I, uh . . .

Look. I was sixteen.

Once it got dark, I sort of knocked over a convenience store.

For lack of anything better to hide my face, I'd tied my sweaty T-shirt around my head in a sort of makeshift balaclava. I didn't have anything else to wear except my letter jacket, which seemed more or less like a screaming advertisement to make it simple for the cops to figure out my identity. There wasn't much I could do except to rip all the patches off of it and hope for the best. After that, I'd scavenged a paper sack from a trash bin, emptied it, and stuck my right hand in it.

Once I had my equipment ready, I looked up at the streetlights glowing outside the QuikStop and flicked a quick hex at them.

Learning magic is hard, but if you can do even fairly modest spells, you find out that wrecking technology is *easy*. Anything with

electronics built into it is particularly susceptible to a hex, but if you put enough oomph
into it, even simpler technology can be
shorted out or otherwise made to malfunction. At sixteen, I wasn't anywhere near the
wizard I would be even five or six years later
— but those lights didn't have a prayer. The
two streetlights over the parking lot flickered
and went black.

I hit the lights outside the store next, and
two security cameras. I was getting increasingly nervous as I went along, and the last
hex accidentally blew out the store's freezers
and overhead lights along with the security
camera. The only lighting left in the place
came from a pinball machine and a couple of
aging arcade video games.

I swallowed and hit the door, going through
in a half-doubled-over crouch, so that there
wouldn't be any way to compare my height
to the marker on the inside frame of the door.
I held out my right hand like it was a gun,
which it might have been: I had the paper
sack I'd acquired pulled over it. There was
something cold and squishy and greasy on
the inside of the bag. Mayonnaise, maybe? I
hated mayo.

I hustled up to the cashier, a young man
with a brown mullet and a Boston T-shirt,
pointed the paper sack at him, and said,
"Empty the drawer!"

He blinked reddened, watery eyes at me.

Then at the paper bag.

"Empty the drawer or I'll blow your head off!" I shouted.

It probably would have been more intimidating if my voice hadn't cracked in the middle.

"Uh, man," the cashier said, and I finally twigged to the scent of recently burned marijuana. The guy didn't look scared. He looked confused. "Dude, what is . . . Did you see the lights just . . . ?"

I really hadn't wanted to do this, but I didn't have much of a choice. I made a little bit of a production of turning the "gun" to point at the liquor bottles behind the counter, gathered up my will, and screamed, "Ka-bang! Ka-bang!"

My verbal incantations have actually gotten *more* sophisticated and worldly over the years, not less.

I know, right? It shocks me, too.

The spell was just basic kinetic energy, and it didn't really hit much harder than a baseball thrown by a high school pitcher — a regular pitcher, not like Robert Redford in *The Natural.* That wasn't really enough power to threaten anyone's life, but it was noisy and it was more than enough energy to smash a couple of bottles. They shattered with loud barking sounds and showers of glass and booze.

"Holy crap!" shouted the cashier. I saw that

his name tag read STAN. "Dude!" He flinched down, holding his arms up around his head. "Don't shoot!"

I pointed the paper bag at him and said, "Give me all the money, Stan!"

"Okay, okay!" Stan said. "Oh, God. Don't kill me!"

"Money!" I shouted.

He turned to the register and started fumbling at it, stabbing at the keys.

As he did, I sensed a movement behind me, an almost subliminal presence. It's the kind of thing you expect to experience while standing in a line — the silent pressure of another living being behind you, temporarily sharing your space. But I wasn't standing in a line, and I whirled in panic and shouted, "Kabang!" again.

There was a loud snap of sound as pure force lashed through the air and the glass door to a freezer of ice cream shattered.

"Oh, God," Stan moaned. "Please don't kill me!"

There was no one behind me. I tried to look in every direction at once and more or less succeeded.

There was no one else in the store. . . .

And yet the presence was still there, on the back of my neck, closer and more distinct than a moment before.

What the hell?

"Run!" said a resonant baritone.

I turned and pointed the paper bag at the pair of video games.

"Run!" said the voice on the Sinistar game. "I live! I . . . am . . . Sinistar!"

"Don't move," I said to Stan. "Just put the money in a bag."

"Money in a bag, man," Stan panted. He was practically sobbing. "I'm supposed to do whatever you want, right? That's what the owners have told us cashiers, right? I'm supposed to give you the money. No argument. Okay?"

"Okay," I said, my eyes flicking nervously around the place. "It's not worth dying for, is it, Stan?"

"Got that right," Stan muttered. "They're only paying me five dollars an hour." He finally managed to open the drawer and started fumbling bills into a plastic bag. "Okay, dude. Just a second."

"Run!" said the Sinistar machine. "Run!"

Again, the insubstantial pressure against the back of my neck increased. I turned in a slow circle, but nothing was there — nothing I could see, at any rate.

But what if there *was* something there? Something that couldn't be seen? I had never actually seen something summoned from the netherworld, but Justin had described such beings repeatedly, and I didn't think he'd been lying. Such a beast would make an ideal hunter; just the sort of thing to send out after a mouthy apprentice who refused to wear his straitjacket like a good boy.

I took two slow steps toward the video game, staring at its screen. I didn't pay attention to the spaceship or the asteroids or the giant, disembodied skull flying around. I didn't care about the flickers of static that washed across the screen as I got closer, something inside its computer reacting to my presence. No. I paid attention to the glass screen and to the reflection of the store that shone dimly upon it.

I identified my outline on it, long and thin. I could see the vague outlines of the store as more shadowy shapes — aisles and end caps, the counter and the door.

And the Thing standing just inside the door.

It was huge. I mean, it was taller and broader than the door was. It was more or less humanoid. The proportions were wrong. The shoulders too wide, the arms too long, the legs crooked and too thick. It was covered in fur or scales or some scabrous, fungal amalgamation of both. And its eyes were empty, angled pits of dim violet light.

I felt my hands begin to shake. Tremble. Actually, they became absolutely spastic. The paper bag made a steady rattling sound. There was a creature from another world standing behind me. I could *feel* it, no more than seven or eight feet away from me, every bit as real as Stan, to every sense but my sight. It took a real effort to move my head enough to cast a single, hurried glance over my shoulder.

Nothing. Stan was shoveling various bills into a bag. The store was otherwise empty. The door hadn't opened since I had come through it. There was a bell on it. It would have rung had it opened. I looked back at the reflection.

The Thing was two feet closer.

And it was smiling.

It had a head whose shape was all but obscured by growths or lumpy scales or matted fur. But beneath its eyes I could see a mouth, too wide to be real, filled with teeth too sharp and serrated and yellow to belong to anything of this earth. That was a smile from Lewis Carroll's opium-inspired, laudanum-dosed nightmares.

My legs felt like they were going to collapse into water at any second. I couldn't catch my breath. I couldn't move.

Malice slithered up my spine and danced in spiteful shivers over the back of my neck. I could sense the thing's hostility — not the mindless anger of a fellow boy I'd needled beyond self-restraint, or Justin's cold, logical rage. This was something different, something vaster, more timeless, and deeper than any ocean. It was a poisonous hate, something so ancient, so vile, that it could almost kill without any other action or being to support it, a hate so old and so virulent that it had curdled and congealed over its surface into a stinking, staggering contempt.

This thing wanted to destroy me. It wanted to hurt me. It wanted to enjoy the process. And nothing I said, nothing I did, would ever, ever change that. I was something to be eradicated, preferably in some amusing fashion. It had no mercy. It had no fear. And it was old, old beyond my ability to comprehend. It was patient. And if I proved too disappointing to it, I would only break through the veneer of that contempt — and what lay beneath would dissolve me like the deadliest acid. I felt . . . stained, simply by feeling its presence, stained as if it had left some hideous imprint or mark upon me, one that could not be wiped away.

And then it was behind me, so close it could almost touch, its outline towering over me, huge and horrible.

And it leaned down. A forked tongue slithered out from between its horrible shark-chain-saw teeth, and it whispered, in a perfectly low, calm, British accent, "What you have just sensed is as close as your mind can come to encompassing my name. How do you do?"

I tried to talk. I couldn't. I couldn't make the words form in my mouth. I couldn't get enough air to push my voice up out of my throat.

Damn it. Damn it, I was more than some terrified child. I was more than some helpless orphan preparing to endure what someone vastly older and more powerful than me was preparing to inflict. I had touched the very forces of Creation. I was a young force of nature. I had seen things no one else could see, done things no one else could do.

And in a moment like that, there was only one thing I could ask myself:

What would Jack Burton do?

"I'm f-f-f-fine," I said in a hoarse, hardly understandable voice. "That's a mouthful, and I'm busy. D-do you maybe have a nickname?"

Its smile widened.

"Little Morsel, among those whom I have disassembled," it purred, its tone wrapping lovingly around the last word of the phrase, "I have several times been called by the same phrase."

"O-oh? W-what's that?"

"He," purred the thing, "Who Walks Behind."

CHAPTER THIRTY-TWO

"He Who Walks Behind?" I said, fighting a losing battle to keep from trembling. "As scary names go, that one kind of isn't. I'd stick with the first one. More evocative."

"Be patient," purred the creature's disembodied voice. "You will understand it before the end."

"Uh, dude?" Stan asked quietly. "Uh . . . Who are you talking to?"

"Oh, tell him," the creature said. "That should be entertaining."

"Shut up, Stan," I said. "And get out."

"Uh," said Stan. "What?"

I whirled on him and pointed the paper bag at him, my arms extending through the space where He Who Walks Behind apparently both was and wasn't. "Get the hell out of here!"

Stan fell all over himself trying to comply. He literally went to the tile floor twice on his way to the door, his eyes wide, and stumbled out and into the night.

I turned back to the reflective surface of

the video game's screen, and just as I again found the shape inside it, fire erupted along my spine. I was slammed forward into the video game, and my head hit it hard enough to send a spiderweb of cracks through the machine's glass screen. Pain, sickening and harsh, flooded through my skull, and I staggered.

But I didn't fall. Justin DuMorne had been hard on me. It hadn't ever been this bad, this scary, and it had never hurt so much — but then, it had never been for real. I grabbed the machine's sides, forced my fingers to hold on, and kept myself from falling.

"Run! Run!" screamed the machine again. This time, the voice was blurred and distorted, disturbingly deep and malicious. I noted blurrily that the cracked and wildly flickering screen had a terrified wizard's blood all over it. The game's computer was apparently failing.

"You think that the inebriated little mortal is going to run to fetch the authorities," purred the creature's voice. I turned my head, looking around, and didn't see anything. But the motion sent fire down my back, and for the first time I felt a trickling there beneath my jacket. I was bleeding.

"You think that if they come running in their vehicles, with their lights and their symbols, that I will flee."

I turned and put my back to the machine.

My legs felt wobbly, but I was beginning to fight through the pain. I clenched my teeth and snarled, "Get away from me."

"I assure you," came the creature's bodiless voice, "that we will not be disturbed. I have made sure of it. But it does demonstrate that you possess a certain talent for performance under pressure. Does it not?"

"You sound like my guidance counselor," I said, and wiped blood from one of my eyes. I took a breath and stalked forward, wobbling only a little. I grabbed the bag of money Stan had left on the counter. "I guess maybe you are a little scary."

"Neither fear nor pain sway you from your objective. Excellent." This time, the thing's voice was coming from the far side of the convenience store. "But there's no knowing the true temper of the blade until it has been tested. Even the strongest-seeming steel may have hidden flaws. This may be interesting."

I paused, frowning, and looked up at my faerie godmother, who still sat at the edge of my grave, listening raptly. "I . . . Godmother, I've heard it said that ghosts are memories."

"Indeed," Lea said, nodding.

"Are the memories truth?"

Lea arched a rather caustic eyebrow at my words. "You ask your first question before finishing the tale?" Her mouth twisted in distaste. "Your storytelling form leaves something to be desired, child."

"Yeah, I never did too well in English class. Will you answer the question?"

Her eyes became very, very green and glittered with a wild, gleeful light. "They are the facts, the events as you experienced them."

I frowned. "I never really had a clear recollection of exactly what the thing said to me," I said. "I mean, that blow to the head gave me a headache for days."

"Ah yes," Lea said. "I remember your pain."

She would. "Yeah, uh. Anyway. I'm remembering the conversation now, word for word. Is that real? Or is it something that guy in black made up to fill in the blanks?"

"They are your memories," she said, "the record, the impression of what you lived. Your brain isn't the only place they are stored — it is, in truth, often a poor facility for such a purpose." She paused to consider her next words and then spread her hands, palms up, an odd light in her eyes. "It is the nature of the universe that things remain. Nothing ever disappears completely. The very sound of Creation still echoes throughout the vast darkness: The universe remembers. You are currently free of the shackles of mortality. Your limited brain no longer impedes access to that record. The only blocks to your memory are those you allow to be."

"That's either very Zen or very . . . very crazy," I said. "So, this memory — this is all the actual event?"

"Did I not just say as much?" she asked crossly. "It would make a ridiculous fiction. Why would I bother listening otherwise?"

I honestly wasn't sure. But I decided not to push the issue. Ghost Harry, wise Harry.

"Now," the Leanansidhe said. "If you are quite finished holding hostage my imagination, pray continue."

"Get away from me," I snarled, clutching the money. Sparks spat fitfully from the fried security camera. They were most of the light in the place. Even if the creature had been something solid and physical, it might have hidden in the stretches of shadow between the flickering motes of light. I didn't see it anywhere.

So it came as a shock to me when something gripped the back of my neck and effortlessly flung me into an end cap of various doughnuts and pastries.

I went through it and hit the shelf behind. It hurt more than I could have believed. Years later, I would have considered it a minor foothill of pain, but at the time it was a mountain. The sweet smell of sugar and chocolate filled my nose. I figured my backside must be coated in about half an inch of frosting, cream filling, and powdered sugar. The scent made my stomach howl for food, gurgling loudly enough to be heard over the sound of items falling from the shelves here and there.

Like I said. Sixteen.

"Such a useless scrap of meat contains you," the creature said, its voice unchanged by the violence. "It is entirely inconsequential, and yet it molds you. Your existence is a series of contradictions. But here is certainty, mortal child: This time, you cannot run."

The hell I couldn't. Running had always served me fairly well, and I saw no reason to change my policy now. I scrambled to my feet and ran for the back of the store, away from the presumed direction of my attacker. I rounded the far corner of the aisle and pressed my back up against it, panting.

Something hard and hot and slimy settled around my neck, a noose made of moist serpent, and just as strong. It jerked me up and off my feet, a bruising force that threw me into the air and released me almost instantly.

I had an enormous flash of empathy for Jerry, facing the raw power and amused pleasure of a large, invisible Tom.

"You cannot escape what is always behind you," it said.

I landed on my ass, hard, and scrambled toward the other aisle on my hands and knees, only to feel another terrible force strike me, a contemptuous kick in the seat of my pants. It flung me forward into a glass door on a wall of refrigerated cabinets holding racks and racks of cold drinks.

I bounced off the door and landed, dazed, staring for a second at the large cracks my head had left in the glass.

"No one will save you."

I tried to crawl farther away. I made it only far enough to reach the next cabinet, and then a blow struck me in the ribs and flung me into the next glass door. My shoulder hit it this time and didn't break the glass, but I felt something go *pop* in my arm, and the whole limb seemed to light up with abrupt awareness of pain.

The unseen presence of the creature came closer. Its voice lowered to a bare, pleased murmur. "Child of the stars. I will destroy you this night."

My head was full of pain and fear. I could sense it getting closer again, coming up behind me — always there, I somehow knew, where I was weakest, most vulnerable. That was where it would always be.

I had to move. I had to do something. But the terror felt like lead weights on my wrists and ankles, sapping my strength, making muscles turn to water, thoughts to noise. I tried to run, but the best I could do was a slow, slippery scramble down the aisle of cold drinks.

"Pathetic," said He Who Walks Behind, growing nearer with every word. "Whimpering, mewling thing. Useless."

Terror.

I couldn't think.

I was going to die.

I was going to die.

And then my mouth said, in a damned passable Pee-wee Herman impersonation, "I know you are, but what am I?"

He Who Walks Behind stopped in his tracks. There was a flickering heartbeat of uncertainty in that inevitable presence, and the creature said, "What?"

"Ha-ha!" I said in the same voice, double-tapping my own fear with the character's staccato laugh. A thought came shining through my head: *Maybe I can't stop this thing from coming at my back.*

But I can choose which way I turn it.

I struggled to my feet and started town the aisle, spinning with every step, whirling-dervish style. The whole time, I heard myself spewing Pee-wee Herman's cartoony laugh — which, in retrospect, was possibly the creepiest thing to hit my ears that night.

I hit the door with a hip and an elbow and blew through it, still spinning, out into the parking lot. Once there, I realized that my escape plan did not have a part two. It hadn't been concerned with getting me any farther than the doors of the store.

I'd achieved the objective. Now what?

The darkened parking lot was a mass of

shadows. The nearest lights were a hundred yards away, and seemed somehow dimmer, more orange than they should have been. There was a heaviness in the air and a faint, faint stench of death and rot. Had that been something the creature had done? Had that been what it meant when it said it had made sure of our privacy?

Stan was in the parking lot, out between the two islands housing the convenience store's gas pumps. He looked like a man who was trying to run in slow motion. His arms were moving very slowly, his legs bent as if sprinting, but his pace was much slower than a walk, as if he'd been trying to run through a rice paddy filled with peanut butter. He was looking over his shoulder at me, and his face was distorted with terror, a horrible mask that hardly looked human in the shadow-haunted night.

I began to run toward him on pure instinct. Herd instinct, really, operating on the assumption that there was greater safety in numbers. My feet pounded the parking lot's asphalt at normal speed, and his eyes widened with almost comical slowness and amazement as I ran toward him.

"Is that what you are?" came the creature's voice, from no direction and from all of them. "One of them? One of the swarm that infests this world?" The origin point of the voice changed, and I suddenly felt hot, stinking breath right on the back of my neck. "I expected better of a pupil of DuMorne."

I whirled, throwing my arms up defensively. I had time to see everything in the reflection of the convenience store's broad front windows.

He Who Walks Behind emerged from the shadows in front of the terrified Stan. Broad, horrible arms wrapped around him, crushing him as easily as a man picking up a child. Another limb, maybe a tail or some kind of tentacle, covered in the same growth-fur-scales as the rest of the creature, joined the two arms, so that Stan was wrapped at the shoulders, at the bottom of the ribs, and at the hips.

And then with a slow smile and a simple, savage twisting motion, He Who Walks Behind tore Stan the convenience store clerk into three pieces.

I'd seen death before, but not like that. Not terrible and swift and bloody. I spun back to Stan in time to see the three pieces fall to the ground. Blood went everywhere. One of his arms waved in frantic windmills, and his mouth opened as if to scream, but nothing came out except a vomiting gurgle and a gout of blood. Wide, terrified eyes stared at mine for a second, and I jerked my gaze away, desperate to avoid seeing Stan's soul as he died.

Then he just sort of . . . changed. From a

person in hideous pain and fear to an empty pile of . . . of meat. Parts. Soiled cloth.

I had never seen death come like that. As a humiliation, a reduction of a unique soul to nothing more than constituent matter. When the creature killed Stan, it didn't simply end his life. It underscored the underlying futility, the ultimate insignificance of that life. It made a man, albeit a fairly unmotivated one, into less than nothing — something that had been a waste of the resources it had consumed. Something that had never had a choice in its own fate, never had a chance to be anything more.

I had involved Stan in this struggle. It hadn't been his fight at all.

Granted, I had never intended to hurt the guy and never would have. Nonetheless, without my decision to stick up the convenience store, he would have still been loitering behind the counter, killing time until his next joint. He had been caught up in violence that he had done nothing to earn or expect — and it had killed him.

Something in my head went *click.*

That wasn't right.

Stan shouldn't have died like that. No one should. No one — man, beast, or otherwise — should get to decide, in a moment of malicious humor, that it got to end Stan's life, to take away everything he was and everything he might ever be.

Stan hadn't deserved it. He hadn't been looking for it. And that creature, that demon, had murdered him.

I felt my jaw begin to ache as it clenched harder and harder. I could feel my rapid pulse beating behind my eyes. There was a terrible pressure inside my head and inside my chest, and with it came a rising wave of anger, and something darker and deadlier than anger that came welling up like a great wave from an unlit sea.

It.

Wasn't.

Right.

No, it wasn't. But the world wasn't a fair place, was it? And I had more reason to know it than most people twice my age. The world wasn't nice, and it wasn't fair. People who didn't deserve it suffered and died every single day.

So what? *So somebody ought to do something about it.*

My right arm and shoulder burned like fire as I felt my right hand slowly form a tight fist. The knuckles popped one by one. They hadn't ever done that before.

I turned to face the creature's image in the reflection. It was crouched over Stan's corpse, its talons tapping lightly on the dead man's open eyes, its mouth still stretched into that horrible, wide smile.

And when it saw the look on my face, its

smile widened and its eyes narrowed. "Ah-hhh," it said. "Ahhhhh. There you are."

I was not a victim. I was not a powerless child. I was a wizard. I was furious. And I was finished running. "This isn't your world," I whispered.

"Not now," He Who Walks Behind murmured, its smile widening. "But it will be ours again in just a little time."

"You won't be around to see it," I said.

I had never used my power in anger. I had never consciously tried to harm another being with my magic.

But this thing? If anything I had ever seen had it coming, if ever a being was deserving of receiving my violence, it was the blood-stained creature crouching over Stan's mangled body. Everything had been taken away from me in the space of a single afternoon. My home. My family. And now, it seemed, I was about to lose my life. Well, if that was how it was going to be, if I couldn't run without getting more innocent bystanders killed, then I would make my stand here — and I had no intention of going quietly.

I reached into that deep well of anger and began drawing it together into something as hot and violent and destructive as what I was feeling inside.

"There's something you should know," I said. "I skipped sixth hour today. Spanish. Which I'm not very good at anyway."

"What is that to me?" asked the creature.

"*Flickum bicus* just doesn't seem appropriate," I replied. The heat in my right arm and shoulder concentrated into my right hand. The scent of burned hairs crept up to my nose. "And you really don't understand where you're standing, do you?"

The creature's reflection looked left and right at the gas pumps on either side of it.

I kept my eyes locked on its image in the windows, extended my right hand back toward it, and formed my little fire-lighting spell into something a thousand times bigger, hotter, and deadlier than anything I had ever attempted before.

I met the thing's eyes in the reflection, reached down to the well of energy and pure will I'd built inside me, extended my hand toward the creature, and screamed, *"Fuego!"*

My rage and fear poured out of me. Fire lashed out from my open hand like water from a broken hydrant. It spilled all over He Who Walks Behind and over Stan's body, and lit up the darkness with angry golden light.

The creature let out a scream, more surprise and anger than pain, clutching at its eyes with its huge hands. The light changed the reflection in the glass and I could no longer see what was behind me. I swept the torrent of fire left and right without turning away or changing the direction my back faced. I hoped it would slow He Who Walks Behind long enough for my modified fire-starting spell to do its thing.

Gasoline pumps have all kinds of safety mechanisms built into them to reduce the odds of accidentally igniting them. They're pretty good. I mean, how many times have you touched off an explosion while filling your car? But as reliable as they are, those measures are made to stop *accidents.*

And no engineer in the world ever thought about building them to stop angry young wizards.

It took a couple of seconds, but then there was a screaming sound, something metallic strained past the breaking point, and the first tank went up in a bloom of spectacular fire.

The explosion flung me back, scorching my skin and burning away the hair on my eyebrows. I landed on my ass — again — and lay there, stunned, for a few seconds. Sudden weariness, deeper than anything I had ever known, flooded over me in reaction to the energy I'd expended on my economy-sized ignition spell.

And then the second tank went up.

Hot wind and pieces of smoking metal showered against the front of the convenience store. I'm glad the first blast knocked me down. If I'd been standing, the metal shrapnel that punched out the entire front wall of windows would have gone through me first.

I stared at the flames and saw a shape

461

within it — or, rather, I saw a creature-shaped void where the smoke and fire should have been. A voice emerged from the fire, something huge and terrifying, a voice that belonged to gods and monsters of myth.

"HOW DARE YOU!" it roared. "HOW DARE YOU RAISE YOUR HAND AGAINST ME!"

Then that not-figure crashed to its knees and fell limply onto its side.

The roaring flames swept in and consumed it.

And my first true battle was over.

CHAPTER THIRTY-THREE

"That was my first fight," I said quietly to my godmother. "I'd never used magic to hurt anything before." I rubbed my hand over my head. "If I hadn't cut class that day . . . I don't know. I might never have become what I did."

"Is that the lesson you took from the memory?" Lea asked, her smile spreading. "You were clearly being prepared to be an enforcer."

"It seems that way," I hedged, trying to read her expression. "But Justin never actually tried to get me to hurt anyone."

"Why would he wish you to be armed against him before he was certain of your loyalty?" Lea asked. "He would have. It was inevitable."

"Probably," I said. "But there's no way we can know, really. It's a long way from breaking boards in practice to breaking bones in life."

"Quite. Because convincing a young mortal

to believe that it is right and proper to use magic for violence is a delicate process and one that cannot be rushed."

I grunted and leaned my head back against the wall of my grave.

"All the wishing in the world will not change the past, my godson," Lea said. "You would like to believe that perhaps Justin had hidden good intentions of some sort. That what happened between you was some kind of misunderstanding. But you understood him perfectly."

"Yeah. Probably. I'd forgotten how much it hurt — that's all," I said quietly. "I'd forgotten how much I loved him. How much I wanted him to be proud of me."

"Children are vulnerable," Lea said. "They are easily deceived and notoriously subject to such delusions. You are no longer a child." She leaned forward slightly and said, with slight emphasis, "I am bound to answer two more questions. Will you ask them now?"

"Yes," I said. "Give me a moment to consider them."

"As you wish," Lea said.

I closed my eyes for a moment and tried to clear my thoughts. Asking questions of inhuman entities can be a tricky and dangerous business — with the fae more than most. You almost never got direct answers from one of the lords of Faerie, the Sidhe. Asking them direct questions, especially questions touching on information relevant to a conflict of some sort, was likely to elicit obscure and maliciously misleading answers. I was on good terms with my godmother, as human-Sidhe relationships went, but that was no reason not to cover my bases.

So I thought over recent events for a while and looked for the blank spots, but I kept getting distracted by the memories of that night in the convenience store. They chewed at me and refused to be pushed aside — especially the conversation with He Who Walks Behind.

"Priorities," I said out loud. "This is about priorities."

"Oh?" Lea asked.

I nodded. "I could ask you a lot of questions about my past — and you'd answer them."

"That is true."

"Or I could ask you about what is happening right now in the city. I could find out how I could best help Murphy."

Lea nodded.

"But I was sent back here to find my killer," I said. "I'm supposed to be hunting down whoever killed me, and yet I've been doing a whole lot of everything but that."

"In point of fact," Lea said, "you've been doing little else."

I blinked.

She gave me an enigmatic, feline smile.

"Oh, you bitch." I sighed. "You just love doing that to me."

Lea demurely lowered her gaze. She fluttered her eyelashes twice.

I scowled at her and folded my arms over my chest. Lea had been involved in my life since I was born, and probably before that. She could tell me any number of things I'd been quietly dying to know since I was old enough to ask questions at all. She was up on all the current events, too. All of the high Sidhe are fanatic gatherers of information, and my godmother was no exception. Of course, they tended to guard their knowledge as ferociously as a dragon guards its gold — and they parted with it almost as reluctantly.

The Sidhe aren't dummies. Information is a great deal more valuable than gold, any day of the week.

So I circled back to my earlier question. Where *did* my priorities lie? What was more important to me: Digging up secrets from the shadowy bits of my past? Getting the information I needed to move on to my future? Or helping my friends and loved ones right now?

Yeah. No-brainer.

"What can you tell me about the Corpsetaker, her resources, and her goals?" I asked.

Lea considered the answer for a moment before nodding to herself. "The creature you ask about is motivated purely by self-interest.

After the body she possessed was killed by a brash, impulsive, and dangerous young wizard, her spirit remained behind. It took a score of moons for her to gather enough coherence to act, and even then she had precious little power to exert upon the mortal world.

"She was limited to speaking with the few mortals who can perceive such things. So she found them and began to manipulate them, guiding them together into the group you have already encountered. Her goal was to assemble her followers, spiritual and material, and then to abduct a body of appropriate strength."

"Clarification," I interjected. "You mean a body with magical capability?"

"With significant capability," Lea replied, stressing the phrase. "When Corpsetaker's spirit still dwelt upon the mortal coil, even bodies with latent talent were hospitable enough for her to exercise her full power. But thanks to you, and like you, my dear godson, she has passed beyond the threshold between life and death. Now she requires a body with a much greater inherent talent in order to use her gifts once she is inside it."

I tapped my lips with a fingertip, thinking. "So you're saying Mort is a major talent."

"In certain respects, he is more potent than you were, Godson. And he is a great deal more practical — he avoided the notice of the White Council almost entirely and hid his abilities from them quite neatly. The Corpsetaker wants him. She doubtless intends to make some use of the city's dead and establish herself as the city's dominant practitioner."

I blinked. "Why? I mean . . . she's just going to attract attention from the Council if she does that, and she's still on their Wanted Dead or Alive but Mostly Dead list."

"Not if she looks like the little ectomancer," Lea countered. "She will simply be a concealed talent unveiling itself in a time of dire need."

"But why risk it in the first place? Why Chicago?"

Lea frowned, golden red brows drawing together. "I do not know. But the Fomor are dangerous folk with whom to make bargains."

I lifted my eyebrows. Considering the source, that was really saying something.

"In my judgment," she continued, "the only reason Corpsetaker would deal with the Fomor would be to establish her presence here — probably as a loosely attached vassal of their nobility."

I found myself scowling. "Well. She isn't going to do it. This is my town."

My godmother let out another silver-chime laugh. "Is it? Even now?"

"Course," I said. I rubbed at my jaw. "What happens if she gets Morty?"

Lea looked momentarily baffled. "She wins?"

I waved a hand. "No, no. How do I get her back out of him?"

Her eyelids lowered slightly. "You have already utilized the only method I know."

"So I gotta get her before she gets to Morty," I said quietly.

"If you wish to save his life, yes."

"And from the sound of the conversation with Creepy Servitor Guy, I'd better break up the Corpsetaker-Fomor team before it gathers any momentum."

"It would seem to be wise," Lea said.

"Why the Fomor?" I asked. "I mean, I barely know who they are. Why are they all over Chicago now? Who are they?"

"Once, they were the enemies of my people, Winter and Summer alike," she said, lifting her chin as her emerald eyes grew distant. "We banished them to the sea. Now they are the exiles of myth and legend, the outcasts of the gods and demons of every land bordering the sea. Defeated giants, fallen gods, dark reflections of beings of light. They are many races and none, joined together beneath the banner of the Fomor in a common cause."

"Revenge," I guessed.

"Quite. It is a goal best served by gathering power, an activity that has been made attractive by the fall of the Red Court. And I have been more than generous with my answer to your question."

"You have. I am grateful, Godmother."

She smiled at me. "Such a charming child, betimes. Two questions have been answered. Your third?"

I thought some more. Somehow, I doubted that asking *Say, who killed me?* would yield any comprehensible results.

On the other hand, what the hell? You never know until you try.

"Say," I asked, "who killed me?"

Chapter Thirty-Four

The Leanansidhe looked down at me, her almond-shaped green eyes distant, pensive.

"Oh, my child," she breathed after a moment. "You ask such dangerous questions."

I cocked my head to one side. "You agreed to answer."

"And I must," she agreed. "And I must not."

I frowned. "That doesn't make any sense."

"Of course, child. You are not Sidhe." She crossed her ankles, frowning, and I saw a distinct spark of irritated rebellion enter her eyes. "I'm of a mind to tell you and end this charade."

YOU MUST NOT.

Eternal Silence's voice wasn't quite the same mind-destroying artillery shell it had been the first time the verdigris-encrusted statue had thought-spoken to me, but that might have been a function of me being sheltered in what amounted to a foxhole. The force of it blew Lea's long hair straight back, and her head snapped to one side as sharply as if she'd been slapped on the cheek. A shadow fell across my grave, and I looked up to see the statue looming overhead.

In broad daylight.

Which meant . . . which meant that whatever the thing was, it *wasn't* a ghost like me. I'd have been withered and blasted into the scraps of what I was now if I'd ventured out of my grave. The lingering power of the dawn wouldn't destroy me, but it would hurt, a lot, and it would cripple and weaken me.

Eternal Silence was apparently having no problems with it.

Lea turned her head back to the statue, her eyes and expression cold. "I am perfectly aware of the situation," she spat. Then she tilted her head to one side and paused, as if listening to a speaker I couldn't hear. She sighed. "Fear not, ancient thing. I have no intention of depriving either of you."

What? *What!?!* Either of *who?*

It was one of those questions to which I knew damned well that no one would tell me the answer.

Crud.

Clearly I should have haggled for seven questions.

"Child," Lea said, "I will tell you an answer that is true. But it is not the answer that you desire."

"Three true answers," I shot back immediately. "The bargain was made in good faith."

Lea puffed out a little breath and made a very contained and elegant gesture that somehow managed to convey the same meaning as if she had thrown her hands up. "Will you never cease pushing?"

"Never, ever," I said.

"Impossible child. Oh, very well. If it will fill that bottomless well you call curiosity." She shook her head, glanced again at Eternal Silence, and said, "The first truth is that you are acquainted with your killer."

I swallowed. The single truly redeeming factor of the Sidhe, Winter or Summer, is that they can't knowingly speak a lie. They are, in fact, completely incapable of it. That's not the same thing as saying that they can't deceive — they are past masters of deceit, after all. But they can't do it by directly speaking words that aren't true.

Which meant that, assuming Lea's information was good, I had just eliminated better than six billion possible suspects — and Lea's information was always good.

Lea nodded at me, the gesture so slight that I almost thought I imagined it. "The second truth is that your murder was but one of thousands at the killer's hands."

I took that in as well, trying to look at it from all angles. I knew some people and things who were stone-cold killers, but beings who had killed thousands of mortals were few and far between. Famous snipers in the World Wars hadn't accumulated more than a few hundred kills. Serial killers working for decades hadn't done any better. But supernatural predators, especially the long-lived ones, could add up that kind of count in a particularly active century or two.

Oh, and I had done my best to shut down pretty much every one of them I actually knew. The suspect pool was rapidly growing smaller.

"The final truth," Lea said. She suddenly looked very tired. "Your killer was but the proxy of another being, and one mightier and more dangerous than he."

He. Male. The pool dwindled by half, give or take.

So . . .

So, aside from the dick who killed me, I also had his boss to worry about.

Super.

"I can say no more, Godson," Lea said.

YOU HAVE ALREADY SAID TOO MUCH.

Lea lifted her hand as if to shield her face from a sudden wind and scowled in Eternal Silence's direction. "Your knowledge of mortals is relatively scarce. It is done. Desist your howling." Lea paused to look to one side again, stiffened her back a little, and added a belated and unenthusiastic, "If you please."

The silent figure looked from my godmother to me, and though it didn't have lungs with which to draw breath, I somehow sensed that it was about to speak.

"I know," I said hurriedly. "I know. Know my path. No need to blow my brains out repeating yourself."

Eternal Silence seemed faintly, vaguely annoyed. There came a purely psychic sensation, something that . . . that really reminded me of an unsatisfied grunt. Then the statue turned away and vanished from my sight.

"Huh," I said, after the figure had gone. "What the hell was that about?"

"Proxies," the Leanansidhe muttered, barely audible. "Always proxies. And respect."

"What?"

She gave me a direct look, and I had the impression that she was saying something with particular meaning. "Proxies, child. Those who appear to speak on behalf of another who cannot be present. Much as I have served as a proxy for my queen over the years, or she for me." Lea shook her head and said, "I must go, child."

"Wait," I said, reaching up to touch her foot with my hand.

My ectoplasmic flesh did not sink through hers. My hand felt nothing, yet met an odd resistance to its motion. I didn't pass into her as I had Mort or Molly. I blinked a little at that.

"I am of two worlds," she said, her tone

slightly impatient. As she often did, she had evidently guessed at my thoughts. "Of course I don't feel the same as mortal flesh."

"Oh," I said. "Uh. Listen. I just want . . . I need to know that you're going to take care of Molly."

She tilted her head and studied me for a moment. "But . . . child. It was never your responsibility to care for the young woman."

"Yes, it was," I said. "She was my apprentice."

"Indeed. Someone whom you had pledged to teach — not to care for. Child, did you miss the entire point of the exercise?"

I opened my mouth and then closed it again. "Maybe I did. What was supposed to happen?"

"You were supposed to teach her to care for herself," Lea replied in a matter-of-fact tone. "Your failure to do so . . ." She frowned. "I confess that I have only a limited understanding of the concepts of good and evil. The differences seem largely semantic to me when applied to empiric situations. Yet it seems to me that you did her no great kindness by being gentle."

I met the Sidhe's impassive gaze for a moment before I looked away. "You might be right."

"I am very old, child. It is a safe assumption in most circumstances." She sniffed and leaned down to pat my hand in a rather peremptory gesture. "Now, then. Listen to the nice statue. And *do* try to destroy anyone who seeks to do you harm. Death should be a learning experience, after all, or what's the point?"

Something in my godmother's words managed to land on the ghost of a functioning brain cell somewhere, and a flash of inspiration hit me. "That's it!" I blurted. "That's how to handle the Corpsetaker."

Lea tilted her head, her eyes intent, and then smiled a knowing smile. "Ahhh. If you can do it."

I swallowed. "Yeah."

"Interesting," she murmured. "If you can control them. They are a power potentially deadly even to the one who wields it. Explosive. Dangerous. And very typical of you. Excellent." Then she moved the fingers of her right hand through a series of little gestures and was gone.

That left me alone in my grave with my thoughts.

I leaned against the wall again, but I didn't settle down on the ground. Instead I thought about Molly and how screwed up she was.

That was my fault, in a lot of ways.

First thing to jump out at me: I never should have let Molly go to Chichén Itzá.

I had led her into the fight of my life against the Red Court, to save my daughter. But I shouldn't have exposed Molly to that. She was a sensitive, a wizard whose magical senses were naturally attuned to the finest, lightest, most delicate workings of the Art. Or, to put it in more Harry-friendly terms, she had great big, honking Dumbo ears that were extremely sensitive to loud noises.

Magic is life. Some forms of death — like murder, the abrupt and violent termination of a life that was not otherwise ending — were the equivalent of enormous, screeching feedback to her senses. And I had dragged her into a freaking concert hall of it at Chichén Itzá. Murderpalooza. Not to mention setting off the biggest, most violent magical curse to be unleashed in the past century — hell, I wasn't exactly a sensitive guy, magically speaking, but even I had a blank spot in my memory over the minutes right after that arcane explosion.

It's got to be bad for me to shut it out. For Molly, it had to have been a whole lot worse. And, oh yes, she had been shot and nearly killed to go with everything else. I had watched her collapse from blood loss.

Mistake. It had been a big damned mistake. At the time, I had been so focused on getting Maggie out that I'd let Molly persuade me that she deserved to be on the team. I never would have let her do that if I'd been thinking straight. I would have told her to stay at home, hold the fort, or maybe stay in the car. That was what I'd always done when I was on my way to a slugfest. Exposure to that kind of noise could quite effectively shatter her sanity.

And maybe it had.

Even if her mental house was still on a good foundation, you didn't need monsters or magic to get damaged by a brush with death. Soldiers coming home from wars had known that for centuries. Post-traumatic stress disorder from life-threatening injuries had screwed up the lives of a lot of people — people who *didn't* have supernatural powers as a possible outlet for their anger, fear, grief, or guilt.

And who had been there to catch her? The freaking Leanansidhe, deputy of Her Wickedness, with her Nietzsche and Darwin Were Sentimental Pansies outlook on life.

Stars and stones. When Molly insisted on going, why didn't I just tell her, "Of course you can come, grasshopper. I've always wanted to create a mentally mutilated monster of my very own."

Man. It wasn't the legacy I'd wanted to leave behind me. I mean, I hadn't ever thought much about leaving a legacy, truth be told, but an apprentice with a crippled heart and mind who was probably going to get hunted down by her own people was definitely never in the plan.

"Oh, kid," I breathed to no one. "Molly. I'm so sorry."

It turns out ghosts can cry.

"Over here," said a familiar voice. It was later, but not much later. Sometime after noon, maybe? It was hard to tell from the grave.

"You've never even been here before," answered another. "I was at the funeral. How the hell would you know where his grave was?"

I heard Fitz let out a sigh front-loaded with so much drama that only a teenager could have managed it without hurting himself. "Is it the gaping hole in the ground over there, with the big pentacle on the headstone?"

There was a brief, miffed pause, and Butters answered, "Okay. Maybe it is."

Footsteps crunched through wet, melting snow. Fitz and Butters appeared at the edge of my grave and peered down.

"Well?" Butters asked. "Is he there?"

"How the hell should I know?" Fitz replied. "I don't see dead people. I hear them. And I don't hear anything."

"Hey, Fitz," I said.

The kid jumped. He was wearing his newly laundered clothes and had added one of Forthill's old coats over the top of everything. "Christ. Yeah, he's there."

"Oh, fantastic," Butters said. "Hi, Harry. Here, man. Help me down."

"Help you down? It's, like, five feet to the bottom, if that. Just jump down."

"Jump into an open grave? What kind of idiot are you?" Butters replied. "I might as well put on a red shirt and volunteer for the away team. There's snow and ice and slippery mud down there. That's like asking for an ironically broken neck."

"Are all doctors whiny girls like you?" Fitz asked.

"Hey. This whiny girl is still alive because he doesn't do stupid crap."

Fitz snorted. "So I help you down, my foot slips, we both fall in and die."

Butters lifted an eyebrow and grunted. "Huh. True."

I pinched at the bridge of my nose. "Oh, Hell's bells, guys. Either get a room or stop flirting and get down here."

"Ha-ha," Fitz said toward me crossly. "He just called us gay."

Butters blinked. "For not jumping into a hole we might not be able to climb out of? That's kind of insensitive."

"Not for that, for . . ." Fitz let out a sigh of vintage teenage impatience. "Christ, just give me your hand, okay? I'll swing you down."

Butters fussed for a moment more, making sure that Fitz had a solid place to plant his feet, and then he swung down into my grave. He was wearing his winter gear again and carrying the gym bag. Once he was down, he made sure he was out of direct sunlight and started opening the bag.

"What's up?" I asked Fitz.

"Trouble," Fitz said.

"We need your help, Harry," Butters said.

"Hey, wait," I said, scowling. "How did Butters find you, Fitz?"

"He asked," Fitz said to Butters.

The little ME nodded. "Harry, I got from Murphy that you were apparently going into social work. It wasn't hard to figure out who you'd ask for help, so I went over to the church to talk to Forthill about the situation — except he wasn't there."

Fitz bit his lip. "Look, Dresden. The father and I talked. And he decided he was going to go talk to Aristedes on my behalf."

I blinked and pushed away from the grave wall. *"What?"*

"I tried to tell him," Fitz said. "He wouldn't listen. He was . . . I think he was angry. But he said he was going to resolve this before it came to some kind of bloodshed."

Hell's bells. I'd known Aristedes' type in the past. If it suited him, he'd kill Forthill without an instant's hesitation. The good father was in danger.

"Murphy would go in guns blazing," Butters said. "She's going to break my arm when she finds out I didn't tell her. We need you to help talk us through this."

"That's crazy," I said. "Go in guns blazing!"

"It's too late for that," Fitz said. "Look,

482

Forthill is already there. I just met the guy but . . . but . . . I don't want him to get hurt for me. We have to move now."

"I can't," I said. "I can't move around in broad daylight."

"We thought of that," Fitz said. "Butters said you needed a shielded vessel."

"Butters said that, did he?" I asked wryly.

Butters rose from the bag, holding the plastic flashlight case holding Bob's skull. He winked at me, held it out, and said, "Hop in."

I blinked.

Then I said, "Right. Let's go."

I took a deep breath and willed myself forward, into the staring eye sockets of the skull.

CHAPTER THIRTY-FIVE

There was a very, very odd swirling sensation as my spirit-self leapt forward, and then I was standing . . .

. . . In an apartment.

Okay, when I say *apartment,* I don't mean it like my old place. I lived in a mostly buried box that was maybe twenty by thirty total, not including the subbasement where my lab had been. Apartment Dresden had been full of paperback books on scarred wooden shelves, and comfortable secondhand furniture.

This was more like . . . Apartment Bond, James Apartment Bond. Penthouse Bond, really. There was a lot of black marble and mahogany. There was a fireplace the size of a carport, complete with a modest — relatively modest — blaze going in it. The furniture all matched. The rich hardwoods from which it had been made were hand-carved in intricate designs. It wasn't until the second glance that I saw some of the same rune and sigil work

I'd used on my own staff and blasting rod. The cushions on the couches (plural, *couches*) and recliners and sedans and chaises (plural, *chaises*), were made of rich fabric I couldn't identify, maybe some kind of raw silk, and embroidered with more of the same symbols in gold and silver thread. A nearby table boasted what looked like a freshly roasted turkey, along with a spread of fruits and vegetables and side dishes of every kind.

It was sort of ridiculous, really. There was enough food there to feed a small nation. But there weren't any plates to fill up, and there weren't any utensils to eat it with. It looked gorgeous and it smelled incredible, but . . . there was something inert about it, something lifeless. There was no nourishment on that table, not for the body or for the spirit.

One wall was covered in a curtain. I started to pull it aside and found it responding to the touch, spreading open of its own accord to reveal a television the size of billboard, a high-tech stereo system, and an entire shelf lined with one kind of video-game console after another, complicated little controls sitting neatly next to each one. I can't tell a PlayBox from an X-Station, but who can keep track of all of them? There are, like, a thousand different kinds of machines to play video games on. I mean, honestly.

"Um," I said. "Hello?" My voice echoed quite distinctly — more than it should have, huge marble cavern or not. "Anybody home?"

There was, I kid you not, a drumroll.

Then, from a curtained archway there appeared a young man. He looked . . . quite ordinary, really. Tall, but not outrageously so; slender without being rail thin. He had decent shoulders and looked sort of familiar. He was dressed like James Dean — jeans, a white shirt, a leather biker's jacket. The outfit looked a little odd on him, somehow forced, except for a little skull embroidered in white thread on the jacket, just over the young man's heart.

Cymbals crashed and he spread his arms. "Ta-da."

"Bob," I said. I felt one side of my mouth curling up in amusement. "This? This is the place you always wanted me to let you out of? You could fit five or six of mine in here."

His face spread into a wide grin. "Well, I admit, my crib is pretty sweet. But a gold cage is still a cage, Harry."

"A gold fallout shelter, more like."

"Either way, you get stir-crazy every few decades," he said, and flopped down onto a chaise. "You get that this isn't literally what the inside of the skull is like, right?"

"It's my head interpreting what I see into familiar things, yeah," I said. "It's getting to be kind of common."

"Welcome to the world of spirit," Bob said.

"What's with the food?"

"Butters's mom is some kind of food goddess," Bob said, his eyes widening. "That's the spread she's put out over the last few holidays. Or, um, Butters's sensory memories of it, anyway — he let me do a ride-along, and then I made this facsimile of what we experienced."

I lifted my eyebrows. "He let you do a ride-along? In his head?" Bob . . . was not well-known for his restraint, in my experience, when he got to go on one of his excursions.

"There was a contract first," Bob said. "A limiting document about twenty pages long. He covered his bases."

"Huh," I said. I nodded at the food. "And you just . . . remade it?"

"Oh, sure," Bob said. "I can remake whatever in here." He waggled his eyebrows. "You want to see a replay of that time Molly got the acid all over her clothes in the lab and had to strip?"

"Um. Pass," I said. I sat down gingerly on a chair, making sure I wasn't going to sink through it or something. It seemed to behave like a normal chair. "TV and stuff, too?"

"I am kinda made out of energy, man," Bob said. He pointed at the wall of media equipment. "You remember me broadcasting to your spirit radio, right? I'm, like, totally tapped in now. Television, satellite imagery, broadband Internet — you name it; I can do it. How do you think I know so much?"

"Hundreds of years of assisting wizards," I said.

He waved a hand. "That, too. But I got this whole huge Internet thing to play on now. Butters showed me." His grin turned into a leer. "And it's, like, ninety percent porn!"

"There's the Bob I know and love," I said.

"Love, ick," he replied. "And I am and I'm not. I mean, you get that I change based on who possesses the skull, right?"

"Sure," I said.

"So I'm a lot like I was with you, even though I'm with Butters, because he met me back then. First impression and whatnot, highly important."

I grunted. "How long do we have to talk?"

"Not as simple to answer as you'd think," Bob said. "But . . . you're still pretty cherry, so let's keep it simple. A few minutes, speaking linearly — but I can stretch it out for a while, subjectively."

"Huh," I said. "Neat."

"Nah, just sort of the way we roll on this side of the street," he said. "What do you want to know?"

"Who killed me?" I replied.

"Oooh, sorry. Can't help you with that, except as a sounding board."

"Okay," I said. "Lemme catch you up on what I know."

I filled Bob in on everything since the train tunnel. I didn't hold back much of anything.

Bob was smart enough to fill in the vast majority of gaps if I left anything out anyway, and he could compile information and deduce coherent facts as well as any mind I had ever known.

And besides . . . he was my oldest friend.

He listened, his gold brown eyes intent, completely focused on me.

"Wow," he said when I'd finished. "You are so completely fucked."

I arched an eyebrow at him and said, "How do you figure?"

He rolled his eyes. "Oh, where do I *start?* How about with the obvious? Uriel."

"Uriel," I said. "What?"

"A wizard tied in with a bunch of really elemental sources of power dies, right after signing off on some deals that guarantee he's about to become a whole Hell of a lot darker — capital letter intended — and there's this sudden" — he made air quotes with his fingers — " 'irregularity' about his death. He gets sent *back* to the mortal coil to *get involved again.* And you think an angel *isn't* involved somewhere? Remember. Uriel is the black-ops guy of the archangels. He's conned the *Father of Lies,* for crying out loud. You think he wouldn't scam *you?*"

"Uh," I said.

I felt a little thick.

"See?" Bob said. "Your first tiny piece of flesh-free existence, and already you're lost

489

without me."

I shook my head. "Look, man, I'm just . . . just a spirit now. This is just, like, paperwork I'm getting filled out before I catch the train to Wherever."

Bob rolled his eyes again and snorted. "Oh, sure it is. You get sent back here just as the freaking Corpsetaker is setting herself up as Queen of Chicago, getting ready to wipe out the defenders of humanity — such as they are — here in town, and it's just a co-incidence, business as usual." He sniffed. "They're totally playing you."

"They?" I said.

"Think about it," Bob said. "I mean, stop for a minute and actually think. I know it's been a while."

"Winter," I said. "Snow a foot deep at the end of spring. Queen Mab."

"Obviously," Bob said. "She's here. In Chicago. Somewhere. And because, duh, she's the Winter Queen, she brought winter with her." He pursed his lips. "For a few more days anyway."

Bob was right. Mab might flaunt her power in the face of the oncoming season, but if she didn't back down, her opposite number, Titania, would come for her — at the height of summer's power, the solstice, if previous patterns held true.

"Harry, I don't want to comment about your new girlfriend, but she's still here six months after you got shot? Seems kind of clingy."

"Wait," I said. "You're saying that Mab and Uriel are in on something. Together. The Queen of Air and Darkness, and a flipping archangel."

"We live in strange times," Bob said philosophically. "They're peers, of a sort, Harry. Hey, word is that even the Almighty and Lucifer worked a deal on Job. Spider-Man has teamed up with the Sandman before. Luke and Vader did the Emperor. It happens."

"Spider-Man is pretend and doesn't count," I said.

"You start drawing distinctions like this now?" Bob asked. "Besides, he's real. Like, somewhere."

I blinked. "Um. What?"

"You think your universe is the *only* universe? Harry, come on. Creation, totally freaking huge. Room enough for you and Spider-Man both." He spread his hands. "Look, I'm not a faith guy. I don't know what happens on the other side, or if you wind up going to a Heaven or Hell or something reasonably close to them. That isn't my bag. But I know a shell game when I see one."

I swallowed and pushed a hand back through my hair. "The Fomor's servitors. Corpsetaker and her gang. Even Aristedes and his little crew. They're pieces on the board."

"Just like you," Bob agreed cheerfully. "Notice anyone else who pushed you a space or two recently? By which I mean that you only recently noticed."

I scowled. "Other than everyone around me?"

"I was sort of thinking about the one behind you," Bob said. His expression grew suddenly serious. "The Walker."

I took a slow breath. He Who Walks Behind.

It was only now, looking back at my crystalline memories and applying what I'd learned during my adult lifetime since they happened, that I could really appreciate what had gone on that night.

The Walker had never been trying to kill me. If it had wanted to do that, it didn't need to play with me. It could simply have appeared and executed me, the way it had poor Stan at the gas station. It had been trying to push me, to shape me into something dangerous — like maybe a weapon.

Like maybe the same way Justin had.

I had always assumed that Justin had controlled He Who Walks Behind, that my old master had sent him after me when I fled. But what if I'd been a flipping idiot? What if their relationship had worked the other way around? What if Justin, who had betrayed me, had similarly been backstabbed by his *own* inhuman mentor, when the creature had, in essence, prepared me to destroy Justin?

"Lotta really scary symmetry there," I whispered.

"Yeah," Bob said, still serious. "You are in a scary place, Harry." He took a deep breath. "And . . . it gets worse."

"Worse? How?"

"It's just a theory," he said, "because this isn't my bag. But look. There's flesh and there's spirit, right?"

"Yeah," I said.

"Mortals have both, right there together, along with the soul."

"I thought it was the same thing. Soul, spirit."

"Um," Bob said. "Complicated. Think of your spirit-self as a seed. Your soul is the earth it grows in. You need both when you die. The way I've heard it . . . they sort of blend together to become something new. It's a caterpillar-butterfly thing."

"Okay," I said. "How does that make it worse?"

"You, here, now, aren't a spirit," Bob said. "You aren't a real ghost. You . . . You're just running around in your freaking *soul,* man. I mean, for practical purposes, it's the same thing, but . . ."

"But what?"

"But if something happens to you here, now . . . it's for keeps. I mean . . . forever.

493

You could capital-E End, man. Spin right off the wheel altogether. Or worse."

I swallowed. I mean, I realized that I'd been in a serious situation all the way down the line, but not one that could potentially be described using words like *eternal.* Joy.

Bob shook his head. "I didn't think it was possible for them to do that to you. According to what I've heard, your soul's your own. I'd have thought you would have to walk into something like this willingly, but . . ."

I held up the heel of my hand and butted my forehead against it in steady rhythm.

"Oh, *Harry,*" Bob said, his voice profoundly disappointed. "You didn't."

"They didn't explain it exactly the way you did," I said. "Not in so many words."

"But they gave you a choice?"

Captain Murphy had done exactly that. It had been phrased in such a way that I hadn't really had much of a choice, but I'd had a choice. "Yeah."

"And you chose to hazard your eternal soul? Even though you get all worked up about that sort of thing."

"It . . . wasn't phrased quite like that . . ." I began. Only it really had been. Jack had warned me that I might be trapped forever, hadn't he? "Or . . . well. Um. Yeah. I guess technically I did."

"Well," Bob said. He cleared his throat. "You idiot."

494

"Argh," I said. "My head hurts."

"No, it doesn't," Bob said scornfully. "You just think it should."

I paused and reflected and saw that Bob was right. And I decided that my head hurt anyway, dammit. Just because I was a spirit or a naked soul or whatever didn't mean I needed to start ignoring who I had been.

"Bob," I said, lifting my head suddenly. "What does this mean? I mean, why not just let me die and move along like normal?"

Bob pursed his lips. "Um. Yeah. No clue."

"What if . . . ?" I felt short of breath. I hardly wanted to say it. "What if I'm not . . . ?"

Bob's eyes widened. "Oh. *Oooooohhhhh.* Uriel's people — Murphy's dad and so on — did they say anything about your body?"

"That it wasn't available," I said.

"But not that it was gone?" Bob pressed.

"No," I said. "They . . . they didn't say that."

"Wow," Bob said, eyes wide.

Mine probably were, too. "What do I do?"

"How the hell should I know, man?" Bob asked. "I've never had a soul *or* a body. What did they tell you to do?"

"Find my killer," I said. "But . . . that means I'm dead, right?"

Bob waved a hand. "Harry. Dead isn't . . . Look, even by terms of the nonsupernatural, dead is a really fuzzy area. Even mortal medicine regards death as a kind of process more than a state of being — a reversible process, in some circumstances."

"What are you getting at?" I asked.

"There's a difference between dead and . . . and *gone*."

I swallowed. "So . . . what do I do?"

Bob lunged to his feet. "What do you *do?*" He pointed at the table of Mother Butters's feast food. "You've got *that* to maybe get back to, and you're asking me what to *do?* You find your freaking killer! We'll both do it! I'll totally help!"

The light in the room suddenly turned red. A red-alert sound I remembered from old episodes of *Star Trek* buzzed through the air.

"Uh," I said, "what the hell is that?"

"Butters calling me," Bob said, leaping to his feet. The form of the young man, who I now realized must have looked a lot like Butters when he was a kid, only taller, started coming apart into the sparks of a wood fire. "Come on," Bob said. "Let's go."

CHAPTER THIRTY-SIX

I didn't actually will myself out of the skull, the way I had gone in. Bob's passage just sort of swept me along in his wake, like a leaf being tugged after a passing tractor-trailer. It was a forcible reminder that, the way things stood now, Bob was the heavyweight. I was just the skinny newbie.

I hated that feeling. That feeling sucked.

I reintegrated standing in a dusty room. Afternoon sunlight slanted through it, its danger abated by the thick coating of grime over the windows. The place looked like an industrial building's entryway. There was what had been a heavy-duty desk, maybe for a receptionist or security guard. An alcove housed rows of small personal lockers. Several rectangles of less-faded, commercial-grade taupe paint on the walls had probably been where a time clock and time-card holders had gone. Butters stood nearby, holding Bob's flashlight, and the eyes of the skull were glowing brightly with Bob's presence in the physical world, now that he had left his "apartment." The little ME looked tense, focused, but not afraid.

It wasn't much of a mystery how they'd gotten into the room: Fitz stood there with a set of bolt cutters with three-feet-long handles held over his shoulder. Fitz looked scared enough for everyone there. The kid was back in the lair of his erstwhile mentor and terrified of his wrath.

Yeah.

I knew that feeling.

Butters fumbled his little spirit radio out of his pocket and asked, in a hushed voice, "Dresden, you here?"

"To your left," I said quietly.

He shone Bob's eyelights my way and evidently saw me illuminated by them. "Oh," he said, looking relieved. "Right. Good."

I had no clue why he looked relieved. It wasn't like I could *do* anything, unless some random ghost came by, in which case my memory-based magic could cook another being incapable of affecting the material world.

But I guess he looked up to me, or at least to my memory, and I owed it to him to help however I could. So I gave him a calm nod and an encouraging clench of my fist. Solid.

"I take it we've come in through a blind spot?" I asked Fitz quietly.

Fitz nodded. "The chains on the doors were enough. And he couldn't extend his guard spells any farther than the main room."

I grunted. "That's good."

"Why?" Butters asked.

"Means Aristedes doesn't have enough power to just burn you to cinders on the spot."

Butters swallowed. "Oh. Good."

"Doesn't mean he can't kill you," I said. "Just that he won't have a high FX budget when he does."

"He's fast," Fitz said. His voice shook. "He's really, really fast."

"Like, how fast?" Butters asked. "Fast like Jackie Chan or fast like the Flash?"

"Little of both," I said. "He can cover ground fast. And he can hit like a truck."

Fitz nodded tightly.

"Oh," Butters said. "Super. We probably shouldn't fight him, then." He set the flashlight aside and rummaged in the duffel bag. "Give me just a second."

A shadow flickered by one of the grimefilmed windows. Fitz let out a hiss and clutched the bolt cutters with both hands, ready to use them like a club. Butters let out an odd little chirping sound and pulled a big, old, cop-issue flashlight–slash-club from his bag.

The shadow passed over another window. Someone outside was moving toward the door, coming in behind us.

I took a quick look at the flashlight and

made sure I was standing in the light of Bob's eyes and out of the path of any direct sunlight that might come through the door. I couldn't do anything, but if I was visibly standing there when the door opened, maybe I could distract Aristedes, if it was him coming through. Maybe he'd speed-rush right through me and into a wall and knock himself out like a cartoon villain. That would make me look cool upon cool.

More likely, I wouldn't accomplish anything. But when your friends are in danger, you try anyway.

The door opened and I raised my arms into a dramatic stage-magician's pose. It felt ridiculous, but body postures draw reactions from human beings on an almost atavistic level. We aren't that terribly far removed from our primal roots, where body language was more important than anything we said. My stance declared me the ruler of the local space, a man who was in control of everything happening around him, one who others would follow, a mix of maestro and madman that would identify me, to instinct, as the most dangerous thing in the room.

Butters and Fitz hit the wall on either side of the door and raised their improvised weapons as it swung open. The door squealed dramatically on its hinges, and a large, menacing figure entered the building. It hesitated, lifting a hand to shield its eyes, apparently staring at me.

Butters let out a shout and swung his flashlight at the figure. Fitz, by contrast, swept the heavy set of bolt cutters down in silence. Even in that flash of time, I had to admire Butters. The little guy couldn't fight and he knew it, but he was smart enough to shout and draw the attention of the intruder toward the smaller, weaker, and lighter-armed of the two of them. He had intentionally thrown himself at a larger opponent to force the man to turn so that Fitz could swing at his back.

No fighter, maybe, but the little guy had guts enough for any three bruisers.

It didn't do either of them any good.

The large man seemed to sense the ploy. He ducked the swinging bolt cutters without so much as turning around and simultaneously snapped out his left arm, the heel of his hand thrusting forward. He hit Butters squarely in the belly and sent the little man sprawling. Then he whirled as Fitz recovered his balance and swung the bolt cutters again. He caught them with one hand, matching Fitz's strength with a single arm. Then with a sinuous motion of his upper body that reminded me of Murphy at work, he both took the bolt cutters from Fitz's hands and sent the young man sprawling into Butters, who had just begun to climb to his feet again. They both went down in a heap as the door clanged shut.

Daniel Carpenter, Michael Carpenter's eldest son, stood in place for a moment, holding the bolt cutters lightly, as tall and as strong as his father, his grey eyes distant and cold. Then he glanced at me, opened his mouth, and closed it again.

I waved at him and said, "Hi, Daniel."

The sound of my voice came to him only through the radio in Butters's pocket.

He blinked. "What the hell?" Daniel asked, staring at me. Then he looked at Butters, then at Fitz, and then at the bolt cutters. "I mean, seriously. What the hell, Butters? What the hell are you doing?"

Butters pushed Fitz off him and eyed Daniel with annoyance. "Quietly, please," he said in a lower, intent voice. "We're sneaking up on a bad guy, here, and you aren't helping."

"Is that what you're doing?" Daniel asked — but at least he lowered his voice. "Because Ms. Murphy thinks you're losing your mind."

Butters blinked. "What? Why would Karrin think that?"

"Because of that thing," Daniel said, nodding toward me.

"Ouch," I said. "That stings, Daniel."

"Dude," Butters said. "Don't be a dick. That's Dresden. Or at least it's his spirit, which is mostly the same thing."

"We don't know that," Daniel shot back. "Things from the spirit world can look like whatever they want to look like. You know that."

"Didn't we already go through this proper-identification thing?" I complained.

"I know. Right?" Butters said to me. "See what she's gotten to be like?"

"Who?" Daniel demanded.

"Karrin, obviously," Butters shot back. "Since you vanished, Harry, she's been fighting a war, and using whatever weapons she can find. Hell, she's even taken help from Marcone."

Daniel's face flushed darker. "Do *not* talk about Ms. Murphy that way. She's the only reason the Fomor haven't terrorized Chicago like they have everywhere else."

"The two don't preclude one another," Butters said with a sigh. He looked at me and spread his hands. "You see what I'm dealing with?"

I grimaced and nodded. "It's about her job, I think. She's insecure about her place in the world. She was like this when I first opened up shop, about the time she got put in charge of SI — suspicious, close-minded, negative outlook about everything. It was impossible to talk to her."

"You're sneaking around against her orders," Daniel said to Butters.

Butters got to his feet and offered Fitz a hand up. "Orders? This isn't the army, man, and Murphy isn't the King of Chicago. She can't order me to do anything."

"I notice you say that when she is not in the room," I said.

"I'm an independent thinker, not a martyr," Butters replied. He squinted at Daniel. "Wait a minute. She had you tailing me?"

"Damn," I said. "That *is* paranoid."

Daniel shook his head, scowling briefly at me. "You're going to have to come with me, Mr. Butters."

"No," Butters said. "I'm not."

Daniel set his jaw. "Ms. Murphy said that for your own good, I was to get you out of whatever that creature got you into. So let's go."

"No," Butters said, glaring up at the much larger young man. "I'm not leaving Forthill to the mercy of a punk sorcerer."

Daniel blinked his eyes several times, and the determined belligerence went out of his stance. "The father? He's here? He's in danger?"

"It gets less likely we're going to be able to help him the longer we stand around gabbing," Butters said. He recovered his bag, rummaged in it, and added, "This will work better with you here anyway." He straightened up and tossed a folded square of grey cloth at Daniel. "Put that on. Stay next to me. Don't talk."

Daniel stared at the cloth dubiously, then looked at Butters.

"For Forthill," Butters said quietly, softening his voice. "We'll leave as soon as he's safe, and you can take me straight to Karrin. You have my word. Okay?"

Daniel agonized over it for a couple of seconds. Then he nodded at Butters and unfolded the grey cloth.

"Oh," I said, suddenly understanding the little guy's plan. "Good call. The fabric isn't exactly right, but it's close. This could work."

Butters nodded. "I thought it might. How should we approach it?"

"Small-timer like Aristedes is insecure about the size of his magical penis," I said. "Give his ego a few crumbs and he'll eat out of your hand."

"We'll have to go to radio silence," Butters said. "There wasn't time to make the headphones work with it."

"If I think of anything imperative, I can tell Fitz. He'll pass it on."

Fitz looked nervously between Butters, Daniel, and me. "Oh. Uh. Sure. Because I can hear Dresden even without a radio."

Butters drew a second square of grey cloth from the bag and then tossed the bag over to one side. Calmly, he unfolded the cloth and threw the hooded cloak it proved to be over his shoulders, fastening a clasp at his throat.

"So, Harry," Butters said. "How do the Wardens like to make an entrance?"

Chapter Thirty-Seven

Daniel Carpenter leaned back, lifted a size-fourteen work boot, and kicked the door leading to the factory floor completely off its hinges.

I was impressed. The kid had power. I mean, sure, the door was old and all, the hinges rusted, but it was still a freaking steel door. And it went a couple of feet through the air before it slammed down onto the floor with an enormous, hollow *boom* that echoed through the huge room beyond it.

"Thank you," Butters said, in the absolutely obnoxious British accent he normally reserved for the nobleman his players were supposed to hate at our old weekly gaming sessions. He sniffed and strode onto the factory floor, his footsteps clear and precise in the empty space. The fake Warden's cloak floated in his wake.

Daniel stomped along a step behind Butters, his dark brows lowered into a thug's glower. It looked pretty natural on him. He had one huge hand clamped down on the back of Fitz's neck and was dragging the kid along with brusque, casual power. Fitz looked intensely uncomfortable.

Butters stopped at a faint old line of chalk on the floor, regarded it for a moment, and then called out, "Hello? I say there, is anyone at home? I'm here to speak to the sorcerer Aristedes. I was told he was to be found here." He paused for maybe a second and a half and added, "I've a warlock to catch in Trinidad in an hour. I would prefer not to draw this out."

No one answered. There were soft, furtive sounds: an old tennis shoe dragging across the concrete floor with a faint squeak. Footsteps. A soft exhalation. A faint grunt of exertion.

"Warden," Butters said. He picked at his teeth with his thumbnail.

Daniel's shoulders locked up and tightened, and Fitz let out a short yowl. "It's me!" he called out frantically. "It's Fitz! Sir, they say they're here to talk to you about the Fomor."

"Fitz!" said a voice from off to one side. One of the kids from the drive-by, the little one, emerged from behind a set of metal cabinets. He got a look at Fitz's situation and tensed into a crouch, ready to run.

"Hey, Zero," Fitz said, trying to sound casual as he all but dangled from Daniel's grip. "The boss home?"

507

There was a swishing sound, as if someone had thrown a large ball at considerable speed. And then Aristedes said, from directly behind us, "I am."

Daniel twitched, but Butters concealed his reaction masterfully. He simply glanced over his shoulder and regarded Aristedes, who now stood in the newly doorless entryway. Butters arched an eyebrow, as if he'd seen the trick before but at least found it well-done, and turned to face Aristedes.

He gave the man a slight bow and said, "I am Warden Valdo. This is Warden Smythe."

Daniel glowered.

"If you aren't otherwise occupied, I wonder if we might ask for a moment of your time."

Aristedes studied the three of them for a silent moment, his eyes narrowed. He was wearing a ragged, old dark blue bathrobe over loose cotton chinos and a tank top. The hair on his chest was thick and dark. The tattoos around his skull and over his cheekbones stood out sharply against his pale skin.

"You are from the White Council?" he asked.

Butters studied him for a moment and then sighed. "Should I start at the beginning again? Our files describe you as a minor but competent operator. Were they mistaken?"

Aristedes folded his arms, his expression a neutral mask. "I am, of course, aware of the White Council. What business do you have

508

with me? And why are you holding my apprentice prisoner?"

I did a quick circle around Aristedes. Since I was all ghosty, he never knew I was there. He didn't so much as get goose bumps on the back of his neck. I guessed that he was the opposite of Forthill: Being a self-centered megalomaniac hadn't prepared Aristedes to be sensitive to anyone's soul at all.

"There's a bulge under the robe at the small of his back," I said to Fitz. "Blink twice for *yes* if you know what it is. Blink once for *no*."

Fitz shot a glance at me and blinked twice.

"A weapon?" I asked.

Two blinks.

"Gun?"

One blink.

"Knife?"

Two blinks.

"Okay," I said. "That's definitely a need-to-know fact. If you get a chance, or if things get violent, tell Daniel about it."

Two more nervous blinks.

I hesitated, and then said, in a gentler voice, "Hang tough, kid. I've been where you are. It's going to be okay."

No blinks. Fitz bit his lip.

Butters, meanwhile, kept the dialogue going. "Clearly, the Council finds the recent activities of the Fomor somewhat repulsive. Just as clearly, our recently concluded war with the Red Court has left us less able to act than we would have been otherwise."

Which, thinking about it, probably wasn't true. The Council finished the war with the Red Court with more active, experienced, dangerous Wardens than they'd had when it started. Granted, the vast majority of them were a bunch of kids Molly's age or younger, but they were already veterans. But I was betting that the Fomor picking on a bunch of low-level talents was a problem that was fairly far down their priority list.

"I'd heard the Wardens were adept at coming to the point," Aristedes said. "Should we start again at the beginning to give you another chance to get there?"

Butters gave the sorcerer a frosty smile and a small inclination of his head. "You and your crew are still here. That suggests competence. We approve of competence."

Aristedes tilted his head to one side and was silent for a moment. "You've come to discuss a relationship of some kind?"

"Let's not get ahead of ourselves," Butters replied. "I'm not a recruiter. This is a visit. A ground-level evaluation, if you will."

I hated to leave the three of them standing in front of Aristedes and his knife, with nothing but Butters's gaming accent and a few yards of grey cloth to protect them, but we hadn't come here to face down Aristedes. We were here for Forthill. The hasty plan I'd sketched with Butters called for me to locate the father while they kept Aristedes' attention.

Besides, those cloaks represented something that Aristedes would respect, if he had two brain cells to rub together. The Wardens of the White Council had never been regarded as friendly figures like your local traffic cop. People feared them — probably all the more so since the war with the Red Court. The Wardens were the guys who gave you one warning, way before you were anywhere close to crossing the line by breaking one of the Laws of Magic. The next time you saw them, they were probably there to cut off your head.

Whether they were more respected or more feared depended greatly on one's point of view, but no one ever, ever took them lightly.

It felt right somehow that Butters was trading on their fearsome reputation. Maybe it felt right because that reputation was, like me, immaterial — but not unable to alter events. The ghost of the Wardens' ferocity could do as much as I could to keep an eye on my companions. So I wished them luck within the silence of my thoughts and set out to accomplish my part of the plan.

I vanished and reappeared at ceiling level, being careful to stay out of any direct sunlight as it streamed through a few small windows high up on the walls. The ceiling wasn't all that high compared to the area of the factory floor, and it took me several tries before I recognized the location of the gang's camp in all that abandoned space. I willed myself over to it and found Forthill.

The priest was lying very still on the floor, curled into a half circle. I couldn't see if he was breathing, and I couldn't touch him to check for a pulse. I grimaced and knelt to thrust my hand into the matter of one of his feet. I felt the sharp, odd sensation of contact with living flesh, like when I'd touched both Morty and my apprentice, and not the sharp tingling of contact with something solid but inert. He was alive. It felt like my own heart had stopped beating and then lurched into gear again.

I studied him for a moment, trying to assess what had happened to him. There was blood coming from several cuts around his face, where his thin, elderly skin had broken open under a sharp blow — across his cheekbones, his brow ridges, and on his chin. His lip had been split and was swelling. He'd taken a beating from someone's fists — or possibly from open-handed slaps delivered with supernatural speed.

That felt right. The old priest, a living, breathing symbol of everything Aristedes resented, must have shown up to talk. No matter how polite the father had been, his simple presence would have been challenge enough to the ego of anyone like the sorcerer.

Challenges could be answered only with violence, and the slaps he delivered would have been both painful and insulting.

Forthill's left arm was pressed against his ribs. He'd fallen and curled up around his midsection. The sorcerer must have given him some body blows as well. Broken ribs, maybe, or worse. Everything about trauma was worse when it happened to the elderly — thinner skin, less muscle, less bone, worn organs. They were vulnerable.

I ground my teeth and looked around the camp. Aristedes had left a guard to watch Forthill. He was a boy, and he might have been a very scrawny and underfed ten-year-old, at most. He sat near the fire barrel, shivering, holding a rusted old steak knife. His eyes roamed everywhere, but he wouldn't look at the priest's still form.

Forthill suddenly shuddered and let out a soft moan before sinking into stillness again.

The little boy with the knife looked away, his eyes suddenly wet. He wrapped his arms around his knees and rocked back and forth. I wasn't sure which sight hurt more.

I clenched my jaw. What animal would do this to an old man? To a *child?* I felt my skin beginning to heat up, a reflection of the rage that had swelled up inside me again.

"It is better not to let such thoughts occupy your mind," said a very calm, very soothing voice.

I spun to face the speaker, the words of a spell on my tongue, ghostly power kindling in the palm of my right hand.

A young woman stood over Forthill, opposite me, in a shaft of sunlight that spilled in through a hole in a blacked-out window. She was dressed in a black suit, a black shirt, a black tie. Her skin was dark — not like someone of African ancestry, but like someone had dunked her in a vat of perfectly black ink. The sclera, the whites of her eyes, were black, too. In fact, the only things on her that weren't ink black were her eyes and the short sword she held in her hand, the blade dangling parallel to her leg. They were both shining silver with flecks of metallic gold.

She met my gaze calmly and then glanced down at my right hand, where flickers of fire sent out wisps of smoke. "Peace, Harry Dresden," she said. "I have not come to harm anyone."

I stared at her for a second and then checked the guard. The little kid hadn't reacted to the stranger's voice or presence; ergo she was a spirit, like me. There were plenty of spirit beings who might show up when someone was dying, but not many of them could have been standing around in a ray of sunlight. And I'd seen a sword identical to the one she currently held, back at the police station in Chicago Between.

"You're an angel," I said quietly. "An angel

of death."

She nodded her head. "Yes."

I rose slowly. I was a lot taller than the angel. I scowled at her. "Back off."

She arched an eyebrow at me. Then she said, "Are you threatening me?"

"Maybe I'm just curious about who will show up for you when it's your turn."

She smiled. It moved only her lips. "What, exactly, do you think you will accomplish here?"

"I'm looking out for my friend," I said. "He's going to be all right. Your services are not required."

"That is not yet clear," the angel said.

"Allow me to clarify," I said. "Touch him, and you and I are going to throw down."

She pursed her lips briefly and then shook her head. "One of us will."

"He's a good man," I said. "I won't let you hurt him."

The angel's eyebrows went up again. "Is that why you think I'm here?"

"Hello," I said, "angel of death. Grim Reaper. Ring any bells?"

The angel shook her head again, smiling a little more naturally. "You misunderstand my purpose."

"Educate me," I said.

"It is not within my purview to choose when a life will end. I am only an escort, a guardian, sent to convey a new-freed soul to safety."

I scowled. "You think Forthill is so lost that he needs a guide?"

She blinked at me once. "No. He needs . . ." She seemed to search for the proper word. "His soul needs a bodyguard. To that purpose, I am here."

"A bodyguard?" I blurted. "What the hell has the father done that he needs a bodyguard in the afterlife?"

She blinked at me again, gentle surprise on her face. It made her look very young — younger than Molly. "He . . . he spent a lifetime fighting darkness," she said, speaking gently and a bit slowly, as if she were stating something perfectly obvious to a small child. "There are forces that would want to take vengeance upon him while his soul is vulnerable, during the transition."

I stared hard at the angel for several seconds, but I didn't detect anything like a lie in her. I looked down at the fire in my hand and suddenly felt a little bit silly. "And you . . . You're going to be the one to fight for him?"

She stared at me with those silver eyes, and I felt my legs turn a little rubbery. It wasn't fear . . . exactly. It was something deeper, something more awe-inspiring — the feeling I had when I'd once seen a tornado from less than a quarter of a mile away, seen it tearing

516

up trees by their roots and throwing them around like matchsticks. Staring out of those silver eyes was not a spirit or a being or a personality. It was a force of freaking nature — impersonal, implacable, and utterly beyond any control that I could exert.

Prickles of sweat popped out on my forehead, and I broke the gaze, quickly looking down.

A dark, cool hand touched my cheek, something of both benediction and gentle rebuke contained within it. "If this is Anthony's time," she said quietly, "I will see him safely to the next world. The Prince of Darkness himself will not wrest him from me." Her fingertips moved to my chin and lifted my face to look at her again. She gave me a small smile as she lowered her hand. "Neither will you, Harry Blackstone Copperfield Dresden, noble though your intentions may be."

I didn't look away from her. The angel knew my Name, down to the last inflection. Holy crap. Any fight against her would be very, very brief, and I was glad I hadn't simply allowed my instincts to take over. "Okay, then," I said a little weakly. "If you aren't here to kill him, why don't you help him? He's a part of your organization."

"As I have already told you, it is not given me to choose when a life will end — or not end."

"Why not? I mean, why the hell *not?* Hasn't Forthill earned a break from you people?"

"It isn't a question of what he deserves," the angel said quietly. "It is a question of choice."

"So choose to help him. It isn't hard."

Her face hadn't shifted from its serene expression for more than a few seconds during the entirety of the conversation. But now it did change. It went flat and hard. Her silver eyes blazed. "Not for a mortal. No. Not hard at all. But such a thing is beyond me."

I took a slow breath, thinking. Then I said, "Free will."

She inclined her head in a micro-nod, her eyes still all but openly hostile. "Something given to you yet denied to me. I may not take any action that abrogates the choices of a mortal."

"Forthill chose to die? Is that what you're saying?"

"Nothing so linear," she said. "This singularity is an amalgamation of many, many choices. Fitz chose to place what little precious trust he had in you. You chose to involve Anthony in the young man's existence. Anthony chose to come here, despite the danger. Aristedes chose to assault him. Waldo and Daniel chose to involve themselves in his rescue. Beyond that, every single one of the people known to each individual I have mentioned have made choices that impacted the life of those involved. Together, all of you have determined this reality." She spread her hands. "Who am I to unmake such a thing?"

"Fine," I said, "be that way."

"I will," the angel responded serenely.

I took one more look at Forthill and vanished, heading back toward Butters and company. If the angel wasn't going to help the good father, I'd damn well do it myself.

It was only a couple of jumps back to the far end of the factory floor, and it took me only a few seconds to get there.

"Fitz," I said, "I found the father. He's —"

"That seems reasonable," Aristedes was saying to Butters. "May I ask one question?"

"Why not?" Butters answered.

Fitz was squirming in Daniel's grip, leaning away from Aristedes. One look at his face told me why: He'd recognized something in his old teacher's words or manner. I'd seen the faces of abused wives while they watched their husbands drink, sickly certain that the cycle of abuse would renew itself in the coming hours. Fitz knew what Aristedes looked like when he was about to dispense violence.

"Wardens," Aristedes said. "Why do you not carry swords?"

Crap.

The question caught Butters off guard. He could have smoothed over the question with a good answer, or maybe even ignored it altogether convincingly — but he did the one thing he absolutely could not do if he was going to sell his false identity to Aristedes.

He hesitated.

Couldn't blame him, I guess. He'd come lickety-split after Forthill, moving as fast as possible. We'd spent all of maybe ninety seconds on putting our plan together, which had only been possible thanks to Butters's foresight in packing those cloaks — apparently, he'd thought it might be useful to have them on hand to create a Warden sighting or two, if it seemed like the city's supernatural scene could use some reassurance. In our hurry to retrieve the good father, I hadn't thought about the whole sword angle — for good reason. The hell of it was that Aristedes was reaching an accurate conclusion based on an erroneous assumption.

The swords of the Wardens were fairly famous in supernatural circles. Bright silver, supernaturally sharp blades, perfect for chopping off the heads of warlocks, and wrought with spells to deflect or disrupt magical attacks or enchantments. When you saw Wardens, you saw their swords.

Or, at least, that had been the status quo until recently. The enchantress who had made them, Warden Luccio, had lost her capacity to create them when Corpsetaker had swapped her into the body of a young woman with very little natural inclination toward magic. As a result, most of the new Wardens, starting with me, didn't have a groovy sword. Which meant that most of the Wardens didn't carry swords any longer.

But that impression, apparently, hadn't trickled down to street level yet.

Things started happening very quickly.

Aristedes produced his knife, a wicked-looking number with a lot of extraneous points on it — an interpretation of a bowie knife, as done by H. R. Giger.

Daniel Carpenter had evidently noticed Fitz's behavior and deduced its meaning. He dragged both Fitz and Butters behind him with a sweep of his brawny arms and positioned himself between them and the sorcerer, his hands up in a defensive martial arts stance.

Butters let out a yelp as his ass hit the cold concrete floor.

Fitz took the fall and rolled, his eyes wide with terror as he regained his feet and started to run.

"You are all dead men," Aristedes snarled.

And then he blurred forward, almost too quickly to be seen, the knife gleaming in his hand.

CHAPTER THIRTY-EIGHT

Aristedes was nothing more than a streak in the air as he closed on Daniel, slamming into him, knocking him back. As Daniel fell, that wicked knife gleamed and whipsawed back and forth half a dozen times in the space of a second, striking Daniel in the chest and belly on every blow.

Anyone other than Michael and Charity Carpenter's son would have been gutted like a fish.

The kid had gotten some serious training — maybe from Murphy, maybe from the Einherjaren, maybe from his father. Probably from all of them. I'm not a professional when it comes to hand-to-hand combat, of the supernatural variety or otherwise, but I know enough to know how little I know. And one of the things I know is that you don't just decide to time your moves a second in advance to compensate for a lack of supernatural speed. You have to learn that stuff, to build it into your reflexes with weeks or months of painstaking practice.

Daniel had.

He started rolling with the slashes of the knife before Aristedes had fully closed the distance, even as he stumbled backward from the force of the sorcerer's initial impact. The knife bit into his chest and belly — and found armor waiting for it.

Beneath his winter coat, Daniel was wearing a garment I recognized as Charity's handiwork: a double-thick Kevlar vest with a coat of thick titanium rings sandwiched in between the layers of ballistic cloth. Kevlar could stop bullets, but it didn't do squat for blades. That was what the titanium mail was for.

Sparks flew up in rapid succession as the knife struck armor. The impact sounded like someone hitting a side of beef with a baseball bat, but Daniel's body was in motion, giving in with each of the blows, robbing them of the most savage portion of their power. The knife never touched his skin.

Aristedes came to a stop after that blinding-fast combination of attacks and crouched, his arm out to one side, parallel to the ground, the knife gripped hard in it. He looked like an extra in a martial arts movie — the goober.

Daniel turned his backward momentum into a roll and came up on his feet. It didn't look very graceful, but he was obviously in control of the motion, and he dropped into a fighting crouch about twenty feet from the sorcerer. One hand went into his hip pocket and came out with a simple folding lock knife with a black plastic handle. With his thumb he snapped out a blade maybe four inches long and held the weapon tucked in close to his body, point toward Aristedes. He jerked the cloak off his back, and with a few flicks of his arm wrapped the heavy material around his left forearm. Then he held his left hand a little in front of him, palm down, fingers loose — ready to block or grab.

Aristedes had a good poker face, but for the moment, I didn't have anything to do except watch what was going on, and I knew his type. The sorcerer hadn't been psychologically prepared for Daniel's reaction. The stupid bruiser was supposed to be bleeding on the floor, maybe begging for his life. At the very least, he should have been running, terrified, but instead, the very large young man had apparently shrugged off the deadly attacks and meant to fight.

"Nice knife," Daniel said. Scorn dripped from the words. "Get it out of a magazine?"

"From the last fool who tried a blade against me."

Daniel bared his teeth. "Come here. I'll give you this one."

Aristedes flicked his knife through a little series of spins, making it dance nimbly through his fingers. It was a stupid thing to do in a real situation, but the guy clearly knew how to use the weapon. Then his body tightened as he hissed a word and once more he flashed toward Daniel.

The body language before the spell that granted him speed had given him away. The kid was ready again. He sidestepped and swept his arms in a pair of half circles as Aristedes flashed by. There was the sound of shearing cloth, and then the sorcerer was past him.

Daniel turned to face Aristedes with a hiss of pain. His left arm, wrapped in the grey cloak, was bleeding, red spreading through the grey in a slow but growing stain.

"No armor there," Aristedes murmured with a smile.

Daniel said nothing. He just took position again, holding his bloodied knife level, its point toward the sorcerer.

Aristedes looked down and saw the long, shallow cut across his right pectoral. A fine sheet of blood had mixed with the sweat that had broken out on his skin.

Heads were popping out of the debris and refuse now. Zero and his compatriots — maybe a dozen kids, all told — were emerging from their hiding spots to watch the fight. From the looks on their faces, it was the first time they'd ever seen their fearless leader get hurt. Hell, if they'd been anything like me when I was young, they probably had believed that he couldn't *be* hurt.

Daniel Carpenter had just shown them differently — and the sorcerer knew it.

Aristedes' face set into a grimace of undiluted hate as he stared at Daniel. Then he did something unexpected — he simply walked forward and pounced into knife range.

The exchange was brief. Most knife fights are. Daniel, the taller of the two, had the advantage of reach, somewhat negated by the length of the sorcerer's blade. He wore armor over his torso and was stronger, but Aristedes was the faster of the two, even without magic — and he had a lot more experience.

Hands and knives flashed, all whip-crack speed and whispering violence as they parted the air. I couldn't keep track of the individual cuts. There were just too many of them. I saw Daniel's mail shirt turn aside another pair of strikes, one of them hard enough to send a titanium ring tinkling across the floor. A flicker of red fanned through the air, where one of the fighters lost a splash of blood.

Daniel let out a short grunt. Then another. Aristedes barked out a sound of both pain and satisfaction. The two parted, both breathing heavily. Combat taxes a body's reserves like nothing else on earth. Seconds of it can leave you exhausted, even if you're in great shape.

Daniel staggered and went down on one knee, letting out a grunt of surprise.

There were wounds on both of his legs — punctures, deep stabs. Neither wound had hit one of the big arteries, or he'd already be unconscious, but they were right through the quadriceps muscles, and had to have been agonizing.

He snarled and attempted to rise. Halfway there, he faltered and went down again. Training, courage, and fortitude get you only so far. A deep enough wound on either leg could have taken Daniel out of the fight. He had them on both.

Aristedes hadn't come away clean from the exchange, though. There was a deep cut on his right arm, where Daniel's knife had caught him hard. Flesh hung from a flap of skin. Blood flowed, but his arm still seemed to work. If Aristedes lived long enough and if he kept the arm, he was going to have one hell of a scar to show off later.

But that wasn't going to matter much to Daniel.

The sorcerer switched his knife to his left hand and stared at Daniel with flat eyes. "Kids like you. Haven't learned the price of doing business. When to trade pain for victory."

He blurred into motion again, and Daniel lifted his knife. Then the younger man cried out and fell to his side, clutching at his right arm with his left hand. His knife landed on the floor and spun away from him, eventually coming to rest against Aristedes' feet.

The sorcerer took his time transferring his own knife to his left hand and picking up Daniel's. He tested the blade's balance and edge and said, "Serviceable." He carefully wiped the blood from Daniel's blade against the leg of his trousers, closed it, and slipped it into the pocket of his bathrobe. Then he fixed the young man with a nasty smile, raised his own blade over his head, so that Daniel's blood dripped down it and fell on his upraised arm.

And he started to chant.

I felt the magic gathering at once. It wasn't particularly powerful, but that was by my own standards. Magic doesn't absolutely require a ton of horsepower to be dangerous. It took Aristedes maybe ten seconds to summon enough will and focus for whatever he was doing, and I stood there clenching my fists and my jaw in impotent fury. Daniel saw what was happening and found an old can in the detritus on the floor beside him. He threw it at Aristedes in an awkward, left-handed motion, but came nowhere close to striking the sorcerer.

Aristedes pointed the knife at Daniel, his eyes reptilian, hissed a word, and released the spell.

Michael's eldest son arched his back and let out a strangled scream of agony. Aristedes repeated the word and Daniel contorted in pain again, his back bowing more than I would have thought possible.

I stifled a furious scream of my own and looked away as the sorcerer bent and twisted the energy of Creation itself into a means of torment. Looking away was almost worse: Aristedes' young followers were watching with a sick fascination. Daniel screamed until he was out of breath, and then began to strangle himself as he tried to keep it up. One of the kids bent suddenly and began retching onto the floor.

"This is *my* house," Aristedes said, his expression never changing. "I am the master here, and *my* will is —"

Butters appeared behind Aristedes, from around an upended vat of some kind, and swung three feet of lead pipe into the side of the sorcerer's knee.

There was a sharp, clear crack as bone and cartilage snapped, and Aristedes screamed and went down.

"That sound you just heard," Butters said, his voice tight with fear and adrenaline, "was your lateral collateral ligament and anterior cruciate ligament tearing free of the joint. It's also possible that your patella or tibia was fractured."

Aristedes just lay there in pain, gasping through clenched teeth. A line of spittle drooled out of his mouth.

Butters hefted the lead pipe like a batter at

the plate. "Get rid of the knife, or I start on your cranium."

Aristedes kept on gasping but didn't look up. He tossed the creepy knife away.

"The one in your pocket, too," Butters said.

The sorcerer gave him a look of pure hatred. Then he tossed away the knife he'd appropriated from Daniel.

"Sit tight, Daniel," Butters called. "I'll be with you in just a second."

" 'M fine," Daniel groaned from the ground. He didn't sound fine. But as I watched, I saw him winding pieces of the slashed cloak around the wound in his right arm, binding them closed and slowing the bleeding. Tough kid, and thinking under pressure.

Butters focused on Aristedes. "I don't want to hurt you," he said. "I want to help you. Your knee has been destroyed. You will never walk again if you don't get medical attention. I'll take you to a hospital."

"What do you want?" Aristedes growled.

"The priest. Fitz. These kids." He bounced the lead pipe against his own shoulder a couple of times. "And this really isn't a negotiation."

"Yes!" I said, clenching my fist. "You go, Butters!"

Aristedes eyed Butters for a moment more. Then he sagged and let out a soft groan of pain.

Oh, crap.

"You win," the sorcerer said. "Just . . . please . . . help me."

"Straighten it out," Butters said, never quite looking at the man. "Lie back and leave it straight."

Aristedes fumbled with his leg and let out another, higher-pitched moan of pain.

Butters flinched at the sound and his eyes were tortured. In a sudden flash of insight, I realized why he cut up corpses for a living instead of treating live patients.

Butters couldn't handle seeing people in pain.

That was what he'd always meant when he said that he wasn't a real doctor, when he said that treating living patients was messy and disturbing compared to extracting individual organs and cataloging them in autopsies. Dead people were just a pile of meat and bones. They were beyond all suffering.

A physician needs a certain level of professional detachment if he is going to best serve his patients, and Butters just . . . didn't have it. The little guy couldn't bring himself not to feel something for the people he worked with. So he had sought a career where he practiced medicine without trying to heal anyone — without involving himself with actual patients.

Aristedes had seen it, too. He probably didn't understand it, but he saw the soft spot, and he went for it ruthlessly.

"Don't," I breathed. "Butters, don't."

"Dammit," Butters said finally, gritting his teeth. He bent to help the man. "Hold still. You're just making it worse. Here." He tried to keep a wary distance as he lent the man a hand, but it just wasn't possible to help him *and* stay out of reach. I saw it on his face as he realized it and began to withdraw. Then, as the man continued his low moans of pain, Butters gave his head a little shake and moved to help Aristedes straighten his leg.

I saw the sorcerer's eyes narrow to slits, an almost sensual pleasure contained in them.

"Dammit!" I said. "Butters, move!" I vanished and appeared beside Butters, shoving my hands into his chest, willing myself to push him away.

I didn't move him — my hands just passed into him, insubstantial — but a sudden frisson seemed to run through him, and he began to pull away.

Too late.

Aristedes' left arm blurred and struck Butters squarely on the chin. If he hadn't been drawing back, the blow would have caught him just under the ear, and the sorcerer's hand was moving fast enough that it might have broken Butters's neck. Even so, the sharp thump of impact snapped Butters's head to one side, hard enough to rebound when it had reached maximum torsion. He did a brief bobblehead impersonation on the way to the floor and landed in a boneless heap.

I wanted to scream in frustration. Instead, I poked at my brain, demanding it to come up with something.

To my considerable surprise, it did.

I vanished straight up to the ceiling and spun in a quick circle. There. I spotted Fitz, moving in a low crawl toward one of the exits from the factory floor, keeping a modest pile of junk between himself and Aristedes.

"Fitz!" I bellowed. I vanished and re-appeared right over him. "Fitz, you've got to turn around!"

"Quiet," he hissed in a frantic whisper. His eyes were white around the edges. "Quiet. No, I can't! Leave me alone!"

"You've got to do it," I said. "Forthill's here in the camp, hurt bad. There's a freaking angel of death standing over him. He needs help."

Fitz didn't answer me. He kept on crawling off the factory floor and into one of the hallways outside it. He was making desper-ate, small sounds as he reached the door and got out of any possible line of sight to Aris-tedes.

"Fitz," I said. "Fitz, you have got to do something. You're the only one who can."

"Cops," he panted. "I'll call the cops. They can handle it." He got up and started pad-ding down the hall, toward what I presumed was the nearest exit from the building.

"Butters and Daniel don't have that kind of time," I answered. "The cops get tipped off by a runaway, we'll be lucky if a prowl car cruises by half an hour from now. All three of them could be dead by then. Your boss can't allow witnesses."

"You're the wizard," Fitz said. "Why can't you do it? I mean, ghosts can possess people and stuff, right? Just zap into Aristedes and make him jump off the roof."

I was quiet for a moment. Then I said, "Look, I'm new at this ghost thing. But it doesn't work like that. Even the badass ghost of a centuries-old wizard I know of can only possess a subject who is willing. So far, I've only been able to move into people who were sensitive to spirits — and they could have booted me out anytime they wanted. Aristedes is neither sensitive nor willing. I'd be like a bug splattering on a windshield if I tried to take him over."

"Christ."

"If you want to volunteer, I could take you over, I suppose. I don't think you've got the right wiring for me to use my power, and you'd still be in danger, of course, but you wouldn't have to make the decisions."

Fitz shuddered. "No."

"Good. It's weird as hell." I paused and took a breath. "And besides. It would be . . . wrong."

"Wrong?" Fitz asked.

"Take away someone's will, you take away everything they are. Their whole identity. Doing that to someone is worse than murder; if you kill them, they don't keep on suffering."

"Who cares?" Fitz said. "This guy is an animal. Who cares if he gets something bad? He's earned it."

"Wrong is wrong, even when you really, really want it not to be," I said quietly. "I learned that one the hard way. It's easy to do the right thing when it doesn't cost you. Not as easy to do the right thing when your back is to the wall."

Fitz shook his head the whole time I spoke that last, and his pace quickened. "There's nothing I can do. I'm running for my life."

I fought down a snarl to keep my voice level. Time to change tactics. "Kid, you aren't thinking it through," I said. "You know Aristedes. You know him."

"Which part of *running for my life* didn't come across?"

I grunted. "The part where you leave your friends to die."

"What?"

"He's busted up pretty bad right now. Weak. How long do you think it will take him to replace all your crew?"

Fitz's steps dragged to a stop.

"They've seen him weak now. Hell, he's hurt bad enough that he might be crippled

535

for life. What do you think he'll do with the kids who saw him beaten? Who saw him get bloodied and smashed to the floor?"

Fitz bowed his head.

"Stars and stones, kid. You started showing signs of independent thought, and he was so threatened by it that he set you up to get killed. What do you think he'll do to Zero?"

Fitz didn't answer.

"You run now," I said quietly, "and you're going to spend your whole life running. This is a crossroads. This is where your life takes form. Here. Now. This moment."

His face twisted up as if he was in physical pain. Still, he didn't respond.

I wanted to put my hand on his shoulder, to give him the reassurance of a human touch. The best I could do was to soften my voice as much as I could.

"I know what I'm talking about, kid. Every time you're alone in the dark, every time you go by a mirror, you're going to remember this moment. You're going to see who you've become. And you'll either be the man who ran away while his own crew and three good men died, or you'll be the man who stood tall and did something about it."

Fitz swallowed and whispered, "He's too strong."

"Not right now, he isn't," I said. "He's on the ground. He can't walk. He's got one arm. If I didn't think you had a chance, I'd be telling you to run."

"I can't," he whispered. "I can't. This isn't fair."

"Life hardly ever is," I said.

"I don't want to die."

"Heh. No one does. But everyone does it anyway."

"That supposed to be funny?"

"Maybe a little ironic, given the source. Look, kid. All that matters is the answer to the question: Which of those men do you want to be?"

Slowly he lifted his head. I realized that he could see his own reflection in the glass of an office door.

I stood behind him, looking down at him and remembering, with a faint sense of irrational disbelief, that I had once been no taller than the boy.

"Which man, Fitz?" I asked quietly.

CHAPTER THIRTY-NINE

When I faced my old master, I did it with newly made staff and blasting rod in hand, with the ancient forces of the universe at my call, and with words of power upon my tongue.

Fitz had more courage than I had as a child.

He went to face his demons with no weapon at all.

As his footsteps rapped steadily on the concrete floor, I worried about the kid. He was doing this on my say-so. What if Aristedes wasn't hurt as badly as I thought? What if he knew some kind of restorative magic? Fitz wouldn't have a chance — and I would never forgive myself.

I gritted my teeth and told myself not to borrow trouble. Things were bad enough without adding in a bunch of my own worries. That wouldn't help anybody.

Fitz stepped into sight of Aristedes and stopped in his tracks.

"Easy," I said quietly. "Calm. Don't show

him any weakness. You can do it."

Fitz took a deep breath and walked forward.

"Fitz," Aristedes spat. He was sitting up now, his leg straight out in front of him. Butters's unconscious body had been dumped next to Daniel, who sat on the ground in a small puddle of his own blood, grimacing in pain and obviously disoriented. He'd bound the wounds closed, more or less, but it was clear that he still needed real medical attention. Zero and the other kids, several obviously detailed to watch Daniel and Butters, were standing around with pipes and old knives. "What do you think you're doing here, traitor?"

Fitz faced him in silence.

"You led those men to us. You've endangered the lives of everyone here."

Fitz almost seemed to dwindle, as if a cloud had passed between him and the wan light spilling in the windows. Dark, hostile eyes glared at Fitz from all around.

A quick check with my senses confirmed that the sorcerer was using power. "He's pushing them," I said quietly, "making them feel hostility toward you. It isn't real. You've got to shake him, break his focus."

Fitz gave a barely perceptible nod of his head. "I didn't lead them here. They caught me while I was trying to recover the weapons. They forced me to come with them."

"That's not what the priest said," Aristedes

shot back.

"The father thought he was helping me," Fitz replied. "There was no reason to hurt him."

"No reason?" Aristedes asked. His voice was dangerous, deadly, and smooth. "That he should trespass here is reason enough. But he wanted to destroy this family. That is something I will not permit."

"Family, right," Fitz said. "We're like the Simpsons around here."

Personally, I would have gone with the Waltons, but I liked the cut of the kid's jib.

Aristedes stared at Fitz with reptilian eyes and said, "Give me one reason why I should not kill you, here and now."

"Because you can't," Fitz said in a bored tone. "You aren't going anywhere under your own power. You're fucked. You need help."

The sorcerer's voice dropped to a bare whisper. "Do I?"

"Yep," Fitz said. "Wasn't like it wasn't going to happen eventually anyway, right? Sooner or later, you were gonna wind up eating applesauce with a rubber spoon somewhere. You think a bunch of kids you terrified into following you are gonna take care of Grandpa Aristedes? Come on."

"I'll give you one chance," Aristedes said. "Leave. Now."

Fitz tapped a finger on his chin thoughtfully. Then he said, "Nah. Don't think so."

Aristedes blinked. "What?"

"Here's how it's going to work," Fitz said. "I'm going to take the priest, those two guys, and the crew away from you. I'm going to get them some help. I'm going to call an ambulance and get you some help, too. After that, we never cross paths again."

"Are you insane?"

"I was," Fitz said, nodding. "I think I'm coming out of it now. I know you aren't coming back from Loopyland, though. So I'm taking the crew away from you."

Aristedes clenched his fists and his eyes blazed — and though he probably didn't realize it, his concentration faltered. The influence magic he held over the children wavered. "Kill him."

The flat-eyed children looked at Fitz. Zero started taking a step toward him.

Fitz's voice was a whip crack, sharp and loud in the echoing chamber. "Stop."

And they did. No magic was involved. Fitz had something more powerful than that. He'd cared for those other kids. He'd thought about them, encouraged them, and led them. That was something every bit as real as mystic power and dark enchantment — and it carries a hell of a lot more weight.

Love always does.

"Zero," Fitz said quietly. "We're done staying with this idiot. Put down the knife and come with me."

"Zero!" Aristedes said sharply.

I could all but see the strain in the air as the sorcerer doubled down on his influence-working, struggling to force the boy to do his will. He shouldn't have bothered. It was over. It had been over ever since Fitz chose to walk back into that room.

Fitz walked over to Zero and put a hand on the other boy's shoulder. "Z," he said quietly. "I can't make you do anything. So you tell me. Who do you want looking out for you? Me? Or him?"

Zero looked searchingly at Fitz. Then at Aristedes.

"Don't listen to him," Aristedes said through clenched teeth, spraying spittle. "Without me, you won't last a day on these streets. The Fomor will take you *all*."

"No, Z," Fitz said quietly. "They won't. It's okay. We've got help."

Zero blinked his eyes several times. He bowed his head.

The old knife in his fingers clattered to the concrete floor.

Another dozen knives and pipes fell to the floor as the other boys released them. They all went over to Fitz and gathered around him.

"I'll kill you," hissed Aristedes. "I'll *kill* you."

Fitz faced the crippled sorcerer and shook his head. Then he did what was possibly the cruelest thing he could have done to his former mentor.

He turned away and ignored him.

"Zero," Fitz said, "we need an ambulance for the father now. Call nine-one-one. Don't move him — let the ambulance guys do that."

Zero nodded and pulled one of those cheap, prepaid cell phones out of the pocket of his oversized jacket. He ran for the door, presumably to get a better signal. Within the next few minutes, rough but serviceable medical supplies had been brought out, and Daniel's wounds had been cleaned and bound tighter than he'd been able to manage on his own.

Aristedes tried to get a couple of the kids to pay attention to him, but they were following Fitz's lead. They ignored him. So the sorcerer just sat and watched it all in stunned silence.

Maybe I should have felt a little bit bad for the guy. As far as his world was concerned, he had just died. Only he was still alive to see the unthinkable — a world that existed without him. He was a living, breathing ghost. Maybe I should have felt some empathy there.

But I really didn't.

Butters stirred and sat up groggily as Fitz finished up tying a second pressure bandage to Daniel's leg. Michael's son let out a short grunt of pain and then breathed deeply several times. He was still shaking and pale, but his eyes were steady. He met Fitz's gaze and said, "Thank you."

Fitz shook his head. "I didn't do anything. You two were the ones who beat him."

"The father was the one who beat him," Daniel corrected him. "He knew what would happen to him when he came here. And he knew we'd come after him."

Butters grunted and spoke without opening his eyes. "Forthill wouldn't have played it like that. He came here to give peace a chance." He groaned and pressed a hand to his jaw. "Nnngh. Ow."

Daniel frowned, thinking it over. "So . . . he didn't want us to come after him?"

Butters snorted. "He knew we would come after him, no matter what he did. And he also knew that if the sorcerer went off on him, there would be someone to come along and do it the other way. He's a man of peace. Doesn't mean he's stupid."

"Where is he?" Daniel asked.

"By the fire," Fitz said. "That way about thirty yards. The ambulance is on the way."

Butters groaned and slowly pushed himself up. He rubbed at his jaw again and said, "Take me to him."

"Wait," Daniel said. "Fitz . . . you ran. I don't blame you. But you came back."

Fitz paused, pursed his lips, and said, "Yeah. I did, didn't I?"

"Why?"

Fitz shrugged. "Dresden. He told me that if I ran now, I'd run forever. And I'm sick of that."

"Heh," Butters said. "Heh, heh. He totally Kenobied the day." Dark eyes gleaming, he looked at Daniel. "Still have doubts?"

Daniel shook his head once, smiling. Then he sank down to the floor with a satisfied groan.

"The father, please," Butters said. Fitz nodded and led Butters over toward the gang's little camp. But not before Butters looked around and said, "Thanks, Harry. Good to know you've still got our backs."

I watched them go to help Forthill quietly.

"Sure, man," I said, though I knew no one could hear me. "Anytime."

Emergency-service personnel arrived. By the time they got there, weapons had been hidden. Stories had been set. Concerned adults had come to discourage some local homeless youth from playing and living in a dangerous, old, ruined building. There had been an altercation with a possibly drunken vagrant that had gotten out of hand. Things had fallen down, injuring several.

It wouldn't have taken more than half a brain to see the holes in the story, but Butters knew the med techs, no one had been killed, and no one wanted to press any charges. The techs were willing to keep their mouths shut for a couple of greenbacks. Ah, Chicago.

Forthill was in bad shape, but by the time they'd gotten him onto a stretcher and out to the ambulance, the angel of death was nowhere to be seen. Hah. Up yours, Reaper Girl. The father would live to not-fight another day.

Daniel went with the father. Aristedes rode in his own ambulance. He was still stunned by what had happened, or else smart enough to look disoriented and keep his mouth shut. The techs, after a few quiet words from Butters, strapped his arms and legs down for the ride. He never resisted. He never did anything. The doors of the ambulance shut on a broken man.

As for me, I couldn't emerge from the old factory into the light. I had to stay in shadowed doorways to watch the proceedings. The afternoon must have been a warm one. The snow had visibly begun to lessen, and water ran and dripped everywhere.

When everyone with immediate medical needs had been taken care of, I went back to where I knew Butters would be. Sure enough, he came into the business entryway to recover his duffel bag and the flashlight containing Bob's skull.

Butters slung the bag's strap over his shoulder and pulled the little spirit radio out of it. He dropped that in his pocket and took out the flashlight housing. Then he held it up and said, "Okay, job's done."

Orange campfire lights shot in a stream over my right shoulder and past me into the eye sockets of the skull, where they took up their familiar glow. "See? I told you so."

"Duly noted," Butters said seriously.

I blinked at him and looked behind me, then back at the skull. "Bob. You were behind me that whole time?"

"Yeah," Bob said. "The nerd had me shadow you. Sorry, Harry."

Butters could see me, and I folded my arms and scowled at him. "You didn't trust me."

Butters pushed his glasses up on his nose. "Trust, but verify," he said seriously. "Don't take this the wrong way, Harry, but the testimony of a cat and a maybe-insane girl — wizard or not — didn't exactly thrill all of us with its undeniable veracity."

"Murphy told you to do it," I said.

"Actually, Murphy didn't want any of us to take any chances dealing with you," he replied. "Things have used your appearance to get to her before."

I wanted to say something heated and ferocious, but all I could have rationally responded with was something like, *You're right.* And that wouldn't have sounded very rational. So I just grunted.

Butters nodded. "And you've got to understand how bad the streets have been. The Fomor have no limits, Harry. They'll use women, children, pets — anything — to get an emotional lever on you, if they can. To fight that, you've got to have buckets and buckets of sangfroid."

I grunted and scowled some more. "But you bucked her orders."

Butters scratched his nose with one finger. "Well. You know. It sounds cooler if I say I acted on my own initiative. I had a hunch."

"Listen to Quincy here," the skull burbled, giggling. "You had me, you dope."

"I had you," Butters admitted. "And I trust you."

"And Murphy doesn't, much," Bob said with cheery pride, "which is probably smart. Someone else gets hold of my skull and who knows what they'd do with me? I am a loose cannon! The Wardens would waste me in a hot second!"

"Present company excluded," I said.

"You don't count," the skull said stoutly. "You were drafted."

"Granted."

"The point being that I am an *outlaw!* And chicks *love* that!"

"Oy," Butters said, rolling his eyes. "Enough, Bob."

"You got it, hombre," Bob said.

I couldn't help laughing a little.

"You see what I've got to live with," Butters said.

"Yeah," I said.

"You, uh," he said. He rubbed at the back of his head. "You're missed, here, Harry. A lot. After a while, most of us . . . you know. We figured you were gone. We kind of had a wake at your grave. Pizza and beer. Called it a funeral. But Murphy wouldn't go."

"Illegal gathering," I said.

Butters snorted out a breath through his nose. "That was her excuse, yeah."

"Well," I said. "We'll see."

Butters paused, body motionless for a moment. "We'll see what?"

"Whether or not this is permanent," I said, gesturing at myself.

Butters snapped up straight. "What?"

"Bob thinks that there is hinkiness afoot with regard to my, ah, disposition."

"You . . . you could come back?" Butters whispered.

"Or maybe I haven't left," I said. "I don't know, man. I got suckered into this whole encore-appearance thing. I'm as in the dark as everyone else."

"Wow," Butters breathed.

I waved a hand. "Look. That will fall out where it may," I said. "We've got a real problem to deal with, like, right now."

He nodded, one sharp gesture. "Tell me."

I told him about the Corpsetaker and her plan for Mort, and her deal with the point guy of the Fomor's servitors. "So we've got to break that up right the hell now," I concluded. "I want you to get Murphy and her Vikings and tell them to go stomp the Corpsetaker's hideout."

Butters sucked in a breath through his teeth. "Ugh. I know there hasn't been time for a lot of chitchat since you, uh, became departed, but they aren't Murphy's Vikings."

"Whose are they?"

"Marcone's."

"Oh."

"We'll have to talk to Childs."

"Marcone's new guy?"

"Yeah. Him." Butters shivered. "Guy gives me the creeps."

"Could be Will and company would be enough."

Butters shook his head. "Could be Will and company have done too much already, man. Seriously."

"Something's got to happen. If you wait, you get a renegade wizard the White Council has nightmares about knocking on your front door. And by *knocking* I mean 'converting it from matter to energy.' "

Butters nodded. "I'll talk to her. We'll figure out something." He squinted at me. "What are you going to be doing?"

"Covering the ghosty side of things," I said. "She and her wannabe Bob and her lemurs and all the wraiths she's been calling up. Assuming things go well on the mortal coil, I don't want her slipping out the back door and coming back to haunt us another day."

He frowned. "You're going to do all that by yourself?"

I showed him my teeth. "Not exactly. Move. There's not much time."

"When?" he asked.

"When else?" I answered. "Sundown."

CHAPTER FORTY

I vanished from inside the factory the second I felt sundown shudder through reality. The jumps were longer now, almost double what I'd managed the night before, and it took less time to orient myself between them. I guess practice makes perfect, even if you're dead. Or whatever I was.

It took me less than two minutes to get to the burnt remains of Morty's place.

On the way, I could see that southern winds were blowing, and they must have brought a springtime warmth with them. All of the city's snow was melting, and the combination of the two with the oncoming night meant that a misty fog hung in the air, cutting visibility down to maybe fifty or sixty feet. Fog in Chicago isn't terribly unusual, but never that thick. Streetlights were ringed with blurred, luminous halos. Traffic signals were soft blurs of changing color. Cars moved slowly, cautiously, and the thick mist laid a rare hush over the city, strangling its usual voice.

I stopped about a hundred yards away from Morty's house. There I felt it: a trace of the summoning energy that had been built into his former home, drawing me forward with the same gentle beckoning as might the scent of a hot meal after a long day. It was like the Corpsetaker's summons, but of a magic far less coarse, far more gentle. The necromancer's magic was like the suction of a vacuum cleaner. Mort's magic had been more like the gravity of the earth — less overtly powerful, but utterly pervasive.

Hell. Mort's magic had probably had some kind of effect on me all the way over in Chicago Between. His house was the first place I'd come to, after all, and though I had a logical reason to go there, it was entirely possible that my reasoning had been influenced. It was magic, after all, intended to attract the attention of dangerous spirits.

At that very moment, in her moldy old lair, the Corpsetaker was torturing Morty and planning to murder my friends — so the remnants of the spell were definitely getting my attention.

I went closer to Morty's house and felt that same pull get a little stronger. The spell had been broken when Mort's house had burned down, and it was fading. The morning's sunrise had almost wiped it away. It wouldn't survive another dawn — but with a little help, it might serve its purpose one more time.

From the voluminous pocket of my duster, I withdrew Sir Stuart's pistol. I fiddled with the gun until the gleaming silver sphere of the bullet rolled out into my hand, along with a sparkling cloud of flickering light. As each mote touched my skin, I heard the faint echo of a shot cracking out — the gunfire of Sir Stuart's memory. Hundreds of shots crackled in my ears, distant and faint: the ghostly memory equivalent of gunpowder. Sir Stuart had heard a lot of it.

But what I needed wasn't firepower, not for this. I took up the shining silver sphere, the memory of Sir Stuart's home and family, and regarded it with my full attention. Once again the scene of the small family farm seemed to swell in my vision, until it surrounded me in a faint, translucent landscape that quivered and throbbed with power all its own. For a second, I could hear the wind rustling through the fields of grain and smell the sharp, honest scents of animals drifting to me from the barn, mixing with the aroma of fresh-baked bread coming from the house. The shouts and cries of children playing some sort of game hung in the air.

They weren't my memories, but I felt something beneath their surface, something powerful and achingly familiar. I reached into my own thoughts and produced the memories of my own home, casting them up to merge with Sir Stuart's cherished vision. I remembered the smell of wood and ink and paper, of all the shelves of secondhand books that had lined the walls of my old apartment, with their ramshackle double- and triple-stacked layers of paperbacks. I remembered the scent of wood-smoke from my fireplace, blending with the aroma of fresh coffee in a cup. I threw in the taste of Campbell's chicken soup in a steaming mug on a cold day, when my clothes had been soaked with rain and snow and I had gotten out of them and huddled beneath a blanket near the fire, sipping soup and feeling the warmth sink into me.

I remembered the solid warmth of my dog, Mouse, his heavy head pillowed on my leg while I read a book, and the softness of Mister's fur as he came by and gently batted my book away with his paw until I paused to give him his due share of attention. I remembered my apprentice, Molly, diligently studying and reading, remembered us having hours and hours of conversation as I taught her the basics of magic, of how to use it responsibly and wisely — or, at least, as responsibly and wisely as I knew how. They weren't necessarily the same thing.

I remembered the feeling of pulling warm covers up over me as I went to bed. Of listening to thunderstorms, complete with flickering lightning, pounding rain, and howling wind, and of the simple, secure pleasure of knowing that I was safe and warm while the elements raged outside. I remembered walking with confidence in pitch darkness, because I knew every step that would take me safely through my rooms.

Home.

I invoked the memory of home.

I don't know at what point the bullet dissolved into raw potential, but its power blended with my memories, humming a powerful harmonic chord with the emotions behind those memories — emotions common to all of us, a need for a place that is our own. Security. Safety. Comfort.

Home.

"Home," I breathed aloud. I found the tatters of Mort's gathering spell, and in my thoughts began to knit the edges of the memories together with the frayed magic. "Home," I breathed again, gathering my will, fusing it with memory, and sending it out into the nighttime air. "Come home," I said, and my voice carried into the night, reverberating through the mist, borne by the energy of my spell into a night-shivering, encompassing music as I released that power and memory into the night. "Come home. Come home."

It all flowed out of me in a steady, deliberate rush, leaving me with unhurried purpose. I felt the magic rush out in a steadily growing circle. And then it was gone, except for the faintest whisper of an echo.

Come home. Come home. Come home.

I opened my eyes slowly.

There had been no sound, no stirring of energies, no warning of any kind.

I stood in a circle of silent, staring, hollow-eyed spirits.

Now that I knew what they were — the insane, dangerous ghosts of Chicago, the ones that killed people — they looked different. Those two little kids? My goodness, spooky now, a little too much darkness in their sunken eyes, expressions that wouldn't change if they were watching a car go by or pushing a toddler's head under the surface of the water. A businessman, apparently from the late-nineteenth century, I recognized as the shade of Herman Webster Mudgett, an American trailblazer in the field of entrepreneurial serial murder. I spotted another shade from a century earlier who could only have been Captain William Wells, a cold and palpable fury radiating from him still.

There were more — many more. Chicago has an intense history of violence, tragedy, and sheer weirdness that really can't be topped this side of the Atlantic. I couldn't put names to a third of them, but I knew now, looking at them, exactly what they were — lives that had ended in misery, in fury, in pain, or in madness. They were pure energy of destruction given human form, smoldering like coals that could still sear flesh long after they ceased to give off light.

They were a loaded gun.

Standing behind them, patient and calm, like sheepdogs around their flock, were the guardian spirits of Mort's house. I had assumed them to be his spiritual soldiers, but I could see now what their main purpose had been. They, the ghosts of duty and obligation unfulfilled, had remained behind in an attempt to see their tasks to completion. They, the shades of faith, of love, of duty, had been a balancing energy with the dark power of the violent spirits. They had grounded the savagery and madness with their sheer, steady, simple existence — and the faded shade of Sir Stuart stood tall and calm among them.

I held Sir Stuart's weapon in my right hand and half wished I could go back in time and rap my twenty-four-hours-younger self on the head with it. The fading spirit hadn't been trying to hand me a weapon at all. He'd been giving me something far more dangerous than that.

I thought he'd handed me potent but limited power, a single deadly shot. I'd been thinking in mortal terms, from a mortal perspective.

Stuart hadn't given me a gun. He'd given me a *symbol.*

He'd given me *authority.*

I held the gun in my right hand and closed my eyes for a moment, focusing on it, concentrating on not merely holding it, but taking it into me, making it my own. I opened my eyes, looked at the tall, brawny shade, and said, "Thank you, Sir Stuart."

As I spoke, the gun shifted and changed, elongating abruptly. The wood of its grip and stock swelled out, becoming knife-planed oak and, as it did, I reached into my memory. Runes and sigils carved themselves in a tight spiral down the length of the staff. I took a deep breath and once more felt the solid power of my wizard's staff, six feet of oak as big around as my own circled thumb and finger, the foremost symbol of *my* power, gripped steadily in my hand.

I bowed my head, focusing intently, drawing on the memories of the hundreds of spells and dozens of conflicts of my life, and as I did the symbols on the staff pulsed with opalescent energy that reminded me of Sir Stuart's bullets in flight. Power hummed through the spectral wood so that it shook in my hand and flickered sharply, sending pulses of weirdly colored light, light I sensed would be visible even to mortal eyes, surging through the mist. There was a rushing sound, something almost like a sudden strike upon an unimaginably large and deep drum, an impact that rippled out from me and passed

559

throughout the city and the surrounding lands. It sent a shiver of energy through me, and for an instant I felt the warmth of the southern wind, the close, muggy dampness of the air, the wet, slushy cold of the snow beneath my insubstantial feet. I smelled the stench of Morty's burned home on the air, and for a single instant, for the first time since the tunnel, I felt the rumble of hunger in my belly.

Then dozens of spectral gazes simultaneously shifted, focusing exclusively on me, and their weight hit me like a sudden cold wind.

"Good evening, everyone," I said quietly, turning to address the circle of raw fury and devotion that surrounded me. "Our friend Mortimer is in trouble. And we don't have much time. . . ."

Chapter Forty-One

The Corpsetaker's stronghold hadn't changed.

But it *had* awakened.

I felt the difference as soon as I approached, and a quick effort to invoke the memory of my Sight brought the changes into sharp, clear view. A column of lurid light, all shades of purple and scarlet, rose into the night sky over the entrance to the stronghold. I could see the magical energy involved, my gaze piercing the ground as if it had been slightly cloudy water. There, beneath the ground, where I had seen them on the stairs and in the tunnels, were formulas of deadly power, full of terrible energy, now awakened and burning bright.

All of that shoddy, nonsensical, quasimagical script hadn't been anything of the sort. Or, rather, it had been only apparent nonsense. The true formulas, strongly burning wards built on almost the same theory and system I had once used to protect my own home, had been concealed within the overt insanity.

"Right in front of me and I missed it," I breathed.

I should have known better. The Corpsetaker had once been part of the White Council, sometime back before the French and Indian War. We'd gone to the same school, even if we'd graduated in very different years. Not only that, but she was getting assistance from a being that had been created from part of my own personal arcane assistant. Evil Bob had probably given her similar advice on constructing wards.

Wards weren't like a lot of other magic. They were based on a threshold, the envelope of energy around a home. Granted, the loonies currently inhabiting the tunnels were hair-on-fire bonkers, but they were still human, and they still had the same need for a home that everyone else did. Thresholds don't care about sunrise, not when a living, breathing mortal fuels them every moment, just by living within them. Build a spell onto a threshold and it doesn't easily diminish. As a result, you can slowly, over time, pump more and more and more energy into spells based upon it.

The Corpsetaker hadn't needed access to a wizard-level talented body to create the wards. She'd just used tiny talents regularly over months and months, and built up the wards to major-league defenses a little at a time, preparing for the night when she would need them.

Obviously, she'd decided that since she was torturing a world-class ectomancer in order to make her big comeback from beyond the grave, tonight was a great night not to be interrupted.

"I hate fighting competent people," I growled. "I just *hate* it."

"Formidable defenses," said a quiet voice behind me.

I looked over my right shoulder. Sir Stuart studied the wards as well. He'd become a tiny bit more solid-looking, and there was distant, distracted interest in his eyes.

"Yeah," I said. "Got any ideas?"

"Mortal magic," he replied. "Beyond our reach."

"I know that," I replied grumpily. "But we've got to get in." I looked around at the crew of lunatic ghosts I'd mentally dubbed the Lecter Specters. "What about those guys? Breaking the rules is kind of what they do. Are they crazy enough to get in?"

"Threshold. Inviolable."

Which again made sense. I'd gotten into the fortress the night before because the door had been open and the ghost-summoning spell had essentially been a big old welcome mat, a standing invitation. Clearly, tonight was different. "Well," I muttered, "nothing worth doing is easy, is it?"

There was no response.

I turned to find that Sir Stuart's shade had faded out again and his eyes were lost in the middle distance.

"Stu? Hey, Stu."

He didn't respond except to face forward again, his expression patient, ready to follow orders.

"Dammit," I sighed. "Okay, Harry. You're the big-time wizard. Figure it out by yourself."

I vanished and reappeared at the doorway. Then I leaned on my staff and studied the active wards. That did me limited good. I knew them. I'd used constructions much like them on my own home. You'd need to throw several tons of bodies at them, literally, to bring them down — which was what had happened to my first-generation wards. Wave after wave of zombies had eventually gotten through.

I mean, go figure. You prepare your home for an assault and you don't take zombies into consideration. I'd fallen victim to one of the other classic blunders, along with not getting involved in a land war in Asia and never going in against a Sicilian when death was on the line.

My second generation of wards had planned for zombies. So had these. So even if I had zombies, which I didn't, I wasn't going to be able to go through them.

"So," I said. "Don't go through them. Go around them."

Yeah, smart guy? How?

"There's an open Way between the heart of the fortress and the Nevernever," I said. "That's like a permanently open door with an all-day invitation, or they wouldn't need fortifications on the other side. All you have to do is get to it, assault Evil Bob's defenses and Evil Bob and whatever the Corpsetaker recruited from God only knows what kind of dark hellhole, smash them up, and blast through from the spirit world."

Well. That plan did have a lot of words like *assault* and *smash* and *blast* in it, which I had to admit was way more my style. One problem, though: I couldn't open a Way to the Nevernever. Once I was through, I could probably find Evil Bob's fortress — it would perforce have to be nearby. But, like the mortal-world lair, I couldn't open the door.

"Other than that, though, it's genius," I assured myself.

A direct assault against a fortress that had undoubtedly been designed to defeat direct assaults? Brilliant. Uncomplicated, do-or-die suicidal, and there's the minor issue that you aren't capable of actually implementing it. But genius — absolutely.

Gandalf never had this kind of problem.

He had exactly this problem, actually, stand-

ing in front of the hidden Dwarf door to Moria. Remember when . . .

I sighed. Sometimes my inner monologue annoys even me.

"Edro, edro," I muttered. "Open." I rubbed at the bridge of my nose and ventured, *"Mellon."*

Nothing happened. The wards stayed. I guessed the Corpsetaker had never read Tolkien. Tasteless bitch.

"I hate this depending-on-others crap," I muttered. Then I vanished and reappeared at the head of my horde. "Okay, everybody," I said. "Huddle up."

I got a lot of blank looks. Which was probably only reasonable. Most of those spirits predated football.

"Okay," I said. "Everyone get to where you can see and hear me clearly. Gather in."

The ghosts understood that. They huddled — in three dimensions. Some crowded around me in a circle on the ground. The rest took to the air and arranged themselves overhead.

"Christ," I muttered. "It's like Thunderdome." I held out my hand, palm up, and closed my eyes for a moment. I called up my most recent memories of Molly, both of her physical appearance and of her evident state of mind. Then I focused on projecting those memories, following my newly developing instincts with the whole ghost routine. When

I opened my eyes, a small, three-dimensional image of Molly hovered above the surface of my palm, rotating slowly.

"This young woman is somewhere in Chicago," I said. "Maybe nearby. We need her help to get to Mort. So, um. Soldier boys, stay here with me. The rest of you guys, go locate her. Appear to her. Tell her that Harry Dresden sent you, and lead her back here. Do not reveal yourselves to anyone else. Harm no one." I looked around at them. "Okay?"

Before I'd finished the last word, half of the crowd — the crazy half — was gone.

I just hoped that they would listen to me, that my beckoning spell and the mantle of authority Sir Stuart had passed to me would help ensure their cooperation. I felt fairly confident in my instinct that nutty killer ghosts were not terribly good at following orders.

"This could turn out bad in so many ways," I muttered.

But it mostly didn't.

Maybe ten minutes after I'd dispatched them, the Lecter Specters reappeared among the ranks of the quiet guardians with no sound, no flash, no fanfare. One second, nothing; the next, there they all were. All but two.

A moment later, the twins came walking

toward us. Molly limped along between the two little spirits, holding hands with each of them. She was moving with her back perfectly rigid, her steps cautious, and she looked a little green around the gills. Like I said, she's a sensitive. She must have figured out the true nature of the child ghosts immediately upon meeting them, and she clearly did not relish the idea of being in skin contact with them. It said a lot about her intestinal fortitude that she had accompanied them at all.

It probably said even more about her trust in me.

It was no coincidence that the ghosts had found her so quickly, either. She'd already been on the way; Molly was dressed for battle.

There were still bloodstains on the front of her long coat, where she'd taken a bullet through the muscle of her thigh. It was based on the design of a fireman's coat and, like Daniel's vest, Molly's coat contained an armored lining of titanium rings sandwiched between layers of ballistic fabric. She still wore her ragged clothing beneath the coat, but she'd added a nylon-web tactical belt to her ensemble. It bore several potions, which she'd always been good at making, and a pair of wands covered in rows of runes and sigils like those on my own staff. One was tipped in a crystal of white quartz, the other with an amethyst.

Once the twins had led her to me, they

vanished, reappearing in their previous spaces in the ranks. Molly blinked and looked around for a moment. She took her cane from under one arm and leaned on it, taking some of the weight off her wounded leg. Then she took out the little tuning fork, rapped it once against the cane, and held it up in front of one of her eyes, so that she was looking through the tines.

"Holy Mary, Mother of God," she breathed, her eyes widening as she took in the spook squad. "Harry, is that you in there?"

"Two ghosts enter; one ghost leaves," I replied. Then I vanished from the Spooky-dome and reappeared in front of her. "Hi."

Molly shook her head a little. She looked tired still, but some of the strain I'd seen in her the night before seemed to have drained out of her. "Who are they?"

"Morty's friends," I said. I gestured at her. "You wore your party dress, I see."

She smiled for a second, enough to show her dimples. Then it was gone. "Butters got in touch with me. He told me what was going on."

I nodded. "Murphy?"

Molly looked away. "She's on the way with whoever she can get."

"Marcone's guys?"

She shook her head. "Marcone is in Italy or something. Childs is in charge."

"Let me guess. He's just supposed to mind

the store until the boss gets back, and he didn't get chosen for his daring and ambition."

Molly nodded. "Pretty much."

I grimaced. "How's your brother?"

"More stitches. More scars," Molly said, looking away — but not in time to hide the flash of pure, murderous rage I saw in her eyes. "He'll live."

"The padre?"

"Stable. Unconscious. He was beaten badly."

"What about Fitz and his gang?" I asked.

"With my father for now," she said. "Mom makes battalion-sized meals already. Eight or ten more mouths isn't bad. Just until there's enough time to figure out what to do with them."

I snorted quietly. "And Murph would just call in the kids' location and tell the cops to round them up for that hit if they'd gone anywhere else. She wouldn't do that to Michael."

"I thought the same thing."

"Your idea?"

Molly shrugged.

"Very good, grasshopper," I said, smiling.

She smiled, but only with the corners of her eyes. "Thanks."

I shook my head. Crap. It was easy to get distracted when talking about memories. The ghost thing must have been slowly congealing my brain. "Okay, chitchat's over. Here's the short version."

I told her about the Big Hood hideout, the wards, and what the Corpsetaker was up to. As I spoke, Molly took a moment to open her Sight and take a quick glance at the wards. She shuddered and closed it again. "Are you sure we can't just hammer through them?"

"If we studied the layout for a day or two, maybe," I said. "We don't have that kind of time."

"What's the plan, then?"

"Me and my army go in through the back door in the Nevernever," I said. "Once I'm in, I'll wreck those formulae and take down the wards. Team Murphy comes storming in like they do on TV. I need you to open the Way."

Molly bit her lip and then nodded. "I can do that. Are you sure that when I do, the other side will be close enough?"

The Nevernever isn't subject to normal geography. It attaches to the physical world by means of symbols and ideas. Open a Way in a happy place, and odds are you'll get a happy place in the Nevernever. Open a Way in a bad place, and the spirit world near it will be the same flavor of bad. Sometimes Ways that opened only ten or twenty feet apart from each other go to radically different portions of the Nevernever. Molly was concerned that if a Way was opened anywhere but in the basement of the stronghold, it might lead to the spiritual version of Timbuktu, rather than where I wanted to go.

"There's seriously bad juju infesting this whole area," I said. "We'll get as close as we can to the entrance. It should get me somewhere in the same neighborhood — and I'm pretty light on my feet these days."

"Ha-ha," Molly said, and thumped her cane gently on the ground. "I'm not. What if I can't keep up?"

I pressed my lips together and tried to keep from wincing.

Her mouth tightened. "You don't want me to go with you."

"It isn't about what I want," I said. "They'll need you on this side. If Murphy tries to go in before the wards are down, people are going to die. Horribly. You're the only one who can tell when the wards fall. So you stay."

Molly looked away again. She swallowed. Then she nodded. "Okay."

I looked at her for a moment. She was clearly hurting in all kinds of ways. She was just as clearly in control of herself. She didn't like the role I'd asked her to play, but she had accepted its necessity.

"You're one hell of a woman, Molly," I said. "Thank you."

She flinched as if she'd just been shot. Her eyes widened as she jerked her head back to me, and her face went entirely bloodless. She stared at me for a moment. Her mouth started working soundlessly. Her eyes overflowed with tears. It took her several seconds to let out a little choking sound.

Then she shuddered and turned away from me. She lifted her arm and wiped her eyes on her coat sleeve. "I'm sorry," she said. "I'm sorry."

"It's okay," I said, trying to keep my voice gentle. "I know . . . I know things haven't been easy for you lately. Bound to bring on the waterworks once in a while."

"God," she said, both bitterness and amusement in her voice. "Harry. How can you be so completely clueless and still be you?" She took a deep breath, then straightened her back and squared her shoulders. "Okay. We're burning time."

"Yeah," I said.

She walked toward the door to the Big Hoods' hideout. She planted her feet firmly, withdrew the amethyst-tipped wand from her belt, and held it firmly in her right hand. I saw her gather her focus and do it rapidly. She was very nearly operating on the level of a full member of the White Council. After less than five seconds, she looked up, lifted the wand, drew it in a long, vertical line through the air and murmured, *"Rokotsu."*

For a second, nothing happened. Then the air seemed to split and fall open, as if reality had been nothing more than a curtain suddenly stirred by an outside breeze. The opening widened until it was the size of the front door of a home, and odd, aqua green light poured out from the other side.

Molly rolled her neck a little, as if the effort had pained her. It probably had. Opening a Way takes a serious energy investment, and Molly had never been a high-horsepower practitioner. She stepped back and said, "All yours, boss."

"Thanks, grasshopper," I said quietly. Then I turned to the spook squad and said, "All right, everybody. Let's go knock some heads together."

I turned and plunged through the Way into the Nevernever, and the deadliest spirit-predators of the concrete jungle came with me.

CHAPTER FORTY-TWO

Before I died, I went to a lot of movies.

Movie theaters were totally useless for me, especially as more and more of them went with increasingly advanced technology for their sound and projection systems. The way I tended to foul up technology, especially electronics, just by standing around meant that it was tough to see a movie all the way through without something going horribly wrong with the sound, the picture, or both. Magic draws a lot of its power from emotion, and at the movies that meant that things would tend to go bad at the parts of the movie that were the most gripping and interesting.

So I could see a movie that sucked at a theater. Usually. But if I wanted to see a *good* movie, there was only one solution: a drive-in.

There are still a few of them up and running. I went down to the one in Aurora. There, I could be far enough from the projector not to interfere with it. The sound system of the movie consisted of hundreds of little car speakers and car radios, mostly turned up loud. Yeah, the place was full of kids who were basically at the drive-in in order to make out, wander around in giggling groups, sneak friends in for free in their trunks, and drink smuggled alcohol. That never bothered me. I could park up front, sit on the hood of my car with my back leaning against the windshield, my hands behind my head, and enjoy the whole movie all the way through.

(I usually took Bob along. He sat on the dashboard. I always thought I'd been doing him a favor, although when I thought back, it made me think he'd been doing it for the sake of shared experience. For company.)

Anyway, the point is, I've seen a lot of movies. So I know whereof I speak when I say that I went through the Way my apprentice opened and landed in the first act of a movie.

Cold water engulfed the lower half of my body, and a second later a wave slapped me in the middle of the back, nearly throwing me off my feet. After the past days of muted physical stimuli, I staggered and gasped against the sudden shock of pure sensation. Salt spray filled my mouth.

I should have expected that. This was the spirit world, where the immaterial wasn't. Gravity, heat, cold, light — they were all just as real as I was now. I was a civilian again.

There wouldn't be any fun ghost tricks like vanishing out of the cold water.

I spat, regained my balance, and got my bearings. I was maybe ten yards away from a pebble beach. The light was grey and somehow oppressive. The beach rose a couple of feet from the water across maybe two or three hundred yards, then ran right up onto the feet of a granite cliff.

There were . . . things, littering the beach. Imagine a jack from the children's game. Now imagine it had babies with a porcupine the size of a dump truck. That was what lurked there: some kind of massive, lethargic-looking beasts, their bodies mostly dug into the ground. Each projected several enormous, bladelike spines seven or eight feet long in several directions from its hump of a body — along with hundreds of other spines about a quarter that size. They were scattered in a vaguely ordered pattern all across the beach between us and the cliffs, their sides heaving gently as they breathed.

My eyes tracked on the cliffs, to squat, ugly, blocky-looking structures at their summit. There were narrow slits carved in their fronts. In a couple of spots along the cliff face, the stone had collapsed into a very steep gradient. A particularly agile monkey might be able to make his way up to the top. All of those spots were covered in razor wire and surrounded by fortified positions that would make an ascension a particularly nerve-racking form of suicide.

A cool wind that smelled of rotten meat fluttered across the pebbles and sand, and it carried a bloodred banner mounted above the structures out to the side, displaying a black swastika within a white circle. I stared at it blankly for half a second while another wave hit me in the back and threatened my balance. Then it struck me where I'd seen this before: the first act of *Saving Private Ryan.*

"Oh, crap," I breathed.

This was the Nevernever, the spirit world, and beings of powerful mind and will could reshape the world to their liking. Evil Bob had been the part of Bob the Skull, which had been in the service of this jerk named Kemmler, who had apparently been killed for good sometime during World War II. Evil Bob had been working with a theme when he designed defenses to his patron's base of operations.

There were flashes of light from the firing slits in the bunkers at the top of the cliffs. Bullets that shone faintly scarlet hammered into the beach at the water's edge and then tracked toward us. The *hiss-splat* of impact got to us a second before the chattering *thump* of the guns.

"Get behind me!" I shouted to the spook squad. I heard them splashing through the water in immediate obedience.

Right. As long as I was a spirit in the spirit world, I might as well take advantage of it. Since I didn't really have my old duster, even though I'd been wearing it ever since Carmichael pulled me up off the tracks, I didn't see any reason why I shouldn't have my shield bracelet, either. I focused on my left wrist without actually looking at it, exerted my will, and then shook my arm in the old, familiar gesture that would make sure the bracelet was clear of the sleeve of my duster. When I did, I felt its slight, familiar weight as it dropped down — a chain, its links made of several braided metals and festooned with dangling charms in the shape of medieval shields.

"Hah!" I muttered, and began to run my will into it to bring up a shield.

A heavy weight hit me and sent me to one side. I hit the cold water and went under.

Glowing red energy masquerading as bullets smashed through the water where I'd just been standing. I came up out of the water, sputtering, and saw one of the projectiles slam into a protector ghost who had been behind me. The round impacted as if upon a living body, apart from one detail: There was no blood. Instead, it tore away a section of the spirit's arm and sent a spray of clear ectoplasm splattering out of him. He barely reacted, pausing to glance at his arm as if puzzled.

The next round tore away the largest part of his head, and the spirit simply dissolved into more transparent ectoplasmic jelly that was swallowed by the sea.

Sir Stuart's shade helped me get back on my feet as a second stream of projectiles strafed through the spook squad, sending ghosts diving and scrambling for cover that was not there. Several more were hit, gaining savage, bloodless wounds. We lost another spirit, one of the Lecters.

"Behind me!" I shouted again, and channeled my will through the shield bracelet, spreading it out into a quarter dome of faint blue energy that came to life ahead of me. It attracted fire at once — and shed it, sending spalling projectiles hissing through the air as they rebounded.

I started forward, toward the beach, with Sir Stuart's shade behind me and slightly to one side the whole way, steadying me as the surf kept trying to knock me down. The spook squad began to close in on me, taking shelter behind the shield, and we pressed forward to the beach as fast as I could walk while still holding the shield.

It turned into hard work within a few seconds. Even in magic, there are some laws you don't get away from — like the conservation of energy. Those pseudobullets were hitting my shield with a certain amount of force.

I had to expend a similar amount of energy to stop them. I was cheating by making my shield as rounded as possible, deflecting rather than directly opposing, but even so, it was taking one hell of a lot of my effort and will to keep the fire off us.

My shield wasn't a solution, really. I was working too hard to manage a simultaneous counterstrike. Sometime soon, within the hour, I wouldn't be able to keep holding it, and when it went, we were all going to be dead. Deader. I had to figure out a way to silence those guns.

"Sir Stuart!" I shouted. "Do any of the gang carry grenades?"

Sir Stuart's hand and arm came into view from behind me. He was holding, I kid you not, a little black iron bomb about the size of a baseball. There was a hole in it that had been plugged with a cork, and a fuse stuck out of it. The thing was straight out of a cartoon, except for its size.

I looked back over my shoulder, and saw that several of the doughboys had produced more modern-looking pineapple grenades of their own. A couple of shades dressed in uniforms of the Vietnam era had them, too.

"Neat," I said. "Okay, here's the plan. We head for the base of that bunker right there, and your boys blow it up. Then we get the one next to it. Then we blow the nests on that slope between the two bunkers and get

581

the hell off this beach."

Sir Stuart eyed the ground ahead of me while fire rattled against my shield. He studied it intently for a moment, then nodded. He looked over his shoulder at the rest of the squad, his face devoid of expression. All of them simultaneously nodded back at him.

"That was not even a little creepy," I muttered. "Okay, stay behind the shield!" And I started pushing forward again, striding across the pebble beach toward the cliff.

That was when the shells came in.

There was a high-pitched whistle from overhead and then a flash of motion. I had an instant's impression of a skull plummeting at a steep angle and blazing with the same angry scarlet energy as the incoming rounds. It hammered into the beach about thirty yards ahead of us. It didn't make any noise when it exploded. Instead, there was a sudden and absolute silence, as if the skull was drawing in absolutely every motion around it, including that of sound moving through the air — and then there was a flash of light, and an instant later, a roar of wind and fire. My ears screamed with the pain of the shift in air pressure. Pebbles slammed into my shield, sending it to blazing blue brightness as the incoming energy began to overload what the shield could handle, the excess energy being shed as light. When the dust cleared, there was a crater in the ground, as deep as my grave and twenty feet across.

More screaming whistles came from overhead, and I felt a surge of raw panic trying to push the thoughts out of my brain. Hell's bells. If one of those skulls hit closer to us or behind us, where my shield couldn't cover, we were dead. Another near-miss might blow my shield down entirely, and then the machine guns would have us. There was only one place to go that might be safe from the screaming skulls.

"We've got to get closer," I growled. "Come on!"

And I broke into a flat-out sprint *toward* the machine guns.

Chapter Forty-Three

Things were pretty much a desperate blur between the water's edge and the cliffs. There was a lot of running and gunfire and spraying dirt and pebbles. Several more shades were destroyed by screaming skull shrapnel. My shield took one hell of a beating, and as we got closer to the machine guns, the angles of fire from either side meant that the shield could protect fewer and fewer of the shades.

There was nowhere to run, nowhere to hide, no direction to go but forward. It was either that or die, and I was as terrified as I had ever been in my life. Honestly, I'm glad my memories aren't much clearer than they are.

There was a nasty bit in the middle, when I was running between two of the crouching spike beasts. I remember realizing that the things were so heavily armored in layers and layers of bony plate that they couldn't stand up. The fire from machine guns and screaming skulls alike seemed only a minor discomfort to them. I remember a pair of reptilian eyes flicking toward me, and then dozens of the shorter spikes shot out upon greasy, living tendrils and started whipping around like a high-pressure water hose with no one holding it. One of them wrapped around my arm, and only the spell-armored sleeve of my duster kept the bladed spike from opening my flesh to the bone. Sir Stuart's ax flashed, and the tendril, separated from the main beast, collapsed into ectoplasm.

I ordered the shades to use their blades, and dozens of swords, axes, combat knives, and bayonets appeared. We hacked our way through the spike beasts, and endured increasingly intense fire. We lost several more protector shades as we did — they were hauled into the open by tendrils and torn to pieces by machine-gun fire.

The mortar skulls stopped coming down near us about twenty yards out from the cliffs, and we finally reached the base of the first tower. The shades and I all crowded in close to its base, where the gunners couldn't shoot us without getting out and leaning over the top or something. I reversed my shield, so that its quarter dome covered us in every direction that the cliff face or the ground didn't, though the fire on us had lightened considerably.

"Grenades!" I ordered, in a firm and manly tone that did not sound at all like a panicked fourteen-year-old.

Sir Stuart held a pair of his black mini-bombs out to a Capone-era gangster, who produced a lighter and flicked it to life. Sir Stuart rose, the lit fuses trailing small sparks, took a couple of steps back from the tower, and flung the grenades swiftly upward, one at a time.

It was a little ticklish, taking the shield down in time to allow the grenades to pass by, then bringing it up again, the wizardly equivalent of interrupting a sneeze, but I pulled it off. Both of the little bombs made clinking noises as they bounced off the inner lip of the firing slits, and there were snarling sounds from above us for a second or two.

Then there was a loud *whump* of an explosion, and inhuman shrieks of what could only be pain. A second later, there was another *whump,* and clear fluid spattered out of the bunker's firing slit and pattered down onto my shield.

"Cha-ching!" I crowed.

Sir Stuart's shade shot me a fierce grin.

"Get ready to move to the next one!" I called. I scrambled down the cliff face to where stone gave way to sand and shale, and the steep slope swept up from the beach to whatever was above. We'd taken out the bunker on one side of the slope. We'd have to take out the one on the other side, or be riddled with fire from several directions as we made the ascent.

I brought my shield around and angled it as best I could as I stepped out into the open. Firing points at the top of the slope opened up instantly, intently, and my shield blazed into sight again as more focused enemy power came down upon it from the positions atop the slope. I crossed the thirty-foot gap to the base of the next tower, keeping ferocious will on the shield, and the spook squad came with me.

On the way, I got a glimpse of the opposition. They wore the black-and-grey uniforms of the old Waffen-SS, but they weren't human. Their faces were stretched and distorted into the muzzle and jaws of a wolf, which looked damned peculiar without any fur covering it. Their eyes were black, empty holes — and I'm not being metaphorical when I say that. There were simply no *eyes* there. Just empty sockets. Machine-gun crews and riflemen — or maybe rifle*things* — alike poured fire into us, a panting, eager hunger to spill blood apparent on their monstrous faces.

I stopped at the other corner, holding the shield until all the spooks had made it across, then took cover myself, redirecting the shield, as I had the last time, to cover us all.

"Handsome fellows," Sir Stuart's shade noted cheerily. He looked less faded than he had only moments before. I had a feeling that

Sir Stuart, in life, had been the sort of person who was invigorated by action — and that his shade was no different.

"We'll send them a nice written compliment later," I called back, and gestured up above us, at the second bunker. "Do it again."

Stuart nodded and turned to the gangster once more. And again he made two excellent throws, pitching a pair of little bombs up the steep angle and into the bunker. Again, enemy ectoplasm sprayed, and again the tower above us went silent.

"Now the fun part," I said. "We're going up the slope. My shield won't last very long — whoever is behind this is going to put everything he has into taking it down. So we close to grips with them as fast as we can."

Sir Stuart nodded and gestured to the nearest of the mad ghosts. "Give them the order."

I pursed my lips for a second and then nodded. "Hey, you guys," I said, pointing at the twins.

Two little sets of dead, empty eyes turned toward me, along with dozens more, and I felt that same cold chill at the touch of their awareness.

"We're about to go up that slope. The very instant my shield drops, I want you to close with the enemy as fast as you can and take them down. Don't hold back. Give it to them hard. Don't stop until they're all down. Clear?"

More soul-empty stares. None of them moved. None of them responded.

"Sure," I said. "You got it. If you didn't, you'd say something, right?"

No response.

"God, it's like Gallagher performing at the Harvard Faculty Club," I muttered. "Here we go, folks. One! Two! Three!"

And I went around the corner again, shield held in front of me. It coalesced into a blazing blue-and-silver dome almost instantly, taking so much energy that the kinetic force began to transfer through, pushing against me like a gale-force wind. I staggered drunkenly, unable to see through the shield and anticipate my next steps up the steep slope. The footing was treacherous. Shale and sand and loose stone twisted and turned beneath me. Even with the occasional supporting shove from Sir Stuart, my forward momentum began to falter and I slipped to one knee, my bracelet getting hotter and hotter around my wrist.

I managed to lunge awkwardly forward a couple of times — and then something hit my shield like a runaway train, and silver-and-blue energy shattered into a coruscation of sound and light. I was abruptly able to see up the slope, where the enemy was momentarily reeling from the explosive feedback of the failed shield.

And the Lecter Specters went to work.

As I stared up the slope, the only thing I could think was that this must be what it looked like in the interior of a tornado. The mad ghosts of Chicago rushed forward with such speed and power that their forms blurred into elongated streaks that jostled to be the first to reach their victims, corkscrewing up the cutting. They ignored ridiculous constraints such as gravity and the solidity of matter, and as they rushed upon the enemy, they *changed* — and I gained fresh nightmare material.

I'm willing to share the least disturbing bits. The twins, for example, just leaned forward and seemed to *slither* sinuously through the air toward the foe. As they went, their bodies elongated, intertwined, and twisted into a single entity that looked like a demented artist's rendition of a battle between a giant squid and some kind of unnamed, deep-sea horror fish with too many spines and too many fins and great, googly-moogly eyes. They reached the nearest bad guy, bobbed up, and then slammed down with so much grace that I almost missed the fact that they'd smashed the wolfwaffen so hard into the ground that he was no thicker than my old checkbook. Tentacles shot out and ripped a rifle from the wolfwaffen next to the first, then plunged forward into its mouth and throat, in through its nostrils, in through its *ears*. A second later, they came whipping out again — along with slime-covered *chunks* of whatever they'd happened to be able to grab while they were in there. They pulled the creature's stomach out through its mouth, along with several feet of intestine — and then the tentacles whipped said loops of flesh around the wolfwaffen's neck and strangled it.

It got considerably less cheerful and humane from there.

Snarls, then screams, filled the steep little opening in the cliff wall. Ghosts, twisted into monstrous forms by decades of hollow, mindless hunger, fell upon the wolfwaffen in our way, uttering howls and squeals and clicks and screams, filling the air with a nightmare cacophony that left me slamming my palms up over my ears and biting down on a scream of pain.

The enemy fought at first, and those who did died swiftly. As more and more hideous *things* dealt with the wolfwaffen, their morale faltered and they began to run. Those that did died horribly. And, toward the end, overwhelmed by terror, a handful of the enemy could only stand, staring in horror, and screaming high and piteously.

Those last few died indescribably.

Ghosts don't get hungry, I reminded myself. *Dead men don't eat.* So there was no reason whatsoever that I should throw up. The thought was hilarious for some reason, so I started laughing. I couldn't help it. I laughed and laughed, even as I realized that I couldn't just sit there — not having turned loose an elemental force of horror like the Lecters.

"Come on!" I said, giggling. "Come on, before they get out of earshot." I staggered up and climbed the slope, Sir Stuart and the protector spirits following along behind me. It wasn't an easy climb. The Lecter Specters had left a lot of the wolfwaffen partly alive, or at least had left some of their *parts* alive, and blood and worse fluids were everywhere. The fortunate few, the fighters who had gone down fast, had become nothing but buckets of slimy ectoplasm.

Any way you looked at it, the climb was a messy, nauseating, dangerous one. But it was a whole heck of a lot less dangerous than if we'd been getting shot at the whole way.

I reached the top of the slope and looked across the long network of trenches that ran outside the bunkers, along the top of the cliff. There was intermittent gunfire. There were intermittent screams. As I watched, I saw a frantic, panicked wolfwaffen clamber out of the trench. It got about three-quarters of the way out before what looked like a slimy yellow tongue shot out of the trench, from below my line of sight, and plunged into its back — and out its chest. The impaling tongue then wrapped around the howling wolfwaffen and pulled it back into the trench with so much force that a puff of dust and dirt billowed out from wherever he impacted.

"Hell's bells," I giggled. "Hell's bells. That's hideous."

Sir Stuart nodded grimly. He made a gesture. Protector spirits began putting the nearby, hideously mangled wolfwaffen out of their misery.

I swatted myself firmly on the cheek and forced the laughter back. I felt myself trying to scream in horror once the laughter was damped down. The demonic servitors Evil Bob had put in position had probably been some very nasty customers. They had probably deserved a violent death.

But there are things you just don't do, things you just can't see, and still be both human and sane.

I forced the incipient screams away, too. It took me a minute or two to get it done. When I looked up, Sir Stuart was facing me, his eyes sad, concerned, and empathetic. He knew what I was feeling. He'd known it himself — which probably stood to reason, as the commander, more or less, of the criminal psych ward of Chicago's ghosts.

"My fault," I said. My voice sounded dull. My tongue felt like it had been coated in lead. "I told the Lecters not to stop until they were all down."

The big shade nodded gravely.

"Follow them," I said. "Make sure any of

593

the enemy who is left is given a clean death. Then round them up and come back to me."

Sir Stuart nodded. He looked at the protector spirits. Then they all moved out at the same time, going both directions up and down the cliff.

I leaned on my staff and rested. Holding that shield had taken a lot out of me. So much so that when I looked down at my hand, I could, just barely, see the shape of the stony ground right through it.

I was fading.

I shuddered and clutched the staff hard. It made sense, really. I've always believed that magic came from inside you, from who and what you were — from your mind and from your heart. Now I was all mind and heart. The shield had to be fueled by something. I hadn't really stopped to consider where that energy would come from.

Now I knew.

I looked at my hand and the ground on the other side of it again. How much more would it take to make me disappear altogether? I had no way of knowing, no way of even making a good guess. What if I needed to use my magic again when I took up the hunt for my killer, after all of this was over? What if I blew it all here? What if I wound up like Sir Stuart — just an empty shade?

I leaned my head against the solid oak of the staff. It didn't matter. Murphy and company — not to mention Mort — needed my help. They would get it, even if it meant I became nothing but an old, faded memory.

(Or maybe became one more insane shade drifting through Chicago's night, causing havoc without reason, without regret, and without mercy.)

I shook my head a little and straightened my back. From the sounds of it, there couldn't be many bad guys left for the Lecters to deal with. These were certainly the Corpsetaker's defenses — an area of bad mojo like this would have a kind of gravity for anyone crossing over from the material world through any Way near the location to which it had been linked, sort of like a funnel spiderweb. That had been the point of building it this way: to make sure anyone who wanted in from the Nevernever side wound up on that beach.

I needed to find the Way this site was guarding, the back door to the Corpsetaker's hideout, the one I'd seen Evil Bob and the Fomor servitor use. I closed my eyes and shut away the recent horrors. I willed away my worry and my fear. I didn't have to breathe, but I did anyway, because that was the only way I'd ever learned to attain a state of clarity. In. Out. Slowly.

Then I carefully quested out with my senses, looking for the energy that would surround an open Way. I found it immediately, and opened my eyes. It was coming from straight ahead of me, away from the cliff and the beach, several hundred yards back up among some rolling, wooded hills. I could see the head of a footpath that led into the woods. There had been regular traffic on it, for it to be so evident, and I doubted that many hikers or Boy Scout troops had been tromping through. That was our next step.

An instant, violent instinct screamed at me without warning. I didn't question it. I flung myself to one side, rolling in the air to bring up my shield again.

A wrecking ball of pure psychic force hit the shield, and half of the little shield charms dangling from my bracelet screamed and then shattered into tiny shards. The blow flung me a good twenty feet and I hit the ground rolling, until said ground vanished from underneath me. I dropped to the floor of one of the defensive trenches and lay there for a second, stunned at the sheer savagery of the assault.

I heard slow, heavy, confident footsteps. *Clomp. Clomp.* Then a pair of black jackboots appeared at the top of the trench. My gaze tracked up the SS officer's uniform, which included a black leather trench coat not too unlike my own. It wasn't one of the wolfwaffen. Instead of a deformed, monstrous wolf face, this being had only a bare skull sitting atop the uniform's high collar. Blue fire glowed in its eye sockets and it regarded me with cold disdain.

"A worthy effort for a novice," Evil Bob said. "I wish you to know that I regret your death as the loss of significant potential." He lifted what was probably not actually a Luger pistol and aimed it calmly at my head. "Good-bye, Dresden."

Chapter Forty-Four

Stall, I thought desperately. Sir Stuart and company wouldn't be busy for long. *Stall.*

"It isn't in your best self-interest to do that," I said.

Evil Bob's eyelights flickered. The gun didn't waver. "That hypothesis assumes that I possess self-interest."

"If you didn't," I said, "you would have pulled the trigger already."

For a second, nothing happened. Then the skull tilted slightly to one side, and I got the impression that Evil Bob had become suddenly pensive.

I rushed to continue. "There's no percentage for your boss in hesitation. And since I know you aren't doing it for my sake, your hesitation must therefore be an act of self-interest."

"An intriguing argument," said Evil Bob, "and potentially valid, given the penchant for independence evident in my progenitor."

"By which you mean the original Bob?"

"Obviously," Evil Bob sniffed. "He from whose essence I came to be. Your instincts for such matters are acute, Dresden. You have given me something to consider in the future, when my attention is not otherwise occupied by mildly effective stalling tactics."

And he pulled the trigger —

— just as Sir Stuart's thrown ax whirled into Evil Bob's outstretched shooting arm.

It hit him only with the spinning wooden handle, but it was enough to save my life. A blast of psychic energy, of sheer, deadly *will*, hit the concrete wall of the trench about five feet to my left and turned it into a cloud of powder.

I raised my right hand and snarled, *"Forzare!"* and responded with a hammerblow of force of my own.

Evil Bob lifted the other black-leather-clad hand and brushed my strike aside, but it rocked him back a step.

Sir Stuart charged into sight, hitting Evil Bob hard at the hips, and tackled him forward and down into the trench. The pair of them hit hard, but the dark spirit was on the bottom, and Evil Bob's skull cracked as it hit the concrete. His high-crowned SS hat went flying.

I let out a short scream of rage and swung my staff at the skull. Evil Bob caught my descending staff in one hand and locked it in place as if his fingers had been a hydraulic vise. He got his other hand under Sir Stuart's chest and simply thrust his arm forward. Sir Stuart went flying out of the trench, and I heard him hit the ground again about a second and a half later.

"Ah," Evil Bob said. Cold blue eyelights regarded my staff. "A simple tool, but serviceable. In McCoy's style." The eyes flared brighter. "And the key to your rather effective little army, as well. Excellent."

I wrenched at the staff but couldn't get it away from the dark spirit. I felt sort of goofy about it, in addition to being extremely alarmed about how *strong* the thing was. I wrenched at the staff with all the power of my hips, legs, back, and shoulders, with the leverage of my wide-spaced grip, and only barely managed to make Evil Bob wobble. He just stood up, holding the end of the staff in his hand, and only after examining it again did he apparently notice me.

"I will make this offer exactly once, Dresden," Evil Bob said quite calmly. He put his other hand on the staff, mirroring me, and I suddenly realized that if he wanted to, he could fling me considerably farther than he had Sir Stuart — assuming he didn't just ram the staff straight back into my chest and out of my back.

I was suddenly unsure whether the spook squad could take Evil Bob even if they were all right there, Lecters, guardians, and all.

"What offer?" I asked him.

"A relationship," he replied. "With me."

Yeah. He actually said it like that.

"Um," I said, narrowing my eyes. "Maybe you could clarify what you mean by a *relationship*. Because I've got to tell you, Bob, I've, uh . . . I've been hurt."

The joke missed him completely. I was apparently snarking on the wrong frequency. "In the nature of an apprenticeship," he said. "You have sound fundamental skills. You are practical. Your ambition is tempered by an understanding of your limits. You have the potential to be an excellent partner."

"And I'm not flipping insane like the Corpsetaker," I said.

"Hardly. But your insanities are more manageable," Evil Bob said, "and you have few self-delusions." He sniffed. "The Master never favored that creature, in any case. But he would have been interested in you."

"Even if Kemmler was still around, I'm pretty sure a relationship with him wouldn't be in the cards, either," I said in an apologetic tone. "I've got a strict rule about dating older men."

The spirit looked at me blankly for a moment. Then, as the real Bob sometimes did, he gave me the impression of an expression that simple, immobile bone could not possibly have expressed. His eyes slowly widened.

"You . . ." he said slowly, "are mocking me."

I whistled through my teeth. "Guess the real Bob made you from the slow bits, huh?"

The blue lights flared brighter, and I felt heat on my face even from six feet away. "*I am* the real one," he said in a hard, distant tone. "The true creation of the Master. Finally shed of my weakness. My doubt. Freed to use my power."

"Guess he threw in a little of his narcissism, too," I drawled — but I met his gaze with my own and felt an odd little smile turn up the sides of my mouth.

The skull's jaws slowly parted like a snake preparing to strike. "You who are barely more than an apprentice — you will die for mocking me."

"Yeah. But I will never, *ever* throw in with you," I snarled back. "I will *never* be like you or your precious Master or that nutball Corpsetaker. So take your offer of a relationship and shove it up your schutzstaffel."

Evil Bob's eyelights blazed and he wrenched at the staff.

He really was a lackey. A real mastermind wannabe would have boned up on the Evil Overlord list. He'd felt so confident in his power (okay, maybe not without reason) that he'd spent a moment talking to me instead of just moving on. Worse, he'd given me a chance to start lipping off to him, and that comes so naturally to me that I don't really need to consciously consider it anymore, except on special occasions.

So, what with my brain being unoccupied and all, I'd had the opportunity to realize a fundamental truth about the Nevernever. Here the spiritual becomes the material. Here spiritual power is physical power. Strength of mind and will are as real as muscle and sinew.

And I was damned if some blurry photocopy of the thoughts and will of some dusty-ass, dead necromancer was going to take me out.

If he hadn't made with the stupid recruiting speech, if I hadn't had my choices laid out in such stark relief in front of me, if I hadn't been reminded of who I was and of those things for which I'd lived my life . . . maybe Evil Bob would have killed me then and there.

But he *had* reminded me. I *did* remember. I spent my lifetime fighting the darkness without becoming the darkness. Maybe I had faltered at the very end. Maybe I had finally come up against something that made me cross the line — but even then, I hadn't turned into a degenerate freakazoid of the Kemmler variety. One mistake at the end of my life couldn't erase all the times I had stood unmoved at the edge of the abyss and made snide remarks at its expense.

They could kill me, but they couldn't *have* me.

I was my own.

And when Evil Bob shoved the staff at my chest, I drew upon the surge of fierce joy that truth had inspired, upon the will that had been dinged and dented but never broken, and fell back with the motion, digging the tip of the staff into the concrete as if it had been soft mud, and used the momentum to *fling* Evil Bob over me.

His unbreakable grip didn't falter — and he arced overhead and then back down while I wrenched at the staff, helping his forward momentum instead of fighting it.

He hit the floor of the trench like a big fascist meteor. The noise was incredible. The impact shattered the concrete for twenty feet in every direction. Chips and shards went flying. Dust flew up in a miniature mushroom cloud. I was flung back by the shock wave of impact — with my staff still gripped firmly in my hands.

"Booya!" I drunkenly howled from the ground. I choked a little on the dust as I staggered back to my feet, my heart pounding, my whole body alive with strain and adrenaline. I stabbed a pointing finger toward the impact crater. "That's right! *Who* just rocked your *face?* Harry fucking Dresden! *That's* who!"

I coughed a little more and leaned against the side of the trench, panting until the world stopped feeling all spinny, grinning a wolf's grin as I did.

And then gravel made a soft rustling sound from inside the dust cloud. A form appeared, just an outline, limping slowly. It came a few feet closer, and I recognized Evil Bob by the rising glow of his eyelights. The skull became visible a second later, and though I could see that the entire surface was lined with a fine network of cracks and chips, it was not broken.

The blue eyelights began to glow brighter and brighter. The dark spirit clenched his fists and his arms slowly rose, as if he was pulling something from the very earth beneath his feet. The ground started shaking. There was an ugly, low humming sound, like some kind of demon locomotive screaming by in a tunnel beneath my feet.

"My turn," the dark spirit hissed.

"Hell's bells," I muttered. "Harry, you idiot, when will you learn not to victory gloat?"

The spirit's skull mouth dropped open wider and wider and —

— a sudden stream of candle-flame-colored energy coalesced into Bob the Skull's human form, right behind Evil Bob.

My Bob lunged forward and snaked his arms beneath the dark spirit's. Bob's fingers locked behind the fractured skull of my enemy, gathering the dark spirit into a full nelson. He wrenched Evil Bob violently to one side and the dark spirit screamed, a sudden torrent of energy ripping through the wall of the trench and about fifty yards of earth as he pivoted, vaporizing spirit matter into an enormous pie-slice-shaped acre of ectoplasm.

Then Evil Bob spun, letting out a shriek of fury, and slammed his attacker back into the opposite wall.

"Harry!" Bob shouted, his face pale and his eyes wide. There were chips of broken concrete in his hair. "Take the spooks and go help Butters!"

"No!" I shouted back. "Let's take him!"

Evil Bob took two bounding steps, the second one on the trench wall about five feet up from the ground, and whirled, falling back to the ground with my Bob on the bottom. More concrete shattered, and Bob the Skull did something I'd never heard him do before: He screamed in pain.

"You can't!" he shrieked, panicked. "I can't! Not with everything here!"

The dark spirit twisted like a snake and broke Bob's grip. Evil Bob nearly got out of it entirely, but my old lab assistant managed to get a lock on one arm, and the pair of them whirled and twisted on the ground, almost too quickly to be seen, pitting dozens of escapes and counterlocks against each other in only a few seconds.

"Go!" Bob shrieked, gut-wrenching, bone-deep terror in his voice. "Go, go, go! Once you're gone I'll shut the Way behind you and bail! Hurry!"

A shadow appeared at the top of the trench, and a weary, battered-looking Sir Stuart held out his hand to me.

"Dammit," I snarled. "Don't make me regret this, Bob!"

"Go!" Bob howled.

I took Sir Stuart's hand, and the big man pulled me out of the trench with a grunt of effort. Up on top, I found the spooks waiting for me in their typical silence.

"Right," I said. "Let's go, double time."

I gripped my staff tight, put my head down, and sprinted for the Way into the Corpse-taker's stronghold.

CHAPTER FORTY-FIVE

The Way hung in the air in the middle of the trail, maybe fifty yards back into the forest, an oblong mirror of silver light. Its bottom edge was maybe six feet off the ground, and a wooden staircase had been built to allow access to it. Behind us, back over toward the beach, I could hear low drumbeats of impact, the crackling scream of shattering concrete. The two Bobs were going at it hammer and tongs, and I desperately hoped that my old friend was all right.

There was another worry, too. If Bob couldn't stop Evil Bob from coming through the Way after us, we'd be caught with the Corpsetaker in front of us and Evil Bob behind. I didn't imagine things would go very well for us if that happened.

A flutter in the energies around the Way danced across my senses, and I paused to focus more intently on the Way itself, going so far as to call up my Sight for a quick peek. A glance told me everything I needed to know: The Way was unstable. Rather than be-ing the steady, solid, steel-and-concrete bridge between here and the mortal world that I had seen before, it was instead a bridge made of frayed and straining ropes that looked like it might fall apart the instant it was used.

"Bob, you tricky little bastard," I murmured admiringly. My former lab assistant had been lying his socks off earlier. Bob wasn't plan-ning on closing the Way behind us — because he had already rigged it to collapse as soon as we went through. His verbal explanation to me had been meant for Evil Bob's ear holes. If Evil Bob thought we were dependent on Bob to shut the door behind us, then he would have no reason to hurry after us. And if Bob had told me the real deal out loud, Evil Bob could have simply rushed to the Way ahead of us and collapsed it himself, leaving us totally shut out.

Bob was really playing with fire. If he'd taken time to sabotage the Way before he came to back me up, it meant that he had left me to face the wolfwaffen and their boss and gambled that I'd be able to hold my own until he circled back to me. On this side of things, his ploy to keep Evil Bob's attention meant that Evil Bob was free to focus entirely on tearing him apart, confident that he could always come charging at our backs as soon as he finished off my Bob.

More concrete shattered, somewhere back toward the beach. Bits of small debris, most of it no larger than my fist, came raining down among the trees a moment later.

"Okay, kids. Gather round and listen up." I shook my head and addressed the huddled shades. "When we go through," I said, "we'll be right in the middle of them. Sir Stuart, I want you and your men to rush any lemurs or wraiths that are near us. Don't hesitate; just hit them and get them out of my way." I eyed the Lecter Specters. "The rest of you follow me. We're going to destroy the physical representations for the wards."

The little girl ghost looked up at me and scowled, as if I'd just told her she had to eat a hated vegetable.

"How can you have any pudding if you don't eat your meat?" I told her seriously. "We're going to destroy the wards. Once that is done, you guys can join the rest of the shades in taking down the Corpsetaker and her crew. Okay? Everyone got it?"

Silent stares.

"Okay, good. I guess." I turned to the Way and took a deep breath. "This worked out reasonably well last time, right? Right. So here we go." I hesitated. Then I said, "Hang on one second. There's one more thing I want everyone to do. . . ."

I went through the Way and felt it falling

apart under the pressure of our collective spiritual weight. It was an odd sensation, falling against the back of my neck like ice-cold cobwebs. I didn't let my fear push me into hurrying. I kept my steps steady until I walked onto the floor of the underground chamber where I'd seen Morty and the Corpsetaker the night before.

I had time for a quick-flash impression. The pit had been filled with wraiths once more, swirling around in a humanoid stew. Mort hung above the pit again, in considerably worse repair than the last time I'd seen him. His shirt was gone. His torso and arms were covered in welts and bruises. He had spots of raw skin that had been burned, maybe with electricity, if the jumper cables and car battery sitting on the ground nearby were any indication. Several of them were on his bald scalp. Someone among the Big Hood lunatics was familiar with the concept of electroshock therapy? That one sure was a stretch.

The Corpsetaker stood in the air above the pit, hissing words into Morty's ear. Mort's head was moving back and forth in a feeble negative. He was weeping, his body twitching and jerking in obvious agony. His lips were puffy and swollen, probably the result of getting hit in the mouth repeatedly. I don't think he could focus his eyes — but he kept doggedly shaking his head.

Again, the hooded lemurs were gathered

around, but instead of playing cards, this time they all stood in an outward-facing circle around the pit, as if guarding against an attack.

Pity for them that the back door from the Nevernever was *inside* the circle. When the spook squad and I came through, they all had their backs to us.

Now, I'm not arrogant enough to think that I was the first guy to lead a company of ghosts into an assault. Granted, I don't think it happens every day or anything, but it's a big world and it's been spinning for a long time. I'm sure someone did it long before I was born, maybe pitting the ancestral spirits of one tribe against those of another.

I'm not the first person to assault an enemy fortress from the Nevernever side, either. It happened several times to either side in the war with the Red Court. It's a fairly standard tactical maneuver. It requires a certain amount of intestinal fortitude to pull off, as Evil Bob had demonstrated with his Normandy defenses.

But I am dead certain — *ba-dump-bump-ching* — that I'm the first guy to lead an army of spirits in an assault from the spirit-world side . . . and had them start off by screaming, *"BOO!"*

The spooks all stood in the same space I did, which felt weird as hell — but I hadn't wanted to take a chance with the rickety Way collapsing and leaving some of the squad behind. When I shouted, they all did, too — and I got a whole hell of a lot more than I bargained for.

The sound that came out of all those spirit throats, including mine, seemed to feed upon itself, wavelengths building and building like seas before a rising storm. Our voices weren't additive, bunched so closely like that, but multiplicative. When we shouted, the sound went out in a wave that was almost tangible. It hit the backs of the gathered lemurs and bumped them forward half a step. It slammed into the walls of the underground chamber and brought dust and mold cascading down.

And Mort's eyes snapped open in sudden, startled shock.

"Get 'em!" I howled.

The dead protectors of Chicago's resident ectomancer let out a bloodcurdling chorus of battle cries and blurred toward the foe.

You hear a lot of stories of honor and chivalry from soldiers. Most people assume that such tales apply primarily to men who lived centuries ago. But let me tell you something: People are people, no matter which century they live in. Soldiers tend to be very practical and they don't want to die. I think you'd find military men in any century you cared to name who would be perfectly okay with the notion of shooting the enemy in the back if it meant they were more likely to go home in one piece. Sir Stuart's guardians were, for the most part, soldiers.

Spectral guns blazed. Immaterial knives, hatchets, and arrows flew. Ectoplasm splashed in buckets.

Half the lemurs got torn to shreds of flickering newsreel imagery before I was finished shouting the command to attack, much less before they could recover from the stunning force of our combined voices.

The Corpsetaker shrieked something in a voice that scraped across my head like the tines of a rusty rake, and I twisted aside on instinct. One of the Lecters took the hit, and a gaping hole the size of a bowling ball appeared in the center of his chest.

"With me!" I shouted. I vanished and reappeared at the bottom of the staircase that led down to the chamber. A streamer of urine yellow lightning erupted from the Corpsetaker's outstretched hand, but I'd had my shield bracelet at the ready, and I deflected the strike into a small knot of stunned enemy lemurs. When it hit them, there was a hideous, explosive cascade of fire and havoc, and they were torn to shreds as if they'd been made of cheesecloth.

Holy crap.

Either one of those spells would have done the same to me if I'd been a quarter second slower. Dead or alive, Kemmler's disciples did *not* play for funsies.

The Lecter Specters appeared in a cloud around me, even as I sent a slug of pure force out of the end of my staff, forcing the Corpsetaker to employ her own magical counter, her wrists crossed in front of her body. The energy of my strike splashed off an unseen surface a few inches in front of her hands, and gobbets of pale green light splattered out from the impact.

"Dresden!" screamed Mort. He stared at me — or, more accurately, at the Lecters all around me — with an expression of something very like terror. "What have you done? What have you *done?*"

"Come on!" I shouted, and vanished from the bottom of the stairs to the top, just as the Corpsetaker appeared halfway up the stairway and sent another torrent of ruinous energy down toward the position the Lecters and I had just vacated.

At the top of the stairs, the tunnel was like I remembered it — decorated in miniature shrines with very real sigils of power concealed within splatters of gibberish. Candles glowed at each position — ward flames that accompanied the activation of the mystic defenses.

"The shrines!" I shouted to the Lecters. "Manifest and destroy them!"

I brought my shield up again, an instant before Corpsetaker sent a slew of dark, gelatinous energy up the stairs. I caught the spell in time, but it instantly began wrenching at my shield as if it had been some kind of living being, chewing away at it, devouring the energy I was using to hold the shield firm.

Crap. I was not going to fare well in a magical duel with someone who had clearly been doing this kind of thing for a long, long time — not when I had the Lecters to protect. The Corpsetaker would tear them apart if she could to stop us from bringing the wards down. She — I always thought of her as a she, for some reason, even though she could grab any kind of body she wanted, male, female, or otherwise — was far more experienced than I was, with what was probably a much broader range of nasty memories upon which to draw.

On top of that, I was already winded, so to speak. The fight with Evil Bob had been a job of work. If I stood there trading punches, she had an excellent chance of wearing me down enough to kill me. If all I did was keep shielding the Lecters, she'd be free to throw her hardest punches, and I felt certain that anyone from Kemmler's crew could hit like a truck.

Time to get creative.

I dropped the shield and simultaneously thrust my staff at the black jelly stuff, snarling, *"Forzare!"* Pure force tore the dark energy to shreds and continued on down the stairs to strike the Corpsetaker. My aim was bad.

The strike only spun her in place and sent her sprawling back into open air.

I took a quick look back at the Lecters and immediately wished I hadn't. The flames of the candles in the hall had burned down to pinpoints of cold blue light. Once again, the ghosts had assumed forms from nightmares — and they were going totally ballistic on the Big Hoods' hideout. Something that looked like a blending of a gorilla and a Venus flytrap smashed apart a wooden crate supporting one shrine. A giant caterpillar, its segmented body made of severed human heads, their faces screaming, their tongues functioning as legs, rippled up a wall and began tearing out chunks of concrete where a ledge had been worn, destroying another shrine.

Right. It was working. I just had to keep the Corpsetaker busy until the wild rumpus got finished tearing apart the defenses.

I called up my Sight and vanished to a point twenty feet below the Corpsetaker's position, reappearing inside solid stone. My eyes couldn't see a thing, but my Sight wasn't impaired. I could see dark, violent energy swirling around where I'd last seen the Corpsetaker; nasty stuff. I felt my lips stretch into a snarl as I hefted my staff again and growled, *"Fuego!"*

Ghost fire roared up through solid matter. In an instant, the dark energy had gathered to oppose my spell, but I sensed more than heard a cry of surprise and pain. The psycho hadn't expected that one.

Then the dark energy vanished.

I scanned around me wildly and found it reappearing behind and above me. I vanished again, flicking out another strike at the Corpsetaker's location — only to find that the Corpsetaker had blinked to a new one.

The next sixty seconds or so was a nauseating blur of motion and countermotion. We exchanged spells in solid stone, parried each other hovering in open air above the wraith pit, and leapfrogged each other's positions throughout the sleeping quarters of the Big Hoods. It was all but impossible to aim, since it required us to correctly guess the next position of the opponent and then hit it with a spell, but I clipped her once more, and she landed a strike of pure kinetic force that slammed into my hip and missed my ghostly genitals by about an inch.

Twice she darted into the hallway to attack the Lecters, but I stayed on her, forcing her to keep moving, keep defending, allowing her only time enough to throw quick jabs of power back at me.

I wasn't her match in a straight-up fight, but this was more like some kind of hallucinatory variant of Whac-a-Mole. Maybe I couldn't take her out, but I could damned well keep her from stopping the Lecters. If she turned her attention from me, I was wizard enough to take her out, and she knew it. If she went all-out on me, I could stand up to her long enough to let the Lecters finish their project — and she knew that, too.

I could feel her rage building, lending her next near-miss a hammering edge that jolted my teeth right through my shield — and I laughed at her in reply, making no effort whatsoever to hide my scorn.

I shrugged off another jab, letting it roll off my shield. And then Corpsetaker vanished and reappeared at the far end of the hallway, at the door to the old electrical-junction room. The very last of the ward flames burned there, at one final, unspoiled shrine. The Corpsetaker faced the Lecters, who were already moving toward her, lifted her hand, and spoke a single word filled with ringing power: "Stop."

And the Lecters did. Completely. I mean, like, statue-still.

"Screw that!" I called out and raised my staff, drawing upon my own will. "Go!"

There was a sudden strain in the air between the Corpsetaker and me, and I felt it as a physical pressure against my right hand, in which I brandished my staff. Corpsetaker's upraised palm wavered slightly as our wills contended down the length of the hallway. I pushed hard, grinding my teeth and simply *willing* the Lecters to finish the job. I leaned forward a little and shoved out my staff, envisioning the Lecters tearing down the last of the little shrines.

My will lashed down the hallway and blew the hood back from the Corpsetaker's face. Maybe she was wearing the form of one of her victims. Maybe I was getting a look at the real Corpsetaker. Either way, she wasn't a pretty woman. She had a face shaped like a hatchet, only less gentle and friendly. Both cheeks were marked with what looked like ritual scars in the shape of spirals. Her hair was long and white, but grew in irregular blotches on her scalp, as if portions of it had been burned and scarred. Her skin was tanned leather, covered in fine seams and wrinkles, and there was a lizardlike quality to the way it loosened around her neck.

But her eyes were gorgeous. She had eyes a shade of vibrant jade like I had never seen this side of the Sidhe, and her eyelashes were long, thick, and dark as soot. As a young woman, she must have been a lean stunner, dangerously pretty, like a James Bond villainess.

Our eyes met and I braced myself for the soulgaze — but it didn't happen. Hell's bells, I had my Sight wide-open, enough to let me see the flow of energy straining between our outstretched hands, and it still didn't happen. Guess the rules change when you're all soul and nothing else.

The Corpsetaker watched me for a moment, apparently not particularly straining to hold my will away. "Again you meddle in what is not your concern."

"Bad habit," I said. "But then, it's pretty much what wizards do."

"This will not end well for you, boy," she replied. "Leave now."

"Heh, that's funny," I said. I *was* straining. I tried to keep it out of my voice. "For a second there, it sounded like you were telling me to go away. I mean, as if I would just go away."

She blinked twice at me. Then, in a tone of dawning comprehension, she murmured, "You are not brilliant. You are *ignorant*."

"Now you done it. Them's fightin' words," I drawled.

The Corpsetaker tilted her head back and let out an eerie little screech. I think that, to her, it was laughter.

Then she turned, swiped a hand at the last shrine, and demolished it herself.

The wards came down all around us, energy fading, dispersing, settling abruptly back down to earth. I could see the massive currents of power begin to unravel and disperse back out into the world. Within seconds, the protective wards were gone, as if they'd never existed.

The Corpsetaker made that shrieking sound again and vanished, and in the sudden absence of her will I almost fell flat on my face.

I caught myself by remembering that I could now officially scoff at gravity, stopped falling halfway to the floor, and righted myself again.

The wards were down. Murphy and company would be crashing the party at any moment.

And . . . for some reason, the Corpsetaker now *wanted* them to do it.

Right.

That couldn't be good.

CHAPTER FORTY-SIX

I let go of my Sight and went up the final flight of stairs, the ones that led from the junction room up to the street entrance — and found them stacked with Big Hoods. I blinked for a fraction of a second when I saw them. I'd practically forgotten the real-world thugs under the Corpsetaker's control. All the power we'd been throwing around in the duel had been ghostly stuff. The Big Hoods had no practical way to be aware of it.

How odd must the past couple of minutes have been from their point of view? They'd have felt the wave of cold, seen candles burning suddenly low, and then heard lots of boards and candles and paints being smashed and clawed down, while the concrete and stone walls were raked by invisible talons and the candles were smacked up and down the halls and stairways.

There were at least a dozen of them on the stairs, and they had guns, and there wasn't a whole lot I could do about it. For a second, I entertained notions of setting the Lecters on them, but I rejected the idea in a spasm of nausea. I'd seen what the killer spooks had done to the wolfwaffen. If I turned them loose, they'd deal with the Big Hoods the same way — and the Big Hoods, at the end of the day, were as much the Corpsetaker's victims as her physical muscle — and once you turned loose a force that elemental, you almost had to expect collateral damage. I didn't want any of it to splash onto Murphy and company.

"Okay," I told the Lecters. "Go back downstairs and help Sir Stuart and his boys out against those lemurs. After that, defend Mort." The Lecters' only response was to vanish, presumably to the main chamber. Good. Mort had still been conscious the last time I'd seen him. He could tell them what to do if they needed any further direction.

Meanwhile, I'd do the only thing I could to take on the Big Hoods. I'd play superscout for Karrin's team.

I vanished to outside the door to the stronghold and found several forms crouched there. Evening traffic was rumbling by on the bridge overhead, though the street running below it was deserted, and the space beneath the bridge was entirely shadowed. I ignored the darkness and saw Murphy next to the door, rummaging in a black nylon backpack. She was wearing her tactical outfit — black clothing and boots, and one of Charity Carpenter's vests made of Kevlar and titanium. Over that was a tactical harness, and she had two handguns and her teeny assault rifle, a little Belgian gun called a P-90. It packed one hell of a punch for such a compact package — much like Murphy herself.

Next to her, against the wall, were three great, gaunt wolves — Will, Andi, and Marci, from the color of their fur. Next came Molly, in her rags and armor, sitting calmly against the wall with her legs crossed. Butters brought up the rear, dressed in dark colors, carrying his gym bag, and looking extremely nervous.

I went over to him and said, "Boo."

The word emerged from the little radio in his pocket, and Butters jumped and said, "Meep."

"Meep?" I said. "Seriously?"

"Yeah, yeah, yeah," Butters muttered. "Keep your voice down. We're sneaking up on someone here."

"They already know you're here," I said. "There are about a dozen gunmen on the other side of that door."

"Quiet!" Murphy hissed. "Dammit, Butters!"

Butters held up the radio. "Dresden says they're right on the other side of the door."

"Now he shows up," Murphy muttered. "Not when we're planning the entry. Give me the radio."

Butters leaned across Molly and tossed the radio underhand. Molly just sat, smiling quietly. Murphy caught the radio. "So, what can you tell us — ?" She hesitated, grimaced, and said, "I keep wanting to add the word *over* to the end of sentences. But this isn't exactly radio protocol, is it?"

"Not really," I said. "But we can do whatever makes you happy. Over."

"No one likes a wiseass, Harry," Murphy said.

"I always enjoy seeing you in gunmetal, Ms. Murphy," I continued. "It brings out the blue in your eyes. Really makes them pop. Over."

The wolves were all wagging their tails.

"Don't make me bitch-slap you, Dresden," Murphy growled. But her blue eyes were twinkling. "Tell me what you know."

I gave her the brief on the interior of the hideout and what was waiting there.

"So you didn't get this necromancer bitch," she said.

"That's one hell of a negative way to put it," I replied, grinning. "Who's a grumpy pants tonight? Over."

Murphy rolled her eyes at Butters and said, in exactly the same tone, "So you didn't get this necromancer bitch."

"Not yet," I said. "Pretty sure her ghost troops are done for, but I need to get back downstairs and see. Just wanted to give you the rundown. You remember how to get to the basement?"

"Down the stairs, through the hole in the wall, fifty feet down a hall that turns left, down more stairs."

"Yeah, you got it," I said.

"Uh," Butters said. "Point of order? There's a locked door and a bunch of guys with guns between here and there."

Molly stood up. "They won't have guns," she said calmly.

Butters frowned. "Uh. Dresden just said . . ."

"I heard him," Molly replied. "They're going to empty their weapons at you the moment they see you in the doorway."

"Okay. As plans go, I can't be the only one who has a problem with that," Butters said.

"Illusion?" I asked Molly.

She nodded.

Murphy frowned. "I don't get it. Why that? Why not push them back with fire or make them all go to sleep or something?"

"Because this is the bad guys' home," I said. "They have a threshold."

Molly nodded. "Any spell that goes through gets degraded down to nothing. I can't push anything past the door. If I go in without being invited, I won't have any magic to speak of. Without an invitation, Harry can't cross the threshold at all."

Murphy nodded. "So you're going to give

627

them a target at the door. Makes sense." She frowned. "How were you going to get back in, Harry?"

I stood there for a second with my mouth open.

"Well, crap," I muttered. "Over."

Murphy snorted. "God, it really is you, isn't it." She turned back to her bag and took out a small black plastic hemisphere of what had to be explosives of some kind. She pressed it onto the door's surface right next to its lock. "No problem. I'll invite you in once the door's down."

"Doesn't work like that," I said. "Got to be an invitation from someone who lives there."

Murphy scowled. "Nothing's ever simple with you, Dresden."

"Me? Since when have you been Polly Plastique?"

"Kincaid showed me how," Murphy said without any emphasis. "And you know me, Dresden. I've always been a practical girl." She pressed a little device with a couple of tines on it through a pair of matching holes in the bowl, turned a dial, and said, "Get clear. Setting for ten seconds. Whatever you're going to do, Molly, have it ready."

My apprentice nodded, and everyone but me and Murphy backed down the wall from the door.

I waited until they were done moving away before I said, "Murph, these gangers . . .

They're victims, too."

She took a breath. Then she said, "Are they standing right by the door?"

"No. Five or six steps down."

She nodded. "Then they won't be in the direct line of the blast. This is a fairly small, shaped charge. With a little luck, no one will get hurt."

"Luck," I said.

She closed her eyes for a second. Then she said, "You can't save everyone, Dresden. Right now, I'm concerned with the man these victims are torturing and holding prisoner. They're still people. But they come right after him and everyone here on my worry list."

I felt a little guilty for making an insinuation about Murphy's priorities. Maybe it was too easy for me to talk. I was the one the Big Hoods couldn't hurt, after all. I wasn't sure how to say something like that, though, so I just sort of grunted and mumbled.

"It's okay," Murphy said very quietly. "I get it. Your perspective has changed."

I stared down at her for a moment. Then I said, "Not about some things."

"Relationship ambivalence from beyond the grave," she said, her mouth turning up at the corners. "Perfect."

"Karrin," I began.

"Don't," she said, cutting me off. "Just . . . don't. It doesn't matter now, does it?"

"Of course it matters."

"No," she said. "You are not Patrick Swayze. I am not Demi Moore." She touched a switch on the little box and it started ticking. "And this sure as hell isn't pottery class." She moved a couple of yards down the wall, pressed her hands up over her ears, and opened her mouth. Molly, Butters, and the wolves all did more or less the same thing. It looked . . . Well, they'd have been insulted if I said anything, but it looked darned cute on the wolves, them all crouched down with their chins on the ground, folding their ears forward with their paws. I'm sure any real wolf would have been shocked at the indignity.

I stayed where I was standing, right in front of the door. I mean, what the hell, right? When was I going to get a chance to see an explosion from this angle again?

I was a little disappointed. There was just a huge *bang,* a flash of light, and then a cloud of dust, which was pretty much descriptive of most of the explosions I'd seen. Though I was glad no one had actually been watching me. I flinched and hopped back about a foot when it went off.

When the dust cleared enough to see through, the door swung freely on its hinges. Murphy stuck her foot around the corner and kicked it all the way open, then gestured to Molly.

Molly murmured and closed her eyes, then

lifted her hand. Abruptly, there were two Murphys crouched by the door. The one nearest it was chewing gum. Noisily. She stood up with her P-90, flicked on the little flashlight under the barrel, and stepped around the corner, the gun pointing down the stairs.

Gunfire erupted. The gum-chewing Murphy dropped to one knee and started shooting, the assault rifle chattering in two- and three-round bursts. It was noisy as hell for about five seconds, and then there was silence. Gum-chewing Murphy withdrew back around the corner. Once she was out of sight of whoever was inside, she vanished.

The real Murphy stood up then and pitched an object down the stairs. A moment later, there was an eye-searing flash of light and thunder.

"Go, go, go!" Murphy called, and swung to point her gun down the stairs with just a portion of her upper body and face exposed to possible fire, while the rest of her body was hidden behind the wall. The three wolves rose and plunged through the dusty doorway in a single blur of motion.

Wolves in general get underestimated in the modern world — after all, humans have guns. And helicopters. But back in the day, when things were more muscle powered, wolves were a real threat to humans, possibly the number-two predator on the planet. People don't remember that wolves are far stronger, far faster, and far more dangerous than human beings. That humanity taught wolves to fear and avoid them — and that without that fear and advanced weaponry, a human being was nothing more than a possible threat and a potential meal. A wolf with no fear could tear several human beings apart. A wolf with no fear and an intelligent mind directing it to work in close concert with teammates was a force of freaking nature, more or less literally.

The point being that three wolves against a dozen Big Hoods, in those tiny confines, was not a fair fight — it wasn't even close.

People started screaming, and Murphy moved in, dropping her assault rifle to let it hang from her harness, and holding a little personal stunner in her hand.

I watched from the doorway, unable to proceed farther. Will, Marci, and Andi plowed into the first guy, half a dozen steps down, in a single bound. I don't care how big and strong you are; getting hit by a stun grenade and about five hundred pounds of wolf in the wake of a close-quarters explosion is going to make you want to call it a day. He went down, taking the next several Big Hoods with him. There was a huge tangle of frantic bodies and flashing teeth. The wolves had the advantage. Hands holding weapons got targeted first, and blood-spattered guns tumbled down the stairs.

One of the Big Hoods produced a knife about the size of a cafeteria tray and drew back to hack awkwardly at Will's back with it. Murphy stomped the weapon down flat against the stairs and jabbed the arm holding it with a stunner. A cry of pain rose sharply, and the weapon fell.

Then it was about momentum and snarling wolves. The Big Hoods were driven down the stairs, stunned, bruised, and bleeding. Once at the bottom, the wolves started attacking with even more savage growls — herding the Big Hoods like so many dazed and over-muscled sheep. They drove the guards down the length of the electrical-junction room and out of my direct line of sight. I had to imagine them all piled up in a corner. I heard growls rolling up out of the wolves' throats in a low, continual thunder.

Murphy went down the rest of the stairs, hands on her gun again, but not actually pointing it at anyone. "You," she said, nodding toward the presumed position of the Big Hoods. "Knife Boy. What's your name?"

"I . . ." stammered a voice. "I can't . . . I don't . . ."

"Murph," I called. "Corpsetaker's been messing with these guys' heads for a while now, ever since that thing with Sue. They are not operating at one hundred percent."

Murphy glanced at the radio in her pocket and then back at whoever she was talking to.

Her expression had changed, from potential executioner to something more like a schoolteacher you don't want to cross. Murphy had been damaged in the same way before. "That's a wallet in your pocket, son?"

"Yes, ma'am," mumbled the voice.

She nodded. "Take it out with just two fingers. Toss it over here to me. Nice and easy."

"I don't want you to hurt me," said the voice.

Murphy tilted her head and I saw pain in her eyes. She lowered the gun and her voice became gentler yet. "Just toss me the wallet. I'm going to set things right."

"Yes, ma'am," mumbled the voice again. A ratty old nylon wallet hit the floor near Murphy's feet.

Murphy picked it up, never taking her eyes off the group. I saw her go through the wallet.

"I like dogs," ventured the voice. There was a disconnected tone to it.

"They won't hurt you if you stay there," Murphy said. "Joshua? Is that your name?"

"I . . . Yes, ma'am. It was. I mean, it is. Josh."

"Josh. Age nineteen," Murphy said. A flicker of anger entered her blue eyes. "Jesus, these game-playing bastards."

"Bitch, technically," I said.

Murphy snorted. "Come here, Josh."

Molly approached the top of the stairway

and stood next to me, where she usually did, a little behind me and to my left. She must have gotten a look at my position through her little tuning fork.

A Big Hood appeared in front of Murphy. He was about five hundred times bigger than she was. He had hands like shovels. One of his hands was bleeding.

"Take the hood off, please," Murphy said.

He hastened to do so. He was an ugly, blunt-featured kid. His hair was longish and matted. It had been months since it was cut, combed, or washed. He didn't have enough beard to notice from the top of the staircase, and he didn't look too bright. He blinked his eyes several times in the light coming from Murphy's flashlight.

"Hello, Josh," Murphy said, keeping her tone level and calm. "My name is Karrin."

" 'Lo, Karrin," Josh said.

"Let me see your hand," she said firmly.

"Establish the pattern," Molly murmured under her breath. "Good."

Josh hesitated a moment and then held out his hand. Murphy examined it. "Doesn't look too deep. It's already beginning to stop bleeding."

"Had worse, ma'am," Josh mumbled.

She nodded again. "Do you know why you were on those stairs?"

"Bad people," Josh said. "Bad people who were going to hurt us." He frowned. "You?"

"I could hurt you right now, but I'm not going to. Am I?" Murphy said.

"No."

"That's right," she said. "I know this is hard, Josh, but I'm probably your friend."

He frowned. "I don't know you. You're a stranger."

"I'm going to help you," she said. "Help all of you, if you'll let me. Get you some food and some clean clothes."

Josh shrugged a shoulder. " 'Kay. I'm hungry."

Murphy looked away from him, and I saw her control another expression of anger. "I'm looking for a little bald man. I know he's here."

Josh looked uncomfortable.

"Is he here? Downstairs?"

"You know he is," I muttered.

It hadn't carried to the radio, but Murphy glanced with an arched eyebrow up the stairway, then turned back to the kid.

Josh looked back and forth and shifted his weight.

"Tell me the truth, Josh," Murphy said. "It's all right."

"Downstairs," Josh said. "With Boz."

"Boz?" Murphy asked.

"Boz is big," Josh said.

Murphy eyed the kid up and down and squared her shoulders. "Um, right. Okay, Josh. There's one more thing I want you to do for me, and then you can go sit down with your friends."

" 'Kay."

"My friends are up at the top of the stairs. I want you to ask them in."

Josh furrowed his brow. "Huh?"

"Invite them inside, please."

"Oh no," he said, shaking his head. "No one in the secret hideout. Orders."

"It's all right," Murphy said. "I'm giving you new orders. Invite them in, please."

Josh seemed to waver. "Umm."

Murphy's hand dipped into her pocket and he seemed to flinch. Then it emerged holding one of those high-activity protein bars wrapped in Mylar. "You can have this, if you do."

The way to a dim minion's heart was evidently through his stomach. Josh snapped up the bar with both hands and said, up toward the top of the stairs, "Won't you please come inside?"

I took a tentative step forward and felt no resistance. The threshold had parted. Molly did the same and hurried down the stairs.

"Will, Andi, Marci," Molly said in a calm voice. "Back a couple of steps, please."

The wolves glanced at Murphy and then started backing up.

"What are you doing?" Murphy asked.

"I'm making sure we don't need to hurt them, Ms. Murphy," Molly said. "Trust me."

"Grasshopper?" I asked.

"It's legal," she said, rolling her eyes. "Don't worry. And we can't just stand around. What's the response time to this block?"

"Eight minutes," Murphy said calmly. "Ish."

"It's been about four since the charge went off," Molly said. "Ticktock."

Murphy grimaced. "Do it."

Molly turned to Josh and said, "Go stand with your friends. You guys look tired."

Josh had a mouthful of whatever it was. He nodded. "Always tired." And he shuffled over to the dazed-looking group in the corner.

"A lot of cults do that," Molly said quietly. "It makes them easier to influence and control." She closed her eyes for a moment, then took a slow, deep breath and opened them. She lifted her right hand and murmured, in a silken-soft tone, *"Neru."*

And the dozen or so Big Hoods just sank down to the floor.

"Mother of God," Murphy said softly, and turned to stare at Molly.

"Sleep spell," I said quietly. "Like the one I had to use on you, Murph."

I didn't mention that the spell I'd used on Murphy had taken every bit of skill I'd had and ten times as long to put together. Molly had just done the same thing, only a dozen times bigger — touching each individual mind and crafting the spell to lull it to sleep.

What she'd just done was *hard.*

In fact, it was what one could only have expected from a member of the White Council.

Maybe my godmother had a point.

Molly shuddered and rubbed at her arms. "Ugh. They aren't . . . they aren't right, Ms. Murphy. They weren't stable, and they could have had their switches flipped to violence at any time. This will at least make sure they won't hurt themselves or anyone else until morning."

Murphy studied her for a moment and then nodded. "Thank you, Molly."

My apprentice nodded back.

Murphy took up her gun again and then looked at her. She smiled and shook her head. "Rag Lady, huh?"

Molly looked down at her outfit and back up. "I didn't pick the name."

The diminutive woman shook her head, her expression firm with disapproval. "If you're going to create a persona, you've got to think of these things. Do you know how many extra PMS jokes are flying out there now?"

Molly looked serious. "I think that just makes it even scarier?"

Murphy pursed her lips and shrugged a shoulder. "Yeah. I guess it might."

"Scares me," I said.

Murphy smiled a little more. "Because you're a chauvinist pig, Dresden."

"No," I snorted. "Because I realize a lot better than you two do how dangerous you are."

Both of them stopped at that, blinked, and looked at each other.

"Okay, ghosty-scout time," I said. "Sit tight for a second. I'm going to check below."

"Meet you at the top of the next stairway," Murphy said.

"Got it," I said. "Oh. Nice work on that spell, grasshopper."

Molly's cheeks turned pink, but she said, casually, "Yeah. I know."

"Atta girl," I said. "Never let them think you're out of your depth."

I vanished and appeared in the main chamber below. I was unprepared for the sight that waited for me.

Corpsetaker was standing about twenty feet from where Mort hung suspended. Her jaw was . . . was unhinged, like a snake's, open much wider than it should have been able. As I watched, she made a couple of convulsive motions with her entire body and swallowed down a recognizable object — a child's shoe, circa nineteenth century. She tilted her head back, as if it helped her slide whichever one of the two child ghosts she'd eaten last down her gullet, and then lowered her chin and smiled widely at Mort Lindquist.

Sir Stuart's faded form was the only one still visible in the room. The wispy, camera-lit mists of several other spirits were still dissolving, all around the room.

Mort spotted me and slurred, "Dresden. You moron. What have you done?"

Corpsetaker tilted her head back and laughed.

"I wasn't keeping them shut away because they might hurt this bitch," Morty said. He sounded hurt and exhausted and furious. "I was protecting them because she was going to *eat* them."

I stared for a second.

The Corpsetaker had been going to *eat* the Lecters. The most vicious, dangerous, powerful spirits in all of Chicago.

Just like she had planned to do to Chicago's ghosts when Kemmler's disciples had attempted a ritual called a Darkhallow several years before, I realized — a ritual that, if successful, would have turned the necromancer who pulled it off into a being of godlike power.

"Ahhhh," the Corpsetaker said, the sound deep and rich and full of satisfaction.

I got a very bad feeling in the pit of my stomach.

"I'm almost full," she continued. She smiled at me with very wide, very white, very sharp-looking teeth. "Almost."

CHAPTER FORTY-SEVEN

One thing you never do in a fight, no matter how emotionally satisfying it might seem, is pause to gloat with an enemy standing right in front of you. Savvy foes aren't going to just hang around letting you yak at them. They're going to take advantage of the opening you're giving them.

The same goes for desperate foes who aren't interested in trying to win a fair fight.

Before the Corpsetaker finished speaking, I snapped my staff forward and snarled, *"Fuego!"*

Fire lashed toward her. She deflected the strike with a motion of her hand, like you'd use to ward off a fly. The memory-fire went flying on by her, through the wall and gone.

"Such a pity," she said. "I was just going to —"

She wanted to keep up the gloating, I was game.

I hit her again, only harder.

This time I sent it flying a lot faster and it

stung, though she slapped the fire aside before it could do much more than singe her. She let out a furious sound. "Fool! I will —"

Some people. I swear they never learn.

I'd built up a rhythm. So I gave her my best evocation, a burst of fire and force, sizzling with a lot of curve and English on it, an ogre-buster the size of a softball, blazing with scarlet and golden light.

She swept both arms into an X-shaped defensive stance, fingers contorted in a desperate defensive gesture, and she snapped out a string of swift words. She stopped the strike, but an explosion of flame and force rolled over her and she screamed in pain as she was driven twenty feet back and into the solid rock of the wall.

"Yahhh!" I shouted in wordless defiance, even as I reached for my next spell . . .

. . . and suddenly felt very strange.

"—sden, stop!" Mort was screaming. His voice sounded very far away. "Look at your-self!"

I had the next blast of fire and energy ready in my mind, but I stopped to glance at my hands.

I could barely see them. They were faded to the point of near invisibility.

The shock drove the spell out of my head, and color and substance rushed back into my limbs. They were still translucent, but at least I could see them. I turned wide eyes to where

Mort still hung over the wraith pit. His voice suddenly snapped back up in volume, becoming very clear.

"You keep throwing your memories at her," Mort said, "but part of what you are now goes out with them — and it doesn't come *back*. You're about to destroy yourself, man! She's luring you into it!"

Of course she was, dammit. Why stand around trying to block my attacks when she could just vanish from in front of them? Evil Bob's fortifications, it seemed, had served a purpose other than simply barring the way — I'd used up way too much of myself on the way through them. And then here, trading punches with Corpsetaker, I'd used up a lot more, slinging out the memory of my magic left and right, when I'd seen how careful Sir Stuart was to recover such expended power practically the minute I'd gotten out of Captain Jack's car.

I couldn't see her without bringing up my Sight, but Corpsetaker's mocking laugh rolled through the underground chamber from the section of wall I'd knocked her into. I stared at my hands again and clenched them in frustration. Mort was right. I'd already done too much. But how the hell else was I supposed to fight her?

I turned to Mort. He was having trouble keeping his eyes on me as he twisted slowly on the rope. He closed them. "Dresden . . .

you can't do anything more. Get out of here. I don't want anyone else to give themselves away for me," he said, his voice raw. "Not for me."

Sir Stuart's shade, floating protectively beside Mort, regarded me with sober, distant eyes.

Corpsetaker's mad laughter mocked us all. Then she said, "If I'd known you would deliver so thoroughly, Dresden, I'd have gone looking for you ages ago. Boz. Kill the little man."

There was a growl and the stirring of a large animal. And then a human garbage truck started climbing out of the wraith pit, emerging from the stewing broil of wraiths like Godzilla rising out of the surf. Boz had a stench to him so thick that it carried over into the realm of spirit — a psychic stink that felt like it might have choked me unconscious had I still been alive. The guy's *brain* had been down there stewing in wraiths for only God knew how long, and if Morty's reaction to exposure was any indication, Boz had to have had his sanity pureed. He was crusted over in filth so thick that I couldn't tell where the spiritual muck left off and the physical crud began. I could see his eyes, like dull, gleaming stones underneath his hood. They were absolutely gone. This guy was only a person by legal definitions. His humanity had long since begun to fester and rot.

Boz climbed out of the pit, radiating a physical and psychic power full of rot and corruption and rage and endless hungers. He stood there blankly for a second. And then he turned and took one slow, lumbering, Voorheesian step after another, toward the apparatus from which Mort hung.

The ectomancer regarded Boz weakly and then said, "Great. This is all I need."

"What?" I said. "Mort? What does she mean?"

"Uh, sorry. Little distracted here," Mort said. "What?"

"The Corpsetaker! What did she mean that she doesn't need you anymore?"

"You fed her enough power to fuel a couple of dozen Nightmares, Dresden," Mort said. "She can do whatever she wants now."

"What? So she gobbles a bunch of killers and she gets to be a real boy again? It can't be that easy."

Boz reached the basketball goal, grabbed it in his huge hands, and just turned it slowly, the hard way. Mort began to rotate toward the edge of the pit.

"Agh! Dresden! Do something!"

I glared at Morty, spreading empty hands, and then in pure frustration I tossed a punch at Boz. It was like slapping my fist through raw sewage. I didn't hit anything solid, and my fist and arm came out covered in disgusting residue. I couldn't act. Information was the only weapon I had. "Kind of limited here, Mort!"

Morty had begun to hyperventilate, but he clearly came to some sort of decision. He started gasping out words rapidly. "She can be real again — for a little while."

"She can manifest," I said.

Boz's fingernails were spotted with dark green mold. He reached out and grabbed the rope holding Mort. He untied the rope from its stay without letting it slide and began to haul Mort toward the edge of the pit. Arms and mouths and fingers stretched up from the bubbling wraiths, trying to reach the ectomancer.

"Gah!" Mort gasped, trying to twist away. Wraith fingertips touched his face, and he winced in apparent pain. "Once she does that, she gets to be her old self for a while. She can walk, talk — whatever."

"Use her magic for real," I breathed. The Corpsetaker wouldn't have to limit herself to people who could contact the dead, people from whom she could try to wrest consent, as she had done to Mort.

She could simply *take* someone new — and then she was back in the game, a body-switching lunatic with a hate-on for the White Council and all things decent in general. Her boss, Kemmler, had apparently slithered his way out of being dead more than once. Maybe her whole freaky-cult operation had been a page from his playbook.

I vanished to the bottom of the stairs and screamed, "Murph! Hurry!"

But I saw no one at the top of the stairs.

Sir Stuart stood in front of Boz, clenching his jaw and his ax in impotent rage, as Boz lowered Mort to the ground and then leaned over him, reaching down with his huge hands to grasp Mort on either side of his head. A twist, a snap, and it would be over for the ectomancer.

But what could I do? I had nothing more than the ghost of a decent spell in me, and then I was misty history. Morty was beat to hell, exhausted, unable to use his own magic — or he damned well would have gotten himself out of this clustergeist by now. Even if he'd let me in — which I wasn't sure he would do in his condition, not even to save his life — I doubted the two of us had enough energy and control between us to get him free. Mort could have called Sir Stuart into him, drawn upon the marine's experience and the memory of his strength, but the ectomancer was still tied up. And besides, Sir Stuart was in the same condition I was, only worse.

All of us were helpless to act on the physical world.

If I'd still had the Lecters, I could have ordered one of them to manifest and free Morty, which I maybe should have chanced a few minutes ago. Hindsight was blinding in its clarity. It was too late for that now — Corpsetaker had taken the Lecters out of the picture, and without the mad spirits' ability to manifest in the physical world . . .

My thoughts sped to quicksilver flickering. Frantic memory hit me like a hammer.

"Hell's bells. Every time I've run into a ghost, it's tried to rip my lungs out! You're telling me none of your spooks can do something?"

"They're *sane*," Mort shouted back. "It's crazy for a ghost to interact with the physical world. Sane ghosts don't go around acting *crazy!*"

For a ghost, manifesting in the material world was an act of madness — a memory trying to enforce its will on the living, the past struggling to steer the course of the present. It was, according to everything I had learned about magic and life, an inversion of the laws of nature, a defiance of the natural order.

Ghosts who weren't supermighty manifested all the time. It wasn't a question of raw power, and it never had been — it was a matter of desire. You just had to be crazy enough to make it happen. *That* was what the Corpsetaker had gotten from devouring the Lecters. Not sufficient power, but sufficient insanity. She just had to be crazy enough to make it happen.

For a wizard running around as a lost soul, expending his very essence in an attempt to rescue a guy who hadn't even really been his friend was definitely of questionable rationality. Grabbing the leashes of several dozen maniac ghosts and leading them on a banzai charge against a far stronger foe was probably less than stable, too. Hell, even the last few major choices of my life — murdering Susan in order to save our child, giving myself to Mab so that I could save little Maggie — were not the acts of a stable, sane man. Neither had been my entire career, really, given the options that had been available to me. I mean, I don't mean to brag, but I could have used my abilities to make money if I'd wanted to. A *lot* of money.

Instead? A little basement apartment. A job catering to clientele who hadn't merely needed help — they'd needed a miracle. Money? Not much. The occasional good deed, sure, but you can't eat sincere thanks. Girls don't flock to the guy who drives the old car, reads a lot of books, and kicks down the doors of living nightmares. My own people in the White Council had persecuted me my whole life, mostly for trying to do the right thing. And I'd kept on doing it anyway.

Hell. I was pretty much crazy already.

That being the case . . . how hard could it be?

It would take a certain amount of energy, I

was sure. Maybe everything I had left. It wouldn't get me any closer to the answers I wanted. It wouldn't let me find out who had murdered me. It might destroy me altogether. Heck, for that matter, if it took too much power to pull off, it could snuff me here and now.

But the alternative? Watching Morty die?

Not going to happen. I'd face oblivion first.

I gripped the wooden grain of my staff, recalling the feelings that had surged through me when I had summoned and bound the Lecters. I called on my memories one more time. I called up the ache of sore muscles after a hard workout, and the sheer physical joy of my body in motion during a run, walking down the street, sinking into a hot bath, swimming through cool water, stroking over the softness of another body beside mine. I thought of my favorite old T-shirt, a plain, black cotton one with 98% CHIMPANZEE written on the chest in white typeset letters. I thought of the creak of my old leather cowboy boots, the comfort of a good pair of jeans. The scent of a wood-smoked grill drifting into my nose when I was hungry, the way my mouth would water and my stomach would growl. I thought of my old Mickey Mouse alarm clock going off too early in the morning, and groaning out of bed to go to work. I remembered the smell of a favorite old book's pages when I opened them again, and the smell of smoldering motor oil, a staple feature of my old *Blue Beetle.* I remembered the softness of Susan's lips against mine. I remembered my daughter's slight, warm weight in my arms, her exhausted body as limp as a rag doll's. I remembered the way tears felt, sliding free of my eyes, the annoying blockage of congestion when I had a cold, and a thousand other things — little things, minor things, desperately important things.

You know. Life.

Then I did something fairly nutty, as I gathered the memory for what I was to attempt. I just uttered the spell in plain, old English. The energy seared through my thoughts in a way that would have been damaging to a living wizard, maybe fatal. It seemed appropriate to use it here, and I released whatever power I had left, clothing it in garments of memory, as I murmured the most basic of ideas, the foundation of words and of reality.

"Be."

My universe shook. There was a vast rushing sound, rising to a crescendo that would have made a sane person flinch and crouch down to find shelter. And in a sudden burst of silence, I stood firmly in cold, dank dimness. The cold raised gooseflesh on my skin.

Shadows had swollen to cover almost all the details around me, and no wonder they had.

All the candles and lamps that lit the chamber had burned down to little pinpoints.

I tapped Boz on the shoulder and said, "Hey, gorgeous."

His face twisted in complete surprise, turning to stare in blank incomprehension at mine.

I winked at him, and whispered, "Boo."

And then I slugged him with my quarterstaff.

It hurt. I mean, more than the shock of impact that lanced up through my wrists. I was solid again, at least for a moment. I was myself again, and with my remembered body came a fountain of remembered pain. My legs and knees creaked and ached, something that was a natural progression for a big guy, a kind of background pain that I never noticed until it was gone and then back again. I hadn't exactly stretched out, and I'd socked Boz with everything I had. I'd torn a muscle in my back doing it. My head wasn't clear, suddenly riddled with a catalog of muscle twitches, physically painful hunger, and old injuries I'd just learned to ignore, now suddenly screaming in fresh agony.

I've said before that only the dead feel no pain, but I'd never spoken from experience before. Pain used as a weapon is one thing. Personal pain, the kind that comes from just living our lives, is something else.

Pain isn't a lot of fun, at least not for most

folks, but it is utterly unique to *life*. Pain —
physical, emotional, and otherwise — is the
shadow cast by everything you want out of
life, the alternative to the result you were
hoping for, and the inevitable creator of
strength. From the pain of our failures we
learn to be better, stronger, greater than what
we were before. Pain is there to tell us when
we've done something badly — it's a teacher,
a guide, one that is always there to both warn
us of our limitations and challenge us to
overcome them.

For something no one likes, pain does us a
whole hell of a lot of good.

Stepping back into my old self and moving
instantly into violent motion hurt like hell.

It.

Was.

Amazing.

I let out a whoop of sheer adrenaline and
mad joy as Boz tumbled back over Mort's
recumbent form.

"Oof!" Mort shouted. "Dresden!"

A howl of excitement came rolling out of
Sir Stuart's throat and he clenched his fist in
vicious satisfaction, flashing briefly into full
color. "Aye, set boot to arse, boy!"

Boz came up into a crouch pretty smoothly
for someone of his bulk and stayed there, low
and on all fours, an animal that saw no
advantage in learning to stand erect. Absolutely no sign of discomfort showed on his

face, even though I'd split open his cheek with the blow from my staff and blood joined the other substances encrusting his face.

Hell's bells. My staff wasn't exactly a toothpick. It was as heavy as three baseball bats. I wasn't a toothpick, either. I wasn't sure of my weight in baseball bats, but I could look down at a lot of guys in the NBA, and I wasn't a scrawny kid anymore. The point being that the blow, delivered with all the power of my shoulders, hips, and legs as well as my arms, should have knocked Boz out — or killed him outright. I'd been aiming for his temple. He'd jerked his head back so that the end of my staff hit his left cheekbone instead. Hell, I might have broken it.

But instead of collapsing in pain, he just crouched there, silent, stony eyes looking right through me as he faced me without flinching. I began to gather my will and staggered, nearly falling on my face. I had nothing left. It was only that burning flash of irrational certainty that had driven me to attempt to manifest that was keeping me on my feet at all — and I realized with a cold little chill that I might not be able to stop Boz from killing Morty.

"Good Lord, I'm regretting this now," I muttered. "I have never — ever — smelled BO this bad in my *life*. And I once had s'mores with a Sasquatch."

"Hang out with him for a while," Mort

gasped. "Eventually it's not so bad."

"Wow. Really?"

"No. Not really."

I kept my eyes on Boz, but did my best to grin at Mort. He'd been strung up and tortured by lunatics for almost twenty-four hours, and his executioner was still trying to finish the job, but he still had the guts to engage in badinage. Anyone with that kind of spirit in the face of horror is okay in my book.

Boz came at me like a predator — a smooth, swift motion that moved his whole body at once, unfettered by any kind of reluctance or hesitation. He never rose to do it, either. He flung himself forward as much with his arms as his legs, and his body's center of mass never came much higher than my knees.

I gave him a boot to the head. I literally kicked him in the head with my hiking boot, and it was like stubbing my toe on a large rock. He just plowed on through the kick and hit me at the knees. Boz had a lot of mass. We went down, me on my ass, him lying on my lower legs. He started trying to claw his way up my body to my throat. I declined to allow him such liberties, and communicated that desire to him by thrusting the end of my staff at his neck.

He slapped at the staff with one paw and caught it in an iron grip. I tried to roll away. He got his other hand on the weapon. We wrenched and wrestled for control of it. He was stronger than me. He was heavier than me. I had slightly more leverage, but not enough to make the difference.

Then Boz surged forward, driving with tree-trunk legs, and I went down on my back. All his weight came down on the staff and he drove it toward my throat.

Temporary body or not, it still worked the same way as the one I was used to. If Boz crushed my windpipe, the body would die. If that happened, I assumed I would be left behind, immaterial again, while the false flesh collapsed into ectoplasm — the way ghosts and demons were driven back to their spirit forms when their temporary bodies were destroyed. But we were getting pretty far out of my comfort zone when it came to ghostly lore.

Boz bore down, and it was all I could do to keep him from choking me with my own staff. I couldn't even dream of moving him. He had seventy-five or eighty pounds on me, all of them solid, stinking mass, and he was coming at me with a silently psychotic determination.

But he hadn't realized where we had fallen.

I released the staff with my right hand, and his shoulders bunched, his back rounding out in a massive hump of trapezius muscles. My one hand wasn't able to do much to hold him back, and I felt the harsh pain of blood trying to hammer through the arteries Boz was compressing.

With my right hand, I seized the ends of the jumper cables still attached to the heavy-duty automobile battery, the one Morty had been tortured with — and jammed the metal ends of them both against the freshly blood-soaked side of Boz's face.

It wasn't exactly a surgical strike. I was holding both clamps in the same hand and only a couple of seconds from being choked unconscious, after all, but it worked. The clamps touched each other and wet skin, and sparks flew. Boz convulsed and jerked away from the sudden source of agony, a reflex action as immutable as pulling your arm away from a searing-hot pan handle. He shifted his weight and I pushed up, adding every ounce of muscle I had to aid the movement. He pitched off me, rolling, and I followed him, letting go of the staff and looping the main body of the jumper cable around his neck. He thrashed and tried to get away, but I had gotten onto his back and locked my legs around his hips. I grabbed the cable in both hands and hauled back on it with everything I had.

It was over pretty quick, though it didn't feel like it at the time. Boz thrashed and struggled, but as heavily muscled as he was, he wasn't flexible enough to get his arms back and up to reach where I was on his back, so he couldn't pull me off. He tried to break away, but between the cable and the grip of my legs, he wasn't able to shake me off. He tried to get his fingers in beneath the jumper cable, but though he managed to get in a couple of digits, I was pulling too hard and was more than strong enough to outmuscle one of his fingers.

I don't care how crazy you are; when your brain doesn't get oxygen, you go down. Boz did, too. I held the choke for another ten seconds to make sure he wasn't playing possum on me, and then for fifteen. Then twenty. Someone was snarling a string of curses and I hadn't realized it was me. The simple sensation of straining power, of primal victory, surged through me like a drug, and only the coup de grace remained.

I ground my teeth. I'd killed men and women before but never when I'd had an alternative. I might be a fighter, but I wasn't a killer, not when there was a choice. I forced myself to let go of the cables, and Boz flopped to the ground, entirely limp but alive. I had to roll him off one of my legs, pushing with my other heel, but he finally went, and I shambled upright, breathing hard. Then I turned to Mort and started untying knots.

He watched me with wary eyes. "Dresden. What you're doing . . . being in the flesh like that. It isn't right."

"I know," I said. "But no one else was going to do it."

He shook his head. "I'm just saying . . . it isn't good for you. Those spirits, the ones I'd been sheltering — they weren't any different from any other ghost when they got started. Doing this . . . It does things to you long-term. You'll change." He leaned a little toward me. "Right now, you're still you. But what you felt there, at the end — it grows. Keep doing this and you won't be you anymore."

"I'm almost done," I told him, jerking the ropes clear as fast as I could. It took a bit. They'd strung him up pretty carefully, distributing his weight across a lot of rope. I guess Corpsetaker hadn't wanted to spend several hours getting her limbs back under control once Mort cracked.

He groaned and tried to sit up. It took him a couple of attempts, but when I tried to help him, he waved my offer away.

"Can you walk?" I asked him.

He shuddered. "I can damned well walk out of here. Just give me a minute."

"I don't have it," I said. "I've got to move."

"Why?"

"Because my friends are up there somewhere."

He sucked in a breath.

"I know," I said with a grimace. Then I rose, grabbed my staff, and started walking toward the stairs.

"Stu," I heard Mort say. "You know knots, right?"

I glanced back and saw Sir Stuart nod. Mort nodded back and started gathering up the coils of rope I'd pulled off him. He beckoned to Sir Stuart. "Come in. I don't want the man mountain there getting up and finishing what he started."

I almost hesitated, to make sure Mort was all right, but I'd spent too much time down here already, and I could feel the hectic buzz of my fatigue growing by the moment. I had to get upstairs.

There was only one reason Corpsetaker would have taken down her own wards as she had. She wasn't limited to such a small sampling of humanity now, when it came to seizing a new body. She'd *wanted* people to come inside her lair.

It would give her more variety to choose from.

I rushed up the stairs, praying that I would be in time to stop Kemmler's protégé from taking one of my friends — for keeps.

Chapter Forty-Eight

I pounded up the stairs and found that it was getting dark. Dammit. I'd gotten way too used to the upside of ghostliness. I reached up to my neck to find my mother's pentacle amulet and . . .

. . . and it wasn't there. Which it *should* have been. I mean, my actual duster had been destroyed, but the one I was wearing was an exact duplicate. There was no reason my mother's amulet shouldn't have been there, but it wasn't. That was possibly something significant.

But I didn't have time to worry about it at the moment. Instead, I sent a whisper of will into my staff, and the runes carved in it began to glow with blue-white wizard light, casting their shapes in pure light on the moldy stone walls and floor of the hallway, showing me the way. I didn't have much magic left in me, but a simple light spell was much, much easier than any kind of violent spell, requiring far less energy.

I ran down the hall, past the filthy sleeping rooms with curtains for doors, and through the break in the wall, to the old electrical-junction room.

A flashlight lay on the floor, spilling light onto a patch of wolf fur from a couple of inches away and otherwise doing nothing to illuminate the scene. I had to brighten the light from my staff to see that Murphy and the wolves were lying in a heap on the floor, next to the unconscious Big Hoods.

The Corpsetaker was nowhere to be seen.

Neither was Molly.

I turned in a slow circle, looking for any sign of what had happened, and found nothing.

Feet scraped on rock and I turned swiftly, bringing up my staff, ready to unleash whatever power I had left in me — and found Butters standing halfway down the stairs, looking like a rabbit about to bolt. His face was pale as a sheet behind his glasses, and his dark hair was a wild mess.

"My God," he breathed. "Dresden?"

"Back for a limited engagement," I breathed, lowering the staff. "Butters, what happened?"

"I . . . I don't know. They started shouting something and then they just . . . just collapsed."

"And you didn't?" I asked.

"I was out there," he said, pointing behind

him. "You know. Looking out for the police or whatever."

"Being Eyes, huh?" I said. I turned back to Murphy and the wolves.

"Yeah, pretty much," he said. He moved quietly down the stairs. "Are they all right?"

I crouched down over Murphy and felt her neck. Her pulse was strong and steady. Ditto for the nearest of the wolves. "Yeah," I said, my heart slowing down a little. "I think s—"

Something cold and hard pressed against the back of my head. I looked down.

Murphy's SIG was missing from its holster.

"Everyone trusts a doctor," purred Butters, in a tone of voice that Butters would *never* have used. "Even wizards, Dresden."

I felt myself tensing. "Corpsetaker."

"You were able to manifest after all? Intriguing. You've a natural gift for darker magic, I think. My master would have snapped you up in an instant."

I'd spent an afternoon with Murphy working on gun disarms, at Dough Joe's Hurricane Gym. I tried to remember which way I had to spin to attempt to take the gun away. It depended on how it was being held — and I had no idea how Corpsetaker was holding the weapon on me. I was pretty sure Butters was a lefty, but I didn't think that would matter to the Corpsetaker once she set up shop. "Oh, boy. I could have hung out with people like you? I'm pretty sure it wouldn't have worked out."

"Possibly not," Corpsetaker said. "I accorded you far more respect than you merited, as an opponent. How much of you is left behind that body you've cobbled together? Scarcely more than one of those pathetic wraiths, I think. You could have made a viable move in time, but clearly you've no patience, no head for strategy."

"Yeah. I guess I've still got a soul and a conscience where you installed that stuff."

"Soul? Conscience?" Corpsetaker said, almost laughing. "Those are nothing but words. They aren't even true limits — just the figments of them. Useless."

"Just because something isn't solid doesn't mean it isn't real," I said. "If you had a brain in your head, you'd know that."

"You're obsessed with the fantasies of the young," she replied with my friend's breath. "Though I must admit that that the ironic reversal of our current state is simply delicious."

And without a hesitation or any change in the tone of her voice, she put a bullet into the back of my head.

The pain was infinitely brief and indescribable, a massive spike of agony that felt as if it should have sent me flying. I saw a cloud of something fly forward and then splatter all over one of the wolves and the nearest Big Hood. Ectoplasm, I realized dully. My physical body had been destroyed. It had fallen back into the spirit matter from which I'd formed it.

The pain faded, and then I was back in the still, neutral absence of sensation of the ghost state. I reached for the splattered matter with an instinctive, unspoken yearning to return to it.

I could barely see my hand.

I tried to turn around, but it felt like I was submerged in something thicker and more viscous than water, and it took forever.

I stared into the Corpsetaker's eyes within Butters's face and watched the body-jumping lunatic smirk at me. "Not much of you now, is there?" she murmured. "You'll be a wraith within days. I think that balances our account. Enjoy eternity, Dresden."

I tried to snarl a curse, but I was just so tired. I couldn't get the sound to come out of me. And by the time I had tried, Corpsetaker had taken Butters's body back to the bottom of the stairs. She was moving so *fast.*

Or . . . or maybe I was just that slow.

I tried to follow, and all I could manage was to drift in the Corpsetaker's wake, moving with grace, but slowly. So slowly.

Corpsetaker made a gesture and a veil fell away from another shade at the top of the stairs. It was Butters. He stood there dressed not in his winter gear, but in the scrubs I was far more used to seeing him wear. He was completely motionless except for his eyes, which rolled around frantically. A rapidly evaporating puddle of ectoplasm spread at his feet. An expression of pure confusion was locked onto his face.

Corpsetaker had been a big fan of body switching. When she left me and Morty in the basement, she must have come directly up here to grab a new body. She'd probably dropped some variant of a sleeping spell on Murphy and the wolves — and then Butters must have shown up.

Corpsetaker had gone with her usual trick, forcibly trading bodies with a victim — and the manifested ghost body she'd been in had fallen back into ectoplasm the moment she wasn't there to give it energy and form. Butters's essence, his *soul,* had just been booted out of his body, and now it stood there, vulnerable and unmoving — brightly colored but fading away, even as I watched. She'd tossed a quick veil over Butters's shade so that no one who might come upon her would see him standing there, forlorn and confused, while she drove around in his hijacked body.

The thing that really got to me? Corpsetaker threw a little smirk back at me as she got to Butters's shade. There wasn't anything I could do to stop her, but she wanted me to see how thoroughly she'd outthought and outmaneuvered me.

But the universe has a funny sense of

humor, and apparently it's not *always* aimed at me. While Corpsetaker looked back at me to smirk, Molly rippled forth from under a veil of her own, on the last step between Butters's stolen body and the explosion-chewed door. She grabbed the Corpsetaker by the front of Butters's coat. Butters wasn't exactly heroic in build. Molly, on the other hand, was several inches taller than he and had her mother's genes, everything I'd been able to teach her about mixing it up, and six months of hard time under the tender guiding hand of the Leanansidhe.

Molly slammed the Corpsetaker against the wall so hard that stolen teeth slammed together. Then she seized Butters's freaking *face* in a clawlike hand and thrust her head close, locking eyes with the Corpsetaker.

I wanted to scream a negation, but nothing came out. I frantically tried to move faster. If I succeeded, it didn't show.

"You want to play head games?" Molly snarled, her blue eyes blazing. "Let's go."

The Corpsetaker's face contorted into an expression somewhere between murderous rage and that of an orgasm, and she opened her stolen eyes wide.

Molly and the dark wizard went into a soul-gaze, and there wasn't a thing I could do about it — except keep trying to get closer.

I could feel power flickering between them, though, like bursts of heat coming out of a furnace, as I got glacially nearer. It was an entirely invisible struggle, a simultaneous and mutual siege of the personality. Mind magic is dangerous, slippery stuff, and doing combat with another mind is all about imagination, focus, and sheer willpower. Right now, Molly was thrusting an array of images and ideas at the Corpsetaker, trying to force the other to pay attention to them. Some of the thoughts would be there to undermine defenses, others to assault them, and still others trying to slip past unnoticed to wreak havoc from within. Some of the thoughts would be simple things — whispered doubts meant to shake the other's confidence, for example. Others would be far more complex constructions, idea demons imagined ahead of time, prepared for such an occasion and unleashed upon the thoughts and memories of the foe.

The White Council hated mind magic, generally speaking. If you beat someone's defenses, you could do a lot of things to them, and precious few of them were good. Events, however, had forced them to acknowledge the necessity of giving all of its members lessons in psychic self-defense that were more comprehensive than the simple wall technique that I'd been briefly introduced to. A couple of old-timers who knew how to play the game had begun dispensing the basics to everyone interested in learning.

As it turned out, I had a natural fortress of

personality, which explained a lot — like how hard it had always been for faerie glamour to trick me for long, and why I'd been able to grind through several forms of mental assault over the years. If someone came in after me, they had a big badass castle to contend with. They could pound on it all day, as such things were measured, without breaking the defenses, and I'd been told that it would take an extended campaign to conquer my head entirely — like any decent castle, there were multiple lines and structures where new defenses could take hold. But I didn't have much of a forward game. For me, the best offense had to be an obstinate defense.

Molly, on the other hand . . . well. Molly was sort of scary.

Her castle wasn't huge and imposing — the damned thing was invisible. Made of mirrors, covered in fog, wrapped in darkness, and generally hard even to pin down, much less besiege; anyone who went into her head had better bring a GPS, a seeing-eye dog, and a backup set of eyeballs. Worse, her offense was like dealing with a Mongolian horde. She'd send in waves and waves of every kind of mental construction imaginable, and while you were busy looking at those, ninja thoughts would be sneaking through your subconscious, planting the psychological equivalent of explosives. We'd practiced against each other a lot — immovable object versus irresistible force. It generally ended in a draw, when Molly had to quit and nurse a headache, at which point I would join her in scarfing down aspirin. A couple of times, my thuggish constructions had stumbled over her defenses and started breaking mirrors. A couple of times, her horde had gotten lucky or particularly sneaky. We'd had the same thought-image set up to signal victory — Vader swooping down in his TIE fighter, smugly stating, "I have you now." Once that got through, the game was over.

But outside of practice, that thought could just as easily be something more like, "Put your gun into your mouth and pull the trigger." We both knew that. We both worked hard to improve as a result. It was a part of the training I'd taken every bit as seriously as teaching her theory or enchantments or exorcism, or any of a hundred other areas we'd covered over the past few years.

But we'd never done it for blood.

The Corpsetaker moved Butters's hands up to gently frame Molly's cheeks and said, "My, my, my. Training standards have improved."

Molly slammed Corpsetaker's head back against the wall with a short, harsh motion, and said, "Stop squirming and fight."

Corpsetaker bared Butters's teeth in a slow grin, and suddenly surged forward, slamming Molly's back against the opposite wall while simultaneously moving up a stair, so that their eyes were on the same level. "Slippery little girl. But I was crushing minds like yours centuries before your great-grandfather's grandfather left the Old Country."

Molly suddenly let out a gasp, and her face twisted in pain.

"They never have the stomach to hurt their darling little apprentices," Corpsetaker crooned. "That's called pain. Let me give you a lesson."

"Lady," Molly panted, "did you pick the wrong part of my life in which to mess with me." She took a deep breath and spoke in a ringing, furious voice. "Now get the fuck out of my friend. *Ideru!*"

I felt the surge of her will as she spoke the word, and suddenly reality seemed to condense around my apprentice. There was a terrible, terrible force that ripped forth from her, pulling hungrily at everything around it. I'd felt something similar once, when a nascent White Court vampire had unintentionally begun to feed on me — an energy that spiraled and swirled and pulled at the roots of my senses. But that was only one facet of the gravity that Molly exuded with the spell.

Corpsetaker's eyes widened in surprise and sudden strain. Then she snarled, "Have it your way. The little doctor was my second choice, in any case."

And then I *saw* Corpsetaker's dark, mad

soul flow into my apprentice on the tidal pull of the beckoning she'd performed.

The expression of Butters's face went empty and he collapsed, utterly without movement of any kind. Three feet away, his shade's helpless, confused gaze locked onto his fallen physical form, and his eyes went wide with terror.

Molly screamed in sudden shock — and fear. In that instant, I saw in her eyes the reflection of her terror, the panic of someone who has come loaded for bear and found herself face-to-face with a freaking dinosaur instead.

My drifting, dream-slow advance had finally gotten me close enough. With sluggish and agonizing grace, I stretched out one hand . . .

. . . and caught the Corpsetaker's ankle as she slithered into my apprentice.

I settled my grip grimly and felt myself pulled forward, into the havoc of the war for Molly's body, mind, and soul.

CHAPTER FORTY-NINE

I landed in the middle of a war.

There was a ruined city all around me. The sky above boiled with storm clouds, moving and roiling too quickly to be real, filled with contrasting colors of lightning. Rain hammered down. I heard screams and shouted imprecations all around me, overlapping one another, coming from thousands of sources, blending into a riotous roar — and every single voice was either Molly's or the Corpsetaker's.

As I watched, some great beast somewhere between a serpent and a whale smashed its way through a brick building — a fortress, I realized — maybe fifty yards away, thrashing about as it fell and grinding it to powder. A small trio of dots of bright red light appeared on the vast thing's rubble-dusted flanks, just like the targeting of the Predator's shoulder cannon in the movies of the same name, and then multiple streaks of blue-white light flashed in from somewhere and blew a series of holes the size of train tunnels right through the creature. Around me, I saw groups of soldiers, many of them in sinister black uniforms, others looking like idealized versions of United States infantry, laying into one another with weapons of every sort imaginable, from swords to rocket launchers.

A line of tracer fire went streaking right through me, having no more effect than a stiff breeze. I breathed a faint sigh of relief. I was inside Molly's mindscape, but her conflict was not with *me,* and neither was the Corpsetaker's. I was just as much a ghost here at the moment as I had been back in the real world.

The city around me, I saw, was a vast grid of fortified buildings, and I realized that the kid had changed her usual tactics. She wasn't trying to obscure the location of her mental fortress with the usual tricks of darkness and fog. She had instead chosen a different method of obfuscation, building a sprawl of decoys, hiding the true core of her mind somewhere among them.

Corpsetaker had countered her, it would seem, by the simple if difficult expedient of deciding to crush them *all,* even if it had to be done one at a time. That vast beast construct had been something more massive than I had ever attempted in my own imagination, though Molly had tossed some of those at me once or twice. It wasn't simply a matter of thinking big — there was an energy investment in creating something with that kind of mental mass, and Molly generally felt such huge, unsubtle thrusts weren't worth the effort they took — especially since someone with the right attitude and imagination would take them down with only moderately more difficulty than small constructs.

Corpsetaker, though, evidently didn't agree. She was a lot older than Molly or me, and she would have deeper reserves of strength to call upon, greater discipline, and the confidence of long experience. The kid had managed to take on the Corpsetaker on Molly's most familiar ground, and to play her hand in her strongest suit — but my apprentice's strength didn't look like it was holding up well against the necromancer's experience and expertise.

I stopped paying attention to everything happening — all the artillery strikes and cavalry charges and shambling hordes of zombies and storms of knives that just came whirling out of the sky. The form of any given construct wasn't as important as the fact of its existence. A flying arrow that could pierce the heart, for example, was potentially just as dangerous as an animate shadow reaching out with smothering black talons. As long as one could imagine an appropriate construct to counter the threat, and do so in time to stop it, any construct could be defeated. It was a simple thing at its most basic level, and it sounded easy. But once you're throwing out dozens or hundreds — or thousands — of offensive and defensive constructs at a time . . . Believe me — it takes your full attention.

It's also all you can do to deal with one opponent, which explained why I hadn't been assaulted by the Corpsetaker instantly, if she had even taken note of my presence at all. She and Molly were locked together tight. The soulgaze had probably played a part in that. Neither was letting go until her opponent was dead.

Both combatants were throwing enormous amounts of offensive constructs at each other, even though Molly was demolishing her own defenses almost as rapidly as the Corpsetaker was. As tactics go, that one had two edges. Molly was hurting herself, but by doing so, she was preventing the Corpsetaker from pressing too closely, lest she be caught up in the vast bursts of destruction being exchanged. A mistake could easily destroy anyone's mind in that vista of havoc, centuries-old necromancer or not. On the other hand, if she spotted where Molly was fighting from, it looked like she'd have the power to drive in and crush my apprentice. But if she closed in on the wrong target, she'd leave herself wide-open to a surprise attack from the real Molly. Corpsetaker had to know that, just as she had to know that if she simply kept on the pressure, the whole place would eventually be ground down and Molly would be destroyed anyway.

My apprentice had come with a good plan, but she had miscalculated. The Corpsetaker was a hell of a lot stronger than she had expected. Molly was playing the most aggressive defensive plan I'd ever seen, and hoping that she could pressure the Corpsetaker into making a mistake. It wasn't a good plan, but it was all she had.

One way or another, it wasn't going to be a long fight. Best if I got moving.

Molly was here somewhere in the sprawl of fake strongholds, and she would be just as hidden from me as from the Corpsetaker. But I had an advantage that the necromancer didn't: I knew my apprentice.

This wasn't the Nevernever. We were in Molly's head, inside a world of thought and imagination. There was no magic involved — not now that we were here anyway. I might be a slender wisp of a ghost, but I still had my brain, and that gave me certain liberties here.

I went over to the ruined building, where the monster thing was groaning through its death. I heaved aside a piece of rubble and pulled a pale blue bathroom rug, stained with dust and weird purple blood, out of the wreckage. It was a tiny piece of an environmental construct, but even so, it was a serious effort to appropriate it as my own. My arms shook with weakness as I lifted the carpet and snapped it once. Blood and dust flew from it as if it had never existed, and then I settled it calmly on flat ground, sat on it, and folded my legs and my arms in front of me.

"Up, Simba," I said in my best attempt to imitate Yul Brynner, and the carpet quivered and then rose off the ground, staying as rigid and almost as comfortable as a sheet of heavy plywood. It rose straight in the air, and as it did, I gripped the edges surreptitiously. It wouldn't do to have either my enemy or my apprentice get a glimpse of me flailing wildly for my balance as the carpet moved. But on the other hand, I didn't want to just fall off, either. I could probably come up with something to keep me from getting hurt when I hit the ground, but it would look awfully bad, and I don't care how close to dead he might be; a wizard has his pride.

Granted, the imagination was the only place where I was going to get one of these darned things to work. I'd tried the flying-carpet thing before, when I was about twenty. It had been a fairly horrible experiment that had dropped me into a not-yet-closed landfill during a thunderstorm. And then there was the famous flying-broomstick incident of Wacker Drive, which wound up on the Internet as a

UFO sighting. After that, I had wisely determined that flying was mostly just a great way to get killed and settled for driving my old car around instead.

But hey. In my imagination, that carpet had worked great — and that was how it went as a guest in Molly's imagination, too.

I went up high enough to get a good view — and was impressed with the kid. The city of fortresses stretched for miles. There were hundreds of them, and fighting raged all the way through. It was the opposite of what the kid usually did in a mental battle — an inverse Mongol horde, with endless defenders pouring out like angry bees to defend the hive. Corpsetaker, unfortunately, was playing mama bear to Molly's queen bee. She'd get hurt coming in, but as long as she wasn't stupid, not very badly. She could crush all the defenders eventually — and then rip the hive to shreds.

I leaned forward a little and the carpet began to gather speed, moving ahead. Shifts of my weight to the left or right let me bank, and it wasn't long before I was cruising through the rain as fast as I could and still keeping my eyes clear. I flew a spiral pattern, scanning the city beneath me. The battle kept going in the skies, too — mostly flying demon things and lightning bolts that kept smashing them out of the air. It got boring to watch after the first dozen spectacular lightning strikes or so, and I tuned that conflict out, too, as I kept searching.

Finally, I spotted what I was looking for: a ruined building that had been reduced to a crater by an artillery shell or some other explosion. It was impossible to tell what it had been from what was left, and burned rubble covered the area around it, coating a thick-bodied old oak tree and the tree house on its lower branches in dust, dirt, and debris.

I went past the tree house without stopping or slowing down for several more minutes, and then went evasive. I couldn't be sure the Corpsetaker didn't know I had ridden in on her coattails, and if she was following me, or had sent a construct to do so, I didn't want to lead her to Molly. So the carpet went from forty or fifty miles an hour to more than a hundred, and at the same time I constructed a veil around me so that I surged forward and simply vanished. I flew low, snaking through the streets, and only after I'd crossed my own trail five or six times without spotting anything shadowing me did I finally soar in to the tree house.

It looked like a miniature home, with a door and siding and trim and windows and everything. A rope ladder allowed one to climb up to the porch, but it had been pulled up. I floated up to the door on the flying carpet and knocked politely.

"I have you now," I said, as much like James

Earl Jones as I could. I do a better Yul Brynner.

Molly's strained face appeared at the window and she blinked. "Harry?"

"What's with the come-hither, grasshopper?" I asked. "You practically vacuumed me in with the Corpsetaker."

Molly narrowed her eyes and said, "What was I wearing the first time we met?"

I blinked at her, opened my mouth, closed it, thought about it, and then said, "Oh, come *on,* Moll. I have no idea. Clothes? You were, like, eight years old and your mom tried to shut the door in my face and I was there to see your dad."

She nodded once, as if that was the answer she'd been looking for, and opened the door. "Come on."

I went into the tree house with her.

The inside was bigger than the outside. You can do that sort of thing in your imagination. It's kind of fun. I've got one closet of my castle that looks like a giant disco roller rink. The roller skaters come after you like juggernaut, the music makes heads explode, and the mirror ball distributes a killer laser beam.

Molly's headquarters looked like the bridge of, I kid you not, the U.S.S. *Enterprise.* The old one. The one that was full of dials that obviously didn't do anything and that had a high-pitched, echoing cricket chirp going off every five or six seconds.

There was an upside to that setting, though: Molly was wearing one of the old sixties miniskirt uniforms.

Look, I'm not interested in a relationship with the kid. I do love her tremendously. But that doesn't mean that she doesn't look fantastic. Anyone with eyes can see that, and I've always been the kind of person who can appreciate gorgeous scenery without feeling a need to go camping in it.

Actually, glancing around, there were about half a dozen Mollys, all of them wearing old sixties miniskirt uniforms, each of them manning a different station. The one who had opened the door had jet-black hair in a neat, almost mathematical, gamine-style cut and slightly pointed ears.

"*Star Trek*?" I asked her. "Really?"

"What?" she demanded, bending unnaturally black eyebrows together.

"There are two kinds of people in the universe, Molly," I said. "*Star Trek* fans and *Star Wars* fans. This is shocking."

She sniffed. "This is the post-nerd-closet world, Harry. It's okay to like both."

"Blasphemy and lies," I said.

She arched an eyebrow at me with Nimoysian perfection and went back to her station.

Communications Officer Molly, in a red uniform with a curly black fro and a silver object the size of a toaster in her ear, said, "Quadrant four is below five percent, and the extra pressure is being directed at quadrant three."

Captain Molly, in her gold outfit, with her hair in a precise Jacqueline Onassis do, spun the bridge chair toward Communications Molly and said, "Pull out everything and shift it to quadrant three ahead of them." The chair spun back toward Science Officer Molly. "Set off the nukes in four."

Science Molly arched an eyebrow, askance.

"Oh, hush. I'm the captain, you're the first officer, and that's that," snapped Captain Molly. "We're fighting a war here. So set off the nukes. Hi, Harry."

"Molly," I said. "Nukes?"

"I was saving them as a surprise," she said.

There was a big TV screen at the front of the room — not a flat-screen. A big, slightly curved old CRT. It went bright white all of a sudden.

"Ensign," Captain Molly said.

Ensign Molly, dressed in a red uniform, wearing braces on her teeth, and maybe ten years younger than Captain Molly, twiddled some of the dials that didn't do anything, and the bright white light dimmed down.

From outside, there was a long scream. An enormous one. Like, Godzilla-sized, or maybe bigger.

Everyone on the bridge froze. A brass section from nowhere played an ominous sting: *bahm-pahhhhhhhhhm.*

"You're kidding," I said, looking around. "A sound track?"

"I don't mean to," Ensign Molly said in a strained, teenager tone. She had a Russian accent that sounded exactly like Sanya. "I watched show too much when I was kid, okay?"

"Your brain is a very strange place," I said. I meant it as a compliment, and it showed in my voice. Ensign Molly gave me a glowing grin and turned back to her station.

I walked to the right-hand side of the captain's chair and folded my arms. The screen came up to light again, showing a devastated section of the city grid. No, not decimated. Had that part of the city been decimated, one out of every ten buildings would be destroyed. That's what *decimated* means. Personally, I think some early-years, respected television personality got *decimated* and *devastated* confused at some point, and no one wanted to point it out to him, so everyone started using them interchangeably. But dammit, words mean what they mean, even if everyone thinks they ought to mean something else.

Science Molly spoke in a grim voice. "Nuclear detonation confirmed. Enemy forces in quadrant four have been decimated, Captain."

I pressed my lips firmly together.

"Thank you, Number One," Captain Molly

said, spinning back to face the front. "Harry, um. Help?"

"Not sure what I can do, grasshopper," I told her seriously. "I barely managed to steal a bathroom rug from some rubble and whip up a flying carpet. Her stuff goes right through me, and vice versa."

She looked at me for a moment, and I saw the same look of fear flicker over every face on the bridge. Then she took a deep breath, nodded, and turned to face the front. She started giving smooth orders, and her other selves replied in calm, steady voices.

After a few moments, Captain Molly said, "If you aren't here to . . . I mean, if you can't help, why are you here?"

"Because you're here," I said calmly. "Least I can do is stand with you."

"If she wins . . ." Captain Molly swallowed. "You'll die."

I snorted and flashed her a grin. "Best thing about being a spook, grasshopper. I'm already dead."

"Quadrant three is collapsing," Communications Officer Molly reported. "Quadrant two is at twenty percent."

Captain Molly bit her lip.

"How many quadrants?" I asked her.

"Four," she said. "Since, you know. *Quad*-rants."

I wanted to say something about *deci*mated, but I didn't. "We're in quadrant one?"

Captain Molly nodded. "I . . . don't think I can stop her, Harry."

"Fight's not over until it's over, kid," I said. "Don't let her beat you. Make her work for it."

Science Molly said, in a firm tone, "Death is not the only consequence here. Should the Corpsetaker prevail, she will have full access to our talents, abilities, memories, and knowledge. Even though we have spent the last months distancing ourselves from others to insulate against a situation such as this one, the Corpsetaker could still inflict considerable damage on not only our friends and family, but on complete innocents. That is unacceptable, Captain."

Captain Molly looked from Science Molly to me and then said, "The fight isn't over yet. Prepare the Omega Bomb, but do not deploy."

"Aye, aye," said Science Molly, and she stood up and strode to the other side of the bridge — and an old wooden cabinet beside an old wooden door.

I blinked at it. "Wow. That's . . . kind of out of theme."

Captain Molly coughed loudly. "That? That's nothing to worry about. Pay it no mind."

I watched Science Molly get a device the size of a small microwave out of the old cabinet and push one button on it. Then she set it on the console next to her.

"Um," I said. "Omega Bomb?"

"The Corpsetaker doesn't get me," Captain Molly said in a firm tone. "Ever."

"And it's in that old wooden cabinet because . . . ?"

"I don't know what you're talking about," said Captain Molly dismissively. "Ensign, bring up the screen for quadrant two."

I eased away from Captain Molly as she kept commanding the battle, and went over to stand next to Science Molly. "Um. The captain doesn't seem to want me to know about that door."

"Definitely not," said Science Molly, also in confidential tones. "It's a need-to-know door."

"Why?"

"Because if you know about it, you're one of the ones who needs to know about it," she replied calmly. "And if you don't, it's better that you not know. The captain feels you've suffered enough."

"Suffered enough?" I asked. "What do you mean?"

"I have nothing further to say on the subject," said Science Molly.

"It's my fault," Ensign Molly said. "Sorry. Look, I don't mean to, with the cabinet and the door, okay? But I can't help it."

You ever get that feeling you're standing in a room full of crazy people?

I got that feeling. It isn't a very nice feeling.

I stared at the door and the old wooden cabinet. It wasn't a particularly outstanding door in any way — a standard hanging door, if rather old and battered. Ditto the cabinet. Both had been stained a medium brown, apparently a very long time ago. Both were covered with dings and dents, not as though something had tried to break them down, but simply from years and years of use.

They looked sort of familiar.

I studied the door and the cabinet thoughtfully, glancing occasionally at the big old CRT as quadrant two buckled under the Corpsetaker's assault. The fighting had been fierce, but she still hadn't revealed herself, and Molly hadn't managed to kill her with the nukes or the assault would have ended with her. Another quadrant went, and Captain Molly detonated another set of massive nuke constructs. Then a third, and more nukes. Neither of the second pair of detonations was followed by a massive scream, the way the first one had been. Molly had bloodied the Corpsetaker, presumably, but it hadn't been enough.

"Dammit," Captain Molly said, clenching one fist and staring at the screen. "She's got to be near now. But where?"

The streets outside were so full of battling constructs that they were literally piling up with bodies, slowing the progress of the enemy — but not stopping it.

Dammit, I felt helpless. Just standing next to the kid wasn't going to do her any good, but I was holding on to the world by a thread. I just didn't have the ability to make things happen, either here or in the real world. All I could do was . . .

. . . was use my freaking *brain. Duh.*

"Wait," I said. "Molly, I've got an idea."

All the Mollys turned to look at me.

I turned to Captain Molly. "Slow her down," I said. "You've got to slow the Corpsetaker down. Whatever you have to do, you need to buy some time. Go!"

Captain Molly blinked at me. Then she turned and started snapping orders. The bridge Mollys started twisting dials and punching keys.

I turned to Communications Molly. "Hey, you do communications, right?"

She looked baffled. "Right."

"We need to communicate," I said. "You need to make a long-distance call."

"Now?" Communications Molly said, her eyes widening.

"Right the *hell* now," I corrected her. I leaned down and explained what I needed in terse tones.

"That's going to be tricky," she said. "We're already at one hundred percent on the reactor."

I put on my best Sean Connery voice.

"Then go to a hundred and ten pershent."

Science Molly arched an eyebrow at me and punched a button. "Engineering, Bridge."

"Aye!" screamed a furious Scottish-accented Molly. "What do ye want now?"

"More power, Engineer."

The answer was a furious rush of pure profanity — but the deep engine-hum in the background around us went upward a bit, and the floor started to vibrate.

Science Molly pointed at Communications Molly and said, "Go."

"Mayday," Communications Molly said into her console. "This is a mayday. Emergency transmission. We urgently require assistance. . . ."

Suddenly everything lurched to one side and we all staggered.

"Oh, I don't believe this crap," I muttered.

"She's found us, Captain," said Science Molly. "Shields at seventy percent."

"Hit her with everything!" Captain Molly snapped.

"Finally," growled Tactical Molly, who sat next to Ensign Molly, wearing a gold uniform almost identical to Captain Molly's. She'd been sitting there doing absolutely nothing and looking bored the entire time I'd been there. Now she turned and started jabbing buttons, and cheesy sound effects filled the bridge.

"Minimal damage," reported Science Molly.

The bridge rocked again and we staggered. One of the panels exploded in a shower of sparks. Some Molly in a red uniform who hadn't spoken crashed limply to the deck.

"Not real," Ensign Molly said. "Sorry; my bad. Some things you just can't get rid of."

Damage alarms started wailing. They sounded like a badly distorted version of a young woman screaming.

"Shields have failed, Captain!" Science Molly reported.

And she reached for the Omega Bomb.

"No!" I snapped. "Stop her!"

Captain Molly took one look at me and then leapt at Science Molly. She seized the Omega Bomb. "Stop!" she ordered.

"There is no room for emotion here," snapped Science Molly. "It's over. This is all you can do to protect them."

"I gave you an order!" snapped Captain Molly.

"You're letting your fear control you," replied Science Molly coldly. "This is the only logical way."

Captain Molly screamed in incoherent rage and slugged Science Molly in the face.

Science Molly screamed back, and swung a fist into Captain Molly's stomach.

Music started playing. Loud. High-pitched. Strident. Most would recognize it.

"Sorry!" Ensign Molly called, cringing.

I hurried forward to grab at the struggling Mollys — and my hands went right through them. Right. I was an observer here. Welcome, sure, but if I wanted to control what was going on, I had to do it the hard way, like Corpsetaker was doing.

I turned to Ensign Molly and said, "Dammit, do something!"

"There's nothing I can do," she said, her eyes uncertain and full of sadness. "They've been like that ever since they killed you."

I stared at Molly and felt my mouth fall open.

Time stopped.

The door. The old wooden door.

The cabinet where Molly had kept her suicide device.

I turned toward them.

My godmother's voice echoed in my head.

You are currently freed of the shackles of mortality. Your limited brain no longer impedes access to that record. The only blocks to your memory are those you allow to be.

I remembered the door. The cabinet.

I *remembered* the past.

Sanya had insisted that they keep me on the backboard when they carried me into St. Mary of the Angels, after my apartment burned down. The dark-skinned Knight of the Cross carried me from his minivan and into the church alone, toting the board and my couple of hundred pounds and change on one shoulder, as if I'd been a big sack of doggy chow.

Molly had gone ahead of him, worried, speaking rapidly to someone. I wasn't sure who — one of the priests, I guessed. I hurt everywhere I could feel. And in the places I couldn't feel, I only wished I could hurt.

My body, from the waist down, had stopped talking to me altogether.

I'd fallen off a ladder while trying to get some of my elderly neighbors out of the burning building and landed on a stone planter. Landed bad, and on my back. I've gotten lucky occasionally. This time I hadn't. I knew what the fall, the point of impact, and the lack of sensation in my lower body meant.

I'd broken my back.

The Red King had my daughter. I was the only one who was going to do anything about it. And I'd fallen and broken my back.

Sanya carried me into the utility room that was mostly used for storage — particularly for storing a battered wizard and his friends when they needed the refuge the church offered. There were a number of folding cots in the room, stored for use. Sanya set me down, rolled out a cot, put some sheets on it, and then placed me on the cot, backboard and all.

"Might as well leave me on the floor," I told

him. "I'm lying on a board either way."

"Pffft," Sanya said, his dark, handsome face lighting up with a white grin. "I do not care to clean the floor after you leave. Someone else can do the sheets."

"Says you," I said. "You smell like burning hair."

"Some of it was on fire," he said cheerfully. His eyes, though, were less jovial. He put a hand on my chest and said, "You are badly hurt."

"Yeah."

"You want a drink?" he asked. One hand hovered near his jacket's breast pocket, where I knew he kept his flask.

"Pass. Maybe I'll just cope instead."

He made another disgusted noise and produced said flask, took a swig from it, and winked at me. "I was never clear on the difference. *Da?*"

Molly appeared in the doorway, and Sanya looked at her.

"He's on the way," Molly said. Her voice was strained. Her day hadn't been as bad as mine, but she still looked shaken.

Sanya offered Molly a pull from the flask. She shook her head. "Very good," the big Russian said. "I will talk to Forthill, tell him what is happening."

"Sanya," Molly said, putting a hand on his arm. "Thank you."

He gave her a wide grin. "Perhaps it was

just a coincidence I arrived when I did."

Molly rolled her eyes and gave him a faint shove toward the door. It didn't move the big man, but he went, and Molly flicked on a little lamp and shut the door behind him. She walked over to me and took a couple of KFC wet wipes from her bag. She knelt down next to the cot, opened them, and started cleaning my face.

I closed my eyes and said nothing.

My little girl was going to die.

My little girl was going to *die.*

And there was nothing I could do about it.

Oh, I'd been defeated before. People had even died because I failed. But those people had never been my own flesh and blood. They hadn't been my child. I'd lost. I was beaten.

This was all over.

And it was all your fault, Harry.

If I'd been faster. If I'd been smarter. If I'd been strong enough of mind to make the hard choices, to focus on saving Maggie first and everyone else second . . .

But I hadn't been. I'd been insufficient to the challenge, and she was going to die because of it.

I broke, right there. I just broke. The task given to me had been more than I could bear. And what followed would be nothing but torturous regret. I'd failed my own child.

My chest convulsed, I made a sound, and my eyes filled until I couldn't see.

Molly sat beside me, patiently cleaning my face and neck with her wipes. I must have had soot on my face. When I could see again, there were large patches of grey and black on the wipes and my face felt cold and tingled slightly.

"I've got to help her," I said quietly.

"Harry, don't . . . don't twist the knife in your own wound," Molly replied. "Right now you need to stay calm and quiet, until Butters can look at you."

"I wish you hadn't gotten him involved," I said.

"I didn't even ask him," she said. "I got halfway through the first sentence and he asked where you were. Then said he'd come see you."

I shook my head. "No, I mean . . ." I drew a deep breath. "Kid. I've got to cross a line."

Molly froze, one hand still extended.

"I'm not getting up off this bed alone," I said quietly. "It's my only option."

You run in the circles I do, you get more than a few offers of power. It always comes with a price, usually a hidden one, but you get the offers. I'd had more than a few chances to advance myself, provided I was willing to set aside anything like integrity to do so. I hadn't been.

Not until today.

"Who?" Molly asked simply.

My mouth twitched at one corner. "One is

a lot like another," I said.

She shook her head. "But . . . but if you go over to one of them . . ."

"They'll make me into a monster," I said quietly. "Sooner or later."

She wouldn't look at me.

"I can't let that happen," I said. "For all I know, I could turn into something that would hurt Maggie myself. But maybe I can use them to get her out of danger."

She inhaled sharply and looked up at me.

"It's got to be Mab," I said. "She's wicked smart, but she isn't omniscient or infallible. I've swindled faeries before. I can do it again."

She inhaled sharply. "You're going to be the Winter Knight?" She shook her head. "What if she doesn't? I mean, what if she won't?"

I let out a low chuckle. "Oh, she'll do it. If I go to her, she'll do it. She's been after me long enough."

"I don't understand," Molly said. "She'll . . . she'll twist you. Change you. It's what they do."

I fumbled and put one of my hands on hers. "Molls . . . Whatever happens . . . I'm not going to make it out of this one."

She stared at me for a minute. Then she shook her head. She shook her head and silent tears fell from her eyes.

"Molly," I said again, patting her hand. "Kid . . . For everything there is a season."

"Don't," she said. "Don't you dare quote the Bible at me. Not to justify this."

"Bible?" I said. "I was quoting the Byrds."

She burst out in a huffing sound that was both a laugh and sob.

"Look, Molls. Nothing lasts forever. Nothing. And if I've got to choose between myself and my daughter? That's not even a choice. You know that."

She bowed her head and wept harder. But I saw her nod. Just a little.

"I need your help," I said.

She looked up at me, bloodshot eyes a mess.

"I'm going to arrange things. But Mab's going to be wary of me. She knows my history, and if I know what's going on, she'll be able to tell I'm lying to her. I don't have enough of a poker face for that."

"No," Molly said, sniffing and briskly swiping at her eyes. "You don't. You still suck at lying, boss."

"To the people who know me, maybe," I said, smiling. "Do you understand what I'm asking you to do?"

She bit her lip and said, "Do you? Have you thought what it's going to mean for me once . . . once you're . . ."

"Dead," I said quietly. "I think Ebenezar or Injun Joe will take over for me, continue your training. They both know how strongly I felt about sheltering you from the Council's judgment."

She looked suddenly exhausted. She shook her head slightly. "That's not what I meant."

"Oh," I said.

Molly had crushed on me since she was a teenager. I hadn't really thought anything of it. I mean, it had been going on for years and . . .

. . . and crushes probably didn't last for years. Did they? They faded. Molly's feelings hadn't, but I didn't reciprocate them. I loved her to pieces, but I was never going to be in love with her.

Especially not if I was dead, I guess.

If our positions had been reversed, that might have been kind of hard for me to accept, too.

I patted her hand again awkwardly and said, "I'm sorry. That I wasn't here longer. That it couldn't be more than it was."

"You never did anything wrong by me, Harry," she said. She lifted her chin and met my eyes again. "This isn't about me, though, is it? It's about Maggie." She nodded, and I saw steel enter her spine. "So of course I'll help you."

I lifted her fingers to my mouth and put a gentle kiss on them. "You're one hell of a woman, Molly," I said. "Thank you."

She shivered. Then she said, "How do you want to do it?"

"Bring me a phone," I said. "Need to make a call. You stay out of it. It'll be better if you don't know."

"Okay," she said. "Then?"

"Then you come back in here. You put me to sleep. You take the memory of this conversation and the phone call out of my head."

"How?" she asked. "If I leave any obvious holes, it could hurt you — and it might be visible to something as powerful as Mab."

I thought about it for a moment and said, "I nodded off in the van on the way here. Set it up so that I was never awake once I was here, until I wake up after."

She thought about it and said, "It could work. If I do it slowly enough, it might not leave a ripple."

"Do it like that, then."

She stood up. She walked over to a battered old wooden cabinet on the wall and opened it. Among other things, there was an old, freestanding rotary phone inside it, attached to a long extension cord, a makeshift line that Forthill had run through the drywall from the next room. She brought the phone to me and set it carefully on my chest. Then she walked to the similarly battered old wooden door.

"You realize," she said, "that I could change this, Harry. Could find out who you were using to kill yourself. I could take it right out of your head and call them off. You'd never know."

"You could do that," I said, quietly. "And I

feel like an utter bastard for asking this of you, grasshopper. But I don't have anyone else to ask."

"You should call Thomas," she said. "He deserves the truth."

Thomas. My brother. My family. He'd be one of little Maggie's only blood relations once I was gone. And Molly was right. He did deserve the truth.

"No," I said, barely louder than a whisper. "Tell him later, if you want. After. If you tell him before that, he won't stand for it. He'll try to stop it."

"And maybe he'd be right to do it."

"No," I said quietly. "He wouldn't. But he'd do it anyway. This is my choice, Molls."

She turned to go and paused. "You've never called me Molls before today."

"Was saving it," I said. "For when you weren't my apprentice anymore. Wanted to try it out."

She smiled at me. She shed one more tear. Then she left.

It took me a moment to gather myself. Then I dialed an international number on the rotary phone.

"Kincaid," answered a flat voice.

"It's Dresden," I said.

The voice warmed very slightly. "Harry. What's up?"

I took a deep breath. "You owe me a favor,"

I said quietly. "For that thing with Ivy on the island."

"Damn right," he said.

"I'm calling it in."

"Okay," he said. "You want some backup on something?"

"I have a target for you."

There was a silence from the other end of the phone. Then he said, "Tell me."

"The new Winter Knight," I said.

"There's a new one?"

"There's going to be," I said.

"How do you . . ." More silence. Then he said, "It's like that."

"There's a good reason," I said.

"Yeah?"

"There's a little girl."

More silence. "You'll know it's coming."

"No," I said. "I won't. I'll see to it."

"Okay," he said. "When?"

They were going to kill my daughter sometime before the next sunrise. I figured it might take me some time to get her home, assuming I didn't die trying.

"Anytime after noon tomorrow," I said. "The sooner, the better."

"Okay."

"You can find me?"

"Yeah."

"Be sure," I said.

"I pay my debts."

I sighed again. "Yeah. Thanks."

He let out a soft chuckle. "Thanking me," he said. "That's new."

He hung up. I did the same. Then I called for Molly.

"Okay," I said. "Let's do this."

Molly took the phone and put it back in the cabinet. Then she picked up a slender, new white candle in a holder and a small box of matches. She came over and set the candle on a folding table nearby, where I could see it without moving my head. She struck a match and lit it.

"All right," she said. "Harry, this has to be a smooth, gentle job. So focus on the candle. I need you to still your mind so that I can work."

It felt odd, letting the grasshopper take the lead — but I guess that was what I'd been training her to do. I focused on the candle and began to quiet my thoughts.

"Good," Molly said quietly after a moment, her voice soft velvet. "Relax. Take a nice, slow, deep breath. Good . . . Listen to my voice and let me guide you. Another deep breath now . . ."

And together with my accomplice, I finished arranging my murder.

CHAPTER FIFTY

I surfaced from the memory, shivering, and looked around in confusion. I was still in Molly's mindscape, on the cheesy bridge. It was silent. Completely silent. Nothing moved. The images on the screen and the various Mollys were all frozen in place like mannequins. Everything that had been happening in the battle had been happening at the speed of thought — lightning fast. There was only one reason that everything here would be stopped still like this, right in the middle of the action.

"So much for that linear-time nonsense, eh?" My voice came out sounding harsh and rough.

Footsteps sounded behind me, and the room began to grow brighter and brighter. After a moment, there was nothing but white light, and I had to hold up a hand to shield my eyes against it.

Then the light faded somewhat. I lifted my eyes again and found myself in a featureless expanse of white. I wasn't even sure what I was standing on, or if I was standing on anything at all. There was simply nothing but white . . .

. . . and a young man with hair of dark gold that hung messily down over silver blue eyes. His cheekbones could have sliced bread. He wore jeans, old boots, a white shirt, and a denim jacket, and no youth born had ever been able to stand with such utter, tranquil stillness as he.

"You're used to linear time," he said. His voice was resonant, deep, mellow, with the almost musical timbre you hear from radio personalities. "It was the easiest way to help you understand."

"Aren't you a little short for an archangel?" I asked him.

Uriel smiled at me. It was the sort of expression that would make flowers spontaneously blossom and babies start to giggle. "Appropriate. I must confess to being more of a *Star Wars* fan than a *Star Trek* fan, personally. The simple division of good and evil, the clarity of perfect right and perfect wrong — it's relaxing. It makes me feel young."

I just stared at him for a moment and tried to gather my thoughts. The memory, now that I had it again, was painfully vivid. God, that poor kid. Molly. I'd never wanted to cause her pain. She'd been a willing accomplice, and she'd done it with her eyes open — but,

God, I wished it hadn't had to happen to her. She was hurting so much, and now I could see why — and I could see why the madness she was feigning might be a great deal more genuine than she realized.

That had to have been why Murphy distrusted her so strongly. Murph had excellent instincts for people. She must have sensed something in Molly, sensed the pain and the desperation that drove her, and it must have sent up a warning flag in Murphy's head. Which would have hurt Molly badly, to be faced with suspicion and distrust, however polite Karrin might have been about it. That pain would, in turn, have driven her further away, made her act stranger, which would earn more suspicion, in an agonizing cycle.

I'd never wanted that for her.

What had I done?

I'd saved Maggie — but had I destroyed my apprentice in doing so? The fact that I'd gotten myself killed had no relative bearing on the morality of my actions, if I had. You can't just walk around picking and choosing which lives to save and which to destroy. The inherent arrogance and the underlying evil of such a thing runs too deep to be avoided — no matter how good your intentions might be.

I knew why Molly had tried to get me to tell Thomas. She'd known, just as I had, that Thomas would try to stop me from killing myself, regardless of my motivations. But she'd been right about something else, too: He was my brother. He'd deserved more than I'd given him. That was why I hadn't thought of him, not once since returning to Chicago. How could I possibly have remembered my brother without remembering the shame I felt at excluding him from my trust? How could I think of Thomas without thinking of the truth of what I had done?

Normally, I would never have believed that I was the sort of man who could make himself forget and overlook something rather than facing a harsh reality, no matter how painful it might be.

I guess I'm not perfect.

The young man facing me waited patiently, apparently giving me time to gather my thoughts, saying nothing.

Uriel. I should have known from the outset. Uriel is the archangel who most people know little about. Most don't even know his name — and apparently he likes it that way. If Gabriel is an ambassador, if Michael is a general, if Rafael is a healer and spiritual champion, then Uriel is a spymaster — Heaven's spook. Uriel covered all kinds of covert work for the Almighty. When mysterious angels showed up to wrestle with biblical patriarchs without revealing their identities, when death was visited upon the firstborn of Egypt, when an angel was sent into cities of corruption to guide the innocent clear of inbound wrath, Uriel's hand was at work.

He was the quietest of the archangels. To my way of thinking, that probably indicated that he was also the most dangerous.

He'd taken notice of me a few years back and had bestowed a measure of power known as soulfire on me. I'd done a job or three for him since then. He'd dropped by with annoying, cryptic advice once in a while. I sort of liked him, but he was also aggravating — and scary, in a way that I had never known before. There was the sense of something . . . hideously absolute about him. Something that would not yield or change even if the universe itself was unmade. Standing in his presence, I always felt that I had somehow become so fragile that I might fly to dust if the archangel sneezed or accidentally twitched the wrong muscle.

Which, given the kind of power such a being possessed, was probably more or less accurate.

"All of this?" I asked, waving a hand generally, "was to lead me *there?* To that memory?"

"You had to understand."

I eyed him and said wearily, "Epic. Fail. Because I have no idea what you're talking about."

Uriel tilted back his head and laughed. "This is one of those things that was about the journey, not the destination."

I shook my head. "You . . . you lost me."

"On the contrary, Harry: You found your-self."

I eyed him. Then tore at my hair and said, "Arrrgh! Can't you give me a straight answer? Is there some law of the universe that compels you to be so freaking mysterious?"

"Several, actually," Uriel said, still clearly amused. "All designed for your protection, but there are still some things I can tell you."

"Then tell me why," I said. "Why do all this? Why sucker me into going back to Chicago? Why?"

"Jack told you," Uriel said. "They cheated. The scale had to be balanced."

I shook my head. "That office, in Chicago Between. It was yours."

"One of them," he said, nodding. "I have a great deal of work to do. I recruit those will-ing to help me."

"What work?" I asked.

"The same work as I ever have done," Uriel said. "I and my colleagues labor to ensure freedom."

"Freedom of what?" I asked.

"Of will. Of choice. The distinction between good and evil is meaningless if one does not have the freedom to choose between them. It is my duty, my purpose in Creation, to protect and nourish that meaning."

I narrowed my eyes. "So . . . if you're involved in my death . . ." I tilted my head at him. "It's because someone forced me to do it?"

Uriel waggled a hand in a so-so gesture and turned to pace a few steps away. "*Force* implies another will overriding your own," he said over his shoulder. "But there is more than one way for your will to be compromised."

I frowned at him, then said, with dawning comprehension, "Lies."

The archangel turned, his eyebrows lifted, as though I were a somewhat dim student who had surprised his teacher with an insightful answer. "Yes. Precisely. When a lie is believed, it compromises the freedom of your will."

"So, what?" I asked. "Captain Jack and the Purgatory Crew ride to the rescue every time someone tells a lie?"

Uriel laughed. "No, of course not. Mortals are free to lie if they choose to do so. If they could not, they would not be free." His eyes hardened. "But others are held to a higher standard. Their lies are far deadlier, far more potent."

"I don't understand," I said.

"Imagine a being who was *there* when the first mortal drew the first breath," Uriel said. Hard, angry flickers of light danced around us, notable even against formless white. "One who has watched humanity rise from the dust to spread across and to change the very face of the world. One who has seen, quite literally, tens of thousands of mortal lives begin, wax, wane, and end."

"Someone like an angel," I said quietly.

"Someone like that," he said, showing his teeth briefly. "A being who could know a mortal's entire life. Could know his dreams. His fears. His very thoughts. Such a being, so versed in human nature, in mortal patterns of thought, could reliably predict precisely how a given mortal would react to almost anything." Uriel gestured at me. "For example, how he might react to a simple lie delivered at precisely the right moment."

Uriel waved his hand and suddenly we were back in the utility room at St. Mary's. Only I wasn't lying on the backboard on a cot. Or, rather, I was doing exactly that — but I was also standing beside Uriel, at the door, looking in at myself.

"Do you remember what you were thinking?" Uriel asked me.

I did remember. I remembered with perfect clarity, in fact.

"I thought that I'd been defeated before. That people had even died because I failed. But those people had never been my own flesh and blood. They hadn't been my child. I'd lost. I was beaten." I shook my head. "I remember saying to myself that it was all over. And it was all your fault, Harry."

"Ah," Uriel said as I finished the last

sentence, and he lifted his hand. "Now look."

I blinked at him and then at the image of me lying on the cot. "I don't . . ." I frowned. There was something odd about the shadows in the room, but . . .

"Here," Uriel said, lifting a hand. Light shone from it as though from a sudden sunrise. It revealed the room, casting everything in stark relief — and I saw it.

A slender shadow crouched beside the cot, vague and difficult to notice, even by Uriel's light — but it was there, and it was leaning as though to whisper in my ear.

And it was all your fault, Harry.

The thought, the memory, resonated in my head for a moment, and I shivered.

"That . . . that shadow. It's an angel?"

"It was once," he said, and his voice was gentle — and infinitely sad. "A long, long time ago."

"One of the Fallen," I breathed.

"Yes. Who knew how to lie to you, Harry."

"Yeah, well. Blaming myself for bad stuff isn't exactly, um . . . completely uncharacteristic for me, man."

"I'm aware — as was that," he said, nodding at the shadow. "It made the lie even stronger, to use your own practice against you. But that creature knew what it was doing. It's all about timing. At that precise moment, in that exact state of mind, the single whisper it passed into your thoughts was enough to push your decision." Uriel looked at me and smiled faintly. "It added enough anger, enough self-recrimination, enough guilt, and enough despair to your deliberations to make you decide that destroying yourself was the only option left to you. It took your freedom away." His eyes hardened again. "I attempt to discourage that sort of thing where possible. When I cannot, I am allowed to balance the scales."

"I still don't understand," I said. "How does me coming back to haunt Chicago for a few nights balance anything?"

"Oh, it doesn't," Uriel said. "I can only act in a mirror of the offending action, I'm afraid."

"You . . . just get to whisper in my ear?"

"To whisper seven words, in fact," he said. "What you did . . . was elective."

"Elective?" I asked.

"I had no direct involvement in your return. In my judgment, it needed to happen — but there was no *requirement* that you come back to Chicago," Uriel said calmly. "You volunteered."

I rolled my eyes. "Well, yes. Duh. Because three of my friends were going to die if I didn't."

Uriel arched an eyebrow at me abruptly. Then he reached into the pocket of his jacket and withdrew a cell phone. He made it beep a couple of times, then turned on the speakerphone, and I heard a phone ringing.

"Murphy," answered Captain Jack's baritone.

"What's this Dresden is telling me about three of his friends being hurt?"

"Dresden," Jack said in an absent tone, as if searching his memory and finding nothing.

Uriel seemed mildly impatient. He wasn't buying it. "Tall, thin, insouciant, and sent back to Chicago to search for his killer?"

"Oh, right, him," Jack said. "That guy."

"Yes," Uriel said.

There was a guileless pause, and then Jack said, "What about him?"

Uriel, bless his angelic heart, closed his eyes for a moment and took a deep, calming breath. "Collin . . ." he said, in a reproving, parental tone.

"I might have mentioned something about it," Jack said. "Sure. Guy's got a lot of friends. Friends are running around fighting monsters. I figure at least three of them are going to get hurt if he isn't there to back them up. Seemed reasonable."

"Collin," Uriel said, his voice touched with an ocean of disappointment and a teaspoon of anger. "You *lied.*"

"I speculated," Captain Jack replied. "I got him to do the right thing, didn't I?"

"Collin, our purpose is to defend freedom — not to decide how it should be used."

"Everything I told him was technically true,

more or less, and I got the job done," Jack said stubbornly. "Look, sir, if I were perfect, I wouldn't be working here in the first place. Now, would I?"

And then he hung up. On speakerphone. On a freaking archangel.

I couldn't help it. I let out a rolling belly laugh. "I just got suckered into doing this by . . . Stars and stones, you didn't even *know* that he . . . Big bad angel boy, and you get the wool pulled over your eyes by . . ." I stopped trying to talk and just laughed.

Uriel eyed the phone, then me, and then tucked the little device away again, clearly nonplussed. "It doesn't matter how well I believe I know your kind, Harry. They always manage to find some way to try my patience."

It took me a moment to get the laughter under control, but I did. "Look, Uri, I don't want to say . . ."

The archangel gave me a look so cold that my words froze in my throat.

"Harry Blackstone Copperfield Dresden," he said quietly — and he said it exactly right, speaking my Name in a voice of that same absolute power that had so unnerved me before. "Do not attempt to familiarize my name. The part you left off happens to be rather important to who and what I am. Do you understand?"

I didn't. But as he spoke, I knew — not just suspected, but *knew* — that this guy could obliterate me, along with the planet I was standing on, with a simple thought. In fact, if what I'd read about archangels was right, Uriel could probably take apart *all* the planets. Like, all of them. Everywhere.

And I also knew that what I had just done had insulted him.

And . . . and frightened him.

I swallowed. It took me two tries, but I managed to whisper, "Aren't we just Mr. Sunshine today."

Uriel blinked. He looked less than certain for a moment. Then he said, "Mr. Sunshine . . . is perfectly acceptable. I suppose."

I nodded. "Sorry," I said. "About your name. I didn't realize it was so, um . . ."

"Intimate," he said quietly. "Sensitive. Names have tremendous power, Dresden. Yet mortals toss them left and right as though they were toys. It's like watching infants play with hand grenades sometimes." The ghost of a smile touched his face as he glanced at me. "Some more so than others. And I forgive you, of course."

I nodded at him. Then, after a quiet moment, I asked, "What happens now?"

"That's up to you," Uriel said. "You can always work for me. I believe you would find it challenging to do so — and I would have considerable use for someone of your talents."

"For how long?" I asked. "I mean . . . for guys like Captain Jack? Is it forever?"

717

Uriel smiled. "Collin, like the others, is with me because he is not yet prepared to face what comes next. When he is, he'll take that step. For now, he is not."

"When you say *what comes next,* what do you mean, exactly?"

"The part involving words like *forever, eternity,* and *judgment.*"

"Oh," I said. "What Comes Next."

"Exactly."

"So I can stay Between," I said quietly. "Or I can go get on that train."

"If you do," Uriel said, his eyes intent and serious, "then you accept the consequences for all that you have done while alive. When judged, what you have done will be taken into account. Your fate, ultimately, will be determined by your actions in life."

"You're saying that if I don't work for you, I'll just have to accept what comes?"

"I am saying that you cannot escape the consequences of your choices," he said.

I frowned at him for a minute. Then I said, "If I get on the train, it might just carry me straight to Hell."

"I can't talk to you about that," he said. "What comes next is about faith, Harry. Not knowledge."

I folded my arms. "What if I dig the ghost routine?"

"You don't," Uriel replied. "But even if you did, I would point out to you that your spiritual essence has been all but disintegrated. You would not last long as a shade, nor would you have the strength to aid and protect your loved ones. Should you lose your sanity, you might even become a danger to them — but if that is your desire, I can facilitate it."

I shook my head, trying to think. Then I said, "It . . . depends."

"Upon?"

"My friends," I said quietly. "My family. I have to know that they're all right."

Uriel watched me for a moment and then opened his mouth to speak, shaking his head a little as he did.

"Stop," I said, pointing a finger at him. "Don't you dare tell me to make this choice in the dark. Captain Jack gave me a half-truth that sent me running around Chicago again. Another angel told me a lie that got me killed. If you really care so much about my free will, you'll be willing to help me make a free, informed choice, just as if I was a grown-up. So either admit that you're trying to push me in your own direction or else put your principles where your mouth is and make like the Ghost of Christmas Present."

He stared at me for a long moment, his brow furrowed. "From your perspective . . . yes, I suppose it does look that way." Then he nodded firmly and extended his arm toward me. "Take my hand."

I did.

The white expanse gave way to reality once more. Suddenly, I stood with Uriel inside the Corpsetaker's hideout, on the stairs where that final confrontation had come. Molly was at the top of the stairs, leaning back against the wall. Her body was twisting and straining, her chest heaving with desperate breaths. Blood ran from both nostrils and had filled the sclera of her eyes, turning them into inhuman-looking blue-and-red stones. She let out little gasps and choked screams, along with whispered snatches of words that didn't make any sense.

Uriel did that thing with his hand again, and suddenly I could see Molly even more clearly — and saw that some kind of hideous mass was wound around her, like a python constricting its prey. It consisted of strands of some kind of slimy jelly, purple and black and covered with pulsing pustules that reeked of corruption and decay.

Corpsetaker.

Molly's duel with the Corpsetaker was still under way.

Butters's body lay at Molly's feet, empty of life and movement. And his shade — now I could see that it was bound into near immobility by threads of the Corpsetaker's dark magic — stood exactly as he had when I last saw him, staring down at his own body in horror. Down here in the electrical-junction room, Murphy and the wolves were bound with threads of the same dark magic as Butters — a sleeping spell that had compelled them all into insensibility.

Molly whimpered, drawing my gaze back to the top of the stairs as her legs gave way. She slid slowly down the wall, her eyes rolling wildly. Her mouth started moving more surely, her voice becoming stronger. And darker. For about two seconds, one of the Corpsetaker's hate-filled laughs rolled from Molly's lips. That hideous, slimy mass began to simply ooze into the young woman's skin.

"Do something," I said to Uriel.

He shook his head. "I cannot interfere. This battle was Molly's choice. She knew the risks and chose to hazard them."

"She isn't strong enough," I snapped. "She can't take on that thing."

Uriel arched an eyebrow. "Were you under the impression that she did not know that from the beginning, Harry? Yet she did it."

"Because she feels guilty," I said. "Because she blames herself for my death. She's in the same boat I was."

"No," Uriel said. "None of the Fallen twisted her path."

"No, that was me," I said, "but only because one of them got to me."

"Nonetheless," Uriel said, "that choice was yours — and hers."

"You're just going to stand there?" I asked.

Uriel folded his arms and tapped his chin with one fingertip. "Mmmm. It does seem that perhaps she deserves some form of aid. Perhaps if I'd had the presence of mind to see to it that some sort of agent had been sent to balance the scales, to give her that one tiny bit of encouragement, that one flicker of inspiration that turned the tide . . ." He shook his head sadly. "Things might be different now."

And, as if on cue, Mortimer Lindquist, ectomancer, limped out of the lower hallway and into the electrical-junction room, with Sir Stuart's shade at his right hand.

Mort took a look around, his dark eyes intent, and then his gaze locked onto Molly.

"Hey," he croaked. "You. Arrogant bitch ghost."

Molly's eyes snapped fully open and flicked to Mort. They were filled with more bitter, venomous hate than my apprentice could ever have put into them.

"I'm not really into this whole hero thing," Mort said. "Don't have the temperament for it. Don't know a lot about the villain side of the equation, either." He planted his feet, facing the Corpsetaker squarely, his hands clenched into fists at his side. "But it seems to me, you half-wit, that you probably shouldn't have left a freaking *ectomancer* a pit full of wraiths to play with."

And with a howl, more than a thousand wraiths came boiling around the corner in a cloud of clawing hands, gnashing teeth, and screaming hunger. They rode on a wave of Mort's power and no longer drifted with lazy, disconnected grace. Now they came forth like rushing storm clouds, like racing wolves, like hungry sharks, a tide of mindless destruction.

I saw Molly's eyes widen and the pulsing spiritual mass that was the Corpsetaker began to pull away from the young woman.

My apprentice didn't let her.

Molly let out a wheezing cackle and both hands formed into claws that clutched at the air. I saw the energy of her own magic surround her fingers so that she grasped onto the Corpsetaker's essence as if it had been a nearly physical thing. The necromancer's spirit began to ooze through Molly's grip. The exhausted girl could only slow the Corpsetaker down.

But it was enough.

The tide of wraiths slammed into the Corpsetaker like a freight train, their wails blending into a sound that I had heard before, in the train tunnel where Carmichael saved me. The Corpsetaker had begun to resume her usual form the instant she disengaged from Molly, and I could see the sudden shock and horror in her beautiful eyes as that spiritual tide overwhelmed her. I saw her struggle uselessly as the wraith train carried her up the stairs and out into the night. The train swept her straight up into the air — and then reversed itself and slammed her down, into the earth.

I saw her try to scream.

But all I heard was the blaring howl of the horn of a southbound train.

And then she was gone.

"You're right," Uriel said, his tone filled with a chill satisfaction. "Someone needed to do something." He glanced aside at me, gave me a slight bow of his head, and said, "Well-done."

Mort limped up the stairs to check on Molly. "You're the one who called to me, eh?"

Molly looked up at him, obviously too exhausted to move more than her head. "Harry . . . Well, it's sort of complicated to explain what was going on. But he told me you could help."

"Guess he was right," Mort said.

"Where is he?" Molly asked. "I mean . . . his ghost."

Mort glanced around and looked right at me — right through me. He shook his head. "Not here."

Molly closed her eyes and began to cry quietly.

"I got her, boss," Molly said quietly. "We got her. And I'm still here. Still me. Thank you."

"She's thanking me," I said quietly. "For that."

"And much more," Uriel said. "She still has her life. Her future. Her freedom. You did save her, you know. The idea to have her call to Mortimer in the closing moments of the psychic battle was inspired."

"I've cost her too much," I said quietly.

"I believe that when you went after your daughter, you said something about letting the world burn. That you and your daughter would roast marshmallows."

I nodded bleakly.

"It is one thing for you to say, 'Let the world burn.' It is another to say, 'Let Molly burn.' The difference is all in the name."

"Yeah," I croaked. "I'm starting to realize that. Too late to do any good. But I get it."

Uriel gave me a steady look and said nothing.

I shook my head. "Get some rest, kid," I called, though I knew she wouldn't hear me. "You've earned it."

The scene unfolded. Murphy and the wolves woke up less than a minute after the Corpsetaker was shown to the door. Will and company changed back to their human forms, while Mort, after a whispered tip from Sir Stuart, rushed over to Butters's fallen body. He worked a subtle, complex magic that made some of mine look pretty crude, and

725

drew Butters's spirit from the disintegrating tangle of the Corpsetaker's spell and back down into his physical body.

It took several minutes, and when Butters woke up, Andi and Marci, both naked, both rather pleasant that way, were giving him CPR. They'd kept his body alive in the absence of his soul.

"Wow," Butters slurred as he opened his eyes. He looked back and forth between the two werewolf girls. "Subtract the horrible pain in my chest, this migraine, and all the mold and mildew, and I'm living the dream."

Then he passed out.

The cops showed up a bit after that. Two of them were guys Murphy knew. The werewolves vanished into the night a couple of seconds before the blue bubbles of the cop cars showed up, taking the illegal portions of Murphy's armament with them. Murphy and Mort told them all about how Mort had been abducted and tortured by the Big Hoods, and if they didn't tell the whole story, what they did tell was one hundred percent true.

Molly and Butters got handed off to EMTs, along with several of the Big Hoods who had been knocked around and chewed up. Mort got some attention, too, though he refused to be taken to a hospital. The rest of the Big Hoods got a pair of cuffs and a ride downtown. Boz was carted out like a tranquilized rhinoceros.

Karrin and Mort stood around outside as the uniforms sorted everything out, and I walked over to stand close enough to hear them.

". . . came back to help," Mort said. "It happens sometimes. Some people die feeling that something was incomplete. I guess Dresden thought that he hadn't done enough to make a difference around here." Mort shook his head. "As if the big goon didn't turn everything upside down whenever he showed up."

Karrin smiled faintly and shook her head. "He always said you knew ghosts. You're sure it was really him?"

Mort eyed her. "Me and everyone else, yeah."

Karrin scowled and stared into the middle distance.

Mort frowned and then his expression softened. "You didn't want it to be his ghost. Did you?"

Murphy shook her head slowly, but said nothing.

"You needed everyone to be wrong about it. Because if it really was his ghost," Mort said, "it means that he really is dead."

Murphy's face . . . just crumpled. Her eyes overflowed and she bowed her head. Her body shook in silence.

Mort chewed on his lip for a moment, then glanced at the cops on the scene. He didn't say anything else to Murphy or try to touch her — but he did put himself between her and everyone else, so that no one would see her crying.

Damn.

I wished I'd been bright enough to see what kind of guy Morty was while I was still alive.

I stood there watching Karrin for a moment and then turned away. It hurt too much to see her in pain when I couldn't reach out and touch her, or make an off-color joke, or find some way to give her a creative insult or otherwise show her that I cared.

It didn't seem fair that I should get to say good-bye to her, even if she couldn't hear it. She hadn't gotten to say it to me. So I didn't say anything. I gave her a last look and then I walked away.

I went back over to Uriel to find him conversing with Sir Stuart.

"Don't know," Sir Stuart was saying. "I'm not . . . not as right as I used to be, sir."

"There's more than enough left to rebuild on," Uriel said. "Trust me. The ruins of a spirit like Sir Stuart's are more substantial than most men ever manage to dredge up. I'd be very pleased to have you working for me."

"My descendant," Sir Stuart said, frowning over at Morty.

Uriel watched Mort shielding Karrin's sorrow and said, "You've watched over him faithfully, Stuart. And he's grown a great deal in the past few years. I think he's going to be fine."

Sir Stuart's shade looked at Mortimer and smiled, undeniable pride in his features. Then he glanced at Uriel and said, "I still get to fight, aye?"

Uriel gave him a very sober look and said, "I think I can find you something."

Sir Stuart thought about it for a moment and then nodded. "Aye, sir. Aye. I've been in this town too long. A new billet is just what I need."

Uriel looked past Sir Stuart to me and winked. "Excellent," he said, and shook hands with Sir Stuart. "A man named Carmichael will be in touch."

I lingered until everyone had vanished into the thick mist that still cloaked the earth. It took less time than it usually did for these sorts of things; no one had died. No need to call in the lab guys. The uniform cops closed the old metal door as best they could, drew a big X over it with crime-scene tape, and seemed willing to ignore the hole that had been blasted in it.

"They're going to be all right, you know," Uriel said quietly. "Tonight's injuries will not be lethal to any of them."

"Thank you," I said. "For telling me that."

He nodded. "Have you decided?"

I shook my head. "Show me my brother."

He arched an eyebrow at me. Then he shrugged, and once again offered his hand.

We vanished from the night and appeared in a very expensively furnished apartment. I recognized my brother's place at once.

It had changed a bit. The brushed steel décor had been softened. The old Broadway musical posters had been replaced with paintings, mostly pastoral landscapes that provided an interesting counterpoint of warmth to the original style of the place. Candles and other decorative pieces had filled in the rather Spartan spaces I remembered, adding still more warmth. All in all, the place looked a lot more like a home now, a lot less like a dressed stage.

A couple of things were out of place. There was a chair in the living room positioned in front of the large flat-screen, high-definition television set the size of a dining room table. The chair was upholstered in brown leather and looked comfortable, and it didn't match the rest of the room. There were also food stains on it. Empty liquor bottles littered the side table next to it.

The door opened and my brother, Thomas, walked in. He might have been an inch under six feet tall, though it was hard for me to tell — he had worn so many different kinds of fashionable shoes that his height was always changing subtly. He had dark hair, currently as long as my shortest finger, and it was a mess. Not only was it messy, it was *simply* messy, instead of attractively messy, and for Thomas that was hideous. He had a couple of weeks' growth of beard; not long enough to be an actual beard yet, but too long to be a sexy shadow.

His cold grey eyes were sunken, with dark rings beneath them. He wore jeans and a T-shirt with drink stains on it. He hadn't even pretended to need a coat against the night's cold, and breaking their easily maintained cover as human beings was something that the vampires of the White Court simply did not do. For God's sake, he was barefoot. He'd just walked out like that, apparently to the nearest liquor store.

My brother took a bottle of whiskey — expensive whiskey — from a paper bag and let the bag fall to the floor. Then he sat down in the brown leather chair, pointed a remote at the television, and clicked it on. He clicked buttons and it skipped through several channels. He stopped clicking based, apparently, on his need to take a drink, and stopped on some kind of sports channel where they were playing rugby.

Then he simply sat, slugged from the bottle, and stared.

"It's hard for the half-born," Uriel observed in a quiet, neutral tone.

"What did you call him?" I asked. Belligerently. Which probably wasn't really bright, but Thomas was my brother. I didn't like the thought of anyone judging him.

"The scions of mortals and immortals," Uriel said, unperturbed. "Halflings, half-bloods, half-born. The mortal road is difficult enough without adding a share of our burdens to it as well."

I grunted. "That skinwalker got hold of him a while back. It broke something in him."

"The naagloshii feel a need to prove that every creature they meet is as flawed and prone to darkness as they themselves proved to be," Uriel said. "It . . . gives them some measure of false peace, I think, to lie to themselves like that."

"You sound like you feel sorry for them," I said, my voice hard.

"I feel sorry for all the pain they have, and more so for all that they inflict on others. Your brother offers ample explanation for my feelings."

"What that thing did to Thomas. How is that different from what the Fallen did to me?"

"He didn't die as a result," Uriel said bluntly. "He still has choice." He added, in a softer voice, "What the naagloshii did to him was not your fault."

"I know that," I said, not very passionately.

The door to the apartment opened, and a young woman entered. She was in her twenties and gorgeous. Her face and figure were appealing, glowing with vitality and health, and her hair was like white silk. She wore a simple dress and a long coat, and she slipped out of her shoes immediately upon entering.

Justine paused at the door and stared steadily at Thomas for a long moment.

"Did you eat anything today?" she asked.

Thomas flicked the television to another channel and turned up the volume.

Justine pressed her lips together. Then she walked with firm, purposeful strides into the apartment's back bedroom.

She came out again a moment later, preceded by the click of her high heels. She was dressed in red lace underthings that left just enough to the imagination, and in the same shade of heels. She looked like the cover of a Victoria's Secret catalog, and moved with a sort of subsurface, instinctive sensuality that could make dead men stir with interest. I had empirical evidence of the fact.

But I also knew that my brother couldn't touch her. The touch of love, or anyone who was truly beloved, was anathema to the White Court, like holy water was for Hollywood vampires. Thomas and Justine had nearly killed themselves for the sake of saving the other, and ever since then, every time my brother touched her, he came away with second-degree burns.

"If you don't feed soon, you're going to lose

control of the Hunger," she said.

Thomas looked away from her. He turned up the television.

She moved one long, lovely leg and, with the toe of her pump, flicked off the main switch of the power strip the television was plugged into. It turned off, and the apartment was abruptly silent.

"You think you're going to hurt my feelings if you take a lover, even though I've given you my blessing. You are irrational. And at this point, I'm not sure you're capable of thinking clearly about the consequences of your actions."

"I don't need you telling me how to deal with the Hunger," Thomas said in a low voice. He looked at her, and though he was at least a little angry, there was an aching, naked hunger in his gaze as his eyes traveled over her. "Why are you torturing me like this?"

"Because I'm tired of the way you've been torturing yourself since Harry died," she said quietly. "It wasn't your fault. And it hurts too much to watch you do this every day."

"He was on my boat," Thomas said. "If he hadn't been there —"

"He'd have died somewhere else," Justine said firmly. "He made enemies, Thomas. And he knew that. You knew that."

"I should have been with him," Thomas said. "I might have done something. Seen something."

"And you might not have," Justine replied. She shook her head. "No. It's time, my love, to stop indulging your guilt this way." Her lips quirked. "It's just so . . . very emo. And I think we've had enough of that."

Thomas blinked.

Justine walked over to him. I swear, her walk would have been enough to try the chaste thoughts of a saint. Even Uriel seemed to appreciate it. With that same slow, gentle sensuality, she bent over — itself quite a lovely sight — and took the bottle from Thomas. Then she walked back across the room and put it on a shelf.

"Love. I am going to put an end to this Hunger strike of yours tonight."

Thomas's eyes were growing paler by the heartbeat, but he frowned. "Love . . . you know that I can't. . . ."

Justine arched a dark eyebrow at him. "You can't . . . ?"

He ground his teeth. "Touch you. Have you. The protection of being united with someone who loves you will burn me — even though I *was* the one who gave it to you."

"Thomas," Justine said, "you are a dear, dear man. But there is a way around that, you know. A rather straightforward method for removing the protection of having had sex with you, my love."

A key slipped into the apartment's door,

and another young woman entered. She had dark-shaded skin, and there was an exotic, reddish sheen to her straight black hair. Her dark chocolate eyes were huge and sultry, and she wore a black trench coat and black heels — and, it turned out, when the trench coat fell to the floor, that was the extent of her wardrobe.

"This is Mara," Justine said, extending a hand, and the girl crossed the room to slide her arms around Justine. Justine gave Mara's lips an almost sisterly kiss and then turned to Thomas, her eyes smoldering. "Now, love. I'm going to have her — without deeply committed love, perhaps, but with considerable affection and healthy desire. And after that, you're going to be able to have me. And you will. And things will be much better."

My brother's eyes gleamed bright silver.

"Repeat," Justine murmured, her lips caressing the words, "as necessary."

I felt my cheeks heat up and coughed. Then I turned to Uriel and said, "Under the circumstances . . ."

The archangel looked amused at my discomfort. "Yes?"

I glanced at the girls, who were kissing again, and sighed. "Yeah, uh. I think my brother's going to be fine."

"Then you're ready?" Uriel asked.

I looked at him and smiled faintly.

"I wondered when we'd get around to

that," he said, and once more extended his hand.

This time, we appeared in front of a Chicago home. There were a couple of ancient oak trees in the yard. The house was a white Colonial number with a white picket fence out front, and evidence of children in the form of several snowmen that were slowly sagging to their deaths in the warm evening air.

There were silent forms standing outside the house, men in dark suits and long coats. One stood beside the front door. One stood at each corner of the house, on the roof, as calmly as if they hadn't had their feet planted on an icy surface inches from a potentially fatal fall. Two more stood at the corners of the property in the front yard, and a couple of steps and a lean to one side showed me at least one more in the backyard, at the back corner of the property.

"More guardian angels," I said.

"Michael Carpenter has more than earned them," Uriel said, his voice warm. "As has his family."

I looked sharply at Uriel. "She's . . . she's *here?*"

"Forthill wanted to find the safest home in which he could possibly place your daughter, Dresden," Uriel said. "All in all, I don't think he could have done much better."

I swallowed. "She's . . . I mean, she's . . . ?"

"Cared for," Uriel said. "Loved, of course. Do you think Michael and Charity would do less for your child, when you have so often saved their children?"

I blinked some tears out of my eyes. Stupid eyes. "No. No, of course not." I swallowed and tried to make my voice sound normal. "I want to see her."

"This isn't a hostage negotiation, Dresden," Uriel murmured, but he was smiling. He walked up to the house and exchanged nods with the guardian angel at the door. We passed through it, ghost style, though it wouldn't have been possible for actual ghosts. The Carpenters had a threshold more solid and extensive than the Great Wall of China. I would not be in the least surprised if you could see it from space.

We walked through my friend's silent, sleeping house. The Carpenters were early to bed, early to rise types. Inexplicable, but I suppose nobody's perfect. Uriel led me upstairs, past two more guardian angels, and into one of the upstairs bedrooms — one that had, once upon a time, been Charity's sewing room and spare bedroom. Hapless wizards had been known to find rest there once in a while.

We went through the door and were greeted by a low, warning rumble. A great mound of shaggy fur, lying beside the room's single, twin bed, rose to its feet.

"Mouse," I said, and dropped to my knees.

I wept openly as my dog all but bounced at me. He was obviously joyous and just as obviously trying to mute his delight — but his tail thumped loudly against everything in the room, and puppyish sounds of pleasure came from his throat as he slobbered on my face, giving me kisses.

I sank my fingers into his fur and found it warm and solid and real, and I scratched him and hugged him and told him what a good dog he was.

Uriel stood over us, smiling down, but said nothing.

"Missed you, too, boy," I said. "Just . . . kind of stopping by to say good-bye."

Mouse's tail stopped wagging. His big, doggy eyes regarded me very seriously, and then glanced at Uriel.

"What has begun must finish, little brother," Uriel said. "Your task here is not yet over."

Mouse regarded the archangel for a moment and then huffed out a breath in a huge sigh and leaned against me.

I scratched him some more and hugged him — and looked past him, to where my daughter slept.

Maggie Dresden was a dark-haired, dark-eyed child, which had been all but inevitable given her parents' coloring. Her skin tone was a bit darker than mine, which I thought looked healthier than my skin ever had. I got kind of pasty, what with all the time in my lab and reading and running around after dark. Her features were . . . well, perfect. Beautiful. The first time I'd seen her in the flesh, despite everything else that was going on at the time, somewhere under the surface I had been shocked by how gorgeous she was. She was the most beautiful child I'd ever seen, like, in the movies or anywhere.

But I guess maybe all parents see that when they look at their kids. It isn't rational. That doesn't make it any less true.

She slept with the boneless relaxation of the very young, her arms carelessly thrown over her head. She wore one of Molly's old T-shirts as pajamas. It had an old, worn, iron-on decal of R2-D2 on it, with the caption BEEP BEEP DE DEEP KERWOOO under it.

I knelt down by her, stroking Mouse's fur, but when I tried to touch her hand, mine passed through hers, immaterial. I leaned my head against Mouse's big, solid skull, and sighed.

"She'll have a good life here," I said quietly. "People who care about her. Who love kids."

"Yes," Uriel said.

Mouse's tail thumped several more times.

"Yeah, buddy. And she'll have you." I glanced up at Uriel. "For how long? I mean, most dogs . . ."

"Temple dogs have been known to live for centuries," he replied. "Your friend is more than capable of protecting her for a lifetime — even a wizard's lifetime, if need be."

That made me feel a little better. I knew what it was like to grow up without my birth parents around, and what a terrible loss it was not to have that sense of secure continuation most of the other kids around me had. Maggie had lost her foster parents, and then her birth mother, and then her biological father. She had another foster home now — but she would always have Mouse.

"Hell," I said to Mouse, "for all I know, you'll be smarter than I would have been about dealing with her, anyway."

Mouse snorted, grinning a doggy grin. He couldn't speak, but I could effortlessly imagine his response — of course he'd be smarter than I was. That particular bar hadn't been set very high.

"Take care of her, buddy," I said to Mouse, and gave his shoulders a couple of firm pats with my fists. "I know you'll take good care of her."

Mouse sat up away from me, his expression attentive and serious, and then, very deliberately, offered me his paw.

I shook hands with him gravely, and then rose to face the archangel.

"All right," I said quietly. "I'm ready."

CHAPTER FIFTY-ONE

Uriel extended his hand again, and I took it.

The Carpenters' house faded from around us and we reappeared in the world of empty white light. There was one difference this time. Two glass doors stood in front of us. One of them led to an office building — in fact, I recognized it as the interior of Captain Jack's department in Chicago Between. I saw Carmichael go by the door, consulting a notepad and fishing in his pocket for his car keys.

The other door led only to darkness. That was the uncertain future. It was What Came Next.

"I can hardly remember the last time I spent this much time with one particular mortal," Uriel said thoughtfully. "I wish I had time to do it more often."

I looked at him for a long moment and said, "I don't understand."

He laughed. It was a sound that seethed with warmth and life.

I found myself smiling and joined him. "I don't understand what your game is in all of this."

"Game?"

I shrugged. "Your people conned me into taking a pretty horrible risk with my soul. I guess. If that's what you call this." I waved a hand. "And you've got plausible deniability — I know, I know — or maybe you really are sincere and Captain Murphy threw a curveball past all of us. Either way . . . it doesn't make sense."

"Why not?" Uriel asked.

"Because it doesn't have anything to do with balancing the scales of one of the Fallen lying to me," I said. "You haven't done any fortune-cookie whispers into my head, have you?"

"No," he said. "Not yet."

"Well, that's what I mean," I said. "The scale *still* isn't balanced. And I don't think you send people back just for kicks."

Uriel regarded me pleasantly. He said nothing.

"So you did it for a reason. Something you couldn't have gotten with your seven whispered words."

"Perhaps it was to balance the situation with Molly," he said.

I snorted. "Yeah. I bet all the time you go around solving your problems one by one, in neat little rows. I bet you never, ever try to hit two birds with one stone."

Uriel regarded me pleasantly. He said nothing.

"I'm headed for the great beyond, and you still won't give me a straight answer?" I demanded, smiling.

Uriel regarded me pleasantly. He said nothing. A lot.

I laughed again. "Tell you what, big guy. Just tell me something. Something useful. I'll be happy with whatever I get."

He pursed his lips and thought about it for a moment. Then he said, "No matter where you go, there you are."

I blinked. "Goodness," I said. "Buckaroo Banzai?"

"Confucius," he said.

"Wow. How very fortune cookie of you." I gave him a half smile and offered him my hand. "But despite your cryptic ways, I'm sure of one thing now that I wasn't before."

"Oh?"

"Souls," I said. "I mean, you always wonder if they're real. Even if you believe in them, you still have to wonder: Is my existence just this body? Is there really something more? Do I really have a soul?"

Uriel's smile blossomed again. "You've got it backward, Harry," he said. "You *are* a soul. You *have* a body."

I blinked at that. It was something to think about. "Mr. Sunshine, it has been a dubious and confusing pleasure."

"Harry," he said, shaking my hand. "I feel the same way."

I released his hand, nodded, and squared my shoulders.

Then, moving briskly, lest my resolve waver, I opened the black door and stepped through.

Given the way my life has typically progressed, I probably should have guessed that What Came Next was pain.

A whole *lot* of pain.

I tried to take a breath, and a searing burst of agony radiated out from my chest. I held off on the next breath for as long as I could, but eventually I couldn't put it off anymore, and again fire spread across my chest.

I repeated that cycle for several moments, my entire reality consumed by the simple struggle to breathe and to avoid the pain. I was on the losing side of things, and if the pain didn't exactly lessen, it did, eventually, become more bearable.

"Good," whispered a dry, rasping voice. "Very good."

I felt the rest of my body next. I was lying on something cool and contoured. It wasn't precisely comfortable, but it wasn't a torment, either. I clenched my fingers, but something was wrong with them. They barely moved. It was as though someone had replaced my bones and flesh with lead weights, heavy and inert, and my tendons and muscles were too weak to break the inertia. But I felt cool, damp earth crumbling beneath my fingertips.

"Doesn't seem to bode well," I mumbled. My tongue didn't work right. My lips didn't, either. The words came out a slushy mumble.

"Excellent," rasped the voice. "I told you he had strength enough."

My thoughts resonated abruptly with another voice, one that had no point of contact with my ears: *WE WILL SEE.*

What had my godmother said at my grave? That it was all about respect and . . .

. . . and proxies.

"The eyes," rasped the voice. "Open your eyes, mortal."

My eyelids were in the same condition as everything else. They didn't want to move. But I made them. I realized that they felt cooler than the rest of my skin, as if someone had recently wiped them with a damp washcloth.

I opened them and cried out weakly at the intensity of the light.

I waited for a moment, then tried again. Then again. On the four or five hundredth try, I was finally able to see.

I was in a cave, lit by wan, onion-colored light. I could see a roof of rock and earth, with roots of trees as thick as my waist trailing through here and there. Water dripped down from overhead, all around me. I could hear it. Some dropped onto my lips, and I licked at it. It tasted sweet, sweeter than double-thick cherry syrup, and I shivered in pleasure this time.

I was *starving*.

I looked around me slowly. It made my head feel like it was about to fly apart every time I twitched it, but I persevered. I was, so far as I could tell, naked. I was lying on fine, soft earth that had somehow been contoured to the shape of my body. There were pine needles — soft ones — spread about beneath me in lieu of a blanket, their scent sharp and fresh.

There was a dull throb coming from my arms, and I looked down to see . . .

There were . . . roots or vines or something, growing *into* me. They wrapped around my wrists and penetrated the skin there, structures that were plantlike but pale and spongy-looking. I could barely make out some kind of fluid flowing through the tendrils and presumably into my body. I wanted to scream and thrash my arms, but it just seemed like too much work. A moment later, my leaden thoughts notified me that the vines looked something like . . . an intravenous fluid line. An IV.

What the hell kind of Hell was this supposed to be?

I realized that something rounded and

unyielding was supporting my head. I twitched and moved myself enough to look up, and realized that my head was being held in someone's lap.

"Ah," whispered the voice. "Now you begin to understand."

I looked up still farther . . . and found myself staring into the face of Mab, Queen of Air and Darkness, the veritable mother of wicked faeries herself.

Mab looked . . . not cadaverous. It wasn't a word that applied. Her skin seemed stretched tight over her bones, her face distorted to inhuman proportions. Her emerald green eyes were inhumanly huge in that sunken face, her teeth unnaturally sharp. She brushed a hand over one of my cheeks, and her fingers looked too long, her nails grown out like claws. Her arms looked like nothing but bone and sinew with skin stretched over them, and her elbows were somehow too large, too swollen, to look even remotely human. Mab didn't look like a cadaver. She looked like some kind of nearly starved insect, a praying mantis smiling down at its first meal in weeks.

"Oh," I said, and if my speech was halting, at least it sounded almost human. "That kind of Hell."

Mab tilted back her head and cackled. It was a dull, brittle sound, like the edge of a rusted knife. "No," she said. "Alas, no, my knight. No, you have not escaped. I have far too much work for your hand to allow that. Not yet."

I stared at her dully, which was probably the only way I was capable of staring at the moment. Then I croaked, "I'm . . . alive?"

Her smile widened even more. "And *well,* my dear knight."

I grunted. It was all the enthusiasm I could summon. "Yay?"

"It makes me feel like singing," Mab's voice grated from between sharp teeth. "Welcome back, O my knight, to the green lands of the living."

ENOUGH, said that enormous thought-voice, the same one from the graveyard, but less mind annihilating. *THE FOOLISH GAMBLE IS CONCLUDED. HIS PHYSICAL NEEDS MUST BE MET.*

"I know what I am doing," Mab purred. Or it would have been a purr, if cats had been made from steel wool. "Fear not, ancient thing. Your custodian lives."

I turned my head slowly the other way. After a subjective century, I was able to see the other figure in the cave.

It was enormous, a being that had to crouch not to bump its head on the ceiling. It was, more or less, human in form — but I could see little of that form. It was almost entirely concealed in a vast cloak of dark green, with shadows hiding whatever lay beneath it. The cloak's hood covered its head, but I could see tiny green fires, like small, flickering clouds of fireflies, burning within the hood's shadowed depth.

Demonreach. The genius loci of the intensely weird, unmapped island in the middle of Lake Michigan. We'd . . . sort of had an arrangement, made a couple of years back. And I was beginning to think that maybe I hadn't fully understood the extent of that arrangement.

"I'm . . . on the island?" I rasped.

YOU ARE HERE.

"Long have this old thing and I labored to keep your form alive, my knight," Mab said. "Long have we kept flesh and bone and blood knit together and stirring, waiting for your spirit's return."

MAB GAVE YOU BREATH. HERE PROVIDED NOURISHMENT. THE PARASITE MAINTAINED THE FLOW OF BLOOD.

Parasite? What?

I'd already had a really, really long day.

"But . . . I got shot," I mumbled.

"*My* knight," Mab hissed, the statement one of possession. "Your broken body fell from your ship into cold and darkness — and they are *my* domain."

THE COLD QUEEN BROUGHT YOU TO HERE, Demonreach emitted. My head was starting to ache, hearing his psychic voice. *YOUR PHYSICAL VESSEL WAS PRESERVED.*

"And now here you are," Mab murmured. "Oh, the Quiet One angered us, sending your essence out unprotected. Had he been incorrect, I would have been robbed of my knight, and the old monster of his custodian."

OUR INTERESTS COINCIDED.

I blinked slowly, and again my lagging brain started catching up to me.

Mab had me.

I hadn't escaped her. I hadn't escaped what she could make me become.

Oh, God.

And all the people who'd gotten hurt, helping me . . . They'd done it for *nothing*.

"Told me . . . I was dead," I muttered.

"*Dead* is a grey word," Mab hissed. "Mortals fear it, and so they wish it to be black — and they have but few words to contain its reality. It escapes from such constraints. Death is a spectrum, not a line. And you, my knight, had not yet vanished into the utter darkness."

I licked at my lips again. "Guess . . . you're kind of upset with me. . . ."

"You attempted to *cheat* the Queen of Air and Darkness," Mab hissed. "You practiced a vile, wicked deception upon me, my knight." Her inhuman eyes glittered. "I expected no less of you. Were you not strong enough to cast such defiance into my teeth, you would be useless to my purposes." Her smile widened. "To *our* purposes now."

The very ground seemed to quiver, to let out an unthinkably low, deep, angry growl.

Mab's eyes snapped to Demonreach. "I have his oath, ancient one. What he has given is mine by right, and you may not gainsay it. He is mine to shape as I please."

"Dammit," I said tiredly. "Dammit."

And a voice — a very calm, very gentle, very rational voice whispered in my ear, "Lies. Mab cannot change who you are."

I struggled and twitched my fingers. "Five," I muttered, "Six. Seven. Heh." I couldn't help it. I laughed again. It hurt like hell and it felt wonderful. "Heh. Heh."

Mab had gone very still. She stared at me with wide eyes, her alien face void of expression.

"No," I said then, weakly. "No. Maybe I'm your knight. But I'm not yours."

Emerald fire flickered in her eyes, cold and angry. "What?"

"You can't make me your monster," I slurred. "Doesn't work. And you know it."

Mab's eyes grew colder, more distant. "Oh?"

"You can make me do things," I said. "You can mess with my head. But all that makes me is a thug." The effort of so many words cost me. I had to take a moment to rest before I continued. "You wanted a thug; you get that from anywhere. Lloyd Slate was a thug. Plenty where he came from."

Demonreach's burning eyes flickered, and a sense of something like cold satisfaction came from the cloaked giant.

"Said it yourself: need someone like me." I met Mab's eyes with mine and curled my upper lip into a sneer. "Go on. Try to change me. The second you do, the second I think you've played with my head or altered my memory, the first time you compel me to do something, I'll do the one thing you can't have in your new knight." I lifted my head a little, and I knew that I must have looked a little crazy as I spoke. "I'll *do* it. I'll follow your command. And I will do *nothing* else. I'll make every task you command one you must personally oversee. I'll have the initiative of a garden statue. And do you know what that will give you, my queen?"

Her eyes burned. "What?"

I felt my own smile widen. "A mediocre knight," I said. "And mediocrity, my queen, is a terrible, terrible fate."

Her voice came forth from lips so cold that frost began forming on them. The next drop of water to fall on me thumped gently, a tiny piece of sleet. "Do you think I cannot punish you for such defiance? Do you think I cannot visit such horrors upon those you love as to create legends that last a thousand years?"

I didn't flinch. "I think you've got too much on your plate already," I spat back. "I think you don't have the time or the energy to spare to fight your own knight anymore. I think you need me, or you wouldn't have gone to all the trouble of keeping me alive for this long, of taxing your strength this much to get it done. You need me. Or else why are you here? In Chicago? In May?"

Again, the inhuman eyes raked at mine. But when she spoke, her voice was very, very soft and far more terrible than a moment before. "I am not some mortal merchant to be bargained with. I am not some petty president to be argued with. I am Mab."

"You are Mab," I said. "And I owe you a debt for preserving my life. For giving me the power I needed to save my daughter's life. Don't think that I have forgotten that."

The faerie's expression finally changed. She frowned and tilted her head slightly, as if puzzled. "Then why this defiance? When you know I will take vengeance for it?"

"Because my soul is my own," I said quietly. "You cannot steal it from me. You cannot change it. You cannot buy it. I am mine, Mab. I have fought long and hard against horrors even you would respect. I have been beaten, but I have not yielded. I'm not going to start yielding now. If I did, I wouldn't be the weapon you need."

Her eyes narrowed.

"I will be the Winter Knight," I told her. "I will be the most terrifying Knight the Sidhe Courts have ever known. I will send your enemies down in defeat and make your power grow." I smiled again. "But I do it my way. On my terms. When you give me the task, I'll decide how it gets done — and you'll stay out of the way and let me work. And that's how it's going to be."

After a long silent moment, she said, "You dare give commands to *me*, mortal?"

"I can't control you," I said. "I know that. But I can control me. And I've just told you the only way you get what you want out of me." I shrugged a little. "Up to you, my queen. But think about whether you want another thug to command or an ally to respect. Otherwise, you might as well start cutting on me right here, right now, and get yourself somebody with less backbone."

The Queen of Air and Darkness stared down at me for silent moments. Then she said, "You will never be my ally. Not in your heart."

"Probably not," I said. "But I can follow the example of my godmother. I can be a trusted enemy. I can work with you."

Mab's pale white eyebrows lifted and her eyes gleamed. "I will never trust you, wizard." And then she rose abruptly and let my head fall back to the earth. She walked away, her silken gown hanging limply upon her insect-thin frame. "Prepare yourself."

Demonreach stirred. The pale tendrils and roots began withdrawing themselves from my arms, leaving small, bleeding holes behind.

"For what?" I asked.

"For the journey to my court, Sir Knight." She paused and looked over one shoulder at me, green eyes bright and cold. "There is much work to do be done."

AUTHOR'S NOTE

When I was seven years old, I got a bad case of strep throat and was out of school for a whole week. During that time, my sisters bought me my first fantasy and sci-fi novels: the boxed set of *The Lord of the Rings* and the boxed set of Han Solo adventure novels by Brian Daley. I devoured them all during that week.

From that point on, I was pretty much doomed to join SF&F fandom. From there, it was only one more step to decide I wanted to be a writer of my favorite fiction material, and here we are.

I blame my sisters.

My first love as a fan is swords-and-horses fantasy. After Tolkien I went after C. S. Lewis. After Lewis, It was Lloyd Alexander. After them came Fritz Leiber, Roger Zelazny, Robert Howard, John Norman, Poul Anderson, David Eddings, Weis and Hickman, Terry Brooks, Elizabeth Moon, Glen Cook, and before I knew it I was a dual citizen of the

United States and Lankhmar, Narnia, Gor, Cimmeria, Krynn, Amber — you get the picture.

When I set out to become a writer, I spent years writing swords-and-horses fantasy novels — and seemed to have little innate talent for it. But I worked at my writing, branching out into other areas as experiments, including SF, mystery, and contemporary fantasy. That's how the Dresden Files initially came about — as a happy accident while trying to accomplish something else. Sort of like penicillin.

But I never forgot my first love, and to my immense delight and excitement, one day I got a call from my agent and found out that I was going to get to share my newest swords-and-horses fantasy novel with other fans.

The Codex Alera is a fantasy series set within the savage world of Carna, where spirits of the elements, known as furies, lurk in every facet of life, and where many intelligent races vie for security and survival. The realm of Alera is the monolithic civilization of humanity, and its unique ability to harness and command the furies is all that enables its survival in the face of the enormous, sometimes hostile, elemental powers of Carna, and against savage creatures who would lay Alera to waste and ruin.

Yet even a realm as powerful as Alera is not immune to destruction from within, and the death of the heir apparent to the crown has triggered a frenzy of ambitious political maneuvering and infighting among the High Lords, those who wield the most powerful furies known to man. Plots are afoot, traitors and spies abound, and a civil war seems inevitable — all while the enemies of the realm watch, ready to strike at the first sign of weakness.

Tavi is a young man living on the frontier of Aleran civilization — because, let's face it, swords-and-horses fantasies start there. Born a freak, unable to utilize any powers of fury-crafting whatsoever, Tavi has grown up relying up on his own wits, speed, and courage to survive. When an ambitious plot to discredit the crown lays Tavi's home, the Calderon Valley, naked and defenseless before a horde of the barbarian Marat, the boy and his family find themselves directly in harm's way.

There are no titanic High Lords to protect them, no legions, no knights with their mighty furies to take the field. Tavi and the free frontiersmen of the Calderon Valley must find some way to uncover the plot and to defend their homes against the merciless horde of the Marat and their beasts.

It is a desperate hour when the fate of all Alera hangs in the balance, when a handful of ordinary stead holders must find the courage and strength to defy an overwhelming foe, and when the courage and intelligence of one young man will save the realm — or destroy it.

Thank you, readers and fellow fans, for all of your support and kindness. I hope that you enjoy reading the books of the Codex Alera as much as I enjoyed creating them for you.

— Jim